HIDING FROM HEMINGWAY

ISBN 0-9701342-3-1

First printing

Point Net Publishing
P.O. Box 759
Petoskey, MI 449770

CHAPTER ONE

Chad Reiger tapped his fingers impatiently on the table in front of him. Looking toward the window, he saw beams of sunlight penetrating through and illuminating his living room. He walked over and squeezed through the space between his desk and the sofa, opened the upper half of the window and let the warm August air flow in as he looked out over Little Traverse Bay. From his second-floor apartment he could see Harbor Springs at the far end.

There had been a regatta the day before and many of the yachters had stayed, enjoying the casual life that came with a Northern Michigan summer. They were the wealthy people who lived the life Chad longed to live. They were the guys who—regardless of their looks—associated with beautiful women. They were the guys who— regardless of their substance—were both popular and looked up to.

Chad shook his head in disgust and dropped himself into the gray swivel chair in front of his desk. He propped his feet on the windowsill and redirected his attention to the activity on the street below. The tourists were beginning to come into town for the day, parking their cars and making the short trek to downtown Petoskey. As was their tradition, they would come into town in late spring and not relinquish their foothold until Labor Day. "Fudgies!" he mumbled.

As he continued his observation a girl came into view, which prompted him to go to the other window and peek through the closed blinds. *Lisa,* he thought. His heart began to race as he searched for a reason to go outside without being conspicuous. He was about to go for the door when he saw a white Mustang pull up along side of her. The door opened, she got in and the Mustang pulled away. *Shit,* he moaned.

He stood at the window for a moment, perplexed by seemingly a lifetime of such luck. He dropped his finger from the venetian blind, went across the room and lowered himself back in his chair. He grabbed a pen that was sitting on the desk and began to fumble with it. He clicked it open, then clicked it shut. He clicked it open and shut again and again until he got to the point where he couldn't stand it. He forced himself out of his chair, went into the bedroom and threw on the clothes that he had set on his still-unmade bed.

As he dressed, he looked in the mirror. He was an average looking guy—not by any means dashing, but still rather handsome in a beatnik sort of way. He was six-foot one and of average build with a face that portrayed honesty and character. He had sky-blue eyes and brown hair that was graying at the temples and which he kept in a 1964 Beatle cut. He liked to dress casual and preferred a tee shirt and jeans to any other attire.

As he studied his face in the mirror, he saw the boy he once was; a boy brimming with youthful exuberance and anticipation. He studied the image, paying particular attention to the emergence of gray in his hair. Lines of age were appearing and his body felt the wear and tear that one feels when coming out of his prime. He scanned through the years of his life and wondered how he had come to be thirty-three so quickly.

He realized that he was living in a cycle of hope, constantly searching for the ideal life. It was a cycle that had now revolved thirty-three times and had left him no closer to his goals. He felt a reluctant acceptance of the way things were, but, with that, had a sense of time lost and an awareness of his own mortality. He understood the importance of time and what revolving seasons can do to a man. He counted the revolutions that remained for him and felt a sense of urgency for what he had to do.

Chad pulled his tee shirt over his head and tucked it into his pants. He laced his shoes then went over to the dresser and grabbed his keys. On the way out he snatched a wad of dollar bills that was lying on his desk and stuffed it in his pocket. Noticing a piece of paper next to the bills, he picked it up, read it, then crumpled the paper and threw it toward the wastebasket. *The things I come up with when I'm stoned,* he thought as he shook his head. He grabbed his cigarettes and headed out the door.

The atmosphere at Pennsylvania Park was festive. There was a folk singer playing in the gazebo at the near end of the park. A crowd had gathered and the people who weren't lucky enough to snatch a bench found makeshift seating on the railroad tracks that ran diagonally through the park. Children were running about, testing their limits with their parents. Some were having lunch under the shade of one of the many walnut trees, while others were eating fudge or licking ice cream cones as they listened to the singer. An Arlo Guthrie song was being sung as Chad planted himself at the base of a tree. He lit a cigarette and inhaled deeply.

Splotches of sunlight laid on the ground under the giant walnut and a gentle breeze blew in from the west. Some pesky ants were trying to reclaim their territory from him and he retaliated by flicking them into the air with a stick. As he was doing this, a girl, about ten years his junior, came up to the base of the tree.

"Hey, can I bum a light?" she asked.

Chad looked up at her. "Sure, no problem," he said. He fumbled through his pockets for his lighter. "This guy's pretty good," he noted, nodding toward the folk singer as he lit her cigarette.

"Yes he is. Mind if I join you?" she asked as she looked for a flat spot under the tree.

"No, not at all," Chad said and scooted over to make room. "My name's Chad," he added.

"Nice to meet you, Chad. I'm Sara."

"Enchanté," Chad said as he shook her hand. "Are you from around here?"

"Yes, I've lived in Petoskey all my life."

"Really? I can't recall seeing you before."

Sara smiled. "Yeah, I can't say that I've seen you before either."

Chad studied the girl as they spoke. She was tall, about five-foot seven, with hazel-green eyes. She had shoulder-length black hair that cascaded down the back of her multicolored sundress. Her skin was creme white and her lips were plush and somewhat pouty. She seemed to have a natural Bohemian way about her—rather intellectual, yet casual and relaxed. Although he didn't know much about her, he found it quite pleasant to have her sitting next to him. "Are you into folk?" he asked.

She smiled at him again. "I'm into any kind of music that has quality and substance," she said as she took a hit off her cigarette and stared back toward the gazebo, seemingly making an effort not to give him too much attention.

As they sat together listening to the singer Chad's mind began to race, searching for something else to say. He felt an instant attraction to the girl and the last thing he wanted was to come across as being dull; however, the only topics he could think of were quite conventional, so he opted to say nothing. He lit a cigarette and leaned back against the tree, sacrificing wit for looking casual. Finally, a topic came to mind that he thought might be of interest. He turned to her and was about to speak when she stood and brushed off the back of her dress. "Well, thanks for sharing your tree, Chad," she said as she held her hand out to him. "And thanks for the light."

Chad shook her hand and smiled. "I enjoyed your company, Sara. Perhaps we'll run into each other again."

"Perhaps we will," she said, showing a hint of a smile. "Have a good day."

She turned and walked down the curving path that ran through the park. Chad watched until she headed down Lake Street and disappeared around the corner. *Dammit, Reiger, you did it again,* he scolded himself. *You couldn't think of anything to say.* He shook his head. No longer in the mood to listen to the concert, he pushed himself up and headed back toward his apartment.

As he walked into the kitchen he noticed the wrinkled up paper on the floor next to the trash. He unraveled it and took another look. "Common sense is the damnedest thing. One can live a comfortable life because of it and fail miserably due to the lack of it. Conversely, one can be successful by disregarding it or an utter failure by following it." Chad flopped his body on the sofa, holding the paper in his hand.

A pounding at the outside door awakened him. He got up, dashed to the door of his apartment and hurried down the stairs. When he got to the entrance no one was there. He stepped out onto the porch and looked down the block. "Miles!" he yelled as he spotted the familiar figure walking back towards downtown.

Miles turned and saw Chad. He made his way back up the block, while Chad lit up a smoke. "Hey Bud," Chad said as Miles sprinted up the steps.

"What the hell? Were you dead to the world? I must've banged on your door twenty times."

"Yeah, I kind of crashed," Chad said with a stretch. "So, anyway, what's up?"

"I need a favor," Miles said as he raised his eyebrows and slightly bobbed his head in an I'll-owe-you-one manner. "I need you to bail me out tomorrow."

"Not the Hemingway shit again?"

"I'm afraid so, Chad. I promised Abbey I'd drive her down to Traverse tomorrow and I totally forgot about the tour. She has a job interview there and Pres has his car in the shop, so I'm the only one in the building with a vehicle."

"Abbey might be moving?"

"Looks that way."

"Shit," Chad mumbled as he contemplated. "Well, okay. I'll do it for her. What time?"

"The tour starts at nine-thirty."

"Do they still begin at the Chamber of Commerce?"

"Yeah. Right in front under the awning," he said as he patted Chad on the back. "Well, I've got to run. Stop over tonight if you're not doing anything."

Chad stayed on the porch and finished his cigarette and watched Miles as he headed back downtown. The last thing he wanted to do on a Saturday morning was escort a group of tourists on a Hemingway tour; however, he did like Abbey and wouldn't want to be the culprit who ruined her chance for a better job.

He decided he'd better brush up on his routine while it was on his mind. He hadn't given a tour in nearly three years and didn't want to be wandering through town aimlessly with a bunch of Fudgies. He sat at his desk and drew up an itinerary.

By early evening Chad began to get restless. He hopped back in the shower, got dressed and took a walk downtown. Along the way he ran into Pres, who shared an apartment with Miles. Pres was cool in a preppy sort of way, but had the misfortune of being born to republican parents in 1971 and they had given him the legal name of President Nixon Smith. Occasionally when one of the gang was drunk enough they would call him Nixon, but for the most part they left him alone on the matter.

They came to the door that led to their place. Chad followed as Pres sprinted up the twenty-four well-worn stairs. When he reached the top he tapped on the first door to the left, then without waiting for a response, unlocked the second door down the hall, took off his coat and threw it on a folding chair next to the card table. As he went into the bathroom, Chad heard a voice down the hall saying, "Where were you guys all afternoon?" He turned and saw Abbey walking through the door that Pres had left open. "Hi Chad," she said as she saw him. She asked where Pres went and Chad pointed to the bathroom. Then, in a voice slightly short of a yell she said, "I need to pick up a few things at the store."

"Damn. And I left my cabby hat at the shop," Pres smirked as he came back into the room.

"Funny, Pres," Abbey scolded. "Actually I was hoping Miles would be with you. I need to get something for dinner. We have a surprise guest tonight."

Pres stopped rummaging through his stack of CDs and looked

at Abbey. "Who is it?" he asked.

"You'll find out around eight."

"Rob?" Chad inquired.

"Perhaps," she replied coyly.

"Oh c'mon Abbey, just tell me," Pres commanded as he dug his fingers into her side and tickled, bringing her to her knees in laughter.

"No, stop it," she screamed, then flopped down on her back and caught her breath. "I told you, you'll just have to wait."

"What's with all this screaming? You guys are gonna piss off everyone in the building."

Chad turned at the sound of the familiar voice. "Hey Monique," he said with a nod. He momentarily stood in appreciation of her natural beauty, as he usually did. Of all the girls he knew, Monique was the finest, with the possible exception of the girl he'd met in the park earlier in the day. She had the typical French look that he had come to love; narrow in the waist but not underweight, flowing brunette hair, full lips and well-defined features. Her face was pure and her skin pale and she carried herself with a sense of propriety without being pompous.

"When Miles gets back do you wanna go for a ride with us? Pres asked her.

"Where are you going? Monique asked.

"We have to take Abbey to the grocery store."

"Yeah, I'll tag along. I want to grab a bottle of Irish Mist anyway."

"Ah ha!" Pres blurted. I had a feeling and I was right. It's Jud!"

"Dammit, Monique," Abbey chastised. "It was supposed to be a surprise."

She shrugged her shoulders in an apologetic manner. "Sorry Abbey, I didn't know I gave anything away."

Abbey explained how everyone knew that Jud drank Irish Mist, while Chad stood back with his mouth frozen in a half smile. A laugh came to him. "Jud's back," he said as he shook his head in disbelief. "You think he's back to stay this time?"

"He'll never be back to stay, Chad. No matter what his convictions are," Pres piped in. "And if I were a trust-fund baby like him, I'd be off seeing the world too."

Pres heard Miles coming up the stairs and he fetched his coat from the chair. With the surprise factor gone, Abbey filled him in on what was happening and everybody headed down the stairs to his car. Jud's return was an event and they all felt rather festive as they packed into his Buick.

As they drove, Chad recalled the last time Jud was in town. Without asking, he had taken the keys to his car and went on a four-in-the-morning drug run. As he was heading down one of the back roads, tripping out on acid, he smashed the car into a tree and nearly ended his existence. He spent two weeks in the hospital followed by ninety days with the county. When he was released there was no, "Sorry about your car, Chad," no, "Till we meet again." Nothing. He simply blew town without a word to anyone. Still, despite it all, Chad found himself anxious to see him.

Pres and Abbey took off to grab some beer and wine, leaving Chad and Monique alone in the snack aisle. Chad picked up a bag of Cheetos and casually glanced over at her—and she was looking at him as well. He smiled awkwardly as he noticed her hair. It looked darker than normal and he wondered if she'd colored it. He wanted to touch her. He wanted to say that he could easily fall in love with her. Instead, he put the Cheetos into the basket that she was carrying and turned his attention back toward the snacks.

Chad had known Pres and Miles for nine years, dating back to when he'd first come to town. Jud had moved back about five years ago after living the previous five years abroad, and Abbey had been born and raised in Petoskey, but Chad hadn't met her until roughly three years ago. Monique was the newest member of the crowd. She was a college friend of Abbey's who had come to town a mere six months ago. She was the kind who seemed to enjoy being on the outside, looking in. In social circles she was more of an observer than a participator; someone who evaluated every nuance of conversation and quietly contemplated it.

Chad first heard of her arrival when Abbey called and said she had an old friend who'd be moving in with her. She invited him, along with the rest of the crowd, to go to the pub so everyone would get a chance to meet her. When Chad asked if she was cute Abbey simply chuckled and said to be down there around eight.

He eyeballed the door in anticipation. After ten minutes the two girls arrived, walking side by side toward their table. Chad's gaze was fixated on the heart-stopping beauty to Abbey's left. She introduced her to everyone and, as Chad stood to greet her, his thigh caught the edge of the table and down went the three glasses of beer—one all over Pres and the other two smashing on the floor below. Pres stood and looked at his lap as the others laughed. Then he looked up at Monique and said, "Don't be concerned. He does this every time we introduce him to someone." The girls laughed as Chad turned red.

Abbey and Pres returned with two bottles of wine and several six-packs of imported beer. Abbey looked in our basket and scolded, "Is that all you could come up with? One bag of Cheetos?"

"Here," Pres said as he reached for the shelf. "This, this and this. There!" He looked over at us with a was-that-so-hard look and sarcastically said, "Are we ready to go now?"

The five of them headed back to the apartment and killed time until seven-thirty, when Chad and Abbey went with Miles to the bus depot. They parked the car and sat on the bench outside, waiting for the bus to arrive. It wasn't due for another twenty minutes and Chad asked Abbey about her interview.

"Well," she began, "it's a job with a computer firm. It's not exactly what I went to school for, but it would pay good."

Chad looked at her and smiled. "You know that I'd hate to see you go, Abbs, but I do wish you luck."

"Thanks. And thanks for covering for Miles tomorrow. If I get this job, I'll owe you one."

"Shit, you won't owe me. Besides, I would rather have Miles owe me," he said with a laugh. He pulled out a cigarette and turned from the breeze to get a light, then turned back and asked Abbey, "Is Sara going to Traverse with you tomorrow?"

"Who?" Miles and Abbey asked in tandem.

"Monique."

"You said Sara," Miles noted.

"Humph, I guess I did," Chad admitted. He felt embarrassed but pressed on. "Anyway, is she?" he asked again.

"No, but who is Sara?"

"Oh, she's a girl I met at the park this afternoon."

"Really? You didn't mention anything when I stopped by." Miles said.

"It's really no big deal. I barely know her."

"Is she cute?" Abbey asked.

Chad smiled at the interrogation. "Yes, I have to say she is." He glanced down at his watch. "Hey, the bus should be pulling in any time now."

It was but a few minutes later that the sound of the diesel engine could be heard and within moments the bus came around the corner. They stood by the side of the bus and watched as the passengers got off. Finally a longhaired, bandanna-clad and bearded Jud emerged, looked at them and smiled.

"Oh my God," Abbey laughed as she went up and hugged him. "What did you do to yourself?"

Jud just smiled his usual wry grin, picked Abbey up and spun her around. "Gotta do what I gotta do," he said with a smile that rose higher on one side. He set his backpack and duffel on the driveway and came loafing up to the bench. He turned back to Abbey. "It's good to see you again," he said. "How have you been?"

Abbey looked at him with gauging eyes. "I'm good, Jud, but how've you been?"

"Why the concern, Abbey baby? I've been good. I'm always good, you know that."

He turned to Miles and shook his hand. "Good to see you, man," he said.

Miles laughed. "It's good to see you too, you fucking rebel."

Jud looked over at Chad as if he hadn't noticed him until that point. He bull-charged him, delivered a fake punch to his gut, then slapped a hard hug on him, almost knocking him over in the process. "Dammit, Chad, how the hell are ya?" he blared.

Chad took a step back and studied his new look. Indeed, it looked like he came straight out of the sixties. "I'm doing good, Jud," he said as he picked up the duffel bag. Jud hoisted his backpack and followed the others to the car. As they drove back to the apartments, Abbey leaned over the front seat and asked Jud what he'd been up to.

"I've been staying in a cabin in the North Carolina woods for the past four months," he began. "I needed to get my shit together. Things were getting a little out of control and I knew I had to change something, so I rented this cabin just outside of Bryson City, toward the western end of the state."

Abbey listened wide-eyed and attentively as he spoke, while Miles occasionally glimpsed back from the rearview mirror. Chad noticed a look of purity in his eyes; a purity he hadn't seen in Jud before. To him, he seemed mellower and lacked his usual cocky insincerity.

"It was a beautiful setting," he continued. "I was right in the heart of the Great Smoky Mountains. The air was sweet and there was no one else around—and that's what I needed most. A man alone tells no lies."

He paused and turned his gaze out the window, seemingly collecting his thoughts for more of his story, but when he looked back at everyone he just smiled and asked what they'd been up to for the last four months.

Chad and Abbey filled him in as Miles pulled into the parking lot behind their building, and they headed up the back stairs. Pres and Monique heard them coming and were standing in the doorway as they rounded the corner. Monique ran up to Jud and enthusiastically embraced him at the top of the stairs while Pres sauntered up to the two of them.

As the rest of the gang huddled, Chad walked into the girls' open apartment. He observed how elaborately the table was set, complete with crystal that he didn't realize they'd had. He noticed that the candles in the center of the table seemed about to be blown out from the wind rushing through the open window at the far end of the living room. He walked over to it, closed the bottom half and slightly reopened the top portion, then sat on the sofa and waited for the others. He saw the gleam in Monique's eyes as she came in holding Jud's hand and wished he was the one who'd been living the fast-paced life, as well as the one who was getting her interminable attention. He sensed himself looking out of place so he hoisted himself up and went into the kitchen to see how Abbey was doing.

"Need any help in here?" he asked as he pushed through the chest-high swinging doors.

"No, thanks though. Everything's gonna be ready in about five minutes." She looked at Chad and studied his face. "You doing all right, Buckshot?" she asked.

"Yeah, doing fine," he said plainly. "Just feeling a little tired."

Abbey smiled and Chad went back into the living room. As he retook his seat, Jud was in the middle of another story—something about a group of college girls who'd stumbled upon his cabin while they were hiking. Chad faced him as he told the tale, but kept eyeballing Monique and contemplating her fascination with Jud. He pictured her in his arms and in his bed, wherever that would be. He looked back toward the kitchen and noticed Abbey studying him. When he did, she smiled and Chad felt somewhat appeased.

The stories continued at the dinner table. The more Chad listened, the more he resented Jud's presence and wished that he'd stayed in Carolina. He gave up any attempt to look interested and plowed into the food in front of him until Jud shouted out, "Hey, what are you so quiet about?"

Chad looked up and saw Jud peering at him, his uncharacteristically long hair and beard making him appear more like a stranger than a friend. He looked around at Monique and Pres and Abbey and realized that he'd become the center of attention.

"You're still pissed about the car," he stated blatantly.

"Chad finished chewing the food in his mouth before saying, "Did I say I was pissed about the car?"

"Bullshit! You haven't said two words all night. Just tell me you're still pissed about it and we'll go from there."

"Well you can read into it as much as you like, but I didn't say a word about the car now, did I?"

"All right, fuck you, Chad!" he lashed. "I haven't seen you in months and you can't even talk to me. What gives, man?"

"C'mon you two," Abbey piped in. "This is supposed to be a fun evening."

"Yeah, you're right, Abbey," Chad conceded as he looked at Jud who was still glaring at him. "Let's just drop it." He lowered his head and took a bite of his mashed potatoes and out of the corner of his eye he saw Monique swirling her hand across Jud's back.

CHAPTER TWO

Sara stopped halfway down the hall and looked out the window. Peering through the pre-dawn gray, she wondered what the day would bring. She lifted the window open and lit a cigarette. Glancing at the alarm clock that rested atop the nightstand in her bedroom, she saw it was five twenty-five. She wasn't used to being up at such an hour, but she found the experience refreshing. She needed to make the most of the day ahead, not for anyone else, but for herself.

Sara lived downtown in an upstairs apartment in the heart of the gaslight district. She worked at a souvenir shop that was down the block and around the corner from her building. She would often stand by the window before getting ready for work and use the streets below as a gauge of how the day would go. The more pedestrian traffic—the worse it would be for her. Today, she found the lifelessness of the early morning streets to be energizing—a reclaiming of her territory. The tourists had worn their wear on her more than usual this summer. She had grown tired of their rudeness and condescending manner. She was tired of pampering people who lived a life much easier than her own.

Today, however, she was determined to put all of that aside. She'd had but a handful of days off all summer and wasn't about to be burdened with anything. She just wanted some time to herself.

Those who didn't know her well would think she wasn't sociable. She could have been part of the "in crowd" had she cared tobe. She was intelligent and had a quick wit and, in a rather unrefined way, she was quite attractive. She was somewhat of an introvert, only revealing who she was to people she knew and trusted. She loved having stimulating intellectual conversations with her closest friends; often nearing the point of argument with impassioned topics. Nonetheless, she was content to spend most of her free time alone.

The youngest of eight children, she was always thought of as *Little Sara* by her family, even though she'd turned thirty in April. Whenever her Aunt Marion from Wisconsin would visit she'd still say, "My, you've grown some more, dear," even though Sara hadn't changed a bit since high school. The fact that she looked much younger than her age added to the situation. Her brothers and sisters still treated her as the baby of the family; constantly offering help and advice although neither would be asked for.

In a way that was unclear to her, Sara was trying to convince herself, too, that she was worthy of adulthood. Her father had died when she was very young and her mother was killed in an automobile accident when she was sixteen. The latter event had, in a way, left her trapped in time. Whenever she would smoke or swear or drink she would still feel a little strange. It was as if the restrictions a mother would put on a sixteen-year-old girl were permanently in place. She had to constantly reassure herself that, if her mother were around, she would certainly endorse her coming of age.

Sara took a final hit off her cigarette and flicked it out the window. Sticking her head out, she took a deep breath. The cool, clean air of late summer had a fresh, awakening effect and she let the gentle breeze push her hair onto her cheeks. She smiled, closed the screen and headed down the hall to the shower.

After a quick breakfast, she walked down to the Lake Michigan shoreline. She casually strolled up the coast, occasionally stopping to look for fossils and Petoskey stones. As she walked, she thought about the guy she'd met the day before at Pennsylvania Park. She found herself intrigued with him, if nothing else. She perceived him to be a little shy, but sensed substance in him. She sat down on a rock near the shore, staring out over the water as she thought. She reminisced about her last two relationships. James had proven to be a boorish, self-centered egotist, and it was only a few months into her stint with Nathan when she realized that he preferred being with men.

A wave came upon the rock and splattered her legs. She got up, took off her shoes and returned to her perch. As she dug her toes into the sand, her thoughts came back to Chad. She resolved that the next time she saw him, she would make a point to talk to him. She sensed that she'd have to be the aggressive one. She pictured him sitting under the shade of the oak tree, looking as complex as he did innocent. She envisioned the honesty in his eyes, as well as the uncertainty that was manifested in the expression he wore. She contemplated the difference: the brooding, introspective person sitting alone, who changed into the bright-eyed and amicable fellow the moment he became aware of her presence.

Over the sound of the waves Sara heard a distant whining. She turned her head toward shore and strained to listen. Faintly, she heard it again. A smile came to her face. She hastily put her shoes on and set out, following the sound. The ancient, haunting melody drew her as if she were summoned by a specter. She could feel the Irish lineage inside her as she approached. Her sojourn took her to the porch of the Perry Hotel; an inn made famous from lodging Ernest Hemingway. A kilt-clad piper strolled the porch as he filled the air with Celtic sound. There was a small gathering of people in front of the hotel who had ceased whatever they were doing and stopped to listen. Sara looked at the eclectic mix of the group: there were men dressed in suits, longhaired kids with tie-dyed shirts, two young mothers with baby strollers and of course the obligatory Fudgies. She stood away from the crowd and listened.

As she did, she looked across the street to the north end of the park. She saw the familiar face of Chad, who was leaning against one of the trees. She crossed the street. Chad saw her coming and his eyes widened as she approached. "Hi stranger," she called out.

"Hey, Sara," Chad replied with an enthusiastic smile.

"How are you?" she asked as she strolled up next to him.

"I'm good," he said. He looked into her warm eyes, then added, "Don't tell me you like this music too. I might have to propose to you right here."

Sara laughed. "Well, I am Irish, you know," she said.

"Well, actually, I don't know."

Sara furrowed her eyebrows in thought, scanning their brief conversation from the day before, then said, "So, I suppose we need to fully introduce ourselves. I mean, if we're going to get married and all. I'm Sara McClair."

Chad held out his hand and took Sara's. "And I'm Chad Reiger," he said, his eyes as focused and piercing as a salesman closing a deal.

"Reiger, eh?" Sara said. "So I take it that you weren't drawn down here by your Celtic bloodlines."

"Probably not as much as you, although I am a quarter Irish. I just love the sound of bagpipes, that's all."

Chad noticed the gleam in Sara's eyes as they spoke. He sensed that she saw it in his, too. He was determined not to crawl into a shell, as he had done the day before. He turned back toward the porch and listened to the music as he thought. He thought about Monique and recalled how she'd gone gaga over Jud the night before and sensed that perhaps it was time to step away from that scenario. Everything about this seemed right. He turned back to Sara. "So anyway, I think we should go out sometime," he said, sounding somewhat mechanical in his delivery.

"You think we should, hey. Humph, that's interesting," Sara toyed.

"You see, that's not really a response though. I was looking for a yes or no answer, preferably a yes."

"Actually, Chad, it is a response. What it isn't, is an answer, because if you're looking for an answer you have to actually ask a question."

"Ah, an intellectual too. And you're right, so let me correct myself. Would you like to go out with me sometime?"

"There, much better, and yes I would," she said with a grin. "So where do you plan on taking me?"

"There's an Irish folk singer playing in the basement of the hotel here tomorrow night," he said, pointing across the street to the Perry.

"Yeah, I know him."

"We could catch a meal and listen to him for a while, and then go from there."

"Sounds good to me. What time are you picking me up?"

"How does seven-thirty sound?"

"Seven-thirty it is?"

Sara turned her attention back to the sound of the pipes and Chad, not wishing to press his luck, bid her a good day. "We'll see you tomorrow then," he said as he nudged her shoulder with the back of his hand.

Sara smiled. "See you tomorrow, Chadders."

"Who?"

"Chadders. I like it, it has a good ring."

"Okay, Chadders it is." He waved and made his way up the hill to his apartment.

Sara sat down on the grass and listened to more of the music. She was comfortable with how the morning had unfolded. She lifted her gaze to the white clouds which graced the blue sky—a sky as blue as Chad's eyes, she thought. She looked forward to the evening that would follow and was proud of herself for taking a chance with someone whom she didn't know well. However, there was something about this guy that made her comfortable—that made her feel like she knew him well from the moment she'd met him. She thought how it was his eyes that won her over. They were trusting and trustworthy, caring and needful. They were the kind of eyes that revealed a person's innermost self. She picked herself up and headed back down Lake Street and to her apartment.

Sara awoke that afternoon from a two-hour nap and took a walk down the street to the gift shop where she worked. As she walked, she scoffed at the idiocy of the tourists that she encountered along her route. *Good job parking that car,* she thought as she came upon a BMW parked diagonally into a gap in the otherwise horizontal parking arrangement of the Petoskey streets. *How stupid can you be?* She shook her head and walked into the gift shop.

"Hey Sara," came the greeting from the girl working the counter that was set up in circular fashion in the middle of the sales floor. "What are you up to today?"

"Hey Jane, not much. Just came in for my check. Is Richard here?"

"Yeah, he's screwing around with something in the back."

"Okay, thanks," Sara said and made her way to the stock room where she spotted her boss tediously trying to assemble a lamp. "Hey Richard, you got my check?" she called out.

"Dammit!" he said as he dropped his screwdriver and grabbed his chest. "Don't sneak up on me like that," he scolded in his somewhat feminine voice. "Oh, anyway, I'm glad you stopped by. I need you to work this evening."

"Sorry pal," Sara said without hesitation. "I just stopped in for my check."

"Well if you want your check, you'll have to work tonight," Richard smirked.

"Listen," Sara began in a firm and direct tone. "That's bullshit and you know it. You owe me a check from last week. I'm not scheduled to work at all today and I want to get paid and go enjoy the rest of my day."

"Well, if you want to get pissy about it, I'll give you your check. Just remember I can get pissy too. I seem to recall that you'd put in a request for the weekend after Labor Day. You don't work to-night—you don't get that weekend."

Sara stood and glared as he buried his head back into his project. "Fine! Take away my weekend. Just give me my check before I call the NLRB."

Richard slammed his screwdriver back on the workbench and opened a small drawer near his desk. "Fine," he snapped as he handed her an envelope. "But I'm not kidding. You just lost your weekend girl."

Sara looked him in the eye, made a frown and shook her head. Then she turned and walked out. After a stop at the bank, she took a walk down to the Bear River and followed a trail that took her upstream and away from the group of fishermen who were gathered at the river's mouth. She found a fallen tree and sat down. Still fuming about the events that transpired at the shop, she lit a cigarette and stared toward the water cascading over a boulder in the middle of the stream. She thought that perhaps it was time to get another job. She had been there five-and-a-half years and it was probably time to move on; however, she liked the convenience of a two-minute walk to work. She thought of how all her sisters had worked there at one time or another, and how the previous owner of the shop was none other than her own mother. She remembered how, when she was a little girl, she would help her decorate for each season and holiday and recalled the pride her mother had in the appearance of the shop. She thought of the division in the family when the decision was made to sell the store and divide the money.

As Sara sat, she found that the tranquillity of the river was outweighed by her frustrations. Reminiscent of the fact that this was supposed to be her day, she headed back to the gaslight district and down to the Seventh Street Coffee House—a hangout for local musicians, writers, painters and other artistic types. She ordered a lattè and took a table near the window as a trendy looking bearded man ogled her frame. She was watching him out of the corner of her eye when she felt a tap on the shoulder. "How you doing, little girl?" a raspy voice greeted.

Sara turned and saw her sister Karen standing behind her. "Hey," she said. "Have a seat."

Karen set a bag from JC Penney on the chair next to Sara, pulled out the chair across from her and sat. "What in heaven's name are you doing in a coffee house?" Sara jested.

"Oh, I've come down with one of these summer colds and I wanted a hot lemon tea," she explained.

"Yeah, I was going to say you don't sound very good. Go ahead and get one. I'll be here for a while."

Karen went up to the counter and, when she returned, asked Sara how she'd been.

"I don't know, Karen," Sara began as she spiraled her finger around the outside of her cup. "I'm really getting fed up with Richard. He's such a little pain in the ass." She paused and looked at her sister for some kind of a reaction. Karen remained placid and Sara continued. "I've had three days off all summer long and that prick tried to coerce me into coming in this evening by not giving me my check."

"What do you mean, he coerced you?"

"He threatened to take away my weekend off—the weekend that I had on the calendar since early May."

"Well, maybe you should've gone in, Sara."

"Did you hear what I was telling you? I've only had three days off all summer. I do need some time to myself," Sara lashed.

"Yes I heard you," Karen said in a calm but somewhat condescending manner, but you're not married and you have to support yourself. You can't count on dipping into your money from Mom."

Sara reached behind her and pulled her purse off the back of the chair. She dug through it, pulled out her wallet and took out her driver's license. She reached across the table and handed it to Karen.

"What's this for?" she asked.

"Look at my date of birth," Sara said.

"I know when you were born. I remember when it happened."

"Then you should know that I'm not a foolish little teenager," she said as she took the license back from her sister's hand.

"Sara, don't be so defensive. I'm just trying to help you, that's all."

Sara sensed the futility in laboring her point and decided to deflect the conversation. "Has anyone heard from Anne?" she asked.

"Yes, Heather got a postcard from California the other day. She said she's doing good and having lots of fun. I worry about her though, so far away from home."

"Yeah, what is it, like a four-hour flight?"

"What is with you today?" Karen commanded. "I can't even talk to you without hearing sarcasm."

"Well why are you worried about Anne? And why do you always have to question my judgment?" Sara stood. "Listen Karen, I don't even care why right now. I've had a rather shitty day and I'm just going to leave this conversation for another time. I hope your cold gets better."

Karen scowled her face into a disappointed look, but then bid her sister adieu. "Hope your day gets better," she reconciled as Sara walked out.

Sara made her way through the park, back down Lake Street and up to her apartment. She rued the fact that her day, which had started off so good, had turned out so badly. She looked forward to the next day and her evening with Chad. There was something there that was new and refreshing, and she felt that was just what she needed. She dug a blanket out of the closet, lay on the sofa and settled in for a nap.

The night was warm and the full moon illuminated the row of white houses on the tree-lined street where Chad lived. The night was so pleasantly mild that it seemed to top any day the summer had yet to offer. It was August eighteenth and the weather would be turning soon. Chad sat on the porch as he thought about the events of the day and especially his encounter with Sara. He got up and began to walk down the street.

He wanted his date with her to go smoothly and was mulling over what he should do. He was concerned with his ability to keep her interested for the duration of the evening. He knew himself well enough that if he got past the first date, he'd be fine. In fact, Sara would have trouble shutting him up. However, he also knew that he could, at times, revert to the shy teenager he used to be when in the company of someone he didn't know well.

In no time he had walked five blocks and found himself at the neighborhood convenience store. He walked in and found his friend Megan working. "Hey there," she casually greeted. "What are you doing out so late?"

"Not much. Just getting some fresh air into my lungs before calling it a night," Chad replied as he grabbed a Pepsi and set it on the counter. "It's too nice outside to go to sleep yet." She rang up the soda and he asked, "Hey, you don't happen to know Sara McClair, do you?"

"Yeah. She's kind of a strange one, isn't she?" she said with a bit of a facial contortion.

Chad cocked his head and asked, "What do you mean, strange?"

"I don't know. She just seems to be one of those artsy types who are a little out there," she replied indifferently. "Why do you ask?"

"Oh, I met her in the park yesterday and I thought she was rather cute."

"Well don't get your hopes up. A girl like her would never go out with you—and don't take that personally. I just know that she only goes out with those freaky, intellectual types."

"So you're saying I'm not smart enough for her?"

"Stop it. That's not what I'm saying and you know it. I just think you would get on her nerves after a while." She handed Chad his change. "I'm just saying don't ask her out, if that's what you're fancying. You'll only get turned down and then you'll be all depressed."

"Yeah, you're probably right," Chad said, opting to end the conversation rather than give the details of what had already transpired. He wished her a good night and started back home. He twisted the top off his soda and took a swig. *What was it about Sara that she seemed not to like?* he wondered. *She said she was kind of strange.*

As he walked back to the apartment he tried to dismiss whatever Megan had said. All he knew was that Sara was cool and that's where he wanted to focus his attention, especially with Monique out of the picture. Still, the conversation with Megan had planted a seed of doubt. *Maybe I am fooling myself,* he thought. *And why would someone like her want to go out with me? And even if she did, how long could it last?*

By the time he got home everything seemed unclear. He sat on the couch, picked up the phone and dialed. "Hello," came a groggy response.

"Hey Greg. Sorry about calling so late but I need your opinion about something."

Greg cleared his throat and coughed several times before saying, "Sure man, throw it at me."

"Well, I met this girl the other day down at the park and there's something about her that I really dig."

Greg chuckled. "You telling me you're in love?" he asked.

"No, it's too soon for that, but there's a lot about this girl that I like."

"But it sounds like something's bothering you."

"Yeah, a couple of things."

"Like what?"

"You remember Megan Drury?"

"Of course."

"Well I ran into her tonight and I was telling her about this girl, Sara's her name, and Megan said that she was a little out there. She said that she was one of those freaky intellectuals and that it would never work with me and her."

"Do you think it could work?" Greg coaxed.

"Yeah, I think it could."

"Then fuck Megan. You have to follow your own heart, man. What else?"

"Well, we're going out for the first time tomorrow and I really want to be at my best. This girl is something special and I don't want to blow it."

"Why would you think you would blow it?"

"I'm just afraid I'll come up empty and not have anything clever to say. With what Megan told me, I feel rather intimidated now—like I have to measure up to the people that she's used to hanging out with."

"So maybe you don't say anything clever. Listen, Chad, this girl apparently sees something in you if she agreed to go out on a date, right? I've known you for a long time and you've got a lot going for you. Maybe you're not as intellectual as the people she hangs with, but she chose to go out with you, not one of them. There's something about you that she likes so just be yourself and everything will be fine."

"So you think I should just wing it."

"Relax and have fun with it. If there's something there, you guys will connect, and that's about all I can offer you, buddy."

"Well, you do make sense and I needed to hear what you said. I'll let you know how it all turns out."

Chad hung up the phone, went over to his desk and lit the night's last cigarette. He'd heard what he wanted to hear, but he also knew Greg was right. If he could relax and be himself, everything would be fine. He finished his smoke, got undressed and headed off to bed.

CHAPTER THREE

Chad lifted his head off the pillow and looked at the clock as he listened to the rain pattering off the overhang. The distant thunder was as tranquil as it was foreboding and he allowed himself another half-hour before getting into the shower. He dreaded giving another tour, and the thought of doing one in the rain made the task even less appealing.

As he was lying in bed, the phone rang. He tumbled to his feet and ran into the living room. "Hello," he answered in an irritated voice.

"Hey Chad, Miles here. I just want to make sure you didn't forget about the Hemingway thing."

"Yeah I had my alarm set," Chad said as he rubbed his eyes. "Is Abbey there?"

"No, we don't have to leave until eleven, but Chad, tell me you're not going to do that Parking Day shit again."

"No, of course not. That was a one time thing."

"Good. I don't feel like answering calls for the next three days and explaining that there's no such thing as Parking Day."

Chad laughed as Miles continued. "Hey, what was that deal with you and Jud anyway?"

"It was no big deal, Miles. The whole thing was blown out of proportion."

"So you're cool with him?"

"Yeah."

"Well that's good. I guess he had a pretty good night after we all left."

"What do you mean?" Chad asked in an anxious tone.

"I guess him and Monique spent the night together."

"Well good for him," Chad said in a low, unsettled voice. "Well, I'd better get ready. Tell Abbey I wish her luck," he said, then hung up the phone. *That fucking little prick!* Chad said to himself. *He's not even in town for one day and he ends up with Monique. Well screw him, and screw her too!* He took the pillow from the end of the couch and rifled it onto the floor. Then he picked it up, set it back and headed to the shower.

⌒ ⌒ ⌒

Chad arrived at the Chamber of Commerce at five to nine. Several of those who were making the tour were already there and waiting under the awning. He introduced himself and joined them as they waited for the others, while the warm summer rain splattered down upon the sidewalk. When everyone arrived, umbrellas in hand, they embarked on the tour. Chad recognized one group member as a student at the college. The others were unfamiliar faces and presumably tourists. They headed through Pennsylvania Park and began at one of Hemingway's favorite watering holes. Single file, the group followed him into the establishment and walked past the well-preserved and intricately carved mahogany bar. Chad waited for the group to form a huddle around him, then explained how Hemingway would frequent the place more often in the winter months and how, with his gruff and adventurous demeanor, he began to earn his reputation as a man of the world. He explained how he would get together with several of his closest friends and share some of his works when they were in the conceptual stage; among them, *Farewell to Arms* and *For Whom the Bell Tolls*.

After Chad delivered his speech, the group looked around and a few took pictures, and then continued their walk through downtown. As they walked, Chad pointed out other hangouts along the route and mentioned any facts, trivial as they may be, that were Hemingway-significant. The more the tour progressed, the more Chad was bombarded with questions. The harder the incessant rain fell, the more he cursed having such a receptive group. He recalled the price the people were paying for the tour and forced a smile to his face.

They went up Mitchell Street and over to the east side of town to a house where Hemingway had once lived. "This is where *Torrents of Spring* was written, am I correct?" came a German sounding voice from the back of the group.

Chad looked back and saw a tall fellow with wavy, blonde hair who appeared to be in his late twenties. "That's right," he affirmed. "And very good. That's a fact that most people don't know, not even the ones who live here."

And with that, despite the rain, the barrage of questions resumed.

"The people who live in this house didn't know Hemingway wrote here?" someone else asked.

"No—I'm not sure if they do or don't but I was referring to the people of Petoskey." Chad answered.

"Is it true that Hemingway has a sister who still lives in the area?" asked a short, rotund woman wearing a bright yellow raincoat which had a brim coming off its hood and made her look like a fat little duck.

"He had a sister in Horton Bay who passed away several years ago," Chad replied.

"Is it true he once was mayor of Petoskey?"

"No, he wasn't, but he did institute one local holiday?"

"What sort of holiday?"

"It's called Parking Day. It started when the area first began to be overrun with tourists during the summer months. One night while Hemingway was sitting in a local tavern, he proposed that on the first day of September all the locals come downtown and park their cars to celebrate getting the town back. It caught on, and although it's since been moved to the day after Labor Day, Parking Day is now a tradition for the locals here."

It was ten after eleven when they made it back to the Chamber of Commerce. Chad gave the group one last list of events in the area and thanked them for their participation. Then, glad that the morning was over, he headed to the pub for lunch.

☞   ☞   ☞

It wasn't until Friday evening that Chad realized he'd failed to ask Sara where she lived. He scurried through the phone book but found no listing for Sara McClair. "Shit! That's just great!" he said aloud as he tossed the directory onto the table. He grabbed his jacket and his keys and ran down the stairs to his car. "Seven twenty-five and you have no idea which apartment's hers," he mumbled. "She's gonna think you stood her up and that'll be the end of it."

He drove down Lake Street, hoping for some sign of Sara. He was dreading the thought of going door to door looking for her when, to his relief, he spotted her down the block and waiting on the corner. He pulled up to her, reached over and pushed the door open and she hopped in the car.

"Forgot to ask where I lived, didn't you, Chadders?"

"I'm glad you realized that and came out to wait for me. I was about to give up and ask that girl across the street if she wanted to go."

"Well, I don't want to hold you back," Sara jested. "You can still ask her if you want to."

"No, I think I'll give it a try with you. If it doesn't work out I can always come back for her later."

Sara laughed. "You are the charming one, aren't you?"

A few minutes later they arrived at the Perry Hotel. Chad parked the car and they walked to the Noggin Room, which was a cozy little pub located in the basement of the building. There was a pleasant breeze blowing in from the west and Chad noted how it gave Sara's hair a sort of wild and sexy look. He momentarily let her get a step ahead of him so he could observe. She was wearing a white stretch top and khaki shorts, through which Chad noticed a shapeliness he had not expected. He surveyed her finely pronounced shoulders, which accentuated her excellent posture, and her soft, shapely bottom, which appeared to suspend ever so slightly over her smooth, white thighs.

"You gonna make it, Reiger," Sara said as she caught Chad lagging behind. "You're not going to get tired and putter out early now, are you?"

Chad, realizing he had just been busted and figuring the easiest way out was to be direct, smiled and said, "Oh, I'll be fine. I just wanted to sneak a quick glance from behind. Is that so bad?"

"Quick? I met three other guys in the meantime."

"Really? Three? Any prospects?"

"Yeah, one was kind of cute but the jury's still out on you."

"But they went into chamber too quick. I didn't get a chance to deliver my closing statement."

"So that works to your advantage. You can call for a mistrial."

They crossed the street and Chad held the door open for Sara and they headed down the steps. As they waited for the host, Chad smiled. He was pleased with the start of the date and he felt at ease with Sara. He was glad that he was able to be himself around her; furthermore, he was relieved that she wasn't one who would force him to carry the brunt of the conversation, offering one-word responses to anything he said. He didn't want the evening to be an exercise in keeping her entertained.

From around the corner came the familiar white-haired host. "Hello, Chad," he greeted as he approached. "Table for two?"

"Yes, Bob, please. And how are you tonight? Looks like you drew a good crowd."

"Yeah we did, but I still have one table open. It's in smoking, though. Does your friend smoke?"

"Like a damn chimney," Chad said, laughing. "Bob, this is Sara. Sara, my friend Bob."

The two shook hands and Bob led them down into the dining area and seated them. "Is Sean going to be playing soon?" Chad asked as he was turning to leave.

"Yes, he's tuning his guitars right now and should be playing within a few minutes," Bob said. Then he nodded and, as he went off to greet another couple, the waitress approached. "Hi, Chad," she said. "The usual to start with?"

"Yes, please," Chad replied. "Mindy, this is my friend Sara. Sara, Mindy."

Sara looked at Chad. "The usual, hey?" she said with a wide-eyed grin. "What is the usual?"

"Guiness, at least when I come here it is," Chad said.

"Well I'll have his usual too, then," Sara told the waitress, then turned back to Chad and commented, "Gee, you don't get down here often, do you?"

"First time here actually," he scoffed.

Sara reached into her purse and pulled out a cigarette. "So," she began as she lit her smoke, "tell me about Chad Reiger."

Chad paused and fidgeted. "Do you want the long story or the short story? he asked.

"Give me the Reader's Digest condensed version for now," Sara quipped. "If everything goes good you can fill me in on the details later."

"Well, okay then. How's this: I guess I'm kind of quiet until you get to know me. I used to be athletic in high school and college but I've lost interest in sports lately—except for hockey. I don't drink much but I go for a buzz every now and then. And I seem to be fond of you."

Sara looked at him with an ever-so-serious expression. "Humph, you're off to a good start, but tell me more," she said without breaking a smile.

Chad dropped the gimmick and proceeded to tell her about himself against the backdrop of Irish music. He told her about his passion for traveling and that he wrote poetry. He reiterated his love of music, told her where he was born, where he had lived and what his hopes were. Then he threw the question back at her and was listening intently until she mentioned her age. "Wait a minute," he interrupted. "You're thirty?"

"That's what I said, isn't it?"

"Thirty?" Chad repeated. "I had you for about twenty-three... twenty-five at the most," he said as he explored her features, looking for signs of age. "I have to say you look great for thirty."

"Why, thank you," she said, showing a genuine, appreciative side that he'd yet to see.

They continued to chat throughout the evening, occasionally stopping to listen to the music. By the end of the night, both feeling comfortable with each other, they left the hotel. "I had a good time tonight, Chad," Sara began as they walked back to the car, "and I feel really good with you."

Chad grabbed her hand. "I feel the same way too," he said.

"So, would you like to spend the night at my place?" she asked with a smile.

Chad turned to her with something of a stupid look on his face. He felt about ten seconds elapse before he forced out, "Yeah, sure." He squeezed her hand as a plethora of thoughts raced through his head. As he walked, he again felt the eerie awkwardness of not knowing what to say. He hadn't expected things to advance this quickly and suddenly he felt out of place—like an impostor posing to be someone good enough for her.

They got to the car and Chad opened the passenger door and by the time he got in, he felt he needed to come clean. "Before we go, I need to introduce you to the side of me that thinks too much." He took her hand again and held it as he spoke. "First of all, I'd love to spend the night with you tonight but you caught me off guard. I feel somewhat…," he paused as he searched for the right word, "somewhat uncomfortable in that I never seem to know what to say in these situations. Anyway, I wanted to tell you this so you didn't think that it was being with you that made me uncomfortable. It's just the way I get."

"Would you rather wait for this?" Sara asked softly.

"No. Just as long as you can deal with me not knowing what to say."

"I think we can handle it, Chadders," she said as she leaned over and gently kissed his lips.

Chad started the car and they pulled out onto Bay Street and even as they did, the discomforting silence had begun. Sara made an attempt at some small talk to lighten him up but it was to no avail. He turned onto Lake Street and parked in front of Sara's building. They headed up the three flights of stairs to her apartment.

Sara unlocked the door and proceeded down the dimly lit hall that led to her bedroom. "You can wait on the sofa for a few if you want," she called out. "And if you want a beer I think there may be some in the refrigerator."

Chad got up, grabbed a bottle of Heineken, then resumed his rigid perch on the sofa. He spotted the remote on the coffee table and turned the television on. He began to channel surf, anxiously killing time until Sara reached over the sofa and pulled the remote from his hand. "You didn't come here to watch TV now, did you?" she said as she turned it off.

"No, I suppose I didn't," Chad said quietly as he gazed into her captivating green eyes. He stared for a moment before leaning to her and pressing his lips against the softness of hers. He placed his hand on her thigh and noticed how warm and smooth it was and he began to feel aroused. Looking down, he found her to be wearing a flannel shirt and nothing else. He had begun to unbutton it when Sara grabbed his hand and softly said, "Come with me, it will be better." Holding his hand, she led him down the hallway and to her bedroom. She shut the door as she went in but Chad opened it halfway as he went in behind her. "I want to see you," he said. The dim light softly illuminated Sara's body as he took her hand and turned her toward him. He resumed unbuttoning the flannel shirt that separated him from her then gently pulled the shirt past her shoulders and off her arms. He held her breasts at arm's length as Sara pulled his polo over his head. He unfastened his belt and stepped out of his Dockers as she pulled back the covers and lay on the bed, waiting for him to follow. He went to her and the two consummated their passions.

He awoke the next morning to the sound of clanking in the kitchen. He slid into his pants and went to find Sara. "This must be the bastard that slept with my sister," came the greeting from a stern-looking man sitting at the table, eyeballing him as he came down the hall. Chad looked over and saw Sara standing at the stove, scrambling eggs.

"Chad, have the pleasure of meeting my dad," Sara said in a caustic tone. "Actually, he's my brother Justin, he just thinks he's my dad at times."

Chad approached the elder McClair and extended his hand. A somewhat reluctant hand came out in response and engulfed his own. It felt like a rock and he hoped that Justin was only jesting with his initial greeting. Chad sat down and looked at Sara. Her hair was wild and nappy, but it seemed to make her look even more tempting. He wanted to make a comment alluding to the fact, but thought better of it as he recalled the cool reception he'd received from her brother. He smiled at her and asked in a rugged, morning voice, "How are you this morning?"

"I'm doing good," she said as she smiled back. "How did you sleep?"

"I slept just great," he said.

She gave him a wink and turned back to the stove and Justin asked, "So, what do you do for a living, Brad?"

"I work in a grocery store, and it's Chad, not Brad," he added, somewhat uncomfortably.

"He's fucking with you, Chadders," Sara told him.

"Hey, you watch your mouth!" Justin scolded.

"And you lighten up!"

Justin paused, then turned back to Chad. "People always have to buy food, right? Sounds like there's job security there."

"Yeah, I guess so. I don't want to make a career out of it though."

"How long have you been doing it?"

"Fifteen years."

"Sounds like you've already made a career out of it," Justin remarked as he turned back to Sara. "Well, I better get going. You kids probably want to be alone anyway," he said to her.

"Aren't you going to stay for breakfast?" she asked.

"Breakfast? It's nine o'clock. Breakfast was three hours ago."

"Well, for you maybe. Just try to remember that it's a Saturday."

Justin went into the kitchen and gave Sara a peck on the cheek. "Tell this young man that he better treat you right," he said, talking loud enough for Chad to hear.

"He will, Dad," Sara replied sarcastically. "Now go do whatever you're in such a hurry to do."

Justin grabbed his jacket from the back of the chair, gave Chad a half nod and headed out the door. "I get the feeling he doesn't like me," Chad chuckled.

"He'll be okay with you, you just have to give him a while," Sara said as she scrapped some eggs and sausages onto a plate and placed it in front of him. "He's that way with everyone I see. He still thinks I'm this defenseless little kid." She went back into the kitchen, then came back and joined him at the table, bringing some toast and coffee with her. Chad dug into his breakfast and didn't say a word until he was finished.

"Are you okay with last night?" she asked as she wondered about the silence.

"Yeah, I'm fine," Chad said plainly.

"You seem a little quiet there, sport. What's the matter?"

"Nothing."

"C'mon. Tell me. You were fine when Justin was here but as soon as we were alone you clamed up on me."

"It's nothing. It just seems a little strange waking up here, that's all," Chad said as he stared at his plate. He paused and added, "And I've never done it on a first date before. I guess I'm kind of old fashioned that way."

"Why didn't you say something last night?"

"Because I wanted you," he replied without hesitation. He looked into Sara's eyes, then went back to fidgeting with the fork on his plate. After a moment he added, "I don't want you to think that last night didn't mean something to me."

"I know," Sara said as she took his hand, drawing his stare from the plate back to her. "So where do you want us to go from here?" she asked.

"I really don't know right now," he replied. He dropped his fork on the plate, stood and pulled her to him, embracing her and kissing her cheek. "You know I could fall for you quite easily," he said. "But for now, I need to go home."

He went into the bedroom and put on his shirt and shoes. On the way back through he stroked Sara's hair and kissed her lips. She stood motionless as he walked out the door.

CHAPTER FOUR

There was a nippy wind blowing in from the north as Chad awoke Wednesday morning. He was feeling the effects of the two-and-a-half packs of Marlboros he'd smoked the night before, so he threw on some jeans and a sweater and went down to the garden in back of the apartment to get some air. Four days had passed since he'd spoken to Sara. He knew he needed to call her soon, but with each day that passed the task was becoming more difficult.

Whatever was wrong with the relationship wasn't clear to him. One thing he realized was that he feared not living up to her expectations. Things had gone exceptionally well on their date, and part of him would rather have the relationship end on a high note, rather than having it be anything less than she anticipated—even if the reasons for ending it had to be ambiguous. All he knew for sure was that he liked her and would rather have her as a friend than lose her, as he did every other girl he had dated.

After four days of mulling it over, it had come to that. There was something about Sara that was too good to risk permanent alienation from a blundered relationship. He went back to the porch and took another deep breath of the crisp, morning air before attempting to make his call. He thought about what he was forfeiting by not taking a chance with the relationship. He tried to anticipate Sara's response to what he was about to tell her.

He looked out over the bay. The trees nearest the lake were already showing the reds and yellows of autumn. Soon, V-shaped flocks of geese would be migrating south and the flowers on the neighbor's porch would be replaced with carved pumpkins. Summer had come and gone again. Chad turned and headed back upstairs.

The notion of having one more encounter before he told her how he felt briefly crossed his mind, but he quickly dismissed it and was angry for even thinking that way. He had too much respect for Sara. Still he knew he would pine for her.

He went to the refrigerator and snatched a half-full bottle of Pepsi, got the phone and brought it over to his desk. He sat down, dialed and on the third ring, she answered.

"Hi there," Chad said, his voice exposing his discomfort.

"Hi," Sara responded in a cold, dry voice.

Chad's face dropped with the chilly reception, but he pressed on. "Sara, I was wondering if you could meet me in the park sometime this afternoon. I'd like to talk to you."

"No, just tell me over the phone," she said bluntly.

"Tell you what?"

"Do you think I'm stupid, Chad? You leave here Saturday morning with a whole cloud of reservations about the night before and then you don't call me for four days? Say what you have to say and we'll be done with it."

Chad put his hand on his head. He felt disheartened that Sara was hurt and he wanted to express himself as clearly as he could, especially with the issue being so vague. He paused to search for the proper words, then began. "Sara, there's nothing wrong with you. There's not a thing about you that I don't like. In fact, I like everything about you and that scares me. I feel I could never be comfortable around you. I feel I'd always have to be at my best and watch everything I say and do."

"What do you mean?" she asked with somewhat softened tone.

"I mean I have you on this pedestal and I don't look at myself as your equal."

"Why would you think that, Chad?"

"It's just everything about you. Everything about you seems perfect for me, but I don't feel that I can offer you what you give me."

"Chad," Sara started.

"No, let me finish," he insisted. "I want to be with you as much as you can stand having me around, but only as your friend. I want to have the luxury of screwing up in front of you and not having to worry about it. I want to be able to tell a lame joke without some-one saying, 'What's she doing with that jerk?' I just want to enjoy the time I spend with you and not feel under pressure."

Sara remained quiet after Chad ended his soliloquy. "You didn't hang up on me, did you? he asked.

"No," came a soft response. "I'm still here. I'm glad you called. I didn't know what to think." She paused and gathered her thoughts. "I wondered if you had just used me. I wondered if you'd seen something in me that you didn't care for. I didn't know what the hell was going on. I *would* like to meet you in the park, but I want to see you now, not this afternoon."

Chad breathed a sigh, one that expressed both relief and regret. "I'll be right there," he said. He swigged down the remainder of his soda and went into the bedroom to change, then hastily ran down the stairs and embarked upon the three-block walk to Penn-sylvania Park. As he walked he felt the relief of having taken care of the situation, but, ironically, he noted that his feelings for Sara were never stronger than they were now. When he arrived at the park he saw her sitting on a picnic table in the shade of an elm. When she saw Chad, she got up and casually walked toward him. "You know," she said as they met, "this isn't what I want to happen."

"I'm sorry, I just sense this is what I have to do. I feel the need to follow my instincts, Sara."

"You didn't give us much of a chance, you know."

Chad looked down, not knowing what else to say about the matter. He began kicking leaves away from the patch of ground where he was standing.

"I'm not giving up on you, Chad," she said assertively.

"And I'm not giving up on you; I'm giving up on me," he said as he looked up at her. "I'm sorry, but this is what I have to do."

"Okay, Chad," she said with a sigh. "If that's the way it has to be."

Chad looked into Sara's sad, green eyes and grabbed her. He

held her tightly and mumbled, "I love you."

"What was that?" she asked.

"Nothing. I didn't say anything," he quickly said in an embarrassed tone.

Sara didn't press him. "You make me sad, Chad. I won't argue with you anymore, but you make me sad." She looked at the unhappiness of his expression and thought how it matched her own feelings. She wondered why he was so unwilling to take a chance. *Had he been hurt in a previous relationship?* she pondered. Finally, she smiled. "So, you say you still want to be friends," she said.

"Yes, Sara, I do."

"Well Chadders, I'm gonna get going. I wish you luck in whatever you're looking for." She zipped up her jacket and tightened her collar. "Be sure to call me sometime then, okay?"

"I will. And you call me too."

They embraced again, then turned and went their separate ways and Chad, again, felt very much alone.

Time passed. Summer had turned to fall and fall was rapidly becoming winter. It was three days before Thanksgiving and Sara was making plans with her sisters for their holiday dinner. A gentle snow was falling as she looked out of her sister Beth's living room window. A storm had blown through the day before bringing significant accumulation. Banks were beginning to appear behind the sidewalks and the trees were struggling to hold onto their last leaves.

Sara had had an uneventful autumn. With the tourist season over she had a lot more free time and spent a good part of it reflecting on her life. She'd often take long walks, mulling over the direction that she wanted it to go; or she would sit at home, put on some Chopin and drift freely to the places where she wished she could be. The classical music would take her to the exotic, romantic places of the Old World. She would fantasize living the life of the elite, a life where she wouldn't have to cater to the wants and needs of social snobs. She thought about the happy homes her siblings had and wondered if such a life would ever fit her. And she tried to

41

make sense out of her brief relationship with Chad.

Since summer, she'd gotten together with him several times. They would go to dinner and a movie, and other times they had just met to chat, either at the park or at the pub. Whenever they got together, though, they avoided talking about the interlude they'd had. Yet, with each encounter, they continued to grow closer.

This particular fall had been a difficult one for Chad. The store where he worked was severely shorthanded and the brunt of the workload was thrust upon him. He was working seventy-hour weeks with no end in sight. His life seemed to be limited to work, a few quick meals and sleep. If he did decide to go out at night, it would come out of his sleep time and he'd have to pay the price the next day. Consequently, he became reluctant to socialize. He tried voicing his concerns to his manager, but he showed no regard for the matter. Other workers were feeling the same frustrations as well, which led to a tense working culture with everyone at each other's throats.

The upcoming holiday added to the problem. The day before Thanksgiving was one of the busiest days of the year and it couldn't have come at a worse time. Business would nearly double for the week and the aisles would be congested to the point where you couldn't work in them. Compounding the matter was the home-for-the-holiday crowd; the people who ran into friends whom they hadn't seen in months and would stop in the middle of the aisles and chat until they were totally caught up.

As Chad's shift on the Wednesday before Thanksgiving had ended, he decided it was time to get out and enjoy himself, so he headed to the pub to unwind. He walked through the doors and into a crowd of people. There were no bar stools available, nor was there standing room at the side bar, so he walked toward the dining section in the back. As he was looking for a seat he noticed Sara and Beth sitting in the corner and made his way toward them. "Hey girls," he said as he approached.

"Hey, Chad," Beth said as Sara flashed a smooth smile his way.

"So, what's happening?" he asked, looking to Beth and then to Sara.

"Not nearly enough," Sara responded.

"I wish I could say the same," Chad said. "They've got me running my butt off at the store, especially this week with the holiday and all."

"Still the same shit, eh?" Sara sympathized.

"Yeah, everything's the same."

Sara's face showed empathy for his situation. Then she smiled and asked, "What are you doing for dinner tomorrow?"

"I'll probably stay home and watch the Lions."

"Would you like to go to Beth's with me? We're having this feast that you wouldn't believe." She turned to Beth and asked, "You wouldn't mind, would you?"

"No, not at all. You'd be more than welcome, Chad," she said with her sincere brown eyes that matched her curly brown hair.

"Well, okay. As long as you're not having turkey or stuffing, cranberry sauce or pumpkin pie. I've seen my share of all that this week," he said with a laugh.

"I'll make you a PBJ," Sara offered.

"A PBJ, hey? Okay, it's a deal then."

Chad borrowed a chair from the group next to them and joined the girls at the table. He caught the waitress's attention and ordered a Budweiser. Looking around, he eyeballed the people in the dining area. With the establishment full and with the holiday, he spotted many people that he hadn't seen in some time. He fought off the urge to mingle and turned his attention back to Beth and Sara. "So what do you girls think of our early winter?" he posed.

"I hate it!" Beth replied without hesitating.

"What do you mean, you hate it?" Sara contested. "You were commenting on how pretty the snow looked when we were making pies."

"Yes, but we were nice and warm then," Beth explained. "And it's much colder tonight. I hate going out in that wind."

Sara threw the topic back at Chad. "How about you?" she asked, her voice sounding as cool and smooth as always. "Are you a winter person?"

"I am, Sara, but I guess it doesn't matter. I don't have time to do anything outdoors," he said with resignation. "And I can't see things changing. Not for the better, at least."

"So why don't you do something about it?" she challenged.

Chad shrugged his shoulders. "What can I do? I've got too many years into the place to quit and there's nowhere else in town where I can start off making the money I make now."

As he said this he noticed Beth taking a glimpse at her watch. He didn't want to portray himself as some sort of blabbering boob, so he looked for a way to excuse himself. After spotting a friend, he rested his hand on Sara's shoulder and said, "Hey, there's my friend Brad. If you girls don't mind I'm gonna run up to the bar and catch up with him."

"All right, then," Sara said. "Are you going to pick me up tomorrow?"

"Sure, What time?"

"About noon-thirty would be good."

"Game time," Chad mumbled.

"What was that?" Sara asked.

"Nothing," Chad said quickly. "Twelve-thirty it is. I'll see you then." He turned to Beth. "Thanks again," he said. "I'll see you tomorrow."

"And, Chad," Sara said as he turned to leave, "don't worry. The guys will be watching the game tomorrow, too."

Chad smiled, then went up to Brad, who was standing at the bar. "Hey there stranger," he called out as he approached. "How was Ireland?"

Brad turned, bearing a grin through his woolly beard. "Hey, sport, good to see you," he said as they shook hands. "And man, Ireland was awesome. You need to get over there sometime. You would love it."

"I know I would. I just wish I could drive there. You know I'm not crazy about flying."

"Man, there's nothing to it," Brad coaxed. "You hop on the plane and you're there before you know it."

"Well, I envy people like you. I wish it were as simple for me, but

I do hope to make it over there someday," Chad said with a face that exposed his own doubt. "At any rate, I'm glad you had a good time."

He chatted with Brad until he saw that Beth and Sara had left. Then, tired from his long day, he bid Brad a good holiday and headed home. As he lay in bed and the work of the day crept into his pre-sleep thoughts, Sara's words tormented him. "Why don't you do something about it?" he heard her ask again. *What can I do about it?* he pondered. *What to do? What to do?* was the mantra he chanted until he became burned out from the seemingly unanswerable question and faded off to sleep.

Thanksgiving morning came and Chad awoke at quarter to eleven. Despite his late-night lamentation he had gotten a restful sleep and, for the first time in weeks, woke up feeling invigorated. He looked forward to spending his afternoon with Sara and briskly made his way to the shower.

He began to get dressed, then realized he didn't know what the proper attire would be. The thought of donning a tie on his day off repulsed him and he looked through his closet, where he spotted a flannel shirt with a good, autumn look to it and opted for that. He was putting on a pair of Dockers, then stopped abruptly. He walked over to his dresser and pulled open the bottom drawer. Digging to the back, he snatched a Detroit Lions sweatshirt, held it up and contemplated if he could get away with wearing it to the gathering. *Hell, Lions football on Thanksgiving is a tradition in Michigan,* he told himself. He put the sweatshirt on, changed into blue jeans, put his shoes on and went into the kitchen. He went to the cupboard, poured himself a bowl of cereal and made toast, then turned on the television and watched the Thanksgiving Day parade until it was time to pick up Sara.

Chad pulled up to her building as she was coming out the door. He noticed how her green dress accentuated her long, black hair. He got out, went around and opened the passenger door of his burgundy Monte Carlo for her. She greeted him with a smile. He hugged her, she got in and they made their way to Beth's.

"You look nice," Chad said as he again ran his eyes over her, seeing a sophistication exposed by her dressy look that he hadn't observed before.

Sara smiled appreciatively and looked over his attire, fixing her gaze on his sweatshirt. "You look nice too," she jested, "but actually, you'll fit right in with my brothers."

"Even Justin?" Chad asked.

"I told you he'd warm up to you if you gave him a chance. You'd have to expect him to act a little strange at first. After all, you *were* screwing his baby sister."

"You have an odd way of trying to make me feel comfortable. Now I picture walking in and everyone will stop what they're doing and glare at me. Then someone will yell out, 'There's the rotten bastard who screwed our baby sister!' And have you noticed that all of your brothers are considerably bigger than me?"

"Stop it, Chad," Sara said, laughing as she envisioned the scenario. "And anyway, if that happens, I'm sure you could outrun them."

After a ten-minute drive they arrived at Beth's. It was a perfect setting for a Thanksgiving get-together. The house stood as an island in the rolling hills of farm field. Off to the side stood a garage, gray and weathered and considerably older than the house. In front of the garage was a pole donning the flag. To Chad, the scene was a realization of a Norman Rockwell painting.

They walked down the sidewalk and up the steps to the house. Sara kicked the snow off her shoes and Chad followed suit and they went inside. As they greeted Beth, Chad saw that all the men were sitting in the living room watching the game. Sara led him to where they were and introduced him to everyone. Then Chad took a seat on the sofa while Sara went into the kitchen to help her sisters.

"Looks like you're quite a Lion's fan," Beth's husband Steve stated.

"Isn't everyone on Thanksgiving?" Chad replied.

"So, how do you know Sara?" her brother Paul asked.

"We're just good friends," Chad said.

46

"Seemed like more than good friends the morning I met you," Justin spouted.

Chad shifted his position on the sofa, as if he were trying to get a solid foothold before responding to Justin's statement. "Well, we dated briefly but decided to just be friends," he said awkwardly.

"What? She wasn't good enough for you?" Justin quipped again in an indiscernible voice that veiled whether he was jesting or delivering a direct attack.

"No, that wasn't it at all. Actually, I felt she was too good for me," Chad stated without hesitation, opting to sacrifice his pride for the sake of getting the statement out. "I couldn't get comfortable and relax around her when we dated. I was always concerned about what to do or say. Now, we decided to be friends and our relationship is great."

Chad's response seemed to appease Justin, as well as befriend him to the other guys. Soon, they were back to talking about football and whether the Lions would ever win a championship in their lifetimes. A short time later, diner was on the table and everyone was summoned to the dining room.

The feast was traditional. There was turkey, sweet potatoes, fresh-baked zucchini bread, stuffing, cranberry sauce, apple and pumpkin pies, and a small plate with a peanut butter and jelly sandwich on it. Everyone paused as Steve said the blessing, then they all dug into the holiday meal.

As the afternoon progressed, Chad and Sara found themselves to be the focus of the dinnertime chat. Sara's aunt remarked how the two made "Such a cute couple," and soon after, the others jumped in on the theme. Chad laid low, occasionally looking up and smiling, while Sara reaffirmed the platonic nature of their relationship. He felt a headache coming on, but at the same time, liked the family's opinion of Sara and him as a couple.

"Touchdown!" Sara shouted abruptly, and suddenly everyone's attention was diverted to the game.

"I didn't know you were a football fan," Chad whispered.

"I'm not," Sara confessed. "But I do know what a touchdown is and it was an opportunity to change the topic."

"Good call," Chad murmured, grinning. "Remind me that I owe you one."

"You owe me more than one for that, Reiger," she said coyly.

They continued on without further encroachment on the topic and when the meal was finished the men went back into the living room to watch the rest of the game. The women, as the family's holiday tradition dictated, put the leftovers away and did the dishes. "You know, the holidays are the only time that I can get away with this," Steve said with a laugh as he kicked back the recliner and popped open a can of beer. The rest of the men chuckled a laugh of familiarity with what he was saying.

The women came back right before the end of the game and sat next to their partners and the size of the sofa dictated that Chad and Sara sit rather close together. After the game, they all stayed in the living room for several hours, drinking holiday punch and beer, sharing stories and reveling in the day's camaraderie. Chad began to feel at ease and found himself genuinely enjoying the get-together.

Around seven, Sara tapped him on the shoulder. "Are you about ready, sport?" she asked. "I'm sure they want to talk about us, so we should leave first so we don't ruin their fun."

"Yes, we don't want to deprive them of that, now, do we?" Chad agreed. They stood up, thanked Steve and Beth for everything, then went around and bid everyone adieu. Chad ran outside and started the car as Beth pulled Sara into the kitchen and handed her a tray of leftovers. Chad fidgeted with the radio till Sara emerged carrying the tinfoil-wrapped plate and, after one final wave, got into the car.

"Turn on the heat, Chad old boy," she said shivering.

"It is on," Chad said. "It'll be a while before she warms up, though." He looked at Sara before backing out of the driveway and added, "If you would've worn a sweatshirt like mine, you wouldn't be cold now, would you?"

"Yeah, whatever," she said impatiently. "Just get us home."

Ten minutes later they pulled up to Sara's building. "Do you want to come in for a while?" she asked.

"Sure, why not," Chad responded without hesitation.

They climbed the stairs that led to her apartment. Sara unlocked the door, went to the refrigerator and tucked her leftovers into the largest available space, while Chad took a seat on the couch. "I've got to get out of this dress," she shouted as she headed down the hall. "Make yourself at home." She reappeared a few minutes later wearing a tee shirt and a pair of well-worn jeans. "Did you enjoy yourself today?" she asked as she softly patted him on the back.

"Actually, yes I did. Thanks for the invite."

"Well, I started thinking about this after I invited you, but I hope I didn't keep you from doing something with your family. You should call your folks tonight and wish them a Happy Thanksgiving. You can phone them from here if you want."

Chad looked up at Sara, then looked down at his hands that rested in his lap. "My mom and dad have both passed away, Sara," he said somberly.

"Chad, I'm sorry," Sara said as she put her arms around him and squeezed softly. "I didn't know. My parents are both gone, too."

He looked up at her. "Yeah, I kind of wondered about that today."

Sara's face showed a subtle smile. "It's funny that we never mentioned this before—and we both have the same situation," she noted. Chad put his arm around her and drew her close to him. She put her head on his shoulder and they sat without saying a word.

He awoke with Sara lying on his chest. He scanned the room, looking for a clock. He found one on the kitchen wall: it was twenty after three. "Shit," he mumbled as he sat up, stirring Sara in the process.

"What time is it?" she murmured.

"We both fell asleep. It's after three in the morning," Chad said dejectedly.

"Well, just put'em in the sink and we'll get'em in the morning," she said as she began to drift off to sleep again.

"Sara! Wake up!" Chad said as he shook her.

She looked at him and sat up, rubbed her eyes and asked, "What's going on?"

"We fell asleep and it's twenty after three," he informed. "I've got to get home."

"Just stay here, Chad," she said groggily.

"I can't, Sara. I have to work early tomorrow… today, actually. I have to go."

She grabbed his hand. "You don't have to do anything. Call in sick."

"I can't call in," he said.

"Then stay here till you have to go."

He was too tired to argue any further, so he acquiesced. Besides, the thought of lying next to Sara was appealing. She took his hand and led him into the bedroom. "You have to set the alarm for me," he said.

"For what time?"

"Six-thirty," he answered.

Sara fidgeted with the clock until it was set for six-thirty. She removed her jeans, took off her tee shirt and undid her bra as Chad stripped down to his underwear. They crawled into bed, snuggled next to each other and faded off to sleep.

Six-thirty came and went. Seven-thirty did the same. At eight there was a knock on the door. Sara woke and sat up. She looked at the alarm clock and then over at Chad. "Oh shit," she said. "Chad! Chad!" she said loudly as she rolled him back and forth till he awoke. "Chad, I'm sorry," she said as he opened his eyes. "I must have set the alarm for six-thirty p.m.—and somebody's here." She got out of bed, put on her tee shirt and jeans and jogged to the door, finding Justin, who had come over for coffee.

"That burgundy Monte Carlo out there looks familiar," he said as he entered.

"Yeah, whatever," Sara said in haste. "Put the coffee on. I'll be right back."

"Well, Reiger, you're two-for-two now with Justin coming over," she said as she reentered the bedroom.

"Did you tell him we didn't do anything," Chad said as he pulled his pants up and fastened them.

"Yeah, I said make yourself at home, I'll be right back. Oh, and by the way, I didn't screw Chad last night."

"I guess we're off to a fine start then. I have to use your phone."

"Just call in sick, Chad," Sara pleaded.

"Can't," he said as he laced his shoes.

Sara moaned. "Okay, do what you have to do," she said, and headed down the hall to the kitchen.

Chad walked down the hallway and into the living room. He knew Sara's brother was sitting at the kitchen table and decided not to put off the unavoidable. He was disappointed that Justin had chosen to come over this morning, particularly after they had started to bond, at least to some extent, the day before. He reluctantly stuck his head in the kitchen. "Good morning," he said as he sent an unassuming nod Justin's way.

"Hey Chad, good morning," Justin responded in a genuine manner which caught him off guard.

Chad exposed a half grin, then said, "I have to make a phone call. I'll be back in a minute."

Several minutes later he came back into the kitchen. Sara was standing at the stove and frying some French toast. Chad leaned in the doorway until she looked over at him. "I've got to fly, kid," he said when he had her attention.

"Sit down and have some breakfast first."

"Can't. They said they'd write me up if I wasn't there in a half an hour and I still have to go home to shower and change."

"So let them write you up. What are they going to do, fire you?"

"You never know," he said as he walked up to Sara and pecked her on the cheek. "See ya, Justin," he said as he turned. Sara watched as he grabbed his jacket and headed out, and she listened until the sound of descending footsteps faded.

"You're boy's in quite the hurry," Justin said as Sara walked back into the kitchen.

"Oh, I set the alarm wrong and now he's late for work," she said with a sigh.

"Wouldn't call in sick?" Justin asked.

"He never calls in sick. Hasn't in ten years."

"Got to give him credit for that. I'm glad to see you picked somebody who's a little more responsible this time."

Sara stopped and looked at her brother, then chose not to complicate the matter by reiterating the terms of the relationship. She also chose to pass on the dig he made on her past relationships. Instead, she smiled wryly and said, "Taking a liking to the boy now, aren't you."

"My intentions were never bad. I just wanted to see what he was made of, that's all."

"Yeah, I know you all too well. Here's Chad's French toast, I know you can eat it. I'm going to jump in the shower."

"Thanks," Justin said as he picked up the fork. "And Sara, I'll probably leave before you get out, but I want to say that I do think this Chad is okay."

Sara smiled a half grin. "Thanks, Justin," she said, then proceeded down the hall.

Chad's workday was miserable. His manager yelled at him as soon as he'd walked through the door, and he spent most of the day wondering how he could get so much flack over such a minor incident. He had always been loyal and hard working and he wondered why the loyalty wasn't being reciprocated. Furthermore, the day after Thanksgiving was traditionally slow. Most people were still full from the day before and everyone had leftovers to consume. The main shopping emphasis of the day was the retail stores, not the supermarkets, and the simple truth was that he didn't even need to be at work. By the end of the day he had developed a 'screw it' attitude and took solace in the fact that he was being paid when there was basically nothing to do.

On his way home he swung by Sara's. He knocked on the door several times but there was no answer. He headed back down the stairs and was about to get in his car when he spotted her coming around the corner. He shut the car door and walked up the street to meet her.

"Hey, Chad," she said with a smile.

"Hey, Peaches," he said as they met.

"Peaches?"

"Yeah, I like it. It has a good ring."

"Copycat," Sara chided. "Are you coming up?"

"For a little while."

"Yeah, that's what you said last night," Sara scoffed.

"And whose fault was that?" Chad chuckled.

"Who fell asleep on the couch in the first place?" She pulled out a cigarette and lit up. "Anyway, how did work go?" she asked.

"It sucked," Chad said vigorously. "It was boring as hell all day."

"They really needed you to rush in, hey?"

"The bastards."

"Well you know what my opinion is about that place," she said as she moved toward the door of her building.

Chad smiled. "I think I'm going to head home now, though. It's been a long day."

"Are you sure you don't want to come up for a little while?" Sara asked, wearing a look of disappointment.

"I want to, but I can't. I just wanted to catch you and thank you for yesterday. I had a great time."

"I had a great time too, Chad. I'm glad you came."

They hugged each other, then Chad got in his car and drove the three-and-a-half blocks to his apartment. Sara stood in the doorway and watched until his car was out of sight. Then she flicked her cigarette onto the street and went upstairs. She pulled one of the kitchen chairs up to the window and thought, as she looked out over the Christmas shoppers scurrying about on the street below. She realized that she liked Chad more with each time she saw him. She liked his simple honesty and character, as well as the way he kept her entertained. She lit another smoke and stared out the third-floor window as she continued to contemplate her feelings.

CHAPTER FIVE

Chad turned off the radio and strolled to the window. The winter snow had come and gone and spring had arrived. The trees had budded before May and were already harboring the bright-red cardinals who each year beckoned the coming of summer. The seasonal Jamaicans and resorters were beginning to trickle in and soon the streets would be congested with tourists. Nothing had changed at the store since fall. Chad was still serving a miserable existence there and was long past the stage of being burnt out. The tension and hostility had escalated, making the task of going into work even more unbearable.

By Memorial Day weekend Chad wondered how much more he could tolerate. Summer was only beginning and the worst was yet to come. On Saturday afternoon, with Sara out of town and a feeling of restlessness coming over him, he picked up the phone. "Miles," he said, "what's up?"

"Not much, Chad. Jud bought an old Harley yesterday and wants to take it for a run to Traverse."

"Well why don't we take a ride, follow him there, then go and see Abbey?"

Miles paused for a moment. "All right. That sounds pretty good. It'll be nice to get out of town before all hell breaks loose. We've got the Hemingway festival next weekend—a hundred Hemingway look-a-likes, not to mention all the others coming in for it. It'll be good to get away. Why don't you stop by in an hour."

When Chad got off the phone he went to gas up his car, then

grabbed some fast food before going to Miles' apartment. When he pulled into the back parking lot Jud was polishing the chrome on his bike and Miles was sitting in a lawn chair on the landing of their fire escape. Chad flagged him a wave and went up to Jud.

"What do you think of 'er?" he asked proudly.

"Looks cool," Chad said, even though it wasn't anything spectacular in his eyes.

"Gotta see what she tops out at today."

"Oh, shit. You do need to do that, man," Chad admonished.

"You don't think I can handle this beast?" Jud challenged.

"I'm sure you can handle it just fine, but why take the chance?"

Jud looked up and grinned. Chad noticed that somewhere along the line he had lost one of his front teeth, but he didn't want to ask and get one of Jud's famous stories. He saw his beard had gotten quite long and the red bandanna on his head was soiled and torn on one side. He was heavier than when he'd last seen him and had the unkempt look of someone who wasn't taking care of himself. Miles appeared and said he was ready. Jud fired up his bike, while Chad and Miles followed behind as they headed down Mitchell Street.

As soon as they got out of the city Jud began to accelerate dramatically, swerving about and passing vehicles on the shoulder. "What the hell's he trying to prove?" Miles asked.

"I don't know, but he's got to be doing ninety."

"Where'd he go?"

"I don't know. He's way up there now."

"I see him," Miles declared. "He pulled off to the side of the road."

Chad crept up to the Harley and was about to pull up behind when Jud gave him a thumbs up and ripped back onto the highway. Chad pulled out behind and, as the road straightened, Jud began to jack the bike back and forth to the point where it nearly touched the asphalt below. Then he straightened it back out and throttled her back up to ninety. "Shit! That crazy bastard's going to wipe out," Miles warned. "Keep up with him."

"And push him so he goes faster?" Chad cautioned. "I refuse to be a catalyst to his destruction."

Up ahead, Jud had slowed down, waiting for Chad and Miles to catch up again. "I'm not going to play this fucking game all the way to Traverse," Chad spouted. "I wanted to get out of town and relax for a day and he has to do this shit."

Miles shook his head. "I want to see Abbey though, and I know she'd like some company."

"I know. This is just bullshit."

Again, Jud had let Chad catch up to him and like before he took off like a rocket, resuming his stunt of jacking the bike into tight, slalom-like maneuvers at a high rate of speed. Miles could no longer watch and was looking out the passenger window when he heard Chad say in a loud, drawn-out voice, "Oh shit!" He looked up and saw Jud bouncing off the pavement and his bike somersaulting down the other lane.

"Oh my God! What happened?" Miles yelled.

"He hit a stone," Chad hollered as he pulled over to where Jud's motionless body was lying in the tall grass beside the ditch. He rushed out and ran toward him, but slowed when he got within a few feet, then turned and, with a horrific face, told Miles, "Don't come any closer."

Miles inched up to the sight, but recoiled instantly. He stood looking the other way, grimacing. "Flag a car down," Chad commanded. "Get someone with a cell phone." Miles slowly walked over to the ditch and sat on the gravel next to it. Chad ran over to him and shook him. "Come on! I need your help now!" he said as he pulled him to his feet. Miles went to the side of the road and tried to flag a car while Chad went back to Jud's side. He stared at his mangled body, not knowing what to do. The flesh was torn off the left side of his face and he was missing his right arm. He was bleeding profusely and Chad reached for a pulse but couldn't get one. A car had pulled over and the occupants ran over to where Chad was. "Do you have a cell phone?" he bellowed.

"We already called. They're on their way," said a girl in her mid twenties.

"I don't know what to do?" Chad cried. "He's going to die."

One of the others from the car, an older man dressed in a white shirt and tie, bent down to Jud, then stood up and looked at Chad and Miles, who had come to the spot but still steered his gaze away from Jud. "You won't be able to do anything, I'm afraid," he said somberly. "He's dead."

Chad turned away and stared out over Lake Michigan while Miles collapsed to one knee. "I fucking knew this would happen!" Chad bellowed. He looked over at Miles, who was staring at him with a blank, vacant face. The others huddled in a separate group until the ambulance arrived. The paramedics confirmed what the older man had said. Chad and Miles gave their account to the police while the ambulance took Jud's body away.

The funeral was held on the Tuesday after Memorial Day. The flags remaining on the street seemed to betray the man that Jud was, and during the service, each time he was referred to as a kind and caring person, Chad could only look away. The two girls took his death hard: Abbey because she was young and had yet to experience death, and Monique, who had become intertwined with him in the recent months. At the cemetery, when they laid him in the ground, Chad held Abbey close. He found his feelings of sorrow and concern were for her and not Jud.

After the ceremony she rode back to the apartment with him, while Miles and Monique went with Pres. Chad pulled into the parking lot before the others and turned to Abbey. "I can't go up there yet," she said, her cheeks tear-stained. "I don't want to be alone."

Chad reached over and held her. "Come on then, let's go sit by that tree for a while," he said, nodding toward an elm at the edge of the lot. They got out and sat on the grass.

Abbey pulled a tissue out of her purse and softly blew her nose. "How's Sara?" she asked in an attempt to infuse a sense of normalcy into the conversation.

"Sara's doing good. She's still out of town though," Chad said with a soft smile.

"She sounds so nice, Chad. I'd like to meet her sometime."

"I'd like that too." Chad put his hand on Abbey's smooth, black dress and gently rubbed her back. "You know," he began, "I feel the need to tell you how much I care about you. You and Miles are true friends. The others, I could take them or leave them, to tell you the truth, but you are an angel." He looked up at the clouds drifting along freely, then looked back at her. "There are certain times when you feel the need to tell people how you feel about them and this is one of those times. I admire your unpretentiousness. I like how you care about others and how you always seem to know when I'm down."

Abbey burst into tears and Chad held her tightly and continued. "I can't go on like this, Abbey. I can't waste my life away. I know there are better things out there and I have to find them." He began to choke up and his voice cracked with emotion. He cleared his throat before going on. "I shouldn't speak badly of Jud today, but I have to say he threw his life away. And if he wouldn't have gotten killed, he was still wasting it. I believe in God and that there's a reason for me being here and it isn't to work in a grocery store and then squander the rest of the hours of the day."

Abbey buried her head in Chad's chest. "I know what you mean," she said, then looked up at him. "Chad, you are such a good guy," she said as she ran her hand across his shoulder. "I know there is something good out there just waiting for you. And I don't know of anyone who deserves it more."

Pres and the others pulled into the lot and Chad and Abbey rose to their feet. "You coming up for a drink, Chad?" Pres yelled.

"This is what I'm talking about," Chad said softly to Abbey. He turned to Pres, "No, I'm going home," he responded. He turned back to Abbey. "How long are you staying in town for?" he asked.

"I'm staying tonight," she said. "I want to make sure Monique will be okay."

He leaned down and kissed her cheek. "These last few minutes, Abbey, I'll remember them always. You take care of yourself," he said and they embraced tightly.

Abbey smiled as he turned and walked back to the car.

A few evenings later, after working a late shift, Chad stopped and sat down on the porch before heading up to his apartment. The night was particularly pleasant and, after having a smoke, he decided to go for a long walk to burn off the stress of the day. He figured it would be a good catalyst for sorting out his thoughts. He got up and started down the block.

As he walked, he thought. He looked at the direction that his life was going and reflected upon his own words to Abbey. He saw himself heading toward a life of unrealized dreams and strolling down a path of compromises. He studied the life he'd been unwittingly etching for himself and shook his head. He began to realize that the world had to turn for him now. He sensed that he was coming to the age where daring would soon be replaced by practicality. He looked ahead and wondered where he'd be at the age of forty. Would he be married? Own a home? Have children? And the further he walked the more the theme embedded itself in his consciousness. *This could be your last chance!* he admonished himself. *Right here, right now... June seventh.* He realized the seriousness of his thoughts and knew that if he didn't act on them now, he never would.

He picked up his step as he passed the old train depot. He began to run through the positives he had in his life as if he were doing a point-counterpoint. He thought of his friends, Miles and Abbey in particular, and thought of the times they'd shared. He looked at the others he knew, worked with, and the ones he'd bump into from time to time. He felt he was liked and respected by them and that, in and of itself, was worth something. And of course there was Sara. She was the biggest positive in his life. His friendship with her was enough to keep him in Petoskey.

Chad abruptly stopped in his tracks. He angrily kicked the gravel below his feet. *You can't think complacently,* he scolded himself. *Things aren't good enough the way they are now.*

A burst of enthusiasm hit him and in that instant he committed himself to pursuing a grand dream one final time. He permitted himself to think big and resolved that he would live life on his own terms and by his own rules. He would give it all he had.

The walk took him into the poorer part of town. As he went on, he studied the rundown dwellings along the route. They were houses with junk in their yard and generally all in a state of disrepair. He wondered if their inhabitants had gotten to the point where they simply didn't care how they lived. His thoughts returned to his scheme and envisioned how it would leave him a changed man. As he left the downtrodden neighborhood he metaphorically equated his plan to walking away from this rundown district.

He headed north for a few more blocks, then turned around and began to head home. Filled with excitement, he quickened his pace. He looked at his watch and saw it was one-thirty in the morning. He'd been walking for over two hours and had to be at work in another five. "I'm calling in sick tomorrow!" he declared aloud. From the time he was a schoolboy he'd never staged an illness, but this was too important.

He arrived at his apartment and sped up the stairs. He unlocked the door and proceeded directly to his desk. He decided he'd stay up all night and lay everything out on paper. He'd make a list of things that needed to be done, calculate expenses, gather the information he would need and make all other necessary preparations. In the morning he'd grab a quick breakfast and call in for work. Then, with everything organized, he'd pay a visit to Sara.

It was around seven-thirty Friday morning when Sara awoke. She'd retired early the night before but she still woke up feeling tired. She got out of bed and went into the kitchen for a glass of water, then went over to the stereo and put on some Tchaikovsky. She went back to her bed to lay down for another half-hour before getting ready for work.

She reached for the cord to the Venetian blinds, pulled them open and looked outside. It was a beautiful start to the early June day, tranquilly overcast but warm, judging by the attire of the people on the street below. Through the crescendos of *The 1812 Overture* she thought she'd heard a knock at the door. She sat up in her bed and listened closely. A few seconds later the knock again made its way into her bedroom. She got out of bed and hastened to the living room. Dressed only in a tee shirt, she asked who it was through the closed door.

"It's Chad, Sara. Let me in."

"Are you alone?" she asked.

"Yeah, why?"

The door opened and Chad's question was answered with his first glimpse. He walked in and followed her into the bedroom. "Why aren't you dressed for work?" he asked.

"Because I felt like sleeping in and now I'm in a rush to get to the shop by nine." She pulled her tee shirt off and grabbed a clean towel from the closet as Chad again found himself appreciating the beauty of her pale-white skin. Sara, aware that she was being ogled, found it somewhat amusing and in a teasing manner turned to him and asked, "So, what are you up to today, Chadders?"

"Well," he began, distracted by Sara's nakedness, "I was hoping that we could chat for a few before you took off. I've got something to throw at you—something quite interesting, in fact. Do you think you can go in an hour late this morning?"

"Not a chance, Chad old boy. And listen to you, Mr. Punctuality, asking me to go in late."

"Well you should know that I called in sick today myself," he said in self-redeeming fashion.

"You did?" Sara asked in a shocked tone. "And obviously you're not sick. What the hell is up?"

"Something is up, Sara, but I don't want to tell you on the fly."

"Then why don't you meet me down at the pub around seven? We can grab some dinner and you can tell me what's on your mind."

"Yeah, I can do that," he said as he turned and began to head for the door. "I'll see you at seven."

"That wasn't what I needed," Chad mumbled as he went down the stairs. He felt anxious and a little nervous about what he had to say and he wanted to get it over with. Now he had to let it simmer for another eleven hours.

When he got home he thought it'd be wise to get a few hours sleep. His mind and body felt ready to go, but he knew he had a propensity to babble when he was overly tired and it wouldn't be a good time for that to happen. He needed his speech to Sara to be coherent and intriguing. Anyway, he was supposed to be sick today and it'd be better for him to lay low and not be seen running all over town. It was bad enough that he'd be at the pub on a Friday night.

At the souvenir shop Sara was having a rough morning. Early in her shift she had been reprimanded for having a cigarette out back. Now she was in the midst of dealing with a difficult customer. A woman had come into the store with an agenda to complain. She would hold up items and loudly proclaim to another woman who was with her how cheaply they were made or how overpriced they were. Sara, observing the woman, looked at the huge stone on her finger and the designer dress that she wore and it made the woman's bickering annoy her all the more.

The woman picked up a picture frame and brought it over to Sara, who was standing behind the counter. "This item is overpriced," she proclaimed. "They would never charge that much in Ohio."

"Then perhaps you should go back to Ohio and get it," Sara said smartly.

With Sara's remark the woman became loud, prompting the manager to approach the counter. "Can I help you, Ma'am?" he asked.

"Yes, thank you!" she said with pursed lips and an adamant face. "This young lady here isn't very polite with your customers. In fact she's downright rude!"

"Well, she's going through the store like she…"

"I'm sorry Ma'am," the manager said, cutting Sara off. "I heard what went on here and I assure you that I will address the matter."

"Thank you. I'm glad that somebody here knows how to take care of your customers."

The woman and her friend left the store and Richard confronted

Sara. "What was the problem there?" he asked her in his snotty, feminine voice.

Sara, annoyed with him for cutting her off, stood mute.

"You know, we're getting tired of this attitude of yours. These tourists are our livelihood. You need to accommodate these people or move on down the road. Your family doesn't own this place anymore and neither do you. You'd better understand that."

Sara didn't argue; she just nodded. It wasn't that she agreed, she was simply fed up to the point where it didn't matter anymore. Inside, though, she was writhing at how the bitch from Ohio had gotten her way, even though she had provoked the incident.

Lunch hour was a welcome respite for Sara. She walked down the street to the corner deli and ordered a sandwich. She exited the back door of the deli—which put her in Pennsylvania Park—found a shady spot under a tree and sat down. She was relieved to get out of the store and the thought of going back to work repulsed her. She dreamed of how nice it would be to stay in the park for the rest of the afternoon.

She looked around and found, like in the gaslight district, the place was crawling with tourists. Even in the peaceful setting of the park, they irritated her. One man—dressed in khaki shorts, a Hawaiian shirt, black socks and donning a safari hat—was taking photos of the black squirrels that dwelled in the park. Another group off to her right was sitting at a picnic table and feeding seagulls. "Yeah, that's smart. Get a whole flock of 'em over here when I'm trying to eat," Sara moaned as she shook her head in disgust.

After finishing her sandwich she kicked off her shoes and lit a cigarette. She thought of how they were just now getting into summer and the tourists were getting to her already. She recalled her morning visit from Chad and wondered what he was up to. She grew anxious to see him. She glanced down at her watch, put her shoes on, got up and threw her trash in the bin. As she started for the store she spotted the woman who had gotten her into trouble. She walked in a line that took her past the woman and as she walked by, she stopped momentarily, glared at her and shook her head. Feeling somewhat vindicated, she went back to the store.

Chad awoke about four in the afternoon. His body was still tired as he lay in bed but he felt too motivated to let it bother him. He sprung up, showered and got dressed.

He went into the kitchen and fixed himself some scrambled eggs and pancakes. As he ate, he gathered his thoughts, trying to find the most efficient way to deliver his idea to Sara. When he felt he was as prepared as possible, he turned on the television to pass the afternoon away.

The day dragged on. He watched a National Geographic special, then a sitcom and then the news. Then, at ten to seven, he headed out the door.

When he arrived at the pub he found Sara already seated at a table toward the rear of the dining area. Judging by the number of cigarette butts in the ashtray, she had been there for some time. "Looks like you made it a little early, kid," he said as a sly smile came to Sara's face.

"It's good to see you, Chad. Sit down, though. You're making me nervous just standing there staring at me," she said wryly.

Chad took a seat, snatched the menu and looked it over. He was too preoccupied to be hungry, but he didn't want Sara to have to eat alone. After ogling it for a while he put it down, reached in his shirt pocket and pulled out a pack of Marlboros. He lit one and took a deep drag. As he exhaled he looked inquisitively at Sara, trying to gauge her mood. He took another hit as he searched for the proper words to begin with. As he was about to speak he noticed that she had just picked up the menu. He turned sideways in his chair and looked at his surroundings as he thought.

The pub was a plethora of antiques, uniques and collectibles. Off to his left and hanging from the ceiling was a bright red torpedo. Sitting atop the torpedo was a black saddle. Next to that, nailed to the ceiling, was a polar bear rug, the fur a yellowish brown from the years of smoke. The ceiling also sported flags from Austria, Ireland, Canada, France, and one other that was too far away for Chad to make out. He turned his attention to the walls. Directly behind him was a goose, mounted as if it were angrily flapping its wings. It was also nicotine stained, although not as yellow as the polar bear rug. There were the mounted heads of a deer, a wild boar, a tiger and the skull of a steer, probably a Texas longhorn. There was a stuffed pheasant, a trophy trout and a swordfish on the other wall. Behind the bar was the head of a large moose. The bartender was known to boast that when it was shot in 1905, it was the largest one ever taken.

There were plaques and posters on the wall in front of him that looked to be from the forties. One promoted a movie that starred Mae West. The others advertised cigarettes and beer. There were musical instruments fastened to the wall also: a saxophone, a banjo, a French horn and a trombone. Off to the far end of the standup bar was a lighted barber pole, and to the near end, a traffic light. Past the jukebox was a bookshelf, which had three shelves. The bottom two were filled with old books, while the top shelf displayed bottles of beer from the past and present. The floors were made of hardwood and were worn in the center from the years of use. They were covered with peanut shells from the front door to the back of the dining area.

Chad turned back to Sara and saw that she'd put the menu down. He took one more hit off his cigarette, rested it in the ashtray and began his pitch. "You've probably guessed that what I have to tell you is grandiose, so, do you want it in a microcosm or do you want it in long form?"

"Well, I know how meticulous you are and I would guess that you spent the afternoon rehearsing what to say," she said smartly. "And we have plenty of time, so give me the long form."

Chad momentarily looked off to his right and took the last draw off his cigarette. Then, with a focused gaze, he looked Sara in the eye. "Is this enough for you?" he asked, moving his hands in an all-inclusive gesture. He wore a sober look as he continued. "I've been feeling discontent lately, Sara. I'm going nowhere in my job, I'm getting bored doing the same old things, seeing the same old people. We have this routine and it never varies." He paused for effect and lifted his gaze into an introspective, squint-eyed stare and at nothing in particular, then turned back to her. "So that's my first question. Is this enough for you? Are you content?"

The waitress came up to their table. "Hey," she greeted. "Are you going to be eating tonight?"

"Yes, and I think we're both ready to order," Sara said as Chad wore an impatient look. "I'll have the Lake Superior whitefish dinner and a black and tan."

"Very well," she said as she scribbled the order onto her pad. She turned to Chad and asked, "And for you?"

"I'll go with the pub club and a Beck's Draft," he said, sounding somewhat irked by the untimely interruption.

She thanked them and went up to the waitress station. Chad reminded Sara of his question and pressed her for an answer.

"You know it's not enough for me, Reiger. I mean it's not like I'm forlorn to the point where I can't function, but I am a bit disillusioned and I do know there's more out there."

"We've always gotten along and enjoyed each other's company, right? And we've known each other for almost a year now."

"Yes we have, Chad, but spit it out. What is it?"

Chad took a deep breath and gazed intensely at Sara. "I'm going to Europe and I want you to come with me."

"Yeah, like I can afford a trip to Europe right now," she spouted. "Come on, Chad."

"I'm afraid you misunderstood me. Think bigger, Sara. I'm not talking about a trip here, I'm talking about expatriating."

"Oh, that's good. I can't afford a trip to Europe but I can afford to run around from country to country for years on end?"

Chad softened his tone, and as delicately as he could, said, "Sara, you have your inheritance."

"That was my mother's money," she said coldly.

"Your mother's dead, Sara. You haven't spent a penny of it in fourteen years. Would your mother want you to take it to the grave?"

Chad paused for a moment, figuring how to state his point with as much sensitivity as possible. Sara had looked away and her vacant stare exposed her contemplation.

"I'm not talking about wasting your inheritance, Sara. I'm talking about taking a chance and trying to better yourself." He took a sip of his beer, then continued. "Once in a while an opportunity comes along that… well… that's in your best interest not to pass up, and I believe that's the situation now. Look at us here. You're not happy, I'm not happy, and the purpose of a life isn't to just get through it, so, dammit Sara, come with me and let's see what the hell's out there."

Sara eyeballed the waitress approaching the table. She pondered Chad's proposal and found herself drawn to the excitement of such a move. She realized that his timing was right for such an adventure—at least for her to even consider it. She hated her job and relished the chance to tell her manager that she was quitting. She thought of how adventurous it would be to live in Europe. She scanned through her daily routine and pondered if there was anything that she wouldn't want to leave. She had her brothers and sisters but, except for her sister Anne, they were all married and had their own lives. She looked back at Chad, who was waiting for some sort of reaction.

"It sounds enticing, Chad, but I'd have to give it a whole lot of thought."

Chad nodded understandingly.

"It would be a major move, to say the least. And as much as I'd like to get away from everything, I've grown up here, I know people here and I have memories here."

"So you will think about it?" Chad asked pensively as the waitress placed their food in front of them.

"Yes, Chad, I will."

"I need to be clear, though. I have to do this and I have to do it soon. I understand the suddenness of all this, and I appreciate all the reasons you'd have for staying, but especially after watching Jud die before my eyes, the time is right for me now." He looked at her and smiled. "Sara, I have to say that I've never been so fired up or so positive about anything in my life and I can't take a chance on letting the enthusiasm wane, so I hope you understand why I can't wait too long."

Sara smiled at Chad's passion. "I'll let you know within a week," she promised.

They finished dinner. When they left the pub, Chad walked Sara back to her apartment. At the base of the stairs he gave her a peck on the cheek and wished her a good night. Then he headed home.

Sara emerged from her morning shower and sat at the kitchen table with her cup of coffee. She hadn't slept much the night before as Chad's proposal dominated her thoughts. She was waging a war with herself and the battle was being fought on many fronts. There was the issue of her inheritance. She saw Chad's point about not ever using the money, but at the same time felt guilty about spending it on anything that might be construed as frivolous. Then there was the issue of leaving the people she knew and loved behind, and that was countered by the opportunity to meet many new and interesting people; diverse people who could offer her new perspectives and ideas. She also found Chad, himself, to be another factor. He was her best friend and much more. Each time she considered telling him that she had to stay behind, she felt the sadness of not having him in her life.

She finished her coffee, got ready for work and headed down the block to the store. The Saturday sidewalks were already filling with tourists and she knew it would be a hectic day. She rounded the corner and walked into the opened door of the gift shop. "Good morning, Sara," Jane greeted in straight-faced fashion. "Richard said to send you to him as soon as you got here."

"Shit, what does he want now?" Sara asked.

"He didn't say but he's being a little prick this morning."

"Great," Sara exhaled, and she headed to the back room. She found Richard at his desk. He took off his glasses and stood at the sight of her.

"No use beating around the bush, Sara," he said with an angry but somewhat quivering voice. "If you have any belongings here pack them up and be on your way."

Sara glared at him. "What the fuck?" she said as she slammed her purse onto the desk. "And what's the reason for this?"

"You can't be swearing at customers. I will not tolerate that."

"What are you talking about?"

"Don't play dumb with me. The woman you had the conflict with yesterday came back in this morning. She said you were in the park and you went up to her and called her a bitch. So there."

"I did no such thing. I may have given her a look, but I didn't say a word to her."

"I don't believe you."

"You know what, you spineless little jerk? It doesn't matter if you believe me or not! And furthermore, I don't really care to work here anymore anyway. You treat all of us like shit. When we had this store everyone was happy. Take a look at your employees now."

"I don't care what you…"

"Just shut up!" Sara admonished as she held up her palm to him. "I don't want to hear another word." She picked up her purse and walked out of the back room, said goodbye to Jane without offering an explanation and walked out of the store.

Chad was getting ready for work when Sara knocked on his door. As he opened it, he was surprised to see her. She marched in without a greeting and dropped down onto the swivel chair in front of his desk. "Well, I just got fired," she said, shaking her head.

"What? Why?" Chad said as he stood next to her.

"I doesn't matter," she said. She paused for a moment, then looked up at him. "I'm going with you, Chad," she said with a look of unfettered determination.

Chad sat down on the couch and Sara turned the chair to face him. "You know, I'd rather you'd take some time and think about this and know for sure. I understand that you've just had a negative experience, but I'd be bummed if you told me yes now and then changed your mind."

"Give me some credit, Chad. I'm not that fickle. You brought up some good points and I gave it a lot of thought all last night. I was about fifty-fifty on it until this morning, but the events of the day were enough to tip the scales." She stood up. "I need some water or something," she said and went into the kitchen.

"There's soda in the fridge," Chad called out.

Sara came back with a bottle of Mountain Dew. "I know this must sound like a rash decision to you, but trust me, it's not. I'm not an illogical person."

"I know you're not," Chad said.

"We have a bond between us, Chad, and I think that'll make this thing work. We love and trust each other. And what would either of us be giving up?" Then she smiled and asked, "So when are we leaving?"

Chad smiled a broad grin. "How about two weeks from today? I don't know why, but I feel that I need to give the store a notice."

"One week from today," Sara corrected. "Screw that store. And if we're going to change our whole fricken' way of life then let's get on with it."

"A one-week notice then," Chad concurred. "That'll still leave me enough time to get everything together. One more thing, though. How long has it been since you went to Italy?"

"It was seven or eight years ago. Why?"

"Okay, your passport is still valid then."

"Yes I still have a valid passport. How about you, though? You've never been anywhere except Canada and Mexico."

"I got mine two years ago, I just haven't used it yet. You know that I like to dream. Well, I picked one up so I'd be ready if the day ever came and now I'm glad I did."

Chad dug out his notebook with the facts and numbers that he'd been toying with and showed it to Sara. She studied it until she saw him come back into the room wearing his white shirt and tie and she realized that he had to get to work. She stood, smiled and hugged him. Neither of them had felt this good about anything in a long time and they both knew it. In another week they were to become a pair of Bohemian adventurers taking their first real run at the world. Together, they walked down the stairs. Sara stood on the porch until Chad drove away.

CHAPTER SIX

The rain had started to fall around four Monday morning and hadn't stopped as of nine. Sara had just finished breakfast and was beginning the task of going through her things, sorting out what she would take with her and what she'd leave behind. Chad had stopped by the night before with Monique, who was moving into her own apartment. She bought Sara's stereo, television and microwave. The day before, a friend of a friend of Sara's had bought her furniture and had agreed to leave it for her to use until the night before she left. As Sara was starting her chore, her sister Beth was pulling up in front of the building. She was adopting her cat and was stopping by to pick it up.

Beth was Sara's oldest but closest sister. After their mother had died, Sara's other siblings would try to be protective and paternal, while Beth took a more subtle approach. She would explain things to her rather than abstractly point out what was right and wrong. She exhibited a tenderness that others in the family, including Sara, lacked.

The two embraced as Beth walked in. "It's good to see you, Beth," Sara said as they hugged.

"Good to see you too, kiddo," Beth replied as she pushed the hair off Sara's face. She smiled and pulled her into another hug. Sara gave her a quick squeeze, then stepped back and motioned for Beth to sit down.

"I don't believe you're leaving us, Sara. And it's so like you to be extravagant."

"What do you mean?" Sara asked.

"I mean that you aren't moving to Wisconsin or Ohio or some-where nearby. You have to go all the way to Europe."

Sara tilted her head in a reflective manner, then said, "Really, if you think about it though, it'd take the same amount of effort to move to Wisconsin. I still have the same amount of things to pack and the same preparations to make. I'll only be on a plane a little longer."

"Yes, but you could come back home more often if you were in Wisconsin." Beth looked off in the distance, smiled, then looked back at her sister. "You always were the restless one, in your own quiet way. Even when you were a kid you were happiest when we were going somewhere. I remember when you were a toddler and we were going to Chicago to visit Aunt Edith. Dad was driving and Mom had you on her lap. You were looking out the window all intense and observational—like a little adult. I remember the rest of us laughing about it. You looked so cute."

Sara showed a quick smile that disappeared as she began to speak. "I feel this will be a good move for me. I needed something to come around and break this rut that I've been in. On the night that I listened to Chad's pitch, I'd had a terrible day at work. I was in a frame of mind where I was receptive to such a scheme. Then I had all that bullshit the next day and I'm actually glad that it all went down that way. If I would've been complacent, how long would this rut have continued?

"I know you probably think it'd be more logical for me to move to Wisconsin or Ohio. Even though I know you were jesting, I also know that you believe that. My thinking is why *not* move to Eu-rope? Some people actually do live adventurous lives, so why can't I? Now that I have this adventure on the horizon, I couldn't possi-bly look at my former day-to-day routine with any enthusiasm."

Beth smiled as she admired her younger sister's spirit. She looked at the stack of boxes on the floor and appreciated the task that she had ahead of her. A few of the boxes were already taped and labeled, others were half full and there was a pile of empty ones behind the sofa. One box sat empty in the middle of the floor with its contents-to-be spewed around it. There was a pile of news-papers next to the empty boxes that Sara was using to wrap her breakables.

"It looks like you have quite the undertaking here," Beth noted.

"Yeah, you could say that. Fortunately, most of this stuff isn't coming with me. I just need to find a home for it until I get situated—just like Daisy here," Sara said as she eyed her cat popping out from behind the curtains. She squatted down and coaxed it over to her. "There there, girl," she said as she picked up the cat and placed it on her lap. "Auntie Beth is going to take real good care of you," she said as she gently stroked the fur on its head. "And she has two little girls who will play with you and love you, so you be a good kitty for me, okay?" She lowered the cat back to the floor as a tear dripped down her saddened face.

"You don't have to do this, you know," Beth said in a quiet voice. "If you don't feel comfortable with it, just call Chad and tell him you changed your mind. He'll understand."

Sara heard the practicality in her sister's voice. She recognized how she herself had been that way so often in her life. *Just call Chad and tell him you changed your mind.* To Beth it was that simple. She realized that Beth was only looking out for her well being, but she also saw a dullness and conservatism that she wanted no part of. She sat on the chair across from her and said, "Beth, certain aspects of this are going to be hard, but I'm going. I want to go. It's going to be the experience of a lifetime and I won't pass it up. Good-byes are going to be difficult, but I'll get through them."

Beth, seeing the determination in her sister's face, stood, grabbed her hand and tugged. "Come on, then. Let's see what we can get packed. I have some free time so I'll stay and help."

Sara smiled. "Thanks, Beth. I'll get us some coffee."

"That would be great," Beth said, and she knelt down by the box in the center of the room. The two spent the next several hours packing Sara's belongings and sorting out what she'd take to Europe and what she'd store. As they packed they chatted about the trip, they chatted about things in general and they reminisced as they came across items of sentimental significance. They cried some and they laughed some.

When it came time for Beth to leave, Sara called Daisy over to her. "Come here baby," she said. She picked her up and held her at arm's length. She looked into her eyes as she spoke to Beth in a little-girlish tone. "Do you promise to take care of my widdle Daisy-waisy for me Beth?"

"I'm sure the girls will spoil her rotten, Sara," Beth assured.

Sara cradled the cat in her arms and gave it one last squeeze before handing it over to her sister. Beth gave the cat a gentle stroke and kissed Sara on the cheek as Sara gave her a one-armed hug. "We'll see you Thursday, hey?" Beth said.

"Yes, we'll see you Thursday. And Beth, thanks again."

Sara went to the window, looked out over Lake Street and watched as Beth put Daisy into her car. As she waved goodbye, she again felt the impact of the move she was about to make. She knew first hand now how she'd have to distance herself from everyone and everything she cared about. The only constant in the scenario was Chad. She realized that if anyone else had proposed this voyage to her, she wouldn't be going. She stayed at the window until Beth's car disappeared from view, then she headed into the living room and lay on the sofa.

Chad took off his rain-soaked shoes and set them outside the door. He had just returned from the travel agency where, playing the role of a prospective tourist, he had gotten a brochure of each country in Western Europe. Prior to that he had stopped at the bank, where he withdrew his savings and closed his checking account. As he took off his raincoat, he recalled his conversation with the bank teller, who had asked if he was leaving town. Chad, having known the woman from many years of doing business there, had obliged her of his scheme. He smiled as he recalled her words of how she'd thought of doing what he was about to do when she was young and how she still regrets the fact that she changed her mind.

Things were coming into place quickly. On Saturday he had managed to sell his car. To his relief, he had garnered a fair amount from the sale. Due to the expediency of his sell off, he was worried that he'd have to let it go for less than its market value. Now, he had enough money to pay for the costs of the move, plus enough to live on for at least one year. His intention, of course, was to become self sufficient before then, but now, at least, he had money to fall back on.

With most of the errands either completed or accounted for, he had only one obstacle left to deal with: his fear of flying. As much as he loved to travel, he had never flown. He had been to every state in the union except Alaska and Hawaii. He had journeyed by bus, car, train and even riverboat. He had come to the point where he was vacationing in places where he'd already been rather than going where he truly wanted to go, simply because he was afraid to fly. In some aspects, however, this would be easier because there was no decision to make. He was going. Like a drone he would get on the plane and whatever happened, happened. He anticipated that he wouldn't particularly enjoy the flight. He fretted about having some kind of anxiety attack that would embarrass both himself and Sara in the process. Still, the most agonizing part was making the decision to go, and that was over.

He sat in his swivel chair and began to reason with his fear. His goal for the day was to put the fear behind him and not taint his remaining days in Petoskey with this unfinished business. He had many times heard how air travel was statistically safer than driving. He thought of the modern technology and safety advances in the airline industry. He thought of all the people he knew who flew on a regular basis, as well as all the sports teams and their constant flying. The latter example seemed to provide a more accurate reality to his perception. He sat back and lit a Marlboro and felt the issue was resolved as well as it could be.

After a quick bite he went back to making the final preparations for his voyage. He began to realize just how soon they'd be leaving and he was getting fired up, and with that, the rest of the day became an adventure, no matter how mundane the task. If he was doing laundry, he was getting his clothes ready because he was going to Europe. If he was scrubbing the floor in his bathroom, he was preparing to vacate his apartment because he was moving to Europe. And so it went for the rest of the day with everything he did. Then, at around nine in the evening, he phoned Sara.

"I'm ready," he said as she answered, not bothering with the formality of a greeting.

It took Sara a few seconds to realize who was on the phone and what they were talking about. When she did, she took a breath and responded, "I think I am too. I felt that I was behind schedule going into the day but everything came together quite well."

"So what are you doing now?" Chad asked. "Do you have time to get together and do something?"

"What do you have in mind, Chadders?" Sara asked as she walked to the kitchen counter, grabbed her soda and took a drink.

"I don't care. I just want to kill some time. Perhaps we could catch the late movie."

"You know," Sara started, "I think I'm going to stay home and relax a bit tonight."

"How about just meeting me at the park for a couple of smokes?"

"Yeah, I could do that."

"Okay, then. I'll meet you there in five minutes."

"Five minutes," Sara affirmed.

Chad arrived at the park before Sara and copped a seat on one of the picnic tables. It had been a hazy, humid day—the type of day that yields itself to a spectacular sunset. Several small groups of tourists were making their way to Sunset Park. Others were headed for the waterfront. All of them were on their way to see what Petoskey was most famous for, with the possible exception of its fudge.

Chad got up and walked to the Lake Street end of the park. He looked in the direction that Sara would be coming and noticed there were five distinct colors in the sky. The blue sky remained on top of the horizon. The setting sun was a deep red and the low clouds in the western sky were three-toned: white, a cigarette-smoke yellowish color and, to the bottom of the clouds, a sort of purple. As he observed he missed Sara's approach, as she came from a different direction than usual.

"Hey, Fudgie," she said as she crept up behind him.

"What do you mean?" Chad said without taking his eyes off the phenomenon. "The Fudgies don't own the sunsets."

"You're high," Sara jested.

"I am not," he said as he turned to her.

"You're stoned as hell. I can see it in your eyes."

"I've seen you naked."

"What does that have to do with anything?"

"Nothing."

"So how did I look?"

Chad looked at her with a raised eyebrow and Sara laughed. "Come on," she said, taking his hand. "Let's sit down and have our smoke."

They went back into the park and propped themselves atop a picnic table. "I can't believe we're doing this," Chad began. "It still seems like a dream to me."

"It's not that big of a deal. We've had smokes in the park before."

Chad fought off the urge to laugh and continued. "Okay, how about this. I can't believe that we're moving to Europe in a few days. It still seems like a dream to me."

Sara looked up at the sky as she exhaled a hit off her cigarette. It was getting dark and the stars were visible. "You know, it's kind of weird," she began. "We're going to be three-thousand miles away from here but we'll still be able to see the same stars."

"That's pretty deep. And you say I'm stoned."

Sara continued to stare at the sky as she asked, "What do you plan on doing with yourself for the next three days?"

"Well, I still have to work on Wednesday and Thursday," Chad said.

"Probably a good thing, hey? It'll keep you occupied."

"Yeah, and get this, they actually did me a favor. They said that on Thursday they'd pay me for all the hours I have in so I won't have to worry about my last check finding me."

"Well, that was cool. It's about time they did something for you."

"Anyway, besides work, I'll make my final rounds and say my good-byes. I would imagine that Miles and Pres are going to have a little going-away bash for me. Other than that, I'll take some long walks and burn off the nervous energy that I'm bound to have, and I'll tie up all my loose ends. How about you?"

"My sister Karen is having a going-away party for me on Thursday night. It's going to be mostly my family, but you can come if you want."

"No, thanks though. Your family will want to shoot me for steal ing you from them," Chad said with a laugh. "Justin will be able to take us to Metro Friday morning?"

"Right."

"Does he know his way around Detroit?"

"Yes he does."

"And he's okay with storing my trunks?"

"Relax, Chad. Everything's in place."

Chad put his arm around Sara's shoulder and squeezed. He wanted to ask if she felt at all apprehensive about their undertaking, but opted not to. He knew it was a good move for her too and didn't want to open any doors. With nothing else to say, he got up from the table. "Well, I think I'm gonna get going," he said. "Sunset at Sunset Park tomorrow evening?"

"Sounds cool," she said as she stood and brushed the dampness from the table off of her jeans. "Have a good night."

"You too, baby," Chad said.

He turned and headed toward the video store. It would be his last night with a television and he figured he'd take advantage of it. He picked out a couple of movies, then crossed the street and went into the convenience store, where he bought a soda and some chips. His friend Megan was working and he filled her in on what he was about to do. In a triumphant manner he reminded her of what she'd said about Sara. Then he went to the back of the counter and gave her a hug, and with that, had his first taste of saying goodbye to someone he knew.

He stayed up and watched movies till quarter to four. Before retiring he got on his knees and said a quick prayer that everything would go well. He opened his bedroom window to get the noise of the street. Then he went to bed.

Chad ceremoniously threw his white shirt and tie into the trash as he left the store for the last time. Clad in a white undershirt, he walked through the store and shook the hands of his fellow workers. He went to his car, took one last look at the place and drove home.

As he approached his lot he noticed an unfamiliar-looking blue Ford parked in his space. As he pulled up behind it all four doors opened and Abbey got out of the driver's side. "How do you like it?" she asked with a broad smile.

Chad went up to Abbey, and with one arm around her shoulder, surveyed the vehicle as Monique, Miles and Pres came up to him. "It's pretty damn sharp, girl," he said.

"We were wondering what you were up to this evening," Miles said. "We tried to call but your phone was already disconnected."

"Well, I need a quick shower," Chad said. "And I don't have any food left in the house, or anything to cook it in, for that matter."

"Then we'll take you out to eat," Pres piped in. "Get your ass in the shower and let's get this party rolling."

They followed Chad up the stairs and into the living room. "Don't you have a TV?" Monique asked.

"Yeah, it's in my suitcase," Chad mocked. "I'm afraid you'll have to entertain yourselves.

They took a seat on the lone couch that remained and chatted as Chad got ready. Fifteen minutes later he emerged, wearing a loud, multicolored Hawaiian shirt and blue Dockers. "You're not going to wear that, are you?" Monique asked.

"Why the hell not. I want you people to remember me."

"You don't have to worry about that, Chadders," Abbey said.

"Oh, shit. Where did you pick up on the Chadders thing?"

"I did meet Sara, remember?"

"Well we can sit here and talk about *Chadders* or we can get something to eat. What's it going to be?" Pres asked in quintessential Pres fashion.

"All right," Abbey said. "Where's it going to be?"

"The pub. It's got to be the pub," Chad said, and everyone agreed.

"You want to take your car Abbey?" Chad asked as they paraded down the stairs.

"Of course. It'll be your only chance to ride in her."

Abbey waited as Chad backed his car onto the street and then the five jammed into her car, Chad and Abbey in the front and the rest in the back. They streamed into the back door of the pub single file and took a round table near the jukebox. Abbey sat to Chad's right and Pres to his left. Miles and Monique sat across from him. Pres flagged a waitress and ordered a pitcher of Manitou. When she came back with it, Chad and Pres ordered food.

Abbey patted him on the knee as the waitress left. "I'm happy for you Chad," she said in a low tone. "I thought about our little chat, the one after Jud's services, and I hoped that you'd find something to make you content. I didn't expect it to be on such a large scale, but I knew that you'd change something." She put her arms around him. "I'm so excited for you," she added.

"Oh great!" Pres blurted. "It's getting sappy already. Come on, love," he said as he took Monique's hand and coaxed her to her feet. They went to the jukebox and stood side by side as they browsed through the selections. Miles got up and headed for the restroom and Abbey started to cry. "I know that this is going to be an adventure for you, Chad, but I'm going to miss you so much."

Chad put his arm back around her. "Come on, Abbs," he said as he snuggled her up to his chest.

Abbey sobbed. "I won't ever see you again," she said. Chad, with his arm around her, sat quietly and stared straight ahead.

For the most part, the rest of the evening was a party. Everyone laughed and chided each other until it came time to leave. Then it got difficult for Chad. Even though he'd tried to console Abbey, he knew she was right. He probably would never see her or any of the others again. They drove back to the house and he said his farewells, saving Abbey for last. He engulfed her into his arms and held her for what seemed like an eternity and found it hard to let go. "You're the one I'll miss the most," he whispered. As he stared into her eyes his throat burned from suppressed emotion. A soft smile came to his face and he kissed her cheek. Then he turned and walked up the stairs without looking back.

CHAPTER SEVEN

To Chad's relief, Friday morning finally arrived. Both he and Sara had been at their respective going-away parties the night before and, with the anticipation of the journey, it seemed to be a never-ending night. When he got back from the pub he had no way to entertain himself. His television and radio had been sold, his phone was disconnected and his friend Mark would be stopping by at any time to pick up his car. Every preparation had been made and he still fought himself in anticipation of the flight. He was too wound up to sleep and he felt the sadness of missing his friends. He set out for a walk but it began to drizzle; nothing much, but he didn't want to take a chance on getting sick—not with everything he had ahead of him.

Justin and Sara would be at his apartment within the hour. All he would have to do then was drop his keys off at his landlord's and they'd be on their way. He took his suitcases and duffel bag to the downstairs hall and set them by the door. He went back upstairs and walked about his vacant apartment, checking for any oversights. With everything in order, he walked up to the window and took one final look at the view of the bay and smiled. He recalled the day he'd moved in—five years earlier—and how the new apartment was a dramatic improvement over his prior place. Now he was hoping that scenario would repeat itself. He smiled again, turned and went to the door. He looked at the apartment one last time, then stepped out, locked the door and went out to the porch. Several minutes later a car pulled up. Mark got out and

Chad walked over to him. He tossed him the car keys and thanked him as Mark wished him well. Then he got in the Monte Carlo and drove away.

He went back to the porch and sat on one of his suitcases as he peered down the street. With the arrival of a blue, Dodge Caravan, their sojourn would begin. The skies were partly cloudy. Chad noticed the bright, white stratocumulus clouds drifting freely in the low sky and the gray ones above them. The drizzle that ruined his walk the night before again appeared to be ominous. Looking across the street he saw Tim taking out his mother's trash. Tim was a nine-year-old who Chad had often seen scurrying about with the other boys from the neighborhood. Seeing him now prompted Chad to think of all the people who he'd probably never see again. He further appreciated how difficult this move had to be for Sara. He was leaving behind his friends, neighbors and coworkers, whereas Sara was leaving her family behind. For as much as he found himself missing his friends, he realized that there was no comparison. He recognized that he was fortunate to have her accompany him.

As he was watching the youngster trot back to his house, he spotted Justin's van coming around the corner. As it pulled up to the curb Chad sprung to his feet, hoisted the blue duffel bag over his shoulder and grabbed his two suitcases. The rest of his belongings, which were contained in two large trunks, had been picked up by Justin the day before. He'd agreed to store them, along with Sara's, until they established residence.

Chad caught Sara's beaming eyes as he trotted up to the van. He dropped his luggage, took her in his arms and spun her around in his exuberance. He set her down and, in the fervor of the moment, bear-hugged Justin too. They squeezed Chad's suitcases and duffel into the van and he took one last look at the building and said goodbye to the world he knew.

He went up to the van and got in the back. As they left town he observed every detail. The stores, parks and ball fields all held memories and he celebrated the swan-song aspect of seeing them for the last time. He eyed the people strolling through the gaslight district and recognized many of them.

After they passed through town and dropped off Chad's keys, they were left with a four-hour ride to Detroit Metro. Chad, no longer needing to look out the window, sat back as Justin began to quiz them. "Where are you kids going to be tonight?" he asked.

"We'll be flying into De Gaulle and getting there around seven Saturday morning, their time," Chad said, taking it upon himself to answer. "We decided that, since we're arriving on the weekend, we'd be tourists and check out Paris."

Justin looked in the rearview mirror and said, "You may as well. You don't get an opportunity like that every day."

"Yes, and Chad will be able to use his French," Sara said as she turned in her seat and looked at him.

"Chad, you speak French?" Justin asked.

"I said I might try," Chad corrected. "I'm not fluent by any stretch, but I can communicate if the conversation stays basic."

"Still, that would be cool," Justin said.

"Then, when we finish seeing Paris we'll head to Germany and begin our search," Sara added.

"And if you don't find what you're looking for in Germany?"

"We decided that we'd start in Germany, that's all. If we don't find anything there we'll move on and we haven't really talked about what the next move would be," Sara said.

"Perhaps the Czech Republic," Chad offered in a nonchalant way.

The dialogue kept them entertained for about a third of the way to Detroit. The rest of the ride turned into waiting: phase two. Chad returned his gaze to the roadside scenery and began reading every billboard they passed while Sara, without realizing the irony, began whistling *This Land Is My Land*. Eventually Justin noticed the lull in conversation and turned on the radio.

They approached Saginaw and Chad read a mileage sign—Detroit 100 miles. He dug into the side pouch of his duffel bag and pulled out his maps of Western European countries. He beckoned Sara and she climbed into the back with him and, for the third time, they scouted the different countries and considered their options. Germany was not only their beginning point, but it was first on their wish list. Besides Germany, they focused their attention on the maps of Italy, Spain, France, The Czech Republic, Switzerland, Austria and The British Isles. Sara showed a preference for the latter while Chad was curious about Spain. The only drawback was that it was another of Hemingway's hideouts and they'd both had enough of Hemingway seekers in Petoskey. After twenty minutes of this, Chad folded up the maps and Sara rested her head on his shoulder and fell asleep.

A little over an hour later they arrived at Metro Airport. Justin stayed with them until they were ready to board. They had another hour to kill, so they found a place to sit and they chatted. They talked about how hot the summer was going to be—at least according to the Farmer's Almanac. They talked politics and talked about baseball, movies, unemployment and the proper way to grill a steak. They observed other passengers bid farewell to their loved ones. Then it was time for Chad and Sara to depart.

Justin turned and offered his hand to Chad. "Looks like you guys are on your way," he said. "And look after my little sister for me," he added, then patted him on the back and turned to Sara. "Have the time of your life," was all he said and he gave her a lengthy hug. Sara looked up at him and smiled. Too choked up to speak, she gave him a wink and turned to board the plane.

Chad took Sara's hand as they walked down the ramp and boarded the plane. They sat and waited for their departure and Sara put her hand on Chad's knee and asked, "Are you doing all right, sport?"

Chad gave her a halfhearted smile and said, "Yeah, actually I am. Once they get this damn thing in the air I'll be fine. Then I should be okay until we come to land."

"Just remember that everything's going to be fine, Chad. Before you know it we'll be setting foot on French soil and you'll feel silly that you even worried at all."

Before Sara could finish her pep talk the plane began to move and, as it got to the end of the runway and turned, the jet engines began to roar mightily. A few short seconds later the plane was aloft and gaining altitude at a rate that had Chad both thrilled and horrified. Sara grabbed a magazine and sat back, deliberately trying to look relaxed. Chad followed suit and seemed to be enjoying the flight. He looked out the window as they went through the clouds and smiled at the serenity of the scene. Then he sat back as Sara pointed out different tidbits from her magazine.

After a while he spotted a tracking screen that was built into the wall in front of them. It showed the flight of the plane in relationship to a map that displayed the northern half of the Western Hemisphere. He looked at the flight data. The plane was flying at twenty-nine thousand feet with an airspeed of five hundred ninety-nine miles per hour. As the trip progressed, he would occasionally glance back at the screen to see if it would eclipse the six hundred mark.

Night came quickly as they traveled from west to east. Chad wasn't tired but he did want to catch some shuteye. With the time change and a full day of sightseeing ahead of them, he knew he could use any sleep he could possibly get. He found himself more at ease than he had anticipated, so he rested his head on the side of Sara's seat and closed his eyes. A short while after he'd fallen asleep, he awoke to the sensation of a vertical drop. Within a few seconds an announcement was made informing everyone that the plane was hitting turbulence. Again, it plunged downward and many of the passengers brandished looks of concern. Chad, however, found himself to be calm. Proud of himself, he glanced over at Sara to reveal the coolness of his demeanor, only to find that she had remained sleeping through the whole ordeal. After another five minutes they had passed through the turbulence and Chad fell back asleep.

Sara awoke to a stream of daylight beaming in her face from the window across the aisle. She nudged Chad with her elbow. "Hey sleepyhead," she mumbled in a cracking early-morning voice. Chad looked over at her and squinted. He straightened his seat and peered through the window across from him. He turned and slid open the blind to his right, looked out and saw that they were now in the middle of a bright, white cloud. He recalled the monitor and looked up at the screen. It showed that they were close to land and approaching the city of Cherbourg. He again looked out the window, this time with his hand on Sara's knee. As he gazed out, he realized how quickly he had awoke. "Look, Sara," he said as he motioned to the screen ahead. "In a few minutes we'll be over Europe."

Sara looked at the monitor, then leaned across Chad and peered through the window. "I'm getting excited, Chad. Today is going to be a cool day."

Chad was the first to spot land as they looked out the window together. Although it wasn't yet defined, it was still discernible. "There it is," he said with a smile as he victoriously clutched Sara's thigh. His voice softened to a near whisper as he continued to stare toward the terrain below and said, "I never thought I'd see this. I thought I'd have to be content reading about it and looking at photos in travel magazines. Now, I look out the window… and there's Europe." He paused momentarily and stared, then continued, as Sara rested her chin on his shoulder and gazed with him. "I'm realizing one of my utmost passions. I thought that I'd be forever incarcerated in my homeland—forever landlocked by the great oceans. Now my foothold on the continent I've longed to see is imminent."

Sara playfully nudged him. "You're being rather dramatic, don't you think?" she said.

"I'm being genuine, Sara. That's how much this means to me."

She smiled. They continued their observance and their view became more distinct. Chad was as full of wonder and anticipation as a child at Christmas, and Sara, in a more stoic fashion, was taking in the view as one would appreciate a work of art. As they got closer, the French farm fields came into focus and turned into a quiltwork of contrasting colors that displayed themselves in an array of square patches blanketing the earth. There were the bright yellow fields of rape, bordered by the greens of newly born vegetation. As they descended further they could see the deep brown furrows of freshly-plowed fields.

Sara's mind began to drift, thinking of all the sights she'd like to encounter. She pictured quaint little Swiss villages tucked between mountain peaks. She imagined the melting, mountain snow forming a stream in the Austrian Alps and the edelweiss showing off its springtime splendor. She envisioned ancient castles lining fabled rivers and Gypsies playing their ethnic songs on a pedestrian thoroughfare. Inwardly, Sara's fervor rivaled Chad's.

The sights of the city came into view as they came to Paris. Off in the distance was the Eiffel Tower and they entered the urban vastness of the megalopolis. Soon the plane was on its final approach and descending rapidly. Chad absorbed the experience, etching it in his memory as if he were recording it on film. Every passing second was another snapshot. The final few feet were gone in an instant. The wheels hit. They were in France.

Chad followed Sara off the plane and set his feet on European soil. A feeling of exhilaration gripped him and he became eager to see the city. He looked at the other passengers getting off the plane and noted their nonchalance. He felt fortunate that the experience moved him as much as it did. He felt thankful for who he was.

Inside the terminal, Sara found a map of the city. She was anxious to see the historical sights: the Arc de Triomphe, the Cathedral de Notre Dame, la Place de la Concorde and the Louvre. Chad wanted to see the Eiffel Tower and walk the Champs Elysees, but other than that, he was up for experiencing the city in any fashion. He was just glad to be in Paris.

Sara suggested that they check into a hotel first. They could drop off their luggage, perhaps grab a quick nap and a shower and still be ready to tour by early afternoon. Chad concurred and they began the task of finding their way around the city. Chad's French was basic at best. He could ask questions but had trouble understanding responses if they were spoken quickly. He had ventured up to Quebec on several occasions and he had some difficulty communicating there. Still, he knew they would get by.

Sara had located a train station on the map named Gare du Nord. Judging by its location, it would be the best sight to depart from, come Monday, and they agreed to look for a hotel in that vicinity. Looking at the map, they planned their way into the city. From the looks of things, they'd have to take a cab from the airport to the Metro station. Then, they'd take a bus from Metro to Gare du Nord and from the hotel they'd take a bus downtown. Sara folded up the map and led the way as they walked out of the terminal. After some encouraging, she got Chad to ask a taxi driver to take them to the Metro station.

He reluctantly approached the man. "Pardon monseiur, nous voulons aux Metro."

"Ah, you are American, eh? The Metro it is right over there," the man said, pointing to his right.

Chad felt a relief in hearing his native tongue. He was self-conscience about speaking French and afraid that he would screw something up, leaving Sara disappointed with him in the process. Beyond that, he was glad to hear that there was a Metro station within walking distance, thus omitting one leg of their journey into the city.

Yet, Chad was curious about how the cab driver knew that he was American. After all, he could have been British, Scottish, Irish or Canadian, or any other non-French speaking nationality for that matter and he couldn't imagine how someone could make the differentiation. He thanked the driver for the directions and asked, "How did you know I was American?"

The cabby smiled. "You do not think I hear many tourists at the airport? I have been doing this for twenty-five years. I can tell where you are from," he replied smugly.

Chad smiled, then went back to Sara and pointed to where the Metro was. They grabbed their luggage, walked to it and bought two tickets to Gare du Nord. They boarded the Metro and began to anticipate what Paris would have to offer. The scenes on route to Gare du Nord contradicted the stereotypical lore of the city. The graffiti along the cement walls that lined their route reminded them more of New York and in the aisle of the coach there was an Asian man playing guitar and singing Bob Dylan songs in English. They found the ride to be quite unique, if not Parisian.

They got to Gare du Nord and found themselves in quintessential Paris. Chad sprinted up the stairs of the terminal to street level and viewed his surroundings until Sara caught up and stood beside him. He put an arm around her and continued his first look at the architecture, boutiques, the abundance of outdoor cafes and the French-scripted signs. He pointed out that the girl on the billboard across the street from them was totally nude, while Sara pointed out that there was a hotel less than a block away.

They walked up to the front of the hotel and checked it out. It was an old, brownstone building that resembled all the others on that block. It had two picture windows on either side of the main entrance and they each had flowerbeds below them. The cement steps were carpeted and there was a cast-iron railing on the left-hand side. Sara looked at Chad and raised her eyebrows and he gave her a why-not tilt of his head and they went up the stairs into the lobby. Chad, knowing his role, approached the front desk.

"Bonjour," he said as he rested his hands palms-down on the counter.

"Bonjour, monsieur. Ca va?" said a middle-aged woman with black hair and white-rimmed glasses that hung off her neck.

"Ca va bien, merci. Je voudrais un chambre pour deux personnes pour ce soir, s'il vous plait."

"Very well," the woman responded. "And would you like a room with a shower?"

"Yes—please," Chad conceded. "But I have to ask, how did you know to answer in English?"

"Chambre is feminine," she said with somewhat of a condescending smile. "Gender errors always give the tourists away."

Chad paid for the room, they got their key, then ascended an old, spiral staircase, which led to their second-floor room. "Now I have to ask again," Chad said as they walked down the hallway, "how did she know to answer in English? Why not German? I'll buy the fact that she knew I was a foreigner from the gender error, but what made her assume I spoke English?"

"I don't know, Chad," Sara said, sounding somewhat impatient with his obsession with the issue. "I guess it's a conspiracy. Perhaps we'd better go back to the states."

Chad dropped one suitcase and fumbled with the room key. "In other words, shut up and get over it, right?" he stated.

"It wouldn't hurt to just enjoy the time we have here."

He unlocked the door and swung it open. The first thing he saw as he entered the room was a hideous painting of a bullfighter that was mounted on the wall between the two double beds. They set their luggage on the floor and Chad sat on one of the beds as Sara walked over to the window and pulled back the curtain. "Chad, check out this view," she beckoned.

Chad looked and saw that their view consisted of the brownish, brick wall of the building next to them. He chuckled. "Are you sure we're not in Omaha?"

"More like Toledo, I think," Sara said.

After a few more jibes they decided to accept the room for its functional value. They hadn't planned to spend a lot of time at the hotel anyway.

They went out and grabbed a bite at a cafe down the street, then came back to the room to rest a while before embarking on a tour of the city. After lying in bed for an hour and a half, Chad gave up and began getting dressed. Sara heard him rustling about and turned toward him. "Did you get any sleep?" Chad asked as he noticed that she was awake.

"Yeah, a little bit. Did you?"

"Sleep doesn't come easy when one's waiting to see Paris for the first time."

"That's pretty profound. You should save that line in case you ever want to write a book."

"All right, that's enough chatter," Chad said as he grabbed her arm and pulled. "Up we go." After a few pulls he coaxed her out of bed. She changed clothes, dug her camera out of her suitcase and they were on their way.

They stopped at the front desk, where Sara inquired about how to get to the Eiffel Tower, and she was told to take bus number sixty-one at the stop down the block. They walked to it and, after a five-minute wait, the bus pulled up. The door opened, some of the passengers got off and Chad and Sara went to get on. "You can't get on here," the driver yelled at Chad, again in English and with nothing to prompt him to do so.

"Shit," Chad exclaimed as he wondered where they'd have to go to catch the proper bus. The driver pulled the door shut and drove off, only to pull to a stop about thirty yards from where they were. He opened the door, stood on the step and yelled to Chad and Sara, "Okay, you can get on now." Chad shook his head and headed for the bus as Sara followed. "That made a lot of sense now, didn't it?" he said with a growing sentiment of disgust.

"Hey, let it go and enjoy this. We're here to experience Paris and how can you experience Paris without at least a taste of rudeness?"

As the bus pulled away, Chad was still going on about it. Sara got stern. "Come on, Chad, enough. At least we're on our way there now."

It wasn't long until the Eiffel Tower came into view. Sara nudged Chad, who was still sulking, and suggested that they get off a few blocks before the tower and walk from there so they could fully appreciate its grandeur as they approached it. They got off at the next stop. It was a splendid afternoon to walk about the city. It was a bit overcast, but around eighty degrees with a slight breeze blowing toward them as they walked down the tree-lined street and toward the fabled tower that dominated their view. Up ahead, groups of tourists were heading to and from the structure as if they were on pilgrimage. When they got to the base of the tower they were surprised by the number of Americans there. They became engaged in conversation with a young couple from Seattle, who had initially taken Chad and Sara to be French. They also chatted with an elderly man from Iowa who said he had been to Paris many times.

He seemed to know the city quite well and told them to take a boat tour down the Seine. He said that he'd taken one on his first trip to Paris and, besides being interesting, it would be a good way to locate all the sights they'd want to visit. It sounded good to Chad and Sara. Their elevator arrived and they thanked the man and bid him a good day, then began their ascent to the top of the tower.

The view didn't disappoint either of them. From their vantagepoint they could see the vast expanse of the city. Chad walked to the rail and looked at a soccer field below. There was a game going on. He tried to spot the ball and, when he did, he challenged Sara to try to find it. She spotted the white dome of the Sacre Coeur and even though it was becoming overcast, the pristine white basilica stood out as if it were illuminated. She noticed how the city blocks of Paris were arranged in triangular fashion with the streets embedded deep within them. Providing the sense of depth was a mass of buildings, one seemingly similar to the other from her nine-hundred-foot perch. Together they formed a sea of grayish-white stone that carried on as far as she could see.

A chorus of German voices caught Chad's attention, prompting him to do a half-turn and pay a closer ear. Sara had quit looking at anything in particular. She simply stood with her hands on the railing, taking it all in. She seemed mesmerized and looked as content as Chad had ever seen her. "It would be too expensive to stay here, you know," she heard him softly say. She didn't say anything. She just turned to him, smiled, then went back to her view. They stayed at the top of the tower for nearly an hour before Chad noted that they still had a lot of the city to see and a relatively short amount of time to play with. On the ride down they decided they'd take the old man's advice and catch one of the boat tours.

They walked down the bank of the Seine, looking for a tour as well as taking in the ambiance of the riverbank as they went. They again found themselves amongst throngs of people who, like them, were leisurely strolling down the walkway. Chad found it unique to hear people speaking French, German, English, Japanese, and a few other languages that were indiscernible to him, all in the same vicinity. It elevated the awareness that he was far from anything he was used to or that he'd ever experienced before. They came upon a bridge and, on the cobblestone bank underneath it, there was a man performing magic tricks to a small convocation. Farther down, there was another man playing the saxophone. There was a synergistic effect to the setting—the eclectic aspect of the performances making the scene more memorable than the sum of each individual act—and it was festive, despite the imminent rain which was made ominous by the dark clouds coming in from the west. Looking upriver they found one of the boat-tour lines. They walked to the dock, purchased tow tickets and began their tour.

Just as the old man had promised, they were delivered an up-close view of the best of Paris. They cruised past the Grand Palais, Notre Dame and The Louvre, and the Eiffel Tower was a breathtaking spectacle when viewed from the Seine. As they passed the Ile do la Cite, Sara observed an old, lonely-looking man standing behind his canvas, painting his surroundings. To her he seemed to depict the very essence of Paris.

In the seat behind them was an American who was being very loud and obnoxious and he was beginning to lessen the enjoyment of the tour. He was being quite the know-it-all and was starting to get on Chad's nerves. Next, the man began talking about how the French would be more disciplined had the Germans won the war. With that, Chad turned sharply to tell the fellow what he thought of him and his opinions, only to be caught off guard when he saw that the man was a paraplegic. However, the look of disapproval was still frozen to his face and his intent was so obvious that he was forced to follow through. He realized that it would have been an insult to the handicapped condition if he ignored the man's comments based on what he saw. So, much to his discomfort, he verbally blasted the man. He brought up the atrocities of the Nazi regime, then told the man that it was people like him who give Americans a bad name and suggested that he be respectful of the French while in their country. By the time he finished, he heard clapping and chants of approval from the others on the boat. The handicapped man wore the look of a little boy who had just been scolded and would have nothing to say for the rest of the tour. Chad, feeling relieved, settled back in his seat as Sara took his hand into hers.

They were both famished by the time the boat returned to the dock. They decided to walk down the Champs Elysees and find someplace to eat along the way. They came upon a quaint little outdoor cafe and sat themselves at a table nearest the street. As they waited for the garçon, Sara persuaded Chad to give his French another try. He asked her what she wanted to eat and rehearsed until the waiter approached.

"Bonjour," he said as he came to the table, hunching slightly to avoid a low-hanging branch of the tree they were sitting under.

"Bonjour. Deux cafe au lait, s'il vous plait."

"Oui, monsieur. And will you be eating today?"

"Yes we will," Chad said politely. "But will you indulge me and speak French?"

"Ah! Oui, monsieur," the young man responded with a compre-hending smile.

After Chad placed their order he gazed at Sara with a look that showed both victory and defeat. "I guess that's what I'll have to do if I want to speak French here, hey?"

"You speak fine French," she reassured him. "So you have an accent. You know how Parisians are."

Chad stretched, then rested his arms on the table. "So you're having a good time?" he asked, changing the subject so Sara wouldn't think he was dwelling on the language situation.

Sara smiled as though she were onto him. "Yes, I'm having a great time, Chadders. How about you?"

He paused momentarily before saying, "I still look around and can't believe that I'm actually here. I know the Eiffel Tower is staring us in the face wherever we go, but it seems so surreal. And, yes, I'm having a great time."

Their food came, and as they ate, they watched the people who passed by. Sara pointed out that it was the first time that they'd been stationary since they started their expedition. As Sara ate she picked out the nuances of the city. She noticed the abundance of the red, white and blue French flags and recalled how they had been seemingly everywhere along their route. She paused to listen to a man who was playing the accordion on the corner across from them and strained to hear his music over the chattering of the birds perched in the tree above her. She noted the variety of nationalities amongst the people who strolled past her and pondered America's claim of being the great melting pot.

They finished eating, then continued their trek down the Champs Elysees and toward the Arc de Triomphe. Sara glanced down at her watch and saw that it was already six o'clock. There was still a lot of the city that they wanted to see but they were beginning to feel the effects of their jet lag. They sat down on a bench along the route to revise their plans, both of them lit a cigarette, then they began discussing the matter. They decided that the walk to the Arc de Triomphe would be their last run of the day, as it would be a rather long one. Then they would pick up where they left off on Sunday.

As they continued down the boulevard, Sara noticed how it had cooled off considerably since they'd begun their tour and she wished that she'd taken a sweater with her. Chad suggested that they jog a block or two to get the blood flowing again, and they did. After a half-mile or so the Arc came into view. It had become twilight and the arch was lit, giving it an even more dominating appearance. They walked down the final two blocks of the tree-lined avenue and up to the roundabout, which was a confluence of twelve avenues. They crossed the traffic circle and walked up to the arch. Upon closer inspection it was more intricate than either of them had imagined. Carved into the structure were angels, soldiers and chariots, and there were names etched into the inner wall. Chad asked Sara about the significance of the names and, when she didn't know, another onlooker informed them that they were the names of Napoleon's generals. They stayed there for a half-hour, circling and observing, and chatting with other sightseers; asking them what they'd seen of Paris and what they'd liked best.

Chad felt as if he was standing on the sacred grounds of hallowed history. As he stood in the presence of the fabled edifice, he began to realize that a life in Europe was imminent. He looked up at the evening sky and took a deep breath. He thanked God that he had the hunger and will to make such a venture. Then, he walked back up to Sara and they began to make their way back to the hotel.

Sara recalled seeing a bus stop near the plaza across from the Eiffel Tower and they headed toward it. The breeze that had cooled the air on the way to the Arc had subsided and their return sojourn was more pleasant. The evening sky had grown dark and the lights of Paris enchanted them as they went along. Chad stopped and looked up to the sky. "There are your stars, Sara," he said.

"My stars?" she asked.

"Yes, the same ones you can see from Pennsylvania Park."

Sara took his hand. "You're half right, Chadders, they're our stars."

They made it to the bus stop and had only a short wait for bus number sixty-one. They grabbed a couple of sodas and some junk food before going up to their room. They sat on their beds and talked until midnight, each rehashing their favorite events of the day. The day had been a full one and neither could believe that they'd flown in a mere fifteen hours earlier. They made their plans for Sunday and talked briefly about getting down to business once Monday came. Then, they called it a night.

CHAPTER EIGHT

Sara awoke Sunday morning to the sound of thunder. She lifted her head up past her pillow and looked at the alarm clock on the bedstand. It was six twenty-three. She plopped back down and listened as a loud ripple of thunder cracked and resonated throughout the early-morning atmosphere. She realized that rain would ruin their plan to finish touring Paris, so she got out of bed, walked over to the window and pulled back the curtain, only to be reminded of the brownish, brick wall of the building next to them. She looked over at Chad and he was sound asleep—oblivious to the storm that was threatening their day. She thought of waking him, but decided to go out for a smoke and see firsthand what was happening with the weather. She threw on the clothes that were on the chair from the night before, snatched the room key and descended the spiral staircase and went out to the front of the hotel.

To her dismay it was pouring. She looked for a puddle and saw bubbles in it—that was something her mother had told her when she was a little girl, *"If there are bubbles in the puddles it will rain all day."* Although Sara always went through the ritual of looking for the bubbles, she couldn't remember ever noticing if it was true or not. However, despite the threatening nature of the storm, she found herself at ease. The rain that was jeopardizing her plans was now mesmerizing her. She watched as it pattered the otherwise quiet street and felt, then and there, that she had Paris all to herself. She lit a second cigarette. She'd been with Chad nearly every minute of the journey and it felt good to have some time alone. She stepped out from under the awning of the hotel and let the rain touch her face. A good storm tended to put her in an introspective mood and prompted her to think about things that she'd normally brush aside. As she stood there she thought of all the challenges they had in front of them. She perceived their undertaking to be a monumental task—if it was to be done to the satisfaction of both of them. In many ways they'd be starting from scratch, just as an eighteen-year-old would when leaving home for the first time.

Sara put out her cigarette and went back to the room. Chad was still asleep and she got undressed and jumped in the shower.

Although the storm hadn't woke Chad, the sound of plumbing in an old building did. Unknowingly, he went through the same ritual as Sara had. He heard the thunder, got out of bed and walked over to the window to see what it was like outside. The sight of the brick wall led him outdoors to get a better look at the weather conditions.

He stood in the doorway and lit a cigarette, trying to wake up as much as anything. He assumed that Sara was in the shower because she was eager to do something. What she wanted to do though, he was trying to discern. It wasn't her nature to be impractical, so he concluded that she must not have known that it was raining. Regardless of her reasoning, he wanted to be awake and ready for whatever she wanted to do.

The front desk clerk saw Chad standing outside and stepped out to have a cigarette with him. He was a small man with un-trimmed sideburns and a goatee. He had dark, black hair and looked very French. "Bonjour," he greeted as he strode up next to Chad.

"Bonjour," Chad replied. "Ca va?"

"Ca va bien, merci. You are American?"

Chad chuckled to himself and smirked, "Why yes, of course," then held out his hand and said, "my name's Chad,"

"Chad, I am Jean Paul," the clerk said as they shook hands. "So tell me then, what is life like in the United States?"

Chad pondered the question before answering, then said, "To tell you the truth I haven't been in France long enough to tell you how it's different. Perhaps it's a little more liberal over here. There are no nude women on our billboards back home," he added with a chuckle.

Jean Paul gave a knowing smile, then asked, "And how do you like our city?"

"I think I like it more than it likes me," Chad said, motioning to the rain. "Did you happen to hear a forecast for today?"

"A forecast? No," Jean Paul said as he extinguished his cigarette before it was a quarter of the way through. "But it looks as though it will rain all day."

"Yeah, it does," Chad conceded.

"Well, you try to enjoy it anyway, eh?" Jean Paul offered with a nod. He gave Chad an encouraging pat on the back, turned to the door and returned to his post behind the front desk.

Chad, appreciating the simplicity of pre-dawn Paris, lit another smoke. Off in the distance he heard jovial voices and a moment later a man and a woman appeared from around the corner. The man was wearing a tan trench coat and the woman had on a blue dress. Both were soaked but seemed oblivious to the fact. The woman teasingly ran ahead of the man, then stopped and taunted him into trying to catch her. When he did he forced his mouth on hers and pressed her back against the building next to the hotel. The woman spotted Chad watching and slapped the man's face, uttering something indiscernible as she did. As he looked over at Chad, the woman ran back down the street and he took off after her.

The rain-darkened buildings, eerily illuminated by the faint streetlights, reminded Chad of how far he was from Petoskey. The unfamiliar surroundings were a refreshing change. They invigorated him and made him think of what was still ahead for him and Sara. He observed that the traffic down the block had picked up since he'd come out and that the city was beginning to awaken. Off in the distance he heard another crack of thunder and he wondered how the day would turn out. He crushed the cigarette under his foot and headed upstairs.

Sara was already dressed when he got to the room. "We've got rain out there, kid," he said.

"I know," Sara answered matter-of-factly. "While you were sleeping I went outside to scope things out. And it's going to rain all day."

"Really? Where did you hear that?"

"I didn't hear it anywhere. I saw bubbles in the puddles."

Any other person in Paris would've thought Sara to be daft, listening to such a statement, but Chad knew all about her bubble theory. He sat on the bed and said, "Well let's hope that your formula is wrong just this one time."

"Why? Don't you like rain, Chadders? What kind of European are you going to be anyway?"

"A dry one."

"With a sense of humor to match, I might add."

They dropped their quipping and Chad took his turn in the shower. He got ready hastily and the two headed downstairs to the hotel restaurant. They were seated next to the window and as they looked out, they realized that the rain wasn't about to let up any time soon. The woman who had been at the front desk when they checked in came to the table, brought them coffee and took their order. Then Sara returned to her gaze to the street.

"Well, it looks like we have a decision to make," she said, her disappointment showing in the tone of her voice.

"I know," Chad conceded, "I've been thinking about that too."

"We've got two options: we can stay here and hope the rain stops or we can continue on our way."

"Touring in the rain is out of the question for you?"

"I'm not particularly fond of the idea, Chad."

"And I don't want to sit in a hotel room all day, even if the hotel is in Paris. If we do continue on, would you feel somewhat satisfied with what we saw yesterday?"

Sara finished sipping her coffee and said, "Yeah, I think I would. At least we saw the highlights, and after all, we did make it to the top of the Eiffel Tower."

The waitress came back with their food and they continued to weigh their options as they ate. "We should come to some kind of a decision quickly, though, "Sara noted. "Checkout time is eleven o'clock and if we do decide to take off we can save a night's lodging if we leave by then." She observed how Chad was quietly staring out the window as she spoke and was about to ask what was on his mind when he turned to her with a gleaming gaze.

"I think I have a compromise though," he said with a smile. "Like you, I don't want to tour Paris in the rain and I don't want to sit in a hotel all day either. Yet, we made a deal that we'd take the weekend and enjoy ourselves and I don't want to relinquish that opportunity either."

Chad's words tweaked Sara's curiosity. "So then—what's the big compromise?"

"We could scoot up to Brussels for the day. If the weather is good there we could check out the city and if it is raining it wouldn't have taken us that far off our route."

Sara's eyes widened and she nodded. "Brussels. I like the idea.

"Done deal then?" Chad asked, and Sara shrugged her shoulders in a why-not manner and said, "Done deal." The two finished breakfast, then went back to the room and gathered their belongings. They checked out of the hotel and ran through the rain to Gare du Nord.

Chad walked up to the ticket window to see what kinds of Eurail passes were available. The woman behind the counter asked to see his passport, handed it back and informed him that such passes would have to have been purchased before he left the United States. This was an oversight in his planning and it would cost them—not just this time but for every leg of the journey. Now, they'd have to buy point-to-point tickets to wherever they were going and, when compounded by the number of tickets they'd have to purchase, it was going to be considerably more expensive. It would also compel them to be more selective in their travel planning. Chad purchased the two one-way tickets from Paris to Brussels.

Sara was looking at the departure board. She saw the listings for trains going to Rome, Vienna, Munich, Geneva, and many of Europe's other cosmopolitan places, and the listing for Zagreb reminded her of a James Bond movie in which the Zagreb train station was featured. A feeling of exhilaration came over her. She felt very free. She thought of what she would've been doing, had she not accompanied Chad, and the thought of it repulsed her. She looked about the station and saw travelers scurrying to get to wherever they were going. Other people were just hanging out, talking or strolling leisurely. As she observed, she thought how all of these people seemed to have a more interesting life than what she'd had. Now, she was one of them.

Chad approached Sara with the tickets in his hand and informed her of his slip up. She took the news lightly though. The disappointment of not touring Paris was gone and she was excited that they were about to see Brussels. She wasn't about to let the ticket situation bother her and she sensed that the day would be a good one.

They stepped inside the terminal and got their first glimpse of the European rail system. Chad had traveled the Amtrak lines before but it was nothing like what he was seeing now. He could sense that the rails were far more a way of life to Europeans than to Americans.

The trains were arranged in lines, waiting to go to their respective destinations. Both Chad and Sara could have been content getting on any one of the trains. They boarded the one bound for Brussels.

Chad was growing anxious to see another country. He knew that they'd be in Belgium in less than two hours—and that would be the fifth country that he'd set foot in. Sara, knowing his wanderlust, let him have the seat by the window. The train slowly began to move, inching its way out of the depot. Once they got away from Paris, they found the scenery similar to Michigan, which bored Chad, as he was geared to see the things that were new and different. He instead took to observing the other people on the train. He looked around and noted the diversity among the passengers and found a large number of them to be young. He heard French coming from all directions. He turned to Sara and asked if she wanted to grab a soda with him, but she said that she was too comfortable and asked him to bring one back for her. He walked to the door at the end of the coach and pulled. When it didn't open he added some muscle and tried again, but it was to no avail. He stepped back and looked at the door in an attempt to figure it out. He sensed that he was becoming the entertainment for the other passengers and was getting embarrassed, not to mention that he felt somewhat stupid. A little girl who was sitting in the front seat got up to help. With her tiny but strategically placed hand she opened the door with one effortless motion. Chad thanked her and she showed him the trick to opening them, then returned to her seat. On the way out Chad glanced back at Sara. Her face was red and she was laughing and had obviously found delight in his humiliation. He lowered his head and went to look for a vending station.

Having learned to use the air-powered doors, Chad began to explore the rest of the train, advancing from car to car, seeing what each one had to offer. He went through the dining car and thought how it'd be a cool experience for one of the longer legs of the journey. He saw a bathroom at the end of the coach and went to use it. When he flushed the toilet he thought that he saw train tracks. He flushed again and, to his chagrin, the contents were indeed being spewed onto the tracks below. He grimaced and moved on.

He found the vending car and bought two odd-shaped cans of Coke. When he returned to his coach he found Sara hunched over her seat and talking with the couple behind them. She'd heard an American accent and turned to ask where they were from. It turned out that they were Canadians. She introduced them. "Chad, this is Bill and his wife Katie," Sara said, motioning as she said each name. "They're from Edmonton, Alberta."

Chad greeted them and they exchanged pleasantries. As they talked, they found that they had some common interests. Sara and Katie shared a passion for art and Katie had just visited the Louvre. Sara explained how they were to have gone and how the rain changed their plans. They then began to talk about music; classical in particular.

Chad sensed the time-killing value of a conversation and began to chat with Bill. The scenery hadn't changed and, aside from entering Belgium, this particular leg of the trip wasn't much of an adventure. As it turned out, Chad found that Bill also loved hockey and they talked about their sport—mainly the Red Wings and the Oilers—all the way to Brussels.

The conversation made time pass briskly and before they knew it the train was pulling into the depot. Katie gave Sara their address and phone number, telling her to get in touch once they got established. Then the couples exchanged hugs and handshakes and went their separate ways.

Sara walked behind Chad as he went into the station. They found a locker, stuffed their luggage inside and headed toward the street. At the end of the corridor was a vending machine where one could purchase Coke, Pepsi and several varieties of beer. Chad stopped to check it out. Like the nude girl on the billboard in Paris, it exemplified how different things were in Europe and he again appreciated how far he was from home.

They took a left from the depot and began to walk the streets of Brussels. Looking around, they appeared to be in a Turkish district. As they passed one of the restaurants Chad pointed to a beastly-looking animal in the window cooking on a rotisserie. The head of the creature was still attached and its eyes seemed to be brandishing its pain as it spun over the fire. The sight proved a little much for Sara and she continued on ahead as Chad took one last look.

A few blocks down they came to an old, gray castle which rested on a knoll. It was a magnificent structure but it seemed out of place with the city built up around it. After strolling a few more blocks they came into an older and more stoic part of the city. The brown buildings were of quintessential European design and the sidewalks were composed of a grayish brick. The street sloped downhill and curved slightly to the right, thus further exposing the architecture that it held. Sara eyed a restaurant and was getting hungry. It was a quaint little place a corner across from an old Catholic church. Sara asked Chad if he had an appetite yet and he said that he could eat something, so they went in.

The waitress came up to their table. "Hello," Chad said as she smiled at them. "Do you speak English?" he asked.

"Yes I do. Most people in Europe speak some English," she said. "And how are you today?"

"I'm doing great," Chad said as Sara nodded in accord.

"And how are you?" Sara asked when it was apparent that Chad wasn't going to.

"I am well, too, thank you. Are you in Brussels on holiday?"

"No we're just here for the day. We're on our way to Prague actually," Chad stated.

Sara shot Chad a look of surprise. "Prague?" she inquired.

"Why? What's wrong with Prague?"

"Nothing. But did you ever mention Prague to me before?"

"We never really talked about anywhere specific."

"That's right. We decided that we would travel until we found a place we both liked." Sara recalled the waitress at the table and looked at her apologetically. She was wearing a look of responsibility for triggering the disagreement and seemed quite uncomfortable. "I'm sorry," Sara said. "We didn't mean to bore you with our little debate here."

"It's okay, you didn't bore me," she assured as a smile came back to her face. "In fact I found you to be very entertaining." She took their order, brought the ticket to the kitchen, then went back to her other customers.

"I don't mind going to Prague," Sara continued after she left. "We can go there and see if it's for us. It's just a decision we both should be making. I have a lot vested in this too, you know. I left my family and my way of life behind so I could find something better and you can't decide what that something is unilaterally."

Chad's face was red and he spoke in a softened voice. "I know and I apologize. I started thinking about Prague while we were at the train station in Paris. I was planning to ask you about it tonight, but I let my enthusiasm get the best of me." He pulled a cigarette out of his shirt pocket and, with a slightly-shaking hand, lit it and inhaled deeply. "Things are starting to happen so fast. I just got a little ahead of myself and, again, I apologize."

Sara looked at him briefly, then brought her gaze out to the streets of Brussels. Chad felt like he'd been scolded and wanted to say something so Sara wouldn't think that he was pouting, but he couldn't think of anything. Suddenly, they heard a loud voice from the back of the restaurant. It was in French and Chad roughly translated it to, "Hey Pappy, do your clap-dance." There was cheering and prodding from a small group in the back that continued until a small, frail man with hair that had been dyed jet black stood up. One of the waiters emerged from the kitchen with a cassette tape player and began to cue it up. The man they called Pappy got up on a table and someone from his clan handed him some castanets. The entourage continued to hoot it up as Pappy waited and when the music started he began to dance. The spectacle was an array of spinning, clapping and stomping. It started off slow but increased in tempo as it progressed, building itself to a crescendo. "Hungarian Dance Number Five," Sara said as she leaned to Chad's ear.

Everyone in the restaurant had turned in their seats and watched the performance and when Pappy had finished they gave him a loud and lengthy cheer. The old man bowed, climbed down from the table and returned to his seat and the rest of the patrons went back to whatever they were doing.

Chad particularly enjoyed the act as, again, it articulated the difference between home and where he was now; furthermore, by the time the Gypsy dance was over, he sensed that the tension over the Prague fiasco had dissipated.

Sara smiled as she fiddled with the food left on her plate. Inside, though, she thought about Chad's slip of the tongue. For most of the journey she felt like it was predominantly his adventure and that she was accompanying him on it. Now she realized that, somewhere in the past two days, she'd become her own entity with her own goals and expectations. She felt the need for closure in the issue with Chad, even though she'd said her piece and he seemed to have gotten over it. She set her fork on her plate, reached across the table and grabbed his hand.

"Hey, I want to wrap up this matter with the Prague thing," she began in a calm yet determined voice. "I know that it's starting to drift away but I don't want issues between us to just drift away. We're too close for that."

"Yes, I agree," Chad said as he nodded rather politely. "I was sitting here and trying to look content, but it was kind of bothering me."

"I just want this to be a fifty-fifty thing, Chad—one person, one vote."

"I agree," he said.

"So are you okay with me or do you think I was being kind of a bitch?"

"I'm very much okay with you and you shouldn't have to even ask."

They finished their meal in accord, then began to peruse the area, continuing down the winding street. "You know, I promised my family that I'd send some postcards from along the way and today would be a good day to do it," Sara said as they walked.

"Shit," Chad moaned. "I never even thought of that yesterday. I wanted to grab a postcard of Paris, but I do need to pick up one from here. I don't know if I ever told you, but I collect postcards."

"Really? That's a cool idea."

"Through the years I've gotten one from every place that I've visited. It gives me something to look back and reminisce upon."

Sara lit a cigarette as they walked past a small park, which was located at the point where the street turned into a boulevard. She looked over at Chad and said, "Anyway, tell me something about Prague. I remember hearing a lot of talk about it recently but I don't know about it in any depth."

"Well, okay, let me think for a minute." He pulled out a cigarette of his own, paused as he lit while Sara stopped and waited for him. He took his time with the question and assembled the facts in his head as they continued to walk. He liked what he'd read about the city and wanted to give a good synopsis. Finally, he began. "Prague is an old and historic city, Sara, dating back roughly to the year seven-hundred seventy. When Czechoslovakia fell into Communist hands it actually helped preserve the city by thwarting modernization." He took another hit off his cigarette and went on. "I've read that recent statistics show Prague to be rivaling Paris as the most toured city in the world. The architecture is splendid and there's a large number of Americans living there—and with all the Americans it might be the easiest place in Europe for us to find employment." He turned back to her in a manner that indicated he was finished.

"It sounds quaint. I'm anxious to see it," she said.

They came to a Belgian chocolate shop and as Chad looked through the opened door he spotted a stand of postcards. They went inside and Chad snatched one for his collection, while Sara picked out several to send out to her family. When they had their cards in hand, Sara said, "I think it would be foolish to come in here and not try the chocolate."

"Go ahead," Chad said. "I'm not a big chocolate person."

"How can you not be a chocolate person?"

"You're acting like a Fudgie, Sara," he jested.

"I just think you should try something indigenous to the area."

"Why don't we go back and grab some of that beast that was roasting in the window?"

"Yeah, that's a fair comparison—yak versus chocolate," she quipped.

Chad sighed. "If I get some will you shut up about it?"

"Of course."

Chad walked up to the counter with his postcard and asked for a small assortment of chocolates. Sara selected some for herself and they went and sat on a bench that was in front of the shop. The sun was beginning to set. It had been a nice day and they were happy with their decision to spend it in Brussels. Sara dug into her purse, pulled out a pen and began to write out her cards. Chad sat quietly and began to observe the people who passed by. When she finished writing, they discussed where they'd go from Brussels. Sara reiterated that Prague was a suitable destination for her, but they decided that they'd first go to Frankfort and spend the night there. Then, after a goodnight's sleep, they would leave for Prague early Monday morning. Sara put her pen and postcards into her purse and they began their trek back to the depot.

Chad was excited about hitting the rails again and was anxious to see Germany. From the pictures he'd seen he considered Germany to be one of the most scenic countries in the world: in its urban architecture, quaint villages and grandiose alpine settings. The land of numerous castles, the Black Forest and the Bavarian Alps intrigued and awaited him.

They arrived at the depot. Sara dropped her postcards in the mail and they grabbed their luggage from the locker. Chad went to the ticket window and got their tickets and was happy to hear that a train bound for Frankfort was scheduled to depart in twenty minutes. They wasted away the final few minutes by browsing through the shops that were in the station. Then they boarded their train. Not long into their trip, a customs officer came around asking for passports and Chad realized that they had entered Germany.

After thirty minutes of traveling Chad talked Sara into taking a walk through the train with him. As they were passing through one of the corridors they came upon a group of young people who were sitting on the floor and passing around a joint. They offered it to Sara as she walked by and she took a hit and passed it on to Chad. They began to chat with the assemblage and eventually joined them on the floor, staying in the corridor until the train reached the Frankfort station.

As they left, Chad saw a hotel across from the depot and they checked in. The day that had begun with a hard rain washing out their Parisian plans had finally come to a close. Tired and travel weary, they called it a night.

CHAPTER NINE

Sleep can have a hold on someone that's as strong as any drug. In the state of semi-consciousness things seem distorted and blurred. In that semi-conscious state dreams get confused with reality and reality with dreams.

Sara awoke earlier than usual Monday morning, eager to begin what they had come to do. She rustled Chad to wake him and they began their routine of showers and gathering their belongings for the next leg of the journey. Although it wasn't yet seven a.m., the sound of traffic from the street permeated their room and the rising sun illuminated the floral pattern on the brownish-red curtain over the window.

Chad pulled back the curtain, looked outside, then opened the window—oblivious to the fact that he was in his underwear. "Trying to give the Germans a bit of a thrill, Chadders?" Sara chided, and he pulled the curtain to a close and smiled. The day was both brilliant and promising and it was hard for them not to feel good.

As they packed, Sara looked for her purse, which she'd placed in her suitcase. Whether it was a sixth sense or not, she had to make sure it was there. She opened the suitcase, dug around to the bottom and to the back and around the sides but couldn't see or feel it. She was getting concerned and wondered what had driven her to look for it in the first place, yet she was realizing that her uneasiness was valid. Then, with growing distress, she picked up the suitcase and dumped the contents onto the floor, sifting through every article of clothing until there was nowhere else to look.

Chad came out of the bathroom and saw Sara's clothes spewed about the floor. "What the hell are you doing?" he jested. "The clothes are supposed to go *in* the suitcase."

"This isn't funny, Reiger. I can't find my purse," she said as she continued to fumble through her scattered garments. "And I had two-thousand dollars in it."

"You are kidding, right?"

She shot him a glare that said she wasn't.

"Why on earth were you carrying that much cash anyway?"

Sara stood up, pulled her hair back with one hand and rested the other on her hip. She looked out the window and sighed, "My passport was in there too."

Chad didn't say anything. With those simple words he envisioned the whole endeavor falling apart before it had even started. He sat on the bed and tried to collect his thoughts as Sara continued to stare out the window. He knew he needed to be calm and not rush to the worst possible conclusion, even though it was hard not to. He knew Sara had enough money—the loss of a couple grand would hurt, but she could continue on. It was the passport that concerned him. *How can we possibly cross any border without a passport?* he thought. *How can we even stay in Germany?* "All right," he began, "let's take a breath and regain our composure." He got up off the bed and began to pace—the type of pace that seemingly helps one think. After a moment he asked, "Are you sure you looked everywhere?"

"Yes I did, Chad—up and down, high and low. I've checked the whole room three times and it's not here."

"Son-of-a-bitch," he said under his breath. "Okay, can you think of anywhere else you might have left it?"

"No, I definitely had it here last night. I remember I had to dig out my passport when we checked in. Then I put it back in my purse and my purse in my suitcase. I know that for a fact. I'm very anal with things like that."

"I know you are," Chad admitted. "Well then, that means it has to be here."

Sara suddenly froze and stared. "Wait a minute, Chad," she said in the hesitant and unfinished manner of someone in mid-thought.

"What is it?"

"Quiet… Quiet for a moment," she said, holding her palm out to him.

Chad stood silently and observed Sara's befuddlement. She had an eerie look about her—perhaps a combination of curiosity and horror would describe it best. She shuddered, paused for a moment, then said, "I had a dream last night that someone was in our room." She stopped and recalled the dream. Her words came slowly as they matched the speed of her recollection. "Yes. I had a dream that I heard someone in here, but I was too tired to look and I fell back asleep. It wasn't a dream, Chad. Someone was in here last night and the son-of-a-bitch stole my purse!"

Sara stood in the middle of the room, seemingly in disbelief of her own words, while Chad sat with an open-mouth stare. If it were anyone other than Sara telling him this he would dismiss the theory as nonsense, but she was the most practical person he had ever known.

He went into the bathroom and came out with an empty glass. Using it as a makeshift ashtray, he lit a cigarette and Sara did as well. Up until now everything had gone smoothly, dating right back to the day he'd asked her if she wanted to come with him. But with this, they had a real problem. Without her passport she could be deported. They had to think.

"Why don't we just go find the U.S. embassy and see if they can help," Sara conceded.

"Not yet," Chad replied quickly and with a warning tone.

"Why not?" she asked, sounding somewhat irritated with his response.

"I'm leery of someone saying that you'd have to be sent home until you got a new passport. For the time being, at least, let's not take that route. And I have to add that we'd face the same problems if we went to the police."

"Well shit, Chad. What option does that leave me?"

"Just for now, Sara, that's all I'm asking. I'll tell you what. Let's check out of the hotel—we have to do that anyway—and go somewhere to mull our options. Then, if you decide to call the police, you can say that you just discovered that the purse was missing."

Sara's frustration showed, but she agreed. She crushed her cigarette into the glass and Chad followed suit. She scooped her clothes off the floor and stuffed them into her suitcase, not bothering to organize them as she did. They checked out of the hotel and proceeded to the train station across the street. They put their luggage in two lockers, then went to one of the restaurants in the depot and grabbed some breakfast. As they ate, they tried to retrace their steps from the night before. It all seemed futile until it finally hit Sara.

"It had to be someone who worked at the hotel. It obviously was someone who had access to our room key because I know that I locked the door and there was no forced entry. And besides, when we checked in I had to dig out my passport. The desk attendant had to have seen my money."

Chad digested Sara's words. Her hunch was sounding like the plot of a detective movie; however, despite its drama, it was the most logical explanation. He began to think aloud. "Okay, so under that scenario we have someone that could be the perpetrator—the front desk clerk. The question is what do we do about it?"

"Maybe we can bait him into doing it again."

"I don't see how," Chad sighed. "If he did steal your purse he'll be too cautious to try it again the very next night."

Sara persisted. "What if we set him up, though? What if… what if we found someone else to check in and flash some money around? We could look for an old woman. Someone that wouldn't threaten or spook him off."

Chad paused and tried to envision Sara's idea. "It does sound interesting," he said. Still, he found himself thinking too many thoughts at once, so he rested his chin on his hands and focused, then asked, "But what could an old lady do if she caught him? She could get hurt."

"Chad, think a little more creatively. The old lady would check in and then give us the key to the room. We would pay her for her efforts and she'd be on her merry way. This is it, Chad. We can do this."

"There is one snag, you know."

"What's that?"

"What if the person you suspect isn't the one who committed the crime?"

Then I may have to go home."

There was nothing else to say. Sara's plan, simple as it might have been, was agreed upon. They decided that it'd be wise to stay out of the hotel's vicinity until nightfall. It'd be better if they didn't run into the perpetrator beforehand, and that he believed he'd gotten away with his crime. They took a long walk through Frankfort, trying to keep their heads as clear as possible. As they walked, they fine-tuned their plan, and it was sounding more plausible with every rehearsal.

They ate lunch; they ate supper. Chad forced himself to eat hearty meals, even though he was too nervous to have an appetite. He realized that he might be in for a scuffle before the night was through and wanted to have as much energy as possible. After dinner they stayed in the restaurant for over an hour. Then at dusk they approached the region of the hotel.

They found a railing on the other side of the train station and leaned up against it, watching the people who passed by and looking for a suitable subject for the task at hand. Within a few minutes they had a candidate. She was a woman of perhaps seventy-two and walked with a cane. Sara approached her but the woman turned and walked back the other way as soon as she started to speak. They leaned for another five minutes or so, passing on one woman who Chad feared was a little too old and frail. Then Sara spotted a tidy-looking woman of about sixty-five. She was rather petite and had a natural pleasantness about her. Sara approached her, asked her if she spoke English, and when she said that she did, she explained what had happened to her as well as the dilemma it had put them in.

She laid out their entire plan for her and the woman nodded as she spoke. Chad had exchanged some American currency for Deutchmarks. He would give the woman a bundle of five hundred, along with his suitcase. She'd pay for the room with this money, trying to show it off some as she searched for the proper bills. Then she'd go up to the room, drop off the suitcase and exit the hotel through the backdoor, where Sara and Chad would be waiting. She'd hand them the room key and the remainder of the money, minus one hundred Deutchmarks for her role.

After listening to Sara's pitch, the woman agreed to help, offering but one condition—she refused to be paid. In their short conversation she'd taken kindly to Sara and felt sorry for her and Chad.

The last bit of preparation was to send the woman in and out of the hotel so she could describe whoever was at the front desk. She went in and browsed through the lobby, making sure to get a good look at the person at the desk, while Chad and Sara stood alongside the building. When she came out she said that there was a man with red hair and a slightly crooked mustache working behind the desk. Sara told her to say no more. They had their man.

The stage was set and they were ready to begin. The old woman reentered the hotel carrying Chad's suitcase, went to the front desk and asked for a room. When the man asked to see her passport he questioned why she needed a room if she lived in Frankfort. She told him that she'd moved in with her son in Düsseldorf, but came back to visit her sister who was in the hospital. He handed back her passport and informed her that the only rooms remaining were on the ground floor and near the street and that it might get a little noisy come morning. She said it wouldn't matter because she was a sound sleeper and added that she was really tired and could sleep through anything.

She paid for the room, displaying the money according to plan. She went to the room, dropped off the suitcase, then went out the backdoor where she found Chad and Sara waiting. "Well, how did it go?" Sara asked nervously.

"It went smoothly," she replied. "And I think I did more than you would have hoped. He told me that the room might get a little noisy come morning, but I said that I was so tired that I could sleep through anything."

"Excellent," Chad beamed.

She told them their room number, then handed the key and the remainder of the money to Chad. "I wish you luck," she said with a somber face, "but please do be careful. The man you are dealing with is a large fellow."

She turned to walk away, but in a soft voice Sara called out to her, "I'm sorry, but I never got your name?"

"Frau Gruber," she said.

Sara whispered one final thank you and the woman disappeared around the corner.

Chad and Sara entered the hotel and quietly went to their room. They each took a turn in the bathroom, then took their positions. Sara stationed herself in bed with her back to the door and the covers pulled up to hide her hair. Chad went back into the bathroom and closed the door slightly. He situated himself so he could see through the opening in the door, as well as through the space between the door and the frame. He positioned the door so he could get through without opening it any further so it wouldn't make any noise. The rest of their luggage had been placed in the bathroom so it would be out of sight. Only the suitcase that Frau Gruber had taken into the lobby was left out. The money was placed on the table next to the suitcase—along with a handkerchief of Sara's and some coin change to make it seem less conspicuous. They gave their scheme a test run with Sara acting as the robber. It went smoothly.

Sara went back to the bed and Chad went up to her. "Looks like everything's a go," he whispered. "Are you damn sure that you're up for this? You know that it could get ugly," he said firmly.

"I can't believe this is really happening—it seems so unreal—but yes, I'm ready. How about you?"

"I'm ready. Let's do it," he replied with a determined look. He turned to go to his post, but Sara grabbed his hand. "Love you," she said softly.

"Love you too," he replied. He let go of her hand and took his position behind the door.

The waiting was monotonous. From ten-thirty at night until two forty-five, nothing had happened. Chad's legs were cramping and he wanted to walk around and stretch but he didn't dare to. He resorted to standing up and squatting back down a few times at fifteen-minute intervals. He thought of what he'd do if Sara had to go back to the states. He felt a debt of loyalty to her for coming to Europe with him and thought, if it came to that, he would go back with her. He realized, though, that if he did go back home, he probably wouldn't come back; perhaps someday as a tourist, but not to pursue this dream. He imagined how good their lives would be if they could only overcome this obstacle. He wondered if, under the circumstances, the authorities would let her stay in Germany until the passport situation was resolved. He felt frustrated because he couldn't be sure of anything.

As Sara lay in bed she thought of Chad. She knew that this wasn't her fault, but she didn't want to have any role in destroying his dream. She still couldn't believe what had happened and just wanted it to come to a conclusion. She was worried for Chad's safety too. Had he not been so insistent, she would've called the police instead. Yet, she understood that everything was on the line for him too. She wondered if the assailant would have a knife—or even a gun. With all the stress she had a ferocious appetite for a smoke, but she forced herself to keep still.

It wasn't until around three in the morning that she heard footsteps coming down the hall. Chad heard them too and his heart began to race. As he glanced at his watch, he hoped it was the perpetrator. He realized that they were running out of time and that if it wasn't him, he may have decided not to try it again. He did one final stand and squat to loosen his knees.

Then he heard a key slowly being put into the door. *This is it!* he thought. *Everything is on the line right here and now, man.* He realized that there would be no second chance to do this and he had to succeed. Frau Gruber's warning about the size of the villain flashed through his head. *"Please be careful. The man you are dealing with is a large fellow."*

Chad listened closely. The door slowly opened and a figure entered the room, carefully shutting the door behind him. Chad had to hold himself from moving in too soon. He peered through the crack between the door and the jam. From his vantagepoint he could see the thief's back as well as Sara on the bed. He wondered if she was aware that they had their company and hoped that she'd keep her composure. In a few more seconds he'd make his move. He wanted to make sure the crook had enough time to take the money. He didn't want to deal with any lame excuses—give the clerk an opportunity to say that he was in the room to check on the air conditioning or any other lie he might invent to explain his presence. He had to catch him cash-in-hand. The robber spotted the money on the table and Chad got on his haunches. *There! He's got it!* Chad took three or four quiet steps toward the thief and then lunged at him with all the force he could muster. As he charged he let out a primal yell, which prompted the thief to turn toward him in wide-eyed shock. Chad lowered his shoulder and plowed him to the floor, then began punching him in the face repeatedly. Sara sprung to her feet and was going to kick the man, but saw that Chad already had him subdued. She bolted to the door and opened it, yelling, "Help! Help us! Helfen! Helfen!" A young man from the room across the hall came out, dressed only in a pair of undershorts, and Sara asked him to call the police. He rushed back into his room, then came back a minute later, this time wearing a pair of pants. He told Sara that the police were on their way and asked what had happened, then helped Chad keep the villain pinned by taking one side as Chad took the other.

It turned out that this large man that Frau Gruber had warned about was no match for Chad on this particular night. The man from across the hall stayed until the police came and, after they asked him a few questions, he returned to his room. After Sara told her story, the robber opted to confess to both of her allegations—his intent to steal the money on the table as well as taking her purse the night before. He told the officers that Sara's purse was at his apartment and that the money had been deposited into his bank account.

The manager of the hotel arrived on the scene and the police briefed him on the situation. He went to Sara and apologized profusely, promising a refund for both nights and telling her and Chad to sleep in as long as they wanted. He offered to go with the police to get her purse and then go with them again in the morning to retrieve her money from the bank. He told her that, if she wanted this done, he'd have everything waiting for her at the front desk. After posing the idea, the manager looked at the police for their approval and they nodded. Sara liked the idea of being able to sleep, after the night they'd had, as well as saving the hassle of running around in the morning and she accepted the manager's hospitality.

She answered a few more questions from the police and it was left at that. The fact that the clerk confessed made it easy and they wouldn't be needed for any further questioning. One of the officers congratulated them for their help in apprehending the robber, but cautioned them against trying anything so dangerous again.

Everyone cleared out of the room. Chad and Sara undressed and climbed into bed. They talked the adrenaline out of their system, then wrapped their arms around each other until sleep came.

CHAPTER TEN

The street was full of activity by the time Chad awoke. As the clerk had told Frau Gruber, the room they were in was not the quietest. He roused from the bed and went to the window, this time only opening enough of the curtain for him to peer out. The street was teeming with traffic, both vehicular and pedestrian, and it was evident that it was a workday. He looked at the clock on the nightstand and saw that it was past noon. He was eager to get moving, but Sara was still asleep and he wasn't about to wake her.

He took a long, hot shower and got dressed and Sara was still sleeping. He snatched the room key from the desk and crossed the street to the train station, where he got their tickets and checked on departure times. In the depot he came upon a magazine stand and picked up a copy of USA Today. Exiting the stand, he spotted a bench, sat down and got caught up on what was happening back home. Then, after a little browsing through the station, he felt he'd killed enough time and headed back to the hotel. He passed a bakery along the way, went in and picked out some pastries for Sara.

When he got back to the room she was dressed and was laying on the bed. She yawned and smiled at him. "Getting anxious to go, aren't you, Chadders?" she said.

Chad smiled back. "Yeah, anytime you are."

"I went down to the front desk to get my things. They had everything except my passport—they weren't able to find it."

"Good. I can travel faster without you," Chad said, grinning. "That wasn't one of your better efforts either. I'm only giving you a two-point-five for it."

"On a scale of three?"

"On a scale of ten."

"I guess I'm not in your league when it comes to bullshit, Chadders."

As they laughed there was a feeling that things were again back to normal. Soon, they'd be on a train bound for Prague and the incidents of the prior two nights would be but a footnote.

Chad walked through the room and gathered his belongings, discussing the day ahead as he did. "When I was at the station I checked the departure times for Prague," he said. "There's a train leaving in about an hour; the next train doesn't leave for another five hours."

"Well I'm ready to get the hell out of here. Aren't you?" Sara replied.

"Yeah—let's roll," Chad said with a look that didn't mask his eagerness.

They checked out of the hotel and the manager came to the desk to see them off. They thanked him for his help and hospitality. As they were about to leave he handed Sara an envelope. Her name was handwritten on the front and misspelled, having an H at the end of it. She thanked him again and they left the hotel. They crossed the street, went to the station and boarded their train. Looking at one of his travel maps, Chad guessed that they'd be crossing the Czech border in a little over four hours.

When they settled in, Sara opened the envelope that the manager had given her. It was a note from Frau Gruber. It read:

"Dear Chad and Sarah,

I was so glad to hear that everything worked out for you. You seem like such a fine young couple. I wish you luck and hope that you find what you are looking for.

Stella Gruber"

Sara showed the note to Chad. "That's pretty cool," he said genuinely. "You need to save that."

"I think I will," she said as she folded the note, put it back in the envelope and placed it in her purse.

They traveled for an hour or so before Chad was back in his element. With their late-night fiasco behind them, he found a tranquillity in gazing out the window and taking in what the German countryside had to offer. Whether it was farmland, rolling hills or the small villages they passed through, it was all new to him. With his interest in the scenery, time passed quickly—even with the anticipation of getting to Prague.

Their fellow passengers on this leg of the journey were mostly businessmen. On their weekend excursion from Paris to Brussels, and then from Brussels to Frankfort, the train was predominantly filled with tourists, which proved to be more interesting. The tourists tended to be friendlier and would chat and romp about the train, whereas the professionals were burying their heads in their work or in newspapers. They were indifferent; both to the scenery and the other passengers.

At what Chad figured to be halfway through their run, they strolled to the dining car for a late lunch. The atmosphere was livelier than in their coach, and after two hours of sitting in the same spot the change of setting was a welcome one. Chad turned to an older couple who was sitting across from them and asked if they were from Prague, but they just shrugged. Chad smiled politely and nodded in return. "Not everyone speaks English, Chadders," Sara poked. The waiter came and they ordered. As they waited for their food they discussed what they'd do upon their arrival and, after discussing their options, Chad returned his gaze to the scenery outside. After a while he brought his stare back to Sara. "Damn! We're almost there," he said with a grin. "I'm getting excited. How about you?"

"Not so much excited as nervously anxious."

"Think of how I'd feel if you weren't with me. I'm glad you came. It would've been a lot harder trying this alone."

"Let me ask you this. What would you have done if I hadn't got my passport back and they deported me?"

"I probably would've continued on with that cute little room-service girl."

"Oh, really?"

"Certainly you didn't expect me to go back to the states with you?"

"It would've been a noble gesture."

"But I'm just a peasant."

"So a maid would be a good match for you."

"Okay, you're pouting now. I would've gone back with you and you know it—so stop."

"Finally—the proper answer."

Sara cleared her throat. Her facial expression went from jovial to serious. She looked at Chad and said, "We'll be in Prague soon and we'll be facing the task of making this thing work. It probably won't be easy and that scares me. Plus, we can waste a lot of money in a hurry if we don't have our act together."

Chad watched as she paused and pulled her hair away from her face. He noticed how long it was getting, as well as how it stood in stark contrast against the softness of her white skin with the back-lighting from the window across from them. He realized that he'd begun to ogle and he re-focused his attention as she continued.

"With all that's happened in the last three days I haven't had time to look ahead. Now we're almost there and I don't have a clue as to what's in store for us."

"I know what you're saying," Chad concurred. "It seems like it's been a week since we landed at De Gaulle. We've had a lot compacted between then and now, haven't we?"

Sara pulled out her first cigarette of the day. Looking out the window, she lit up, took a hit and said, "You know, Chad, I think we should ease our way into this—be diligent and focused, but not allow ourselves to be overwhelmed." She took another hit before continuing. "We toured Paris and Brussels and learned a lot about those cities. Why don't we take today and do the same with Prague? We need to explore to find where things are anyway."

Chad nodded. "That sounds logical to me. We do need to gain

our sense of direction. Then, if the city works for both of us, we can begin to establish ourselves the next day."

"I just think that a day to adjust would be good. I mean, you find yourself in a totally strange environment and you start to look for work and an apartment on the first day? It seems a little overwhelming."

"I know," Chad said as he rearranged himself in his seat. "I have to admit I feel it too. If we were coming here to visit I'd be ready to roll, but with the magnitude of this, I think a little time to absorb everything would be cool." He pulled out a smoke of his own and said, "Sara, we'll do whatever it takes to make this work—and if that means easing in, then we'll ease in."

Sara extinguished her cigarette and excused herself to use the bathroom. Shortly after she left the waiter arrived with their food. Chad crushed his smoke into the ashtray and took a sample bite of his lunch before waiting for Sara to return. Although the atmosphere in the dining car was quaint, they couldn't boast about the quality of their food. When she came back they ate, then returned to their coach. A short while later a customs officer entered. They had made it to the Czech Republic.

The agent worked his way from the back of the car to the front. About halfway up he came to Chad and Sara. He was a burly man with Slavic features and a stoic face. He said something in Czech and Sara pulled out her passport. She handed it to him and asked, "Do you speak English?"

"Ya ya. Vhat do you do in Czech Republic?"

"We want to visit Prague," she said, much to Chad's relief. They hadn't discussed getting through customs and he was glad she didn't say they were looking to live there.

"How long you stay?" he asked, his tone sounding more like a statement than a question.

"We're staying about four days," she responded.

He examined her passport photo, then glared back at her. After a long, hard stare he handed the passport back and took Chad's. "You are vit her?" he asked.

"Yes."

And that was that. He handed Chad back his passport and proceeded to the next passenger. When the official was out of sight Chad said, "I didn't want to say anything earlier but I'm kind of glad we're out of Germany."

"Why?" Sara asked, curious about his remark.

"I doubt if anything would've come from it, but in the back of my mind I wondered if the desk clerk would have thought about pressing charges against me for hitting him. I realize that he robbed us and all, but you know that strange things like that happen."

Sara raised her eyebrows. "I never thought about that. You did get a few good shots in, didn't you. And I do remember hearing about a thief back in the states suing the owners of the house that he robbed because he tripped on something going down the stairs."

Chad smiled. "Yeah, I think I heard that one too. Anyway, we got through customs. That was step one. Now we have to see if we can legally work here. If not, we can find jobs where we get paid under the table until we sort things out—get our citizenship or a visa, or whatever it is we have to do. We'll try to ask an American what the procedure is.

"I think it is a visa that we'll need, Chad. It's too bad we didn't think of that sooner."

"Well it wouldn't have done any good anyway, Sara. We would've had to know what country we were settling in, and we didn't."

"That's true," she conceded. "Shit, Chad, now I'm getting nervous about all this."

"Don't be nervous. It's going to work out. Trust me. Essentially, we'll pose as tourists for a while, even after we have our apartment and jobs. The city is large enough for us to blend in and remain relatively anonymous."

"You're not exactly helping me relax here, Reiger," Sara said wryly.

"I'm sure it sounds more intimidating than what it'll be. I'm just laying everything on the table. It'll work out, though," Chad said in a reassuring tone, "and if it doesn't, we'll move on."

They reached Prague at mid-afternoon and again had a hotel across from the train station. They checked in, dropped off their belongings and went to explore the city.

They walked several blocks into town and, for the first time since Chad had known her, Sara displayed more enthusiasm than he did. She twirled about, smiling and marveling at everything around her. "Oh! This is wonderful!" she beamed. From the pictures Chad had seen, he knew that there was still much more that she'd be awed by too. He observed the wonder in her eyes and he felt good.

She only needed to go as far as the Karlûv Most, or the Charles Bridge, to totally fall in love with Prague. It did what she hadn't deemed to be possible: it surpassed the beauty and splendor of any sight she'd seen in Paris—including the Eiffel Tower. She stood motionless and looked past the pedestrian-filled street and out toward the tower at the end of the bridge. She eyed the colorful buildings with their reddish-brown roofs at the far end of the river, and further on, the many domed buildings—each representative of a different culture that had left its mark on the city. She observed the bridge's brick street and the dark, gray statues that lined it. The combination had a synergistic quality. She turned and saw the other bridges spanning the Vltava River and the city in the background. There was a haze in the air that gave the scene a postcard-worthy effect. It was the most inspiring sight she'd ever beheld.

Touring further into Prague added testimony to the diversity of architectural styles. The city had been a crossroads for many years and each culture that passed through added to its uniqueness: Gothic and Romanesque designs, edifices with baroque facades and the mosques and temples of Eastern influence.

They walked down a thoroughfare and into a district called Old Town Square. The street was lined with old and unique buildings and the detail on these structures was incredible—both in the style of the buildings themselves and in the intricate murals painted on them. Many of them also were adorned with spired balconies.

Leaving Old Town Square they ascended the brick walkway of Castle Hill to Prague's one-thousand-year-old Hradcany Castle. The buildings which lined their ascent were as marvelous as the ones in the square and the walkway was brimming with sightseers. "It's kind of refreshing to see this many tourists and not hear a word about Hemingway," Chad had to jest.

The summit of the hill offered a breathtaking vista. The sun's reflection off of the numerous domed structures gave the city a golden hue. They saw how the Vltava divided Prague into two distinct halves with the old separated from the new, similar to what they'd seen in Paris.

They scouted the city for several hours, then returned to the hotel.

"I have to admit, I like what I saw," Sara said as she kicked her shoes off and reclined on the bed.

"I know. I could tell. I like it too."

"I think this would be an interesting place to live, Chadders, but it seems weird that we found a location this easily."

"So, we both agree on giving it a go here?"

"Yeah… why not?"

"Cool," Chad replied. "Then why don't we take a little break—maybe hang here for an hour or so." He lay back on the bed and took his pillow and fluffed it to a thickness that suited him, then continued. "I want to look for some Americans. Hopefully we can find one that can answer a few of our questions. Maybe we can run into an entrepreneur who started the way we'll have to, or someone who's sympathetic to what we're trying to accomplish—someone who can either give us a job or a lead on one."

"We do need to look into this visa issue though," Sara advised.

"We will. I'd just like to get settled in first."

"I know. You're afraid of being sent home before you get started, right?"

"I don't want to get sent home at any time or under any circumstances. But to answer your question, I just want to feel things out for a while."

"Well, Chad, I don't want to get all domesticated on you, but we need to do some laundry too."

"And you need to call your family."

"But this bed is feeling too good right now."

"I know," Chad said as he turned onto his side and cradled the lower half of his pillow.

A half-hour later Sara got up, looked at her watch and nudged Chad. "Time to get moving," she said. She slipped her shoes on and went down to the lobby and called her sister Beth from the pay phone. Chad sat on the edge of the bed and began browsing through his map of the city. When Sara returned to the room they were ready to do the town again. Their plan was to hit a coffeehouse where perhaps they could run into someone who could give them a little direction. They found one about ten blocks from the hotel and went in. They spotted an empty booth and sat down. In a short while a waitress came over to them.

"Dobre den," she greeted.

"Hello," Sara replied. "Do you speak English?"

"Some little English, yes."

"Two coffees please," Sara said, looking at her to see if she comprehended.

"Very good, two coffee. I come right back."

"There, that's a good sign," Sara said.

"I told you that they do speak English here, especially the younger people."

"I know. It's just good to actually hear it."

"This is a quaint little place," Sara said. "I can see coming down here quite a bit."

"Depending on where we find an apartment," Chad added.

"That's true. At any rate, I like the coffee house atmosphere."

"We used to go to the one in Petoskey from time to time. You never seemed all that enthralled with it then."

"Chad," Sara said with a look that spurned his remark. "You can't seriously be trying to compare the Eighth Street Coffee House with this?"

"The Seventh Street Coffee House, and no, I won't compare the two," he said with a chuckle."

"Hi there," came a voice from the booth behind them. "Pardon my intrusion but I couldn't help overhearing. You're from the States, right?"

"Red-blooded Michiganders," Chad beamed. He stood and offered his hand to the stranger. "I'm Chad Reiger and this is my friend, Sara McClair."

"Pleased to meet you. Floyd Mayor from Pittsburgh P.A."

Sara, who was sitting with her back toward him, turned and shook his hand as well. If ever there was a man who could be described as plain and average looking, Floyd was it. He was wearing gray dress pants with a bluish-gray flannel shirt. His hair was slicked over to the left and he had a couple day's of beard growth going. His voice was average—not high or low in pitch—and he looked to be about five-foot ten. Still, despite his ordinary appearance, his weathered face showed character. Sara looked him in the eye and said, "Pardon my prodding, Floyd, but are you here on vacation or do you live here?"

"Well, Sara, I'm over here taking advantage of the free market actually."

Sara raised her eyebrows and glanced at Chad. "So you live here," she voiced.

"Yes I do. I was divorced about two years ago. I had four restaurants in the Pittsburgh area but my wife—ex-wife, thank you—cleaned up in the settlement. So after twenty-five years of building the businesses and putting everything I had into them, I was left with nothing." Floyd held up his finger, gesturing to give him a second while he reached over to his table for his coffee. He took a sip and continued. "Anyway, I heard a lot was happening over here and I needed a fresh start." He took another sip, then concluded, "So here I am."

"Why don't you scoot over here and join us?" Sara offered.

"That sounds like a good idea, let me grab my stuff," he said as he reached around to the booth behind them and grabbed a paper bag and a plaid tam. Chad relinquished his seat and moved across the table beside Sara. Floyd set his bag and hat on the seat and sat down.

"So what do you do over here?" Chad asked.

"I have an authentic American restaurant—Floyd's American Cafe. We serve steaks, hamburgers, fries, apple pie… all the delicacies of home," he said with a smile. "And how long have you folks been in town?"

"This is our first day here," Sara answered. She then asked, "Is there a language barrier, Floyd?"

"Not really, Sara. Most of the service people speak English, with the exception of the older ones. You should be able to get around, though." He took another sip of his coffee and asked, "How long will you be staying in Prague?"

Chad explained their situation to Floyd and asked if he could either help them or offer some advice. When he voiced his concerns about the visa situation, Floyd told him that he already had his visa when he came over and that he didn't know how it would work without one. However, he offered to let one of them wash dishes at his restaurant. That way they'd be able to work in the kitchen and remain out of sight. In addition to the job opportunity he told them about an employee of his, Staneslous Volf, who was to be married on the coming weekend and was looking for someone to sublet his apartment.

Sara looked over at Chad and smiled, then told Floyd she'd gladly take the dishwashing job and asked how they could get in touch with Staneslous. He told her that Stan waited tables for him and that he'd be there the following day for the lunch shift. He explained where the restaurant was and told her to stop by around nine. He'd put her to work and introduce her to Stan. Then Floyd finished his coffee and put his tam on, grabbed his bag and bid the two farewell. Chad and Sara finished theirs as well and headed back toward the hotel.

As they walked in the cool night air, Chad smiled at Sara and said, "Well, mission accomplished." He then elaborated, "I'd have to say, just like that, we're way ahead of schedule on our list of objectives."

"I just hope that Stan's apartment is cool."

"My feeling is that unless it's a total dump we should take it."

"I know, Chad. I still hope it's cool though," she said, then gave him a playful shove and ran off ahead of him, stopping in front of a movie theater. Chad caught up to her and they looked at the posters of the films that were playing and decided to catch one—an American comedy—before returning to their room.

As they got back to the hotel they stood outside and had a smoke before going up to their room. They talked about the city, how much they liked it and how everything came together for them. They were anxious for the next day and to get more of a flavor of how things would be. They were curious as to what Stan's apartment looked like and where it was located. And, when all the day's business was done, they wanted to explore more of the city. Sara extinguished her cigarette into the ashtray and furrowed her eyebrows in a way that asked, are you ready? Chad crushed his, then followed her up to the room.

CHAPTER ELEVEN

It was October first and Chad and Sara had been living in Prague for nearly three months. The was a bit of a chill in the air and the trees nearest the river were accruing the orange leaves of autumn on their north sides. The two were beginning to settle into the city. They had taken the apartment from Staneslous Volf, Sara was working at Floyd's American Cafe and Chad found work loading freight at a warehouse. Both of them were being paid under the table and the apartment was still in Stan's name. As far as any official in the Czech Republic knew, they didn't exist.

Their living quarters were tight, to say the least. The bedroom consisted of a bed, one dresser and enough extra room to squeeze past the two pieces of furniture. The bathroom was proportionately as small and basic as the bedroom and they had a walk-through kitchen. Their only other room served as a living room and dining area and was compressed into the size of an automobile. This was the room that contained the heat pipes which, according to Stan, kept you warm and cozy as long as you were within a three-meter radius.

The walls were painted in bland colors and showed signs of previous tenants. Sara dressed them as best she could by mounting a painting she'd purchased at the market along with a couple pieces of her own. Chad added to the decor by having a couple photos that he'd taken in Paris blown up and framed.

The floors were always cold and they creaked. There was no carpeting, only tile in the kitchen and bathroom—a rather ugly red and white square pattern—and worn, hardwood floors throughout the rest of the apartment. Their bathtub and sink bore the stains of hard water and the bathroom faucet had a continuous and seemingly unfixable drip. Their walls were thin and they would often hear their neighbor's sexual conquests at night. From their one window they could catch glimpses of the river, provided that the wind blew enough to rustle the leaves on the tree which stood directly in front of it.

In spite of it all, the apartment was theirs and they loved it. They were living abroad and things were going much the way they'd envisioned. Both of them had jobs and neither had dipped into their bankrolls, except to occasionally treat themselves.

The lives they led were simple—not void of interest, but free of the fast-paced, stress-filled days that they were used to. Chad had gotten into a routine of stopping by a bakery on his way home from work. A young woman who worked there had caught his eye and he made a point of selecting something every day just so he could see her.

Sara had begun painting again. It was something she had loved to do when she was in her teens, but she stopped when her mother was killed. Shortly after they moved into their apartment she decided to try it again. She would get back from work before Chad and paint while she had the apartment to herself. Then when he arrived they'd go and grab a bite at one of the area restaurants.

They loved taking the evening to enjoy the city. Whether it was walking down its streets, taking in live music in the coffeehouses and nightclubs or staring out over the town via the Charles Bridge, they found a contentment that they hadn't experienced in Michigan. They fed off the city's timelessness and admired its grandeur. They were thankful that it was their home. Chad told Sara that he felt like he'd become a better person since he came to Prague. He was enjoying life again and nothing was a chore. He was living a Bohemian lifestyle in the heart of Bohemia.

The people they had come to know found Chad and Sara to be likable. Some of their new friends were American but most of them were Czech. There was one couple in particular that they'd grown close to—Gustav and Martina. Gus worked at the warehouse with Chad and had come to his aid when he couldn't understand what the foreman was screaming at him about. He spoke enough English to resolve the situation and looked after Chad from that point on.

Gus and Martina were a handsome couple. They both had dark, brown hair and were roughly the same height. They shared certain facial characteristics; both had big brown eyes and angular faces. It was a couple that one could look at and affirm that they were meant for each other. When Chad and Sara were still new to Prague, Gus and Martina would take them around town and show them the inside scenes of the city. Now, they would catch a movie or stop at a coffeehouse, then, later into the night, they'd hit one of the area nightclubs.

Gus was a huge soccer fan and had taken Chad to some games. Chad had been indifferent to the sport, but with his new exposure he began taking an interest. He enjoyed the fact, again, that it was something he wouldn't have done if he were back in the states.

When they weren't socializing or out on the town, their nights consisted of casual conversation about their day with a glass of burgundy or merlot, while lounging on their lone piece of living-room furniture; an old couch with worn springs and a bad floral pattern. Later into the evening Chad would grab his transistor radio and they'd explore the Czech airwaves, sometimes looking for English music and other times listening to the local Eastern European sound. Then Chad would rummage through the refrigerator, looking for a late-night snack, and within an hour they would be in bed. Even though the size of the apartment dictated that they sleep in the same bed, they maintained their platonic relationship. On occasion, one would wake in the night with an arm around the other, but aside from that they remained absolute in their friendship. More than anything else, they were soul mates. Chad could talk to Sara about anything and Sara could, likewise, if it were her nature.

One day after Chad got home from work he told Sara how he had an eye for a girl that worked at the bakery. He told how he would flirt with her and how he could always make her smile, regardless of the mood she seemed to be in. He said that he hadn't noticed a ring on her finger and that he was thinking about asking her out.

Sara looked at him with honest and reassuring eyes. "If you like this girl you should ask her out," she said, fighting off her own feelings of jealousy as she spoke. She knew that he hadn't been with anyone since they were together and the thought of this was disconcerting to her, yet she cared for him and wanted him to be content. She focused on his enthusiasm and asked, "So, what's this girl like?"

Chad smiled as he spoke. "She's about five-five and has medium-length brown hair with soft curls. She has green eyes—just like you—and a cute little turned-up nose." He stopped and thought, still sporting a grin, then added, "She looks to be about twenty-five and she seems kind of shy, but I think she digs me."

"What's her name?"

"Irena."

Sara turned back to the laundry she'd been folding before he came in and said, "She sounds attractive, Chad."

He stepped up behind Sara and fluffed her hair. "Still not as attractive as you, though," he said, and he gave her a playful peck on her cheek.

That night as Sara lay in bed, she tried to sort out her relationship with Chad. It was obvious to her that she was still in love with him, and contrary to what he'd told her about Irena, she sensed that he was still in love with her too. She tried to decipher the situation but her thoughts became tangled to the point that she gave up and fell asleep.

The next morning Chad figured it was time to ask Irena out. He went to work and spent much of the morning thinking about what he would say. He knew that he'd have to express himself in basic English and he searched for the right words as he drove stacks of pallets into an empty freight car. He thought of how, as little as three months ago, he would've dismissed the idea of asking a stranger out, considering it a foolish whim. Now he had the resolve to take chances—a resolve he didn't have while he lived in Petoskey.

When his shift came to an end, he hurried out of the warehouse and toward the bakery. He hastened his pace until he was within a few blocks, then slowed down so he wouldn't be out of breath when he went in. He came to the door, stepped inside and saw three other customers ahead of him. He pretended to shop around and looked at all the other baked goods until he was the only customer. Then he approached the counter.

"How is Irena today?" he asked, trying to look calm and cool.

"I am good. And how is the American?" she said with her usual pleasantness.

"I'm good too, thanks."

"You have usual today?"

"Yes, but I have something to run past you, too."

"Yes? You want to run past me—but why?" she asked with a befuddled look.

"No, I don't really want to run past you," he said with a snicker. "It's just an American expression. What I mean is that I have something to ask you. Do you want to go to a movie with me tonight?"

"No I don't. I have too much class for that now."

Chad's expression froze at her response, leaving him with a foolish-looking half grin. He waited for her to crack a smile but she didn't. He forced himself to save face and asked for his usual loaf of bread, then wished her a good day and walked toward the door, craving the point where he'd round the corner and be out of sight and distant from his embarrassment. On the way home he replayed the scene in his head. He had thought Irena was sweet, but he had obviously misread her. He wondered if she'd been acting hospitable for the sake of the bakery—just as a waitress would occasionally flatter him for the sake of a better tip. He figured that he must have mistaken this business-at-all-costs attitude for her having a genuine interest in him. Either way, he felt humiliated and vowed not to go back there again.

He reached the apartment and walked in with his loaf of bread. He set it on the table and took off his jacket. Sara heard him and came into the living room. "I see somebody's been to the bakery," she said coyly.

"Yeah, whatever. There's nothing happening there," Chad said as he tossed his jacket onto the back of the chair.

"What happened? Did you ask her out?"

"Yes I did," he answered, keeping his head down to avoid eye contact as he spoke. "She said I wasn't good enough for her."

"Oh she did not!"

"She said she had too much class for a guy like me."

"Really?" Sara said, somewhat surprised at such an outcome. "Well screw her then," she admonished.

Chad picked up the jacket he'd tossed on the chair and walked it over to the closet. He felt rather emasculated telling Sara of his rejection—especially with it being such a cold one—and wished that she would've been out of the apartment when he'd gotten home.

"Come on, Chadders," she said as she watched him mope. "Why don't we go out to a nice restaurant tonight."

"I don't know," he said without looking at her. "I'm not hungry."

"Okay then, why don't you get undressed and go to bed at six in the evening. Obviously your life is over now and you have nothing else going for you."

"I know, you think I'm pouting, but shit, Sara, I got knocked down pretty hard back there."

Sara softened her tone. "I understand your disappointment, Chad, but how long have you known this girl? Three months at the most. I don't mean to be crass with you, but if you get your mind off of her it'll do you good."

Chad let out a groan. "So where are you taking me?" he conceded.

Sara smiled. "It's a surprise. Just get ready—and dress up for it."

Sara went into the bedroom, changed into a dress and put her hair into a French braid while Chad hopped into the shower. "I don't know why I feel so bad," he shouted over the sound of the water. "I didn't know her that well. Maybe I would've felt a little more like I belonged here if I was dating a local."

"Open your eyes, Chadders. You do belong here. You fit in and it's become your home. You don't need anything else to happen for that to be true. And even if you are kind of homely, you'll find someone else. Now hurry up. I'm getting hungry."

They went to the corner, flagged a taxi and went down to the Nebozzizek, a highly touted restaurant that had a spectacular view of the castle. As they entered they spotted Floyd. He waved them over to his table.

"Well, stranger, I don't believe I've seen you since the day I hired this pretty young lady of yours," he said as he stood and gave Chad a pat on the back.

Chad, who offered no correction to Floyd's interpretation of their relationship, shook his hand and said, "It has been a while, hasn't it? It's good to see you again."

"So what do you think of our city, now that you've had a chance to feel it?"

"I love it, Sara loves it… it's a fantastic place to be," he replied with a grin.

"Well unless you two want to dine alone, why don't you join me?"

Chad glanced over at Sara and she nodded. "Thank you, Floyd," she said. "I think we will."

Floyd remained standing until the two were seated and then asked, "So, Chad, how are things with your job?"

"Good enough to get by, I guess. It's not a particularly fun job and the pay could be better, but it's keeping me afloat until I find something else. The main thing about that job is that it's simple. I know what I have to do, so the language barrier doesn't come into play."

"But you must be picking up a little Czech by now?"

"Yes, actually I am. I still think it'll be a year before I can really communicate though."

Sara sat quietly and watched the two converse. She'd come to look at Floyd as something of an uncle, always caring and eager to help her along. Now she sensed that Chad looked at him in such a light as well. Since she'd come to Prague, Chad and Floyd were the people she felt the closest to and it was good to have them both together with her.

Floyd's meal had come shortly after Chad and Sara had placed their orders, so he finished well ahead of them. When he did, he stood and thanked them for their company and told Chad that he'd keep an ear open for a better job for him. Then motioned to the waiter, paid his bill and picked up the tab on Chad and Sara's as well. They tried to say that it was a nice gesture and that they'd pay their own, but he insisted, so they thanked him and he went on his way.

Chad and Sara leisurely finished their dinner. They opted to walk back home and enjoyed their stroll through the autumn evening. Chad thanked Sara for dragging him out of the apartment and assured her that he was already feeling better about things. When they got home they resumed their routine of listening to the radio and talking until they were tired enough to sleep.

Things continued to go smoothly until the middle of November. Until then, Chad had worked six days a week for four-and-a-half months without incident. On November seventeenth that all changed.

A woman he worked with had come to suspect him of being an illegal immigrant. She wondered why he didn't speak Czech and had observed him being paid in cash the day before. She'd taken it upon herself to call immigration and report Chad's suspicious nature.

This woman was the bitter type. Things at work hadn't turned out the way that she'd hoped and she took to making everyone else's life miserable at every possible opportunity. She would parade around the warehouse, flaunting an authority that she didn't have. She believed that she knew everything and thought everyone was afraid of her while, in reality, she was the running joke of the warehouse. Chad had noticed how the guys had a name for her and asked Gus what it meant. He laughed and said, "It means 'The Queen.' And she really believes that she is," he added with a laugh.

For Chad, though, this would be no laughing matter. A short while into his shift, two men from immigration were in the warehouse looking for him. They found the foreman and inquired about an English-speaking employee. He led them to Chad and they began to interrogate him.

"Dobre rano," the taller of two said.

"Dobre den," Chad answered. "But I'm afraid I don't speak much Czech," he said apologetically. He sensed who they were and what they were there for and his heart began to race.

"We though you might not. You are obviously not Czech citizen."

"No, I'm an American," Chad admitted. His mind was racing ahead and he imagined himself being deported, but he rebuffed the thought and tried to stay calm.

"Let me see your pass," said the taller agent who appeared to be in charge.

"Do you mean my passport?"

"Did I ask to see your passport? Show me your long-term residency pass."

Chad hadn't a clue about what he was referring to. His heart was beating even faster and his palms grew cold and sweaty. "I don't have one," he conceded.

"Then you will need to come with us."

The two officials led him out the door and into a black car that was waiting outside. As he left he saw Gus, who had snuck out to see what was happening. He bore a look of resignation, but nodded to Chad as he got into the vehicle. The smaller man closed the door behind him and he saw the woman who'd turned him in standing on the dock, looking quite satisfied. As they drove off, Chad continued to contemplate his fate. He realized that this would probably happen sooner or later, but he still wasn't prepared for it. He wondered what they were about to do and what the ramifications would be. His only wish now was that he wouldn't be deported. Anything short of that he was willing to endure.

They arrived at the Department of Immigration and led him into a small, windowless room. A third official entered—a middle-aged and very proper-looking woman. She asked Chad to sit and pointed to the chair that she wanted him to use. The two men who'd brought him in sat facing him while the woman remained standing and they continued their questioning.

"So, from the information in the complaint against you, I understand your name is Chad Reiger," the woman said in an English that was markedly better then her counterparts.

"Right," he replied.

"Tell me, Chad, what are you doing in the Czech Republic?"

"I came here to start a new life."

"What do you mean by this? You were a criminal?"

"No… no, not at all. What I mean is that I was tired of living where I was. I wanted to be somewhere that was new and exciting and I heard things were happening here. I'd become bored with everything back home and I was going nowhere." He cleared his throat and added, "That's why I came here."

The woman stepped up to him. "Let me see your passport," she said in a tone just short of a command. He handed it to her and she handed it to the shorter of the two agents who had brought him in. He took the passport, left the room and the interrogation continued.

"How long have you been in Prague?" she asked.

"About four-and-a-half months."

"And working here?"

"About the same."

"And where do you live?"

"Four twenty-two Hlucin Square."

"And are you here alone?"

"No, I have a friend, Sara McClair. She came over here with me."

"And is she working here?"

"No."

She paused and glared at Chad for what seemed to be an eternity. He sensed that she was waiting for him to change his answer under the pressure. He wasn't a particularly good liar and he was beginning to feel uncomfortable with the woman's staring. Yet, he didn't want to involve either Sara or Floyd in this situation and he forced himself to stay composed. He recalled the stressful night with the thief in Germany and found a resolve in that. Finally she turned and the questioning resumed.

"So this woman, you take care of her?"

"No, she takes care of herself. She inherited some money. She pays her own way."

The woman paused again and Chad, sensing the need to clear the matter up, decided to expedite the process.

"Do you mind if I speak?" he asked.

"No, go right ahead. That's why we brought you here." Her tone was polite but her pose was of someone waiting for the gift horse of self-incrimination.

Chad cleared his throat and began to explain his position. "I realize now that I missed a step when I didn't get a visa, but if you do a background check on me you'll find that I have a clean record and so does Sara. I put a lot into this move: I quit my job, sold my car and gave up a good apartment in order to come here. I love Prague and I'd really like to stay.

"I sought a job that would pay me in cash when I learned that I couldn't work here legally. I had hoped to be able to speak Czech before I applied for a visa because I thought I'd have a better chance of getting one." He looked back at the woman and concluded, "So if there's any way I can stay I would very much appreciate it."

The woman that Chad addressed his statement to didn't answer. Instead, the taller of the two men—the one who seemed to be in charge when they'd brought him in—stood up and walked over to him. "We will check your history. If what you say is true we will not trouble you. Instead, we will help you go in right direction. First of all you will not need visa. An American does not need visa in Czech Republic. You will need long-term residency pass. If everything checks out with you, getting one will not be problem. We will need to speak with this Sara though."

Chad nodded and breathed a sigh of relief. Four-and-a-half months of concern were coming to an end. He looked back at the woman—the one who spoke the best English—and asked one final question. "Will my employer be in much trouble from this?"

"Your employer will be in some trouble, yes. There are other jobs available to Americans right now. If you get your pass it may be wise to start with a new job."

The official who had left with Chad's passport came back into the room. He huddled briefly with the other man and the woman, then came to Chad and handed him his passport. They finished their business and gave him the information he'd need to obtain a pass, then led him back to the black car, which was again running and waiting for them.

They drove him back to the warehouse, escorted him inside and waited as he gathered his belongings. Along the way he caught eyes with Gus and gave him a wink and a quick grin to let him know that things had worked out. Then, when he had everything, he left the warehouse for the last time.

He walked with the agents to the car and they offered him a ride back to the apartment. He declined, but thanked them for their assistance and bid them farewell. He took one last look at the warehouse, zipped his jacket tight to the collar, then turned and faced the stiff November breeze and began his trek home.

Sara was in the living room working on a painting when Chad walked in. She was surprised to see him home at such an early hour and asked if everything was all right. He explained what had happened and told her that the immigration officials needed to talk to her too, but they didn't clarify when. He cautioned that they'd probably be watching them for a while and advised her not to work for the time being.

Sara, like Chad, felt relieved that the issue was coming to resolution. She agreed that she shouldn't work and they decided to take a walk to the cafe to tell Floyd what had happened. They walked in and found him in the kitchen and Sara explained what had occurred. She told him that she'd better quit for now, but would eventually apply for a residency pass too. Floyd looked surprised at the development, but thanked her for telling him. He told her she was welcome to come back when things were settled, but reminded her that she could get a much better job once she had her pass. She conceded and thanked him for his role in getting them started, but added that if she learned to speak Czech well enough she'd come back and wait tables for him. Floyd chuckled and accepted her offer. He wrapped an arm around each of them and wished them luck. They shook hands, then Chad and Sara headed back to their apartment. They would never see Floyd again.

About a month later, Stan Volf came by and informed them that Floyd had died of a massive stroke. As he left, Sara turned to Chad. A tear was running down her cheek and he held her close to him as they stood together by the door. The news had come as a shock. Floyd was the first person they'd met in Prague. He'd taken them under his wing and had even seemed paternal at times. They'd since made other friends, but Floyd was the one who genuinely cared about them. He was the one friend they had who'd taken the same path they were taking and understood their challenges. Sara recalled the night they met him and how he had come to their table when she realized they were Americans. She and Chad exchanged many stories about him.

Floyd had been gone for a week by the time the news got to them. His body had been flown back to Pittsburgh and there had only been a small memorial service for him in Prague. Sara was heavy-hearted about missing the tribute and wanted to somehow pay her respects. She had taken the first crown she'd earned at the diner and saved it as a souvenir. She took the crown, inscribed 'Thank you Floyd' on it and stuffed it into her pocket. She put her coat on and set out for the Charles Bridge.

Sara stood on the bridge alone. She looked at her breath being exposed by the frosty air and noticed patches of snow along the riverbank. Christmas would come soon. She thought how she would've gotten a special gift for Floyd and when she pictured him wearing his plaid tam she had to fight the urge to cry. She reached into her pocket and took the crown with the dedication and dropped it into the river.

CHAPTER TWELVE

It was December twenty-third and a Christmas snow was cascading past the apartment window. Carolers were on the street corners and Sara was going through the Christmas cards she'd gotten from home. The streets were filled with the hustle and bustle of the holiday rush and there was a sense of cheer in the air. Prague had delivered their first European Christmas in good fashion.

Sara glanced out the window at the falling snow as she sat on the sofa, then opened a card from her sister Beth. She had written about how they were off to an unusually harsh winter in Petoskey and that thirteen inches of snow had fallen the day before. She said how everyone would be getting together at her place on Christmas Eve and how it would seem strange without her there. Hearing this saddened her. The holidays were always special to her and she'd always been home for them.

As she sat with the card on her lap, Chad heard her sobbing. He looked towards her but her hair was covering her face as she leaned forward. He called her name and when she didn't answer he went over to the sofa and sat beside her, rubbing her back with his hand. "It's being away from home during the holidays, isn't it?" he asked and she nodded. He took his forefinger and lifted her chin, turning her face until he saw her tearstained green eyes. "But you know what?" he began with a reassuring smile. "You're about to have a special Christmas. I promise you that. And it'll be one you'll remember for the rest of your life."

Sara gave him a halfhearted smile. "Thank you," she said softly.

Christmas decorations hadn't been on their list of priorities when they packed for Europe, so consequently they didn't put up a tree. Instead, Sara took the Christmas cards they'd received and taped them to the wall in the shape of a tree. She'd bought two candles which were to be saved for Christmas Eve, one red and one green, and that was the extent of their ornamentation. They took the presents they'd gotten each other, along with one that Sara's family had sent her and Chad's gift from Abbey, and placed them on the floor under their makeshift tree.

It had been a month since either of them had worked and being cooped up in the apartment was starting to make them restless. "I need some fresh air," Chad said as he went over to the coat rack. "I'm going to take a walk and check out some of the decorations around town."

"Hold on," Sara said as she got up off the couch. "I'll go too."

"Okay," he said as he pulled his boots on. "I'll be outside waiting."

Chad headed down the stairs while Sara took her time and bundled up. She'd barely made it out the door when a snowball plucked her in the shoulder. "You bastard!" she said as she scooped up a handful of snow. She chucked it at Chad but missed, causing him to heckle her. He kept up his taunting until she nailed him in the face and, with that, he rushed her and tackled her into a snow bank. He grabbed a handful of snow and smeared it in her face. Sara conceded as Chad sat atop her in triumph. After a few moments of gloating he brushed the snow off her face and helped her to her feet. Sara stepped back, stuck her tongue out and raced back up the stairs. Chad shook the snow off his clothes and followed her up to the apartment. Wet and winded, they changed into dry clothes and ventured back out to see what was playing at the cinema.

As they were walking, Chad spotted Irena from the bakery. He pointed her out to Sara and, as they passed, Irena stopped him. "Well hello, Mr. American," she greeted with a cheery smile. "Where have you been? I miss you at bakery."

"Hello, Irena," Chad replied. "I've been busy and haven't been able to stop in," he said as he put his arm around Sara and pulled her next to him. "I'd like you to meet Sara," he said, making a point not to use the word friend.

"Hello, Sara. It is pleasure to meet you," she said as she held out her hand.

"It's nice to meet you too," Sara replied cordially.

"So, Irena, what have you been up to?" Chad asked.

"Up to? she questioned, sporting a puzzled look.

He recalled the extent of her English and clarified. "What have you been doing lately?"

"Oh," she said with a nod that indicated that she understood his previous question. "Well, because of Christmas I no longer have class. And because of this I have much time."

The words had barely come out of her mouth when it became apparent what she'd been trying to say at the bakery. "So you're not taking classes at school now," he stated.

"No, we have break."

Chad glanced at Sara. She gave him a nod and said, "I'm going to take a look in this shop. Come get me when you're ready to go." She walked into the store and Chad turned back to Irena.

"It is good to see you again," she said as she smiled. "It has been long time."

"I have to tell you—when you said you had too much class to go out with me, I didn't know that you were talking about school. I thought you meant that I didn't have enough class to be seen with you."

"Oh my, no! I am sorry. My English is not always good," she said apologetically.

"Anyway, that's why I haven't been back to the bakery."

"And now you have met another," Irena stated.

"Sara is just a friend of mine," Chad admitted as he looked over at her through the shop window. "She and I lived in the same town back in America."

"So tell me, is it too late to still go to movie with you?"

Chad again looked over at Sara before answering. "I would like that," he said with a smile. "But perhaps we could wait until after Christmas. Sara is already feeling homesick and I don't want her to be alone during the holidays."

"I understand and you are very nice to think of her. You stop by bakery after Christmas then."

Chad nodded. "I will," he said. "And you have a Merry Christmas."

Irena stretched up and gave him a peck on the cheek. "And you too have Merry Christmas," she said with a smile, then turned and continued in the direction she'd been heading.

He watched for a moment as she walked away, then went into the store. It was a shop that sold items imported from the East. He spotted Sara looking at vases and walked up to her. She turned to him and asked, "So, how did Mr. American do?" she asked coyly.

"I think we have everything cleared up."

"Did you say that you couldn't see her now because she didn't have class?"

"Stop it."

"Oh, come on," Sara teased. "I can't believe you couldn't figure out what she was trying to say. You knew that she didn't speak English as her first language. And then you come back to the apartment pouting, "She says she has too much class for a guy like me."

"Okay, so I screwed that one up. Are you ready for a movie or what?"

"Yeah, in a second," she said as she picked up a vase and held it at arm's length, spinning it around as she observed its intricate pattern. "What do you think of this one?" she asked.

Chad rolled his eyes. "It's a spectacular vase, Sara."

"Don't you think it'd look nice on the ledge?"

"We don't have a ledge. We have bricks that stick out too far— but not a ledge."

Sara turned from the vase to Chad. "It's a ledge," she stated in a corrective tone.

"Okay, it's a ledge. And that vase would look spectacular on it."

"Well, I wasn't sure about it, but seeing that you like it so much

I feel compelled to get it."

Sara bought the vase and they made their way to the cinema. In theme with the season, *It's a Wonderful Life* was playing. Chad had yet to see the movie but it was one of Sara's all-time favorites.

As they sat toward the back of the theater Chad tried hard to appreciate the movie that had meant so much to Sara, but his mind raced ahead as he stared at the screen. He couldn't help flashing back to his encounter with Irena. Until a few minutes ago, it had been a while since he'd seen her and she hadn't been in his thoughts since perhaps three or four days after the episode at the bakery. He thought of Sara and how important they were to each other—especially now in this holiday season. As much as he tried not to complicate things he couldn't get around the fact that, somewhere along the line, he had reacquired feelings for her. He told himself to focus on the movie, but as he sat he could only think of how good her hair smelled and how pleasantly warm her arm felt against his. He reenacted their snowball fight and thought of all the good times they'd shared over the past couple of years. He noted how his rekindled romantic feelings for Sara hadn't been clear until he ran into Irena. Suddenly, the thought of going out with anyone but her seemed utterly wrong.

The movie ended and he turned to Sara and saw a tear trickling down her face. She turned to the vacant seat next to her to grab their coats and her purse and he noticed her trying to discretely wipe off her cheek. He wanted to embrace her but fought the urge, knowing it would embarrass her if she was caught crying over a movie. He searched for some sort of comment, but couldn't come up with one that seemed appropriate.

"So, you liked it?" Sara asked as she turned and handed him his jacket.

"I loved it," Chad lied, hoping she wouldn't ask him about any specific part.

They exited the theater and Chad pulled out a smoke. The night was pleasant for December and they decided to walk up the bank of the river for a ways before returning home. Along the way they

150

passed a young couple who were passionately kissing and unaware of anyone's presence. They continued to walk silently until Sara broke the stillness. "You must be anxious to see Irena," she said in a barely audible voice.

Chad's mind froze and he felt put on the spot. He didn't want Sara to know how he was feeling about her, but he didn't want to mislead her about Irena either. "I don't know," he began. "So much time has passed since I saw her last and I didn't really know her that well to begin with. Now, I'm feeling like it was more of an infatuation."

"But you're still going out with her, right?"

Sara's question sounded as much like a directive than anything else. *You're not getting any funny ideas about me?* is what Chad translated it to. Deliberately, he answered, "Yeah, I guess," trying to sound as unenthusiastic as possible.

"I think you and her would be cool together."

Chad didn't reply. He didn't know if Sara was sincere or simply trying to be nice. Either way, he wished that they hadn't run into Irena. He wondered if Sara shared any of the feelings he was experiencing. The only thing he knew for sure was that he felt comfortable with her and was as content as one could be just walking down the bank of the river with her. He decided not to broach the topic for the time being—not until he could get a better read on the situation—and he didn't want to violate any unspoken trust they might have had.

As they walked along Sara sensed a silence. She noticed Chad's hesitancy when he spoke of Irena and was curious about it. Still, she didn't want to labor the topic now. She turned to him and said, "Tell me, Chadders, what was Christmas like for you when you were a kid?"

"Christmas when I was young," Chad contemplated. "Probably some of the best memories of my life. I remember my dad would come home with the tree. I never knew exactly when it would be. It was always a matter of waiting. My mom and I would wait by the window each day at five-fifteen until the day he showed up with it. I think he liked to make it an event.

"We'd put the tree in front of our bay windows, which meant rearranging the furniture. I always got a kick out of having the furniture in a different place and I would bounce around from the couch to the chair as if it were something special.

"We always had a lot of company from out of town. My mom would get on the piano and play for them and my dad would sing. Then on Christmas Eve we'd go to my aunt's house and I was allowed to open the presents I got from my aunt and cousins on Christmas Eve. When we got home I was sent right to bed. If I put up a fuss, Dad would come up to my room and say something like, 'I think I heard some sleigh bells up on the roof, so you better get to sleep.' Then I'd wake up early in the morning and, voila! Santa had come."

Chad smiled upon finishing his story, then nudged Sara and said, "Okay, your turn. Christmas past for little Sara McClair."

"All right, but I think we should turn around before we end up in Vienna."

The two began heading back toward the apartment and Sara began. "Christmas when I was a little girl," she said in a reflective manner. "Well, I really don't remember any with my dad, but my mom was a baking fool during the holidays. She'd bake tray after tray of Christmas cookies and I'd have the job of cutting them out. I remember how she'd always hand me some of the trimmed dough to eat before we rolled it back out.

"Justin and Paul would go out to the woods with Mom to pick out the tree while Beth looked after the rest of us. When they got home we'd all help decorate with these ornaments that looked like they'd been passed down for five generations. I remember Paul would call me over to him when the tree was just about done. Then he'd hoist me up and I'd put the star on the top." She stopped and chuckled. "I remember Anne used to get all pissy, but I was the youngest so I had the honor.

"We would go to midnight mass. It was the only night of the year that I was allowed to stay up past midnight and I'd always look forward to it for that reason. When we got home, Anne and I would be sent to bed while the others got to stay up. When we got up the next morning Santa had all his goodies waiting for us. Then around noon we'd have Christmas dinner." Sara turned to Chad, smiled and said, "And that was Christmas for little Sara McClair."

Chad smiled back and added, "I remember these special bulletins from the Civil Air Defense saying that their radar had picked up an unidentified flying object in the sky. They'd say that it looked like one large object being pulled by eight smaller objects."

"Yeah, I remember those. And they usually spotted it over Saskatchewan or somewhere like that."

"Yeah—and I remember thinking how stupid they were for not figuring out that it was Santa Claus."

They continued to rehash old memories until Chad looked up and found they'd come to the street where they lived. They rounded the corner and embarked on the final few blocks. When they got there he told Sara to go up ahead of him and that he'd be up in a minute. He lit a cigarette and began to think. Regardless of the direction that his relationship with Sara would go, he was enjoying every moment he spent with her. He resigned himself to the fact that whatever happened, happened—and whatever didn't, didn't. He took a final hit and flicked the butt onto the street, then went upstairs to talk about their plans for Christmas.

There was a fresh blanket of snow on the ground when Christmas Eve morning arrived. "Better get your johnnies on today," Sara yelled into the bedroom as she witnessed a thick cloud of frosty breath being exhaled from a man on the street below. "She's gonna be a cold one."

Chad emerged from the bedroom and, while Sara went in to get dressed, he snatched some loose change from the top of the dresser and ran down to the pay phone in the entrance to give Gus a call. He wanted to see if he and Martina would like to have a holiday lunch with them, but when he reached the bottom of the stairs he saw the cord dangling without a receiver. He tried to picture where the closest phone booth was and realized that it was six blocks away. Not willing to brave the elements, he stuffed the change back into his pocket.

He sprinted back up the stairs, resigned to the fact that they'd have to dine alone—not that he was opposed to the idea, but he wanted to make things as festive as possible for Sara. He thought of Floyd and how, if he were around, they would've had a dining partner lined up. He smiled at the memory of Floyd. After all, it was Christmas and Christmas was the time for memories.

He reentered the apartment. "Well, it looks like it'll just be you and me, kid," he said as he walked into the bedroom and sat on the bed.

Sara smiled at him. "That's not such a bad thing now, is it?"

Chad smiled back. "Of course not," he said.

With their anticipation of Christmas Eve, morning passed slowly—as did the afternoon. When evening arrived Sara suggested they go for a walk through the city to see what was happening. They got bundled up and walked down to Old Town Square and found the streets to be alive. There were carolers on nearly every corner. Some were singing Christmas songs in Czech while others sang them in English. They passed more who were singing in German and what sounded to be Polish. An old woman was handing out candy to children and across the street from her a line of kids waited to see Santa Claus.

They passed through the square and wanted to go to the Charles Bridge. However, once they neared the river they found a fierce wind whipping at them, so they decided to forgo the bridge and continued on toward St. Vitus Cathedral to see if they had a service at midnight. St. Vitus, a Gothic-style basilica which rested atop Castle Hill, was the most visible landmark in Prague. Construction on the church had begun in the year thirteen forty-four and wasn't completed until nineteen twenty-nine. Sara had wanted to attend a midnight mass for nostalgic reasons, as much as anything else, and thought it would be fitting that their first service in Prague would be at a church with such historical significance.

They found that there would indeed be a midnight service, then they headed back to their apartment. Sara wanted to call Beth and, recalling what Chad had said about the phone in the hall, looked for a phone booth as they walked. The farther they went the more the frigid wind numbed their cheeks and Chad's gloveless fingers felt like they would soon fall from his hands. After twenty minutes of walking through the bitterly cold streets of Prague, Sara found her pay phone in the lobby of the hotel where they had stayed on their first night in the city. She dialed up the long-distance operator and placed a collect call. As she waited she realized that it was not quite three o'clock in Michigan and Beth's guests would still be trickling in. She didn't want to miss anybody, but figured that this would be her only chance to call. She waited anxiously and when she finally heard Beth's voice she smiled broadly.

She spent about forty-five minutes on the phone, talking with each family member and friend, while Chad sat patiently in the lobby. When he saw her come back he stood and went to her. "How is everything back home?" he asked quietly, respectful of the fact that she was probably a little sad.

Sara sniffled slightly and said, "Everyone is good, Chad, and they all wish you a Merry Christmas."

"That's nice," he said as he put an arm around her. "And I hope you passed a greeting onto them from me, too."

"Of course."

"So how are you doing?"

"I'm a little down, Chadders, but I'll be okay. I feel bad for you, though—not having any family to call."

"Don't feel bad for me. I'm used to it, hon. Besides, I think the whole Christmas season thus far has been pretty unique and I dig spending it in Prague."

Sara smiled softly. "Are you ready to roll?" she asked.

Chad nodded and extended his hand in a lead-the-way fashion and followed her to the door.

When they got back to the apartment they huddled together in front of the stove until the frost crept out of their bones. The dim light seeping into the living room from the kitchen cast a warmth that seemed to offset the wind that howled past their window with a fierceness that rustled the curtain. Chad looked over at Sara who was draped chest-high in a blanket and looking quite cozy. Her black hair was getting quite long, but she had adopted the curl-under look that was popular with the Czech girls. Her summer freckles were completely gone and her skin seemed as white and pure as the Slavic snow.

"Tell me, what are you thinking, Chadders?" Sara said, aware of the fact she was being ogled.

"I was just thinking how quaint this is."

"What do you mean?"

"Well, perhaps it's the innate consolation of having shelter from the storm; sitting here all warm and comfortable by the stove."

"But Chad, it's fifty degrees in here," Sara said with a distressed look as she pulled the blanket up to her neck.

Chad paused, knowing he was in danger of saying more than he wanted. He looked toward the window. "Maybe we'd better grab a bite before we get dressed for church," he said. He got up, walked to the refrigerator and pulled open the door. "How about a salad?" he asked.

Sara turned toward him. "That sounds good, but no dressing. I miss having products labeled in English. I don't know what that stuff I bought is, but it's nasty."

"Very well. One plain salad coming up."

They each had a salad and some bread, then changed into their dress clothes for the midnight service. The busses had quit running but they managed to hail a taxi at the end of their block.

As they entered St. Vitus Cathedral they were fascinated by the detail and grandeur of the edifice, just as they'd been with Prague's other buildings when they first arrived in the city. An usher came and led them to a pew about three quarters of the way from front and, as they walked, Sara looked through the congregation. She noticed many youngsters dressed in traditional Christmas garb and as she looked at them she wondered what Christmases were like for them. Soon after they were seated, the mass began. It was a long and elaborate service and the fact that it was said in Czech didn't diminish the splendor of a midnight Christmas service.

Unlike Sara, Chad was grateful when the service concluded. His focus had waned with the lack of English and he'd begun to get restless. They stood and waited as the congregation left the building in processional style, beginning with the front row and working its way to the back.

By the time they got out the door it was past one-thirty and there wasn't a cab in sight. The wind had subsided and it was actually quite calm, but the temperature had dropped even more. Sara wrapped her scarf tight around her neck and Chad stuffed his hands into his coat pockets as they embarked on their walk back to the apartment. They hadn't gone three blocks when a van pulled up next to them and the side door slid open, exposing the faces of two small children. Chad peered toward the front of the vehicle but couldn't see who it was, but then heard a woman say, "You—American. Get in, we give you ride." She then said something in Czech to the children and they scooted over to make room.

Chad took Sara's hand and led her into the warmth of the van. As he sat, his eyes widened as he realized whom this Samaritan was. "Thank you," he said as Sara slid the door to a close.

"Where do you go to?" the woman asked.

"Cross the next bridge, take a left and then go down about two kilometers," he said.

Sara looked at Chad for some clue as to who the woman was, but he just stared straightforward until they came to the street that their apartment was on. "This will be good," he said and the woman inched the van up to the curb. Sara slid the door open and the two got out. "Thanks again," Chad said and, "Yes, thank you," Sara added.

"It was no problem. And Merry Christmas."

"Merry Christmas," Chad repeated as Sara waved. Then the children scooted back into their original positions, the door slid shut and the woman drove off.

"All right, Chad, who was that mystery woman?"

"That, Sara, was The Queen."

"That's the woman who turned you in to immigration?"

Chad raised his eyebrows. "That was her."

"She's nothing like I'd pictured her to be. I thought she'd be fat—or at least big bottomed—and rather ugly." She turned and began walking toward their door, which was halfway down the block. "Well, it was nice of her to give us a ride."

When they got up to the apartment Sara walked over to the ledge and lit her red and green Christmas candles. Chad sat on the floor under their makeshift tree and began sorting out their presents. When they both had their gifts in a little pile, Sara joined him and they began unwrapping. Sara went first. She turned and smiled when she lifted a green, button-down sweater out of its box. "Thank you. I love it," she beamed as she held it up to her shoulders. Chad's eyes widened as he pictured it on her and how its color would compliment her hair. Then he picked up one of the presents in front of him and, unlike Sara, hastily tore off the wrapping paper. "You are a kid at Christmas," Sara chided. He smiled and threw the paper on the floor, opened the box and pulled out a pair of gloves—something he'd neglected to bring with him when they moved. Again, it was Sara's turn and she suggested that they open their gifts from Beth and Abbey next. She carefully unwrapped the paper, took the cover off a box and pulled out a wall clock that was made of Petoskey stone and was polished into the shape of the state of Michigan. Chad's gift from Abbey was a biography of Bob Dylan and he held it up for Sara to see. She picked up another gift from Chad. This time he'd gotten her a stuffed puppy that said something in Czech when it was squeezed. "Oh, he's so cute," Sara said, her eyes looking warm and radiant.

"I tried to ask the girl at the store what it was saying, but unfortunately the dog spoke more English than she did."

"So we should make something up and pretend that's what he's saying."

"What do you suggest we have him say?" Chad asked.

"How about, 'I want some fudge?' It would remind us of home."

"Why don't we just name him Hemingway?" Chad mocked.

"I suppose we should just have him say, 'I love you.' You do love me, don't you, Chadders?"

"If I didn't would I have gotten you a puppy that said I did?"

"All right," Sara said, smiling. "I do believe it's your turn to open."

Chad tore the paper off another present and this time came out with an incense burner. "You're always complaining about the building having a musty smell," Sara offered, "and maybe now you'll finally shut up about it."

"As a matter of fact, I think I'll light some right now," he said as he sifted through a variety of scents that she'd picked out and selected one that smelled like balsam. "Here—now at least it'll smell like we have a tree," he said. He lit the incense and sat down next to her as she opened her final present—a multicolored assortment of wool socks. Then she handed Chad his last box. He opened it and found a new watch.

They both loved what they'd received, if for no other reason than they'd gotten them from each other. Except for the stuffed puppy, they were all items that they needed and could use right away. They picked up the wrapping paper and snuggled together on the floor by the stove. "So," Chad began as he put his arm around her, "I assured you that this would be a special Christmas. Did I keep my promise?"

"Yes you did, Chad," she said with a glow. "It was as magical as when I was a kid. I'll never forget it."

Chad looked deep into her eyes—so deep that he could feel her soul. "I'm glad I spent it with you, Sara," he said in a low voice.

"I'm glad I spent it with you, too," she said as she returned his gaze. "I just hope I didn't screw up your plans with Irena."

"Not at all. I'm glad that we spent the day together," he assured as he caressed her back. "With all that we've been through these past few months I feel close to you and there's no one I would rather have been with tonight. After all, on Christmas Eve you should be with the one you care about the most."

They stared into each other's eyes, neither willing nor able to say anything more until finally Chad stood and smiled. "There is one more thing I got for us." He went into the kitchen, opened the cupboard and returned with a bottle of cabernet sauvignon, two glasses and a corkscrew. He popped the cork, filled their glasses and offered a traditional holiday toast, "Peace on earth—good will toward men."

By the time they polished off the bottle it was three-thirty in the morning. Sara conceded that she needed to get to bed and opened her arms to embrace Chad. He took her in his arms and held her close. He stroked her hair, then softly kissed her lips. "Merry Christmas," he said as he let go.

"Merry Christmas," Sara replied. She returned Chad's kiss with a soft, slow one of her own—a kiss that could have been taken as a romantic one. Then she said, "We'd better get some sleep."

To his reluctance, Chad agreed and wished her a good night's sleep. He told her he was going to stay up for a while and that he would blow out the candles.

He sat alone amidst the warmth of the stove and his passion. As he sat he recalled the events of the day and particularly the evening. He realized that somewhere in the last six months he'd fallen in love with Sara and he felt good about it. He smiled to himself. *What a great time to feel this way,* he thought. *Christmas time.*

He picked himself off the floor, blew out the red and green candles and went to bed.

CHAPTER THIRTEEN

It wasn't until January that Chad received his long-term residency pass. It had been two months since he last worked and he'd been restless—and the situation was putting a dent in his bankroll. In the weeks after Christmas he went through the English-speaking papers and through the town, scouting potential job opportunities. He talked to prospective employers about his upcoming availability. He needed to have a job ready and waiting when the pass arrived.

One job that was of particular interest to him was a bookkeeping position for an American firm that purchased and exported authentic Czech goods. He had some computer skills and was good with numbers, so he felt like it was a job he could handle. Most of all, though, he'd be in an English-speaking environment. Even though he was starting to pick up some Czech, his limited vocabulary would limit the number of jobs for which he'd be considered.

Meanwhile, Sara was having more success in sustaining herself. After Christmas she began to sell her paintings in Old Town Square and had garnered a handsome price for several of them. She too was waiting for her residency pass, but her accomplishments had made the wait more tolerable. In fact, she contemplated whether she should seek employment at all, once she had the pass, and simply continue to sell her paintings in the square.

Chad had kept his date with Irena without mentioning a word of it to Sara beforehand. He went to the bakery to pick her up, then they went to a quaint little coffee house which Irena frequented, before taking in a movie. They chatted over cappuccinos and cafe lattès, soaking in the warm atmosphere of the establishment as they got to know each other. As they talked, Chad explained how a lot had happened since he'd originally asked her out. He told her how he thought she was extremely attractive and pleasant to be around, but told her about his past with Sara and how he'd come to fall in love with her again. He explained how he hadn't mentioned anything to her about this yet and how he was concerned that, if she didn't feel the same way, it would complicate their situation.

Irena gave him an understanding smile. "It is okay for me to just be your friend, no?" she said.

"Yes, that would be great," Chad said with a relieved sigh and a smile. "In fact, it would do me good to have a woman to talk to. Other than Sara, I haven't had a female friend since I left the United States."

Irena took a sip of her cappuccino and said, "So tell me more of your situation and I give you my perspective."

Chad raised an eyebrow.

"What is it? Did I say it wrong?"

"No, on the contrary. I was impressed with your English."

"I do not have problem with words as much as your slang expressions. But still speak slowly and I will tell you when I do not understand."

Chad chuckled as he recalled his own misinterpretation. "And I promise to do the same."

"Yes, Chad, you have no class," Irena mocked with an accent so sensual it could easily bring a man to his knees.

"You know, maybe we could meet somewhere, say once a week, and you can teach me some Czech."

Irena smiled. "Yes, we could do that. But you know my Czech is not perfect either and I found it to be very difficult language to learn."

Chad looked puzzled. "Yes, I heard that. But you grew up speaking it?"

"No, I was not born in Czechoslovakia. I am Bulgarian."

"Really?"

"Yes. I lived there until I was seventeen." She took another sip of her cappuccino and continued. "By the time I was five both my parents were dead. I was raised in an orphanage—a shithole as you Americans would say. The place was very crowded and I had to sleep many nights on the floor—and a cement floor in winter does not make good bed. The orphanage did not always have money and sometimes we ate only one meal per day."

Chad leaned forward and listened intently as she continued.

"They put us to work when we were twelve. By the time we were sixteen we would get brave and sneak out during the night and go to dance club. We did this for over one year with never being caught. Then, one night as I went to club, I met Lars. He was from Sweden but lived in Prague. Together we left the club and he took me out to his car, it was a Porsche, and I let him have his way with me. He was seven years older but was handsome man—you know the Swedes and the blond curls. Anyway he asked me to go back with him and I did. We left that same night and I have never went back to Bulgaria."

"And whatever happened to Lars?" Chad asked with a look of concern.

"I stayed with him for two years. In that time I began to become myself. Become myself, is that right?"

"Yes—you found out who you were and what you wanted."

"Yes, exactly. Anyway, when I did this I began to meet more people and I became bored with him. Because he was older and I was staying with him he would try to be boss of me and I never liked that. I began working at bakery and I moved in with another girl who worked there and it was so-long, Lars." She looked at Chad and smiled. "But things are good now and that is enough about me. Tell me about Sara."

Chad began with his dilemma and they ended up talking for several hours. To her credit, Irena spent most of the evening listening to him talk about Sara. She listened closely so not to misinterpret and asked about what she didn't understand. She encouraged him to make his move, offered him advice on how to broach the topic and told him he would regret it if he didn't at least try. As it turned out, Irena was an outlet he hadn't had since he'd left Petoskey and, in an ironic way, Irena was taking the role of friend and confidant that Sara used to have while Sara was now the one who had Chad's heart.

By the time they finished talking it was too late to take in a movie and Chad walked Irena back to her apartment. He thanked her for listening to him ramble and made arrangements to go to coffee with her the following week. He gave her a hug, then turned and began the walk back to the apartment.

Two days later Chad was on the bus, coming back from an excursion into town. On his way home he decided that it was time to make his move with Sara. After mulling it over for three weeks he was ready to take his chance. He began to plan everything out as he stared out the window of the bus. He figured he'd take her to a fancy restaurant and then to a movie or perhaps a play. Then, when the mood was right, a kiss without forewarning or explanation— the kind of kiss that would not be confused with one that is given by a friend.

Although he had a picture of how all this would play out, he was still nervous and his hands were cold and sweaty and he began to envision the worst of all possible outcomes. He even let himself imagine Sara being so upset with him that she packed her bags and moved home. He broke his stare from the window and told himself he was being ridiculous. He needed to relax. He was aware that he'd be treading over an unspoken trust that they had, but if she wasn't interested she would tell him so and leave it at that. Still, he remained confident that she harbored feelings for him as well.

When he arrived at the apartment Sara was gone. He showered and changed and by the time he was done she was walking in the door, carrying a bag of groceries. She looked up at him and noticed his attire. "Gee, Chadders, I don't think I've ever seen you in a tie before. Going somewhere special tonight?"

"Yes, I'm taking you to dinner tonight so you better get ready.

And we're going to someplace nice—so dress up."

Sara flashed him a quirky grin, then went to the cupboard with her bag. "And just where are you taking me, Chad old boy?" she asked as she began putting the groceries away.

"I was thinking Parnas in Old Town."

Sara stopped what she was doing and bent so she could see him through the gap between the cupboards and the counter. "Parnas? What's the occasion? Did you get your job?" she asked excitedly.

"No—no special occasion. I just thought I'd take you out to dinner and maybe a movie."

"You're buying, right?" she jested.

"Of course."

She came back into the living room with a folded paper bag and a curious look. "Okay then, let me get ready," she said, and she headed into the bedroom.

They arrived at Parnas and Chad's table was ready after a five-minute wait. The waiter came and, as Sara ordered, Chad rubbed the sweat from his palms onto his pants. He cleared his throat and assembled his thoughts and when the waiter left he started. "So…," he said as he brought his hands atop the table, looking awkward as he tried to decide where they should be.

"So…?" Sara repeated with one eyebrow raised.

Chad fidgeted with his water glass, spiraling it on its base until it spilled. He set the glass down, put his hands back under the table and grinned stupidly. "Anyway," he began again, "what would you think about…"

When he hesitated again Sara interrupted, "Let me guess. You're moving back to Michigan, getting a conventional job and you want me to go with you."

Chad smiled and seized the words that Sara had unwittingly dangled in front of him. "Yes, I want you to go with me."

"Say again?" Sara said with a frozen expression.

"I want you to go with me—as in go out. I think it's time for us to be a couple again."

She smiled a perplexed grin. "What about Irena?" she asked.

"Irena who?"

"You know, Irena I wanna lay-ya."

"Oh, you mean Irena," he toyed. "Well I guess we just won't tell her."

Chad liked the way Sara was being playful with the topic. It was a good sign and his confidence bloomed. He looked her in the eye in a manner that prompted an answer. She smiled softly and said, "Yeah, Chadders, we can give it a try."

They flirted back and forth until their food came. As they ate, the conversation deepened as Sara recalled why their relationship was broken off the first time around. Chad reminded her that they were much closer now and how he could relax and be himself. By the end of their dinner they both concurred that it was a logical choice.

From Parnas they strolled to the theater, goofing off the whole way there. Chad held Sara's hand as she skipped down the sidewalk, prompting smiles from an elderly couple who passed them. Chad bellowed out a few verses from a Czech folk song that they'd been hearing on the radio and Sara joined him on the chorus.

The movie proved to be lame and they couldn't wait to get out. When it finally ended they took a walk down to the Charles Bridge. As they came to rest in the middle of the structure, Chad gazed into her green eyes and, as he looked deeply into them, he saw a Sara that was different from the girl he'd dated when they were in Petoskey. The dependence they had on one another had drawn them closer. She was someone he could trust with everything he had—including his emotions. He brushed her hair from her face and pulled her into him. He kissed her—slowly at first—but his passion soon burst and he drew her body into his as if they were one. He ravaged her lips and slid his open mouth down her neck as she let out a moan. He reached inside her coat and palmed her breast, caressing her nipple with his thumb. Sara pushed her thigh between his legs and slowly moved it up and down. "I think we need to get back to the apartment," she whispered.

"Uh huh," Chad replied.

They walked hand-in-hand back to their building and Chad had Sara back in his arms before the door closed behind them. He unbuttoned her coat and slid the scarf off her neck, tossing both on the kitchen chair behind him. Sara unzipped his jacket and, as he finished pulling it off, she loosened his tie, unbuttoned his shirt and pulled it open. She ran her hands across his bare stomach, causing him to recoil from the cold. When he did she stepped back, removed her blouse and bra and pulled him toward her, then pushed her hands inside his trousers and warmed them on his buttocks.

Chad groaned as Sara pulled herself close to him. They kissed madly. "I want you," Chad said as he tried to slide Sara's skirt down over her hips. She let go of her embrace. "Wait here," she said and she went into the bedroom. Chad took off his trousers and rested them over the back of the couch, then stood waiting, wearing only his briefs. Sara reemerged from the bedroom, wrapped in a blanket and carrying two pillows. She sauntered across the room and over to the heat pipes, where she peeled off the blanket and spread it out atop the hardwood floor. She set the pillows at the head of the blanket and Chad came up behind her. She rolled onto her back and he pulled off his briefs and slowly lowered himself into her.

Chad woke in the middle of the night, shivering from lack of a blanket. He took the one that they were laying on, wrapped it around her and went into the bedroom. He looked at the clock—it was quarter past five. Quietly, he got dressed, grabbed a pack of cigarettes, descended the stairs and went outside. He lit up a smoke and began walking.

The night was bitterly cold, colder than any he could remember—either in Prague or back in Michigan—and the street was lifeless. Steam ascended heavenward from the neatly spaced chimneys, rising straight and unaltered into the still, night sky. Their frigid columns formed a quasi-Siberian setting, transforming the city he had come to know into a strange and desolate wasteland.

As he exhaled, ice formed on the mustache he'd been growing for the past month and he wondered why he was out. He stopped at the corner, three blocks from his apartment, and stared into the night sky. While he stared, he contemplated his interlude with Sara. He compared it to their previous attempt and appreciated how much had changed since then. He wondered how things would evolve, but realized how relaxed he felt. He knew he could finally be himself around her and not worry about what to say or do.

He looked up to the heavens. "Dad, she's the one," he said aloud. "I think you'd like her." He smiled and flashed a wink, then dropped his head, stomped out his cigarette and returned down the windless street.

When morning arrived Sara found herself back in their bed. She turned and found Chad next to her and still asleep. She shrugged her shoulders and, as she went into the kitchen to make breakfast, a smile came to her as she thought about the night before. A little while later Chad came stumbling into the living room. "Hey," she said as he smiled at her.

"How you doing, darling?" he asked.

"I'm good. And you?"

"I'm good too." He walked up and held her waist as she scooped eggs from a frying pan onto two plates. "What do you have planned for tomorrow?" he asked.

"Just another day of painting, I suppose. Why?"

Chad rubbed his face and ran his hand through his hair. "Do you want to get out of town for a couple of days?"

Sara turned to him and pondered. "I suppose we could," she said.

"We haven't been out of Prague since we moved here."

"Yes, but it's the middle of winter, Chadders."

"So we'll go south—catch a train to the French Riviera or Italy. Now would be a good time to go. Once I find a job I won't be able to for quite some time."

"That's true," Sara noted. "Yeah, why not."

As they ate breakfast they debated on where to go. In the afternoon they walked down to the train station and bought two tickets for the Côte d'Azur. The Riviera in January wouldn't provide beach weather, but it would at least be springlike.

On Thursday morning they caught their train for the South of France and Chad's wanderlust kicked in as soon as it pulled out of the station. He grabbed Sara's hand as he looked out the window. Along with seeing the Côte d'Azur, they'd also be passing through Austria and Italy. In his head he counted the countries he'd been to. Then he sat back, smiled and turned to Sara. "Thirty-four," he said.

"Thirty-four what?" she asked.

"I can't believe in all the time we've known each other you've never asked me when my birthday was."

Sara stared at him with an open mouth, contemplating what he'd said until she realized it was true. "You bastard," she grinned. "Today is your birthday and you never told me."

"You never asked," he retorted.

She stared at him—her mouth still gaping. She shook her head and wrapped her arms around him. "Well happy birthday, Chadders," she said, and she kissed him. "How did it happen that we never talked about your birthday?"

"I don't know. You never asked and I chose not to disclose."

"But you disclosed it now."

"Yes. And you feel guilty about not getting me anything."

"You got something last night."

"Yes, but that present wasn't wrapped."

Sara grinned and swatted him. "I'll get you a wrapped present, dear, so don't fret."

By the time they'd finished discussing the matter the train had built up speed and was rapidly on its way toward their destination. Sara got up to use the restroom and Chad began meandering through the train. In a short while, she caught up and joined him on his excursion.

As they strolled Chad caught sight of two girls, one wearing a University of Michigan sweatshirt and the other wearing one from Ohio State. He tapped Sara's shoulder, pointed, then approached the girls. "Excuse me," he said, "I'm Chad and this is my girl-friend, Sara. I noticed your sweaters and assume that you're from the States?"

The girl in the aisle seat stood and extended her hand. "Hello, I'm Connie and this is my friend, Stephanie. We're from Michigan. We spent a couple of days in Prague and now we're on our way to St. Moritz to do a little skiing."

"What part of Michigan?" Sara asked.

"Stephanie's from Ann Arbor and I'm from Traverse City."

"Traverse? No shit!" Chad smiled. "We're from Petoskey."

"Really?" Connie gasped. "Wow. Like they say, it's a small world, isn't it?"

"You know, if you girls would like, why don't we go over to the dining car?" Sara suggested. "We both have quite a ride ahead of us and a good chat would kill some time."

Connie looked over at Stephanie and shrugged her shoulders in a why-not manner. Stephanie nodded and the four headed to the dining car and snatched a table. Chad and Sara sat across from the girls, both of whom looked to be in their early twenties. Connie was the more attractive of the two, with light-brown hair that was cut in a Cleopatra style. She had brown eyes and full, sultry lips. She was about five-five and was wearing tight blue jeans that Chad couldn't help but notice while they were walking to the dining car. Stephanie was pretty but had more of a common look to her. She was a few inches taller and had dishwater-blonde hair and blue eyes. She seemed genuinely friendly but acted more reserved than Connie.

Chad grabbed the ashtray from the end of the table and slid it toward him. "Do you girls mind?" he asked and when they didn't he lit his cigarette.

"So, what have you guys seen over here?" Stephanie asked.

"We live here, actually," Chad proudly stated. "We came over in late June and have been living in Prague."

"That would be so cool," Connie said. "What do you do for a living, if you don't mind my asking?"

"Did you visit Old Town Square when you were in Prague?" Chad asked.

"Yes we did," Stephanie answered.

"Well Sara's an artist and she sells her paintings there. I've been off work for a couple of months and have been waiting for a residency pass. Now I have it and it looks like I'll be working for an American exporting firm."

"Stephanie," Sara began.

"Steff—call me Steff."

"Okay—Steff. You said you were from Ann Arbor, right? I have to ask what you're doing with an Ohio…"

"An Ohio State sweater?"

Sara smiled. "Yes."

"I grew up in Ann Arbor and everything was Michigan, Michigan, Michigan. I wanted to be a little different, that's all."

"Different or defiant?" Chad asked.

"Maybe a little of both," Steff answered.

"So where are you guys off to now?" Connie asked.

"We're heading down to the South of France. We wanted to get out of town and roam around a bit before Chad started his new job," Sara said as she pulled Chad's ashtray toward her and lit a smoke of her own. "We haven't been out of Prague in seven months," she added.

"I don't know if I've ever been in one city for seven months without getting out," Connie said.

"But if you had to, Prague would be a good place to be," Steff said.

"Oh! I have to tell you guys what happened to us last night," Connie interjected. "We were in this nightclub back in Prague and these too goofy-looking guys were hitting on us all night long. We kept trying to blow them off but they never got the hint. The funny part was that they were trying to be so cool but they were both dorks. It kind of reminded me of the wild and crazy guys on Saturday Night Live."

"How fitting," Chad said. "The guys in that skit were Czech too."

The foursome stayed in the dining car for an hour and a half—not eating, but sharing travel stories and taking about life in Europe as well as back in Michigan. Customs had come through and the train had entered Austria and would be pulling into the Vienna station in about fifteen minutes. Connie and Steff would be on the train as far as Innsbruck. From there they would change for St. Moritz. When they pulled into Vienna everyone decided they'd go back to their respective coaches and kick back until then.

Chad took his customary window seat and stared out at the Vienna station, wishing they would've had time to check out the city. Sara squirmed in her seat until she was comfortable, then closed her eyes.

Soon, the train was rolling again and Sara was asleep. Getting to the Mediterranean would take a day and a night, so a nap wasn't a bad idea. Chad, however, wouldn't afford himself the luxury. As long as it was light enough to see out the window he would keep his post, keeping an eye out for something new and interesting. He was checking out the mountains that they were approaching when he felt a tap on the shoulder.

"I didn't think she'd be sleeping so early."

"Hi, Connie," Chad said as he turned. "Yeah, she doesn't always have the same sense of adventure that I do," he said as he smiled at Sara and patted her lightly on the leg.

"Well, we're going to be getting off at Innsbruck and we were wondering, if you two had the time, if you wanted to spend the night there. We could all go out on the town and it would be cool if you guys came."

"It's up to you, Chad, I don't care," Sara muttered as she straightened herself in her seat. "After all it's your birthday."

"It's your birthday?" Connie asked with surprise.

"Yeah, he doesn't tell anybody."

"Well, then you have to come. What's the sense of riding on a train all night when it's your birthday?"

Sara sat up. "How long till we get to Innsbruck?" she asked.

"We should be getting there in about an hour."

"Well, Chad?" Connie prompted.

Chad looked at Sara and said to her, "It's cool with me if you want to."

"Yeah, it sounds like a good time," Sara said as she looked up at Connie. "You said we have about an hour. So why don't we meet in your section in about forty-five minutes. If we're going to go out tonight I'm gonna kick back for a while longer and make sure I'm ready."

"Okay, forty-five minutes. We'll see you then."

As Connie went back to her coach, Chad turned to Sara and asked, "Are you sure you won't mind staying in Innsbruck?"

"No, I don't care. Besides, it'll give you a chance to stare at Connie's ass a little more."

Chad froze. "What are you talking about?" he asked, red faced.

"I saw you checking her out. Anyway, Connie's cool and so is Steff and I don't mind hanging out with either of them."

Chad continued to stare open-mouthed, still not knowing what to say.

"Don't worry about it, Chadders. It's your birthday so that one's a freebie."

Chad eased up. "Okay, so I'm busted. But you have to admit, she does have a cute little tush."

"But don't push it, Reiger."

Chad, not wanting to dig a deeper hole, sat back and closed his eyes. Sara dug into her travel bag and pulled out a brochure of France, which Chad had gotten before they'd left Petoskey. After a quick browse through it, she shut her eyes and envisioned what the night ahead might bring. She liked the idea of stopping in Innsbruck and was looking forward to hitting the town with their new acquaintances.

The sound of the rails had put Chad to sleep and he woke abruptly. "What time is it?" he asked as he rubbed his eyes.

"It's almost time to go," Sara said as she dug through her purse.

Chad looked out the window and it was dark outside. He figured he'd slept for a half-hour but it seemed longer. Sara stood and gathered her belongings from the overhead and Chad followed suit. They headed down the aisle and through three cars to the girl's coach. "Hey there," Sara said as they approached them. "Are you ready for a little night on the town?"

"Yeah, we're ready," Stephanie answered.

The train began to slow as Sara set her luggage on the floor. They were coming into Innsbruck and would be at the station in a few minutes. Connie and Steff gathered their things and the four walked up to the door and waited for the train to come to a stop. When they got off they were pleasantly surprised at the temperature—it was at least fifteen degrees warmer than it was when they'd left Prague. "Maybe we'll get lucky and hit a warm front when we get to Nice," Chad said.

"That would be nice," Sara jested.

Connie sensed Chad and Sara's experience with European cities and let them lead the way, with Chad eventually taking over. "He's trying to satisfy his sense of purpose," Sara whispered.

"Typical male," Steff replied.

Chad led them out of the depot and onto the street. They walked several blocks, stopping when they came to a hotel. "Does this place look all right to you girls?" he asked.

"Looks fine to me," Connie said and Steff nodded.

They walked in and Chad and Sara approached the desk.

"Guten Abend," the clerk greeted.

"Guten Abend," Sara replied. "Ich möchte zwei doppelzimmer für huete nacht, bitte."

"Mit Dusche?"

"Ja. Heir ist mein Paß." She turned to the rest of the party, gathered their passports and handed them to the clerk. He checked them and handed them back to Sara.

"Zwiehundret zwanzig Deutch Marke, bitte," he said.

Sara told the girls how much it had come to. They paid her and she paid the clerk. She got the keys, turned and handed them to Chad.

"What the hell was that?" he asked.

"What the hell was what?" she said with a smug grin.

"Since when do you speak German?"

"Seems like we both have our little secrets, don't we, Chadders?"

The four Michiganders walked up the stairs and to their adjacent rooms on the second floor. They dropped off their luggage, met again in the hall and headed back to the street. All agreeing that they were hungry, they stopped at a little cafe which they had passed on route to the hotel.

As they waited to be served, Connie asked them to tell her more about life in Europe. She was especially curious about what drove them to put everything aside and make such a move. She said that she wished she could be more like them and do something so dramatic, at which point Chad informed her that neither him nor Sara would've made the move either when they were in their early twenties.

Steff had gotten into a conversation with a couple of guys who were seated next to them. They told her that she and the other two girls with her were very attractive and asked where they'd be later in the evening. She asked them for some suggestions and they gave her the names of a couple of nightclubs.

When they finished eating, the foursome went up the street to one of the places the guys had recommended. They went in and found the only open spot at the bar. The music was loud and the atmosphere festive. In the center of the establishment was a large dance floor and it was filled. Connie asked if anybody wanted to dance—which essentially meant Chad—and when he didn't answer she grabbed his arm and pulled him into the crowd.

"I hope you don't mind her forthright manner," Stephanie told Sara. "She tends to act first and think later. She really means no harm."

"I'm not worried about it, Steff. I do think she has somewhat of a crush on Chad though. He has one on her too, I'm sure."

"You don't seem too upset about it though."

"We all look around to some degree. I trust Chad. He has a good heart. I think he senses that Connie has something for him and he's flattered that someone as attractive as her is showing interest in him."

"Don't sell yourself short, Sara. You're very pretty. You and Chad make a great couple."

"Thanks, Steff," Sara said. "We do get along great. He tends to be a little more rambunctious than me, but we offset each other well."

Connie and Chad returned from the dance floor, Chad out of breath and Connie bouncing and ready for more. "Have another smoke, Chadders," Sara ribbed.

"Don't mind if I do," he retaliated as lit a cigarette.

"Mind if I have one of those?" Connie asked.

"You don't smoke, you dufus," Steff scolded.

"I'm on vacation and I want a cigarette!"

"Here you go," Chad said as he handed her one, pulled out his lighter and lit it.

"Thanks, Chadders."

Sara took Chad's hand. "Put out your smoke," she said. "It's time for us to dance." She led him down to the dance floor and pulled him into a slow dance. "You don't have to encourage her, you know," she said.

"What do you mean?"

"She just called you Chadders. She turns into a schoolgirl when you're around."

"It's not like I'm trying to…"

"I know. That's not my point. It's just that you're ignoring me."

"I'm sorry, baby."

"Listen, I know it's nice to meet new people and that's cool, it really is. I'm just saying that you can make this night either good or bad for me."

Chad held her tightly. "It won't be bad. I promise."

As Chad and Sara were on the dance floor, Stephanie scolded Connie. "What do you think you're doing?" she admonished. "You need to back off of that boy. He's taken."

"I know," she said as she took a swig of beer and avoided eye

176

contact. "Nothing would ever come of it. I just think he's cute. But if he wasn't spoken for I would definitely screw him."

"You're drunk."

"Uh uh, not drunk—horny," she said as she took another gulp.

"Either way, you have to be respectful of Sara. After tomorrow we're never going to see these people again, but Chad and Sara are going to have a life together. Don't complicate things for her."

Chad and Sara returned from the dance floor. They all stood at the end of the bar, feeling somewhat awkward, until Sara suggested they finish their drinks and take a walk through town before stopping at the other nightclub.

They went out to the street and flagged a taxi, asking him to take them somewhere that was interesting but not too far away. He took them to Innsbruck's old town and dropped them off near the pedestrian district. They got out and began to meander about. The district possessed an abundance of medieval architecture, complete with painted facades and stucco ornaments. They followed Herzog-Friedrich-Strasse past the Goldenes Dachl, a splendid example of sixteenth-century architecture. Chad and Sara would've been content to stroll the streets for hours, but their younger counterparts were dropping hints that they wanted to get back to the night-life scene. The taxi ride hadn't been a long one and they remembered the route, so they began the hike back to their point of origin.

They spotted the other club about a block ahead and headed for it. As they approached, Connie grabbed Chad's bottom. "Hey Chadders, are you gonna dance with me again?" she blurted.

"You know what? I think Sara and I are going to call it a night." He turned to Sara and said, "Give me a minute to talk to Connie and I'll fill you in as we walk to the room."

"I saw what she did," Sara said. "Go ahead and do what you have to do."

Sara took a few steps and started reading a poster on a light pole as Chad walked up to Connie, who was being scolded by Stephanie. "I just want to say goodbye tonight. We'll be taking the first train out in the morning and we likely won't be seeing you."

He gave them both a hug and Stephanie, sensing Chad had more to say to Connie, turned and waited by the door of the nightclub.

Chad smiled as he stood alone with her. "You know, if I weren't attached I think you and I would've had a lot of fun tonight."

"I think so too," Connie replied with a slight smile.

"But I am in love with Sara."

They smiled at each other as they conceded to reality. "I'm glad I got to meet you," Chad said.

"Me too. I had a good time all day long." Connie looked into Chad's blue eyes one last time, gave him a hug and told him she wanted to say something to Sara. She walked a few steps, then turned and added, "Have a good life, hey."

Chad smiled. "You too," he said.

Connie walked up to Sara and put her hand on her shoulder. "I behaved badly tonight," she confessed, "and I'm sorry. Chad's a great guy and he loves you a lot. You're a lucky girl. And if it means anything to you I've learned a lesson or two tonight."

Sara offered her a forgiving smile. "You're not a bad person, Connie. I can sense that. And I appreciate the effort you made in coming to talk to me."

"Thanks, Sara."

"I hope you enjoy the rest of your vacation."

"I think we will." She extended her hand and bid Sara farewell.

Chad and Sara talked lightly as they walked back to the hotel. Sara told him that she forgave Connie for her youthful exuberance and that she was proud of how he handled himself. Chad apologized for flirting in the first place and, as they walked through old town Innsbruck, told her how he put himself in her shoes and imagined how he would feel if she'd been flirting with another guy. He told her how he thought it was all harmless until he saw it through her eyes.

They got to the room, checked out the train schedule and went to bed.

The alarm went off at seven-thirty Friday morning. Chad got out of bed and jumped in the shower while Sara began organizing her suitcase. When Chad came out, the two reversed roles.

They got everything together and headed out. As they went into the hall they found Stephanie there too, waiting for Connie. "Good morning," she mumbled and it was obvious she wasn't quite awake yet.

"Good morning," Chad said, as did Sara.

"What time do you leave for St. Moritz?" Sara asked.

"About ten minutes ago," Stephanie countered. "Our little prima donna couldn't get ready on time, though, so we'll have to catch the next train."

Connie popped her head out into the hallway. "Good mornin'," she said. "Did I hear you guys talking about me?"

"Of course not," Steff said sarcastically.

Connie went back into the room, then came out with her camera in hand. "All right, everyone get together and smile," she said as she motioned everyone into a tight group. "Cheese!" she said, then snapped a picture.

"Okay," Sara said as she dug into her bag for her own camera. "Likewise." Connie and Steff flanked Chad for one shot, then Chad took a picture of the three girls.

"Well, we'd better get cutting," he then said as he handed the camera back to Sara. After one more round of hugs and good-byes they headed down the hall and up the street to the train station.

They arrived in Nice by late afternoon. The weather was pleasant—about sixty-five degrees with a gentle breeze coming off the Mediterranean. They took a taxi and began to explore, looking for a bed and breakfast near the sea.

When they got to a quaint-looking area, they got out and began to walk. Soon, they came upon their bed and breakfast, which was snuggled cozily amidst other eighteenth century structures, halfway down the curving hill on which they trekked. They broke off their cobblestone path and went in. There was a room available and they rented it for the weekend. They went in and set their luggage on the floor, then simultaneously flopped on the bed.

The next thing Chad saw was the clock on the nightstand reading seven forty-four. He looked out the window and saw it was dark. He reached over and grabbed Sara's shoulder and gently shook her. "Hey baby, wake up," he coaxed.

Sara opened her eyes, then shut them again. "What's up?" she asked.

"Hey, it's almost eight o'clock."

"So, I don't have to work today," she said in a falling-back-asleep voice.

Chad laughed. "Man, you are out of it. Sara, wake up! We're in France, remember?"

"Then go get me a croissant or some cheese. Just leave me be for a while longer."

"Sorry, kid, no can do," he said as he took her arm and hoisted her into a sitting position. "We've got things to see tonight. You can sleep all you want when we get home."

Apprehensively, Sara swung her legs over the edge of the bed and, after a stretch and a moan, got up and put her shoes on. "So what do you want to do?" she asked through a yawn.

"I'd like to stroll through the city," Chad said in a plain and matter-of-fact tone. "I don't necessarily have an urge to go to any nightclubs tonight, though. How about you?"

"I just want to get something to eat along the way."

They walked down to the road that ran parallel to the sea. It was festive compared to the frozen streets of Prague, with people strolling in plenitude and lots of neon lighting. They came to an Italian restaurant, looked at the menu that was posted in front and went in. Taking a table next to the window, they gazed out to the action on the street as they waited.

"Buon giorno," the waiter greeted as he came to the table. "Français ou Italiano?"

"Anglais?" Sara asked.

"Yes, go ahead," he said in a thick Italian accent.

"What do you recommend?" she asked.

"Our spaghetti here is il la cosa migliore in questo mondo—the best in this world," he boasted flamboyantly.

"Well I'll have to have it then. And a cup of black coffee."

"Very well. And you sir?"

"Un cafe, noir aussi, et de lasagna s'il vous plait."

"Oui monsieur."

"Sorry, Chad," Sara said as the waiter left. "I forgot about your French."

Chad smiled and lit a cigarette. The waiter came back with their coffees and Sara hastily downed a third of it. "There. That's what I needed," she said.

Chad sat back and gazed into her green eyes. "This is going to be a cool weekend. I can feel it."

"It's nice here, isn't it?"

"Is that another play on words?" Chad quipped.

"No, it's not. It's exquisite here, how's that?"

"You're exquisite. How's that?"

"You're not going to get all feisty on me before we get a chance to see the city, are you?"

"Well you're the one who wanted to stay in bed."

"But I'm up now, buddy boy."

They kept up their banter until the food arrived. As they ate their Italian cuisine they came to realize how close to Italy they actually were. When they finished, they returned to the streets of Nice. They came to rest at a spot where a waist-high stone wall lined the walkway and they looked out over the sea. "I'm glad we went to Prague before we came here," Sara said.

"Why?"

"Because if we had come here first I would have fallen in love with the place and never would've left." She turned to Chad and added, "But I love Prague even more."

They walked hand-in-hand down the cobblestone street, emancipated by the warmth of the night. When they came to a souvenir shop, Chad went in to get a postcard for his collection. "I should get some to send out to the family," Sara said as she followed him. "And it's about time you sent some to Miles, Pres and Abbey."

They sat on the steps in front of the building and Sara began writing out her cards as Chad stared into the night sky. As he stared he wondered what Connie and Steff were doing. He wished that Connie hadn't been so cumbersome on Sara and that they all could have spent more time together. He glanced over at Sara and smiled. She'd finished writing her card to Beth and had decided to write the rest at the room. It was getting late and they were ready to kick back and call it a night.

Saturday's agenda was much the same, except that they toured in the daylight. They browsed through more shops and ate five times, according to Chad—four according to Sara. They checked out a nightclub in the evening, but it was crowded and they only stayed a half-hour.

By Sunday morning they were both satisfied with Nice and ready to get back home. They pulled into Prague after dark and scurried through the snow-filled streets back to their apartment.

CHAPTER FOURTEEN

Winter turned to spring and Chad had taken employment at the American export firm. After being immersed in Prague and its culture for ten months, it was refreshing for him to be around other Americans. Although there were others living in the city, neither Chad nor Sara had an American friend since Floyd died.

Chad's work was simple. It consisted of logging all the company's transactions onto a computer, seeing that their invoices were paid promptly, and until a few weeks ago, making sure the front of the building was shoveled. He had a good rapport with his coworkers and he genuinely liked the job.

Meanwhile, Sara was enjoying the life of an artist. She liked the freedom it gave her, not to mention the profit she found she could make. She realized that if she sold two paintings per week she could make a decent living, but some weeks she'd sell three or four. She'd stay in the square from eleven in the morning till three in the afternoon. Then she'd return to the apartment and paint until Chad came home from work and when he went to bed she'd paint into the wee hours of the morning.

She had stockpiled eighteen paintings during the winter months and now her supply was getting low. She found that she could paint two per week and realized that soon she wouldn't have any on backup. Also, she was running out of ideas for subjects and found it redundant to paint the same scene twice.

A lot of her paintings were scenes from Michigan. Some were of Prague's more popular landmarks, while others were the conjured faces of people she imagined. Of all she painted, it was the latter that she enjoyed doing the most.

Two of Sara's sisters, Beth and Anne, had planned to fly in for a week's stay. Beth had wanted to make the visit a surprise to Sara and had made detailed plans with Chad to arrange it. She'd written a letter to him, with the address written in someone else's handwriting. In the letter she told him of their plans, along with the day they'd be arriving. She had Chad write back with directions to a public place where they could casually meet, along with the exact time of day for their rendezvous.

On Monday, the twenty-third of April, Beth and Anne arrived in Prague. According to Chad's plan they were to take a taxi to the Charles Bridge and be there by one o'clock.

Meanwhile, when Sara woke up that morning she found Chad still at the apartment and sitting half-dressed on the couch. "What's the deal, Reiger?" she asked with concern.

"I'm not going into work today, Sara," he said in a monotone voice.

"Why, what's wrong?"

He sat and stared straight ahead. "I don't know. I just feel real low, you know?" And he put on a morose face.

"Was it anything I did?"

"No, baby. I don't know what it is."

"Is there anything I can do?"

Chad paused for effect, then looked her in the eyes and said, "Yeah, could you stay home with me today? Maybe we could do a lunch somewhere. And maybe a brisk walk to the bridge will help me come out of this."

At eleven-thirty they went down to Stan Volf's restaurant—the one he and two coworkers had bought, once Floyd's estate was settled. Sara figured that Chad hadn't seen Stan in some time, and with whatever was troubling him, he wanted to be among friends. In truth, Stan's place was the closest restaurant to the bridge. Chad had visited Stan the day before and told him of the scheme, asking for an assurance that they could be served quickly and be out by one o'clock.

As they ate, Sara pried, trying to find out what was bothering him. Chad acted as ho-hum as he could, telling her he didn't want to talk about anything. "You didn't get fired, did you?" she finally asked.

He seized what she had dished up and planted a seed of speculation. "Really, Sara, I don't want to talk about it."

"You were fired," she sighed. "What did you do."

"Sara, just let me relax and get over this for a while, okay, and I'll talk about it when we get home. As for now, I just want to get out for a while and get it off my mind."

"Okay then, Chadders," she conceded.

After they ate Chad glanced at his watch. It was one o'clock and time to get to the bridge. He wanted to allot the girls a little extra time to get there, in case there was a delay. In the essence of the scheme it was imperative that Beth and Anne arrived at the bridge before they did, but with a ten-minute walk ahead of them, it was time to roll.

Chad spotted Sara's sisters as he approached the bridge. They were standing in the middle, about fifty yards straight ahead of them. He diverted Sara. "Hey," he said, motioning her to come to the other side, but still trying to sound somewhat depressed. "Check out these triangular things sticking out of the water."

"Chad, we've seen them fifty times before."

"I know, but I never really paid attention to them… come on, keep walking."

"Do you want me to look at them or walk with you?"

"Both. There are more down here. I wonder what they're for?"

"Chad, I don't know. What don't you just talk to me and tell me what happened?"

"It's a nice spring day and I don't want to spoil it yet. Come… let's walk down here."

Anne spotted Sara coming down the bridge and clued Beth in on her arrival. The two girls turned their backs to her, concealing their identity. Chad played his role in Oscar-winning fashion, leading Sara

185

directly behind her sisters but redirecting her attention from them. Now that they were within earshot Chad issued his cue phrase. "I miss Ernest Hemingway," he said loudly as he stared off into the distance.

Sara looked inquisitively at him, trying to discern where the statement came from. As she eyed him, Anne came from the other side and bumped her as she walked by.

Sara turned around and sarcastically yelled, "Excuse me!" and as she did she heard a voice from behind say, "I told you not to talk to her like that."

Sara noticed a familiarity in the voice but still it was vague and out of place. She turned to see the beaming face of her sister Beth. "Oh—my—God!" Sara said as she stood with her mouth agape. "Oh—my—God!" she repeated. Anne walked up to her and, upon seeing her too, Sara put her hands on her cheeks and stared, a bewildered smile frozen to her face. "Oh—my—God!" she said again.

Anne gave her a wry grin and said, "So we traveled all this way and all you have to say is Oh my God over and over again?"

"I don't know what to say," Sara bellowed. "I'm flabbergasted." She shot Chad a glance that said *You got me, you little shit,* then opened her arms to Anne and said, "Come here." The two hugged for a moment, then Sara turned to Beth. Her smile broadened.

"Hey baby girl," Beth said as she squeezed her sister. Then she took her shoulders and held her at arm's length, scanning her in the process. "You look great!" she complimented.

Beth and Sara were in deep conversation and Anne looked out from her perch on the bridge. "I love your city," she told Chad, who had taken the role of an observer.

"Wait till you get to see all of it," he boasted.

Anne smiled. "We could probably go see it now and come back in two hours and these two wouldn't even know we'd been gone."

Chad laughed. "I know what you're saying."

Sara looked over to Chad, shrugged her shoulders and smiled a giggly smile that he'd never seen from her before. She leaned back against the brown, stone wall of the bridge, still trying to collect herself from the surprise. In an instant she'd gone from chastising what she thought was a rude pedestrian to being in the arms of her sisters. She recalled how, for a second or two, it didn't even register to her that Beth and Anne didn't belong in Prague and how what she was seeing seemed surreal. She asked how they'd pulled off the visit without her knowing about it and Beth and Chad filled her in on the scheme, as Anne continued to look out over the Charles Bridge. Sara shook her head, her mouth still half-open in disbelief.

"Happy birthday, Sara," Chad hailed.

"Yes. Happy birthday," Beth repeated.

Sara gave Chad a scowl. "You brat," she said. "And I thought I was about to get even with you."

They walked toward the end of the bridge. Sara and Chad took the girls on a quick tour of the city before going back to their apartment. Anne was as impressed with Prague as Chad and Sara had been, while Beth was content to be chatting with her baby sister.

They circled the city and returned home. "I don't know where we're going to put you," Sara said as they entered their abode. "As you can see, we don't have the most spacious place in Prague." Chad went back out and the girls settled in. Sara sat on the floor while her sisters parked themselves on the couch. "So I have to ask—what's the occasion?"

"We all missed you so much at Christmas time, honey," Beth said. "It didn't seem the same without you around. Then Anne, Karen and I tossed around the idea of coming here to see you. It turned out that Karen couldn't make it, but Anne and I got our passports in February and started our planning. We figured the weather would be getting good by your birthday and... here we are."

They talked for several minutes, then the conversation paused at the sound of Chad coming up the stairs. He came in carrying a birthday cake and set it on the table. "All right everybody, gather round," he said as he stuck candles into the cake and lit them. They shared the cake as Sara's sisters filled her in on what was happening back home and Sara described life in the Czech Republic and told them about her and Chad.

When they finished eating Chad got up and took the empty plates to the kitchen. "How long will you girls be staying?" he asked. "And what do you want to do while you're here?" Sara added.

"Tell her we want to do a little running around," Anne directed. Anne was three years older then Sara but was far less assertive and lacked the self-confidence that her younger sister had. By most accounts, however, she was the most attractive member of the family. She had soft, cheek-length brunette hair and big, brown eyes. Her lips formed a perpetual pout that gave her a certain erotic quality. She was thinner than Sara and a little shorter. Of all her sisters, Anne was the most distant. She had come to Prague in part to see Sara, but mostly because she sought the adventure of seeing a foreign country—that, and the fact that Beth had paid for her ticket.

"Yes, Sara," Beth began, asking Anne's question for her. "We were thinking of staying here three or four days. Then, maybe we could all go on a little trip, perhaps to one of the nearby countries."

"Hey, that sounds great," Sara smiled. "How 'bout you, Chadders? You up for it?"

"Not a chance in hell, I'm afraid. I had a tough enough time just getting today off. I can't press my luck any farther. You girls go, though. Go to Vienna or Salzburg."

"Salzburg sounds cool," Anne piped in.

"Okay, I'm in," Sara said. "It'll give me an opportunity to photograph some subjects to paint."

"It sounds like we have a plan then," Beth said, looking back and forth at the other two for confirmation. "So how are we going to get there?" she asked.

"The train's your best bet, Beth. It's a fun way to travel and it takes you right into the center of town. Sara and I had a blast when we came here from Paris—and again this past winter when we took our excursion to the Mediterranean. You get to see everything along the way and you get to meet a lot of people."

It was agreed upon that they'd stay in Prague until Thursday morning. Then, they'd take a train to Salzburg and return Sunday afternoon. In the meantime they could visit, relax and see what Prague had to offer.

Thursday came quickly. Beth and Anne minimized their luggage into three days worth of clothes while Sara said goodbye to Chad. She lamented the fact that he wouldn't be able to go with them and thought of how much more fun it would be for her if he went. She told her sisters how close they had gotten and how she pined for him. Beth, the only one of the three who was married, advised that a little time apart was always good for a couple and that everything would be all that much better when she returned.

Packed and ready, they said goodbye to Chad and took a taxi to the train station. After a brief wait in the depot they boarded and began their excursion. The train sped out of the Czech Republic and toward Austria. Anne enjoyed the trip the most. While Beth and Sara chatted, she checked out the sights along the route—barely paying attention to her sisters. She reminded Sara of Chad in the way she picked out the differences between Europe and the States.

They arrived at the Salzburg station around two in the afternoon. As they passed through the depot they exchanged some of their crowns and dollars for schillings, stuffed their luggage into lockers, then commenced their expedition. They exited the depot and found a bus stop directly ahead of them. Sara suggested that a loop through the city on the bus would orient them and they could decide what they wanted to catch. When they did, they found that most of what they wanted to see was within walking distance of the depot. They got off the bus when it had gone full circle and began a walking tour.

It was a gorgeous day, somewhat overcast but warm April. The girls passed through the nouveau cosmopolitan district and headed toward Old Salzburg, following a walkway that skirted the Salzach River. There were beautiful, stately homes on the opposite bank and a municipal park on the side that they walked. People were out in plenitude and it seemed like a summer day. They passed women with strollers and romping children, an old man walking his dog who greeted them heartily and young lovers nestling on the riverbank.

They reached one of the older parts of the city, which had been modernized into a shopping district. The area was centered by a pedestrian thoroughfare that led up the hill to Salzburg Castle. They strolled down, browsing through shops and collecting souvenirs. Sara looked at an assortment of postcards and selected her favorite to bring back for Chad's collection. Anne was getting hungry and wanted to eat and Beth had gotten wind of a *Sound of Music* tour and suggested they take it.

They continued down the street until Anne spotted an Italian restaurant, which was located on the second floor of one of the gift shops. They all agreed that Italian sounded good and went up. All the seats that looked out over the street were taken and they were seated in the back, making the restaurant appear the same as any the girls would frequent back home. The ordinary setting seemed to prompt ordinary conversation.

"How do you like your new job?" Sara asked Anne.

Anne delivered her answer in fragments. "It's a job. It pays the bills. Nothing special."

"But you like working with Mrs. Higgins?" Beth said.

"Mrs.? She's five years older than me, Beth. Does that make me Ms. McClair?"

"I was just asking," Beth said with a hint of disgust.

Their food came and they talked as they ate.

"So tell me, Sara," Anne began, finishing her mouthful of spaghetti and then continuing, "are you really doing okay over here? Don't get me wrong, I love it to death, but you're so far from home. Don't you ever miss the real world?"

Sara resented the question but answered calmly. "This is the real world, Anne. And as far as being far from home, I did get homesick at first, but I haven't lately. I've gotten into a routine and I've been busy. Besides, Chad and I have gotten very close and this is where I want to be."

"I don't know. You don't convince me, Sara. I just don't see you staying in Prague that long," Anne commented.

"Well that shows how little you know about me."

Anne took a drink of her coffee and again asked," Have you had any other guys since you've been here?"

"Do you think that I'm going to slut around like you?" Sara snapped in a steady but smart tone.

"Sara!" Beth admonished.

"I don't care. That remark was uncalled for. If she wants to be a little bitch then it's coming right back at her."

Anne but raised an eyebrow at Sara and Beth, in motherly fashion, diffused the situation. Soon the conversation resumed in a proper and civil tone and they finished their lunch. It was clear to Sara, however, that Anne had come to Europe to sightsee and didn't give a damn about her or her feelings. She wished that Karen could have come instead, but resolved not to let Anne spoil their time in Austria. But, in an ironic, way the exchange had returned things to normal. Sara and Anne could drop their facades and resume the relationship they were accustomed to.

The girls left the restaurant and continued to stroll through the town. They took the *Sound of Music* tour for Beth's sake, then returned to the depot and picked up their luggage. They had spotted the hotel they wanted about ten blocks from the station and they took the bus back to it.

Later that night, after Anne had gone to bed, Beth and Sara went for a walk. The unseasonably warm Austrian air felt good against their faces and they enjoyed being able to talk without Anne's negativity and sarcasm.

Beth wanted to be sure Sara was okay before she went back to Michigan. If she wasn't, she was prepared to stay and help her return home. "It's really awesome over here, Sara," she said as she eyed her surroundings. "Indeed it is." She stopped and took her sister's hand and looked her in the eye. "But before I leave, I need to know that you're all right."

Sara gave Beth's hand a tug and they resumed their walk. She fixed her gaze straight ahead as she spoke. "You know, I'm thriving over here, Beth. Not in a financial sense—but inside. I feel so inspired—so emancipated from who I used to be. Everything is fresh and new and I feel alive inside and I hadn't felt that way for a long time."

"How *are* you doing financially, if you don't mind my asking?"

"I'm holding my own, Beth. My savings is basically intact."

"And what about young Mr. Reiger?"

Sara grinned and returned the question. "What about young Mr. Reiger?"

"You know what I'm asking."

"I have to say things look good, Beth. Real good." Sara stopped and filled her lungs with the springtime air. She looked at her sister and said, "If he asked me to marry him, Beth, I would."

Beth put her hand on Sara's shoulder. "Well, then, I'm happy for you, kid," she said, beaming proudly. "I'm well aware that I can act too motherly at times, but I do care about you. I came here in part to make sure you weren't trapped into something that you didn't want. After these past four days I see you're doing fine and I know down inside that you're self-reliant and capable of doing anything that you put your mind to." She paused and cleared her throat. Her eyes were beginning to well, but she composed herself enough to finish with a calm and proud voice. "It's time for me to look up to the sky and tell Mom that her little Sara is going to be just fine."

Tears began pouring down their cheeks and Sara grabbed Beth and held her. They had just experienced a passage. Beth let go of her maternal responsibilities that night and Sara and her became peers.

The three sisters spent the next two days sightseeing before returning to Prague. They spent most of Sunday at her apartment, visiting and relaxing, and on Monday Beth and Anne returned to the States.

The visit had empowered Sara with the knowledge that she'd become her own woman. Her conversation with Beth made her realize how strong and independent she had become. She overcame her ghosts that weekend. Now she was free.

CHAPTER FIFTEEN

By the time July arrived the streets of Prague were bustling with tourists. Sounds of ethnic music permeated Old Town Square and the atmosphere in the city was festive. The days were again warm and life was good.

The feelings that Chad and Sara shared continued to grow. In June, they moved into a more modern and spacious third-floor apartment. With both of them bringing in a good income, they were able to afford a flat that overlooked the river. It also afforded them the privacy that wasn't possible in their previous, thin-walled apartment. Their spirits were high as they customized their new abode to suit their needs. Besides a full-sized bedroom, living room, kitchen and bathroom, there was an extra room that Sara converted into her studio. Its window also overlooked the river and provided an inspirational view when she painted; however, the feature they enjoyed the most was a balcony that projected from their living room and looked out over the city.

They finally had enough room to have Justin ship them their trunks. Sara was anxious to look through them, as a year had passed and she'd forgotten what all she had packed away. Because she had only brought the basic necessities with her to Europe, she craved some of the comforts and conveniences that the arrival of the trunks promised.

Their careers continued to progress as well. Chad was enjoying his work at the firm and was looking at a promotion in the near future. Sara had made a connection with the owner of an art gallery and sold her paintings there, while still continuing to sell them in the square.

The influx of tourists had given Prague an energetic infusion. Looking out their window to a walkway by the river, Chad vicariously experienced the freshness and magic of Prague through the virgin eyes of first-time visitors. Now when he walked through the city's streets he'd find himself telling the history of the city to curious onlookers, just as the locals had explained it to him, one year earlier.

Chad was helping Sara put the finishing touches on the apartment when they decided to go to the market. It was a pleasant evening and a gentle breeze swept their faces as they walked. Chad held Sara's hand as she stopped to browse in one of the shop windows. "I wonder how I would look in that hat?" she asked as she looked at the display.

"It looks a little old fashioned. I think it'd look better on your grandma," Chad remarked.

"But my granny's dead."

"That's what I mean."

"You don't like it because it would make me stand out from you."

"No, Sara. I'd hate to see people laugh at you—for you to become the talk of little children in school yards."

"Sara sighed. "Yes, you're right. I should learn to take fashion tips from someone who wears a thirty-year-old hairstyle."

"It's a Beatle cut, Sara. And may I point out that the Beatles are as popular now as they ever were."

"I guess that's why everyone's wearing that hairstyle, hey Chadders? No—wait, I was wrong. It's only you that wears it."

Chad yanked Sara's hand." Come on, let's go. You win. I'll shave it all off tomorrow, okay?"

They arrived at the market. Chad grabbed a cart and they circled through the aisles, shopping in a whimsical manner. Sara would put something in the cart and Chad would put it back on the shelf, selecting something in its place; conversely, she'd do the same to him. In the end they'd garnered an assortment of food that could not be construed as either nutritious or healthy.

On the way home as they passed the boutique, Chad again chided Sara about the hat in the window. "There it is again—the hottest fashion accessory in all Czechoslovakia."

"There is no more Czechoslovakia, dear boy."

Chad shifted the grocery bag to his left arm and took Sara's hand with his right. "You know," he began as he looked into her charming green eyes, "I might change my mind about asking you to marry me if you were to be wearing that hat all the time."

Sara gave him a measuring stare. "So you're saying... if I didn't get the hat...?"

He looked at he with a grin that stirred her curiosity. She repeated herself. "If I didn't get the hat...?"

"Oh, all right, Sara, I'll take you even with the hat." He pulled her hand to his chest, looked into her hazel-green eyes and said, "Sara, will you marry me?"

She looked back into the blue of his eyes as if she were looking into his soul, trying to ascertain if he was serious. She didn't want to overreact and look the fool if he was kidding, seeing that their afternoon to this point had been filled with levity. She thought for a moment and said, "You shouldn't joke about something like that, you know."

"I'm afraid I'm not joking, Sara," he replied. "So you'll have to give me an answer."

Sara looked at him again and this time she saw it in his eyes. It was the look of someone deeply in love. "You know what, Chad?" she said, smiling, "it's the best offer I've had in days and I'm going to take it." She clenched his hand. "I love you!" she beamed.

"I love you too," he said with an unwavering stare.

Chad realized that he was still holding a bag of groceries, lowered them to the sidewalk and grabbed her, kissing her lips—softly at first but progressing to an explosive flurry. He clutched her, picked her off the ground and twirled her around, then rushed her back to the apartment and they made love.

They stayed in bed for a half-hour after consummating their passion. They laid silently in each other's arms until Sara softly asked, "So when do you plan on marrying me?"

Chad smiled. "How about August?"

"That's not even a month away?"

"What? Do you need to get to know me better?"

"Planning!"

"What's to plan? We go somewhere and we get married."

"I'd like my family to be able to come. One month is a rather short notice, you know."

"September then."

"I can live with September."

She kissed him, then went to the phone and called her sister Beth, who was overjoyed with her news. When she got off the phone, Sara prepared a quick supper. Then, along with a bottle of merlot, they went out to christen their new balcony. They stayed there till the wee hours of the morning, talking about their future together, their hopes, dreams and aspirations. The wine smoothed their senses and they again made love.

When Sara awoke the next morning she found that Chad had already left for work. He had placed a teddy bear on the pillow where he had been, along with a love note. She picked up the stuffed bear and hugged it, then reached for the note and unfolded it. It read:

Sara,
    Didn't want to wake you. I'll be thinking about
    you all day long. Can't wait to see you this evening.
        Hugs and kisses.
            Your loving Chadders

Sara took the note and held it to her heart. She made the bed and placed the bear back on Chad's pillow, then went into the living room and wrote a note of her own for him. She took her note and placed it back on the pillow so it was halfway under the bear.

She strolled into the shower and prepared for her daily routine. Then she set out.

It was a brilliant morning. The streets were alive and the sun beamed warm on Sara's face as if God himself was helping her celebrate. The birds chirped gleefully in the trees that lined her walk, prompting her to reveal the smile that she'd been wearing inwardly.

She turned off Zborovská and onto one of the side streets. It was narrow and lined with parked vehicles and, although it wasn't a one-way street, it was apparent that it would be a struggle for two cars to pass through at the same time. The activity continued, unfazed by the shadows cast from the buildings that blocked the sunlight which had given such vivacity to the other streets she'd taken.

Up ahead of her, some children were kicking a soccer ball back and forth along the sidewalk while a group of older kids leaned against the building and watched, wasting away the hours of their adolescence. They had music playing loudly and were laughing and shouting in Czech, apparently harrying the younger boys as they practiced. As Sara approached, one of the older kids kicked the ball away from the younger ones and out onto the street. One of the other younger kids ran between the parked cars to fetch the ball and, as he picked it up, looked back and laughed at the one who'd kicked it into the street. Sara, who'd been watching this, noticed a bus coming swiftly around the corner and flailed her arms and yelled, "Watch out!" but the boy only looked at her. She raced to him as the bus rapidly came up behind and she pushed him hard, tripping on the cobblestone street in the process.

Within a second Sara heard the screeching of brakes. She thrust her arms and pushed herself into an upright position and saw the boy lying on the street, but clear of the bus. Then, her vision was supplanted with a bright, multicolored flash.

The people on the sidewalk came running up to her. She lay on the street—bloodied and in a semiconscious state—groaning and mumbling something in English.

Several minutes passed before ambulance siren was heard. Faint and distant, it grew louder until it came to park in the street where Sara lay. Two paramedics got out and rushed up to her. One of them was frantic while the other kept his composure. The calm one addressed Sara until a bystander told him that he'd heard her speaking English. They prepped her for transport and rushed her to the hospital.

When the doctor examined her he told the nurse that the outlook wasn't good. Sara was coherent, but there was a lot of internal damage and she had suffered a blow to the head. The doctor dispatched the nurse to summon someone who spoke adequate English. A minute later, another nurse came into the room. She leaned down to Sara and explained that she was about to undergo a series of operations and, in a frank manner, told her that her chances of pulling through weren't good.

Sara shook her head, not wanting to undergo anything until she saw Chad. She mumbled out his name and where he worked and said to get him right away. The doctor, hearing the translation, softly tilted his head, motioning to the other nurse to do as Sara had requested. If there was any doubt in Sara's mind about her chances, it ceased with the doctor's lack of argument with her decision. She prayed that they'd find Chad quickly and get him to the hospital. She took a breath, concentrated and fought to stay alive. She recalled the note she'd left for him and wished she had said so much more. She wished she had told him everything she wanted him to know about her. She fought with all the fortitude she had so she could see him one last time. She knew that was her only achievable goal.

As the room where Sara lay began to fade in and out, a police officer rushed into the office of the export firm. "Is there a Chad Reiger here?" he asked in Czech.

"Yes," said the secretary. Sensing the urgency in his voice, she hastily rose from her seat. "Follow me," she said as she hurried toward a cubicle in back and pointed to Chad.

The officer approached him. "There had been accident. You must come with me now."

Chad stood and took a couple of slow steps—his eyes fixated on the officer. "Come now!" the officer said, motioning with his hand for him to hurry.

"No. Tell me! What is it?"

The secretary went to him and took his hand. "Go, Chad," she ordered and pulled him toward the waiting police car.

Chad opened the door and got in. He took a deep breath, then demanded, "Tell me what's happening!"

The officer had gotten no further than saying "Sara," when Chad felt his heart drop into his stomach. "What?" he interrupted.

"This Sara has asked for you. She has been in accident." The policeman turned to him and in a low and solemn voice added, "She is not good. Be ready for that."

Chad felt his worst fears becoming reality. He slapped his hands on his legs as though the action would make the car go faster. Everything was a blur—the buildings they passed, the people on the street, the traffic—they all blended into a gray-like fog. "Is she going to live?" he asked, forcing the question through his swollen throat. "I mean—she asked for me, she must be all right?"

The officer stared straight ahead, prompting Chad to repeat the question even more impetuously. "Is she going to live?"

"I do not know," he answered, then thought for a moment but decided not to say any more.

At the hospital, Sara was desperate to see Chad. She could feel herself fading out and she knew she didn't have much time left. Then, she came to the point where she'd waited as long as possible and could wait no more. The nurse was standing next to her and Sara groaned to get her attention. She looked at the nurse and forced out the words she needed to say. "Tell Chad… tell Chad I love him." She paused as she collected her breath, then continued slowly. "Tell him I still… like… the hat." She paused again and took another breath. A small smile appeared at the corner of her mouth as she continued. "Tell him… I'll be… with him." She gathered her breath for one last sentence. "I will be with him always!" Then she relaxed and let go.

Everything grew dark and the pain, that had been so terrible, subsided. Her mind eased and in an echoed distance she heard frantic voices, but soon they also faded. She felt an inner peace—unlike any she had felt before. "There really is a tunnel," she mumbled. Then Sara exhaled her final breath.

Chad arrived at the hospital and rushed through the front door. He ran to the desk and asked for Sara McClair, while the officer who had followed him in translated to the receptionist. She picked up the phone and dialed a number and moments later a nurse arrived. She led Chad into a small room and asked him to sit down. The officer followed them and gave Chad a pat on the shoulder, then turned and walked out.

After a few minutes the doctor came in, wearing a solemn look. He sat across from Chad and, in a straight and forthright manner, told him that Sara had died. Chad let out a wail and collapsed to the floor in a fetal position. "No! This isn't possible!," he cried. "This can't be happening!"

The nurse who had spoken to Sara came into the room. She dropped to her knees and put her arm around him and held him, speaking somberly into his ear. "Your Sara has left a message for me to tell you."

Chad stopped crying and looked up at her.

"She wanted me to tell you that she loves you. She said she will be with you always."

Chad's head dropped back down to the floor as he sobbed uncontrollably. Each passing second heightened the reality of the tragedy. "Oh no!" he hollered out. "Not Sara!"

The nurse ran her hand across his back. "One more thing," she added, her voice, as well, cracking with emotion. "She wanted me to tell you that she liked the hat."

Chad wrapped his arms around Sara's messenger and held her as if she were Sara. He felt like a child—helpless and afraid. He let out a breath and pulled himself together, wiping his running nose with his hand. He stood and looked at the nurse through watery-red eyes and said, "Take me to her. I want to see Sara."

One of the doctors who had tended to her had come into the room. The nurse turned to him and, in Czech, told him of Chad's request. The doctor looked at him and shook his head. "Not good idea," he said. Then he said something in Czech to the nurse and she turned back to Chad. "Her injuries were very bad. You do not want to remember her like this."

"I don't care!" Chad said with vehemence. "I love her and I want to see her, dammit!"

The nurse put her hand on Chad's chest and looked back to the doctor, again saying something in Czech and this time seemingly pleading on Chad's behalf. This time the doctor nodded and motioned for Chad to follow. He led him into a dimly-lit room where Sara lay, then went up to her, pulled the sheet that covered her down to her shoulders and stepped out of the room.

Chad looked at his motionless love. Her face was bruised and her lip swollen, but she didn't have the look of someone who'd been in a life-ending accident. He ran his fingers through her hair and began to cry. He stared for a moment before speaking, then softly said, "Baby, I tried to get here. I didn't want you to die alone. I didn't want you to die!"

Chad, choking up, forced himself to stay composed. He grabbed onto the sides of the bed, leaned over her and said, "You are the love of my life, Sara. How can I leave this room? How can I leave you here? We should have never left each other's side."

Again he tried to fight off his tears but this time the dam had burst. He knew they wouldn't let him stay in the room long so he spoke through his emotions. "I will love you every day of my life, baby. I will pray for you every night before I go to bed, and baby, you put in a good word for me too. I love you, Sara." He leaned across her and rested his head on her chest. Then he stood back up. He put his hand on her hair, like he would at night when she was going to sleep, and gently stroked it. "This is the last time we'll have together, honey," he murmured. Then he smiled. He bent down and kissed her cheek. "I love you so much, baby," he cried. "I'll love you always!... But now I have to go." He lowered his head, wiped his eyes and walked out.

He spotted the doctor and nurse in the hall. He wiped his eyes, looked at the doctor and simply said, "Thank you." He turned to the nurse and embraced her. "Thank you," he said emphatically. "Thank you for telling me."

"Chad," the nurse began, "she seemed like an angel and I am sure she is with them now." Then she walked him to the door. "They will have papers they will need you to fill out and you will have a lot of preparations during this hard time. So, now you go. Go outside and be alone for a while."

Chad nodded without looking up and walked through the doors—the same doors that had at least offered hope, the last time he passed through them. Now there was no hope. There was no life—not for Sara and not for him. His body was numb. The sounds of the city—the honking horns, people's voices, construction workers—seemed distant and from another time. He walked down the street until a panic came over him and he began to run. He ran through the crowded city, oblivious to anyone or anything in his way. He ran as fast as he could until he reached the boutique where Sara had seen the hat in the window the night before. Despite his agony, he was relieved to see it was still there and he rushed inside. He found a sales clerk and told her that he had to have the hat in the window—not one like it, but the actual one on display. He managed to purchase the hat and make it outside before he broke down. Crying uncontrollably, he squeezed the hat as a child would hug a stuffed animal. Then he clenched it in his hand and labored back to his apartment, still numb and far removed from the chirping birds and the shinning sun.

He got to the apartment and stood at the door. He wanted to collapse on the bed. He wanted to go back to work and pretend that none of this had happened. He wanted to jump off the balcony. But he admonished himself and told himself that he had to be strong. Sara had services that needed to be arranged and they would be nothing less than perfect. He went to her dresser and dug out her address book, then looked up Beth's number and went to the phone.

"Hello," came the just-awakened voice of Sara's sister.

Chad couldn't speak.

"Hello," she said again, louder this time.

"Hi, Beth, this is Chad," he began. His voice was cracking but he forced himself to continue and said, "I have something terrible to tell you." He paused and steadied his trembling hand with the other, then continued. "Sara was…," he paused again and put his hand on his forehead, staring blankly at the floor as he went on. "She was hit by a bus and she died, Beth."

"She what? Chad… Chad… what happened?"

Chad could hear Steve talking in the background. He held the phone at his waist, then put it back to his ear. "She's dead, Beth," he sobbed. "She died at the hospital. And I didn't even get to tell her goodbye!"

The he lost what little composure he had left. Beth, who was herself crying and shocked, sensed that Chad needed her. She gathered herself, grabbed a tissue and cleared her throat. She told him that the rest of the family had to be told and said that she would call Karen and she could get in touch with the others and she would call him back as soon as she got off the phone with her.

"I was told she died a hero," he added. "She saved a deaf boy's life. Tell the others we can be proud of her."

A half-hour passed before Beth called Chad back. He talked with her for several hours, both sharing his grief and making tentative arrangements for a service. At times the conversation was light, as when Chad told of how they had come to be engaged and the role that a fur hat in a shop window had to play in it all. He talked about a lot of the things they had done together over the past year. Then he shared the words that Sara had left him with.

When their conversation ended, Chad didn't know what to do with himself. He wanted to go outside and walk, but he couldn't deal with running into anyone he knew. Instead, he went into the bedroom to lie down. When he got there, he found Sara's note on the pillow. He picked it up. It read:

"Dear Chadders,

Can't wait to see you tonight either. You'll probably make it home before me but I won't be far behind you. Just remember—even when I'm not there—I love you and I'm with you wherever you go.

All my love,
Sara"

And for the first time since the tragedy occurred, Chad felt an inner peace.

EPILOGUE

I remember those final days with Sara as if it were yesterday. I had never felt more alive or filled with love than I did in that time. We were soul mates, we were friends and we were extremely happy. Our lives were good. We weren't rich, but we'd found what we were searching for—both in Prague and in each other.

If I say the memories of my final days with Sara are vivid, then I must add that my recollection of the accident is nothing less than absolute. I was obliterated. I lost my will to live—my ability to function. That is until I realized that there was now a void in the world and I had to become Sara's torchbearer. I found relief to my misery in doing things in her stead. I took to volunteering in the children's ward of the hospital—the same hospital where she died—because that was something that Sara would have done. Much of what I did was inspired by her and I found her existence perpetuating through me.

Sara's family agreed that I would have the final say in the funeral planning and I decided that she would be buried in Prague. She had a Christian service in a small church and was laid to rest in a beautiful little cemetery that was situated on a hill and overlooked the Vltava. All her family came, as did Abbey and Miles. I will always love them for that.

Beth and Justin stayed with me for another day after the funeral. They said that the family had decided that I should have Sara's inheritance, because that's what she would've wanted. I felt close to Beth. She'd always been Sara's favorite sister. But I also felt close to Justin and in the end, he felt close to me as well. I recall our first encounter and how he seemed to dislike me, but as Sara had assured, he was just being protective of her. As time passed I kept in touch with both of them. I would always be invited to Beth's for Christmas and on a couple of occasions I did fly back to Michigan to attend.

The seasons passed. I'd go up the hill daily and visit Sara—as I still do. It never mattered to me if it was raining or freezing or if I was under the weather, I found comfort by her graveside. I'd bring her flowers and talk to her and by the time I would leave I'd feel better. I'd go down to the Charles Bridge and stay there for hours, thinking of all we used to do and all we'd been through. I remember one time in particular, standing there and looking out over Prague and thinking about the day Sara had agreed to come to Europe with me. That memory made me smile.

Eventually, I quit my employment at the export firm and took a job at the art gallery where Sara had displayed her work. It was only a security position, but I felt closer to her there. In fact, one of her paintings remains on display with a special dedication to her on a plaque underneath it.

I relinquished our new apartment—it was too big for me—for a smaller one, all the time waiting for our old apartment to come available again. It's still occupied but if it opens up I'll take it in a heartbeat. Most of our memories were in that building.

From time to time I ponder my future: whether I should leave Prague and whether I should move on with my life. But it's been five years now since Sara died and I still can't let go. In time, I believe I may. I think that's what Sara would've wanted from me. Still, with her resting atop that hill, it's a pretty big reason to stay. She had to die alone in the hospital and I don't think I could ever bear to leave her alone again.

In the meantime, I walk through the city and I enjoy what it has to offer, just as we used to do together. On occasion I dig into my cigar box and pull out the note that she had left me on the day she died. Or I'll go to the closet and pull out the hat from the boutique and I'll just hold it. Of all the possessions I have, I cherish that the most.

But more than any possession, I cherish the words that she had left with me. "Remember, even when I'm not there, I love you and I'm with you wherever you go."

And I know she is.

ZEUS

Sovereign ruler of the universe, controller of the weather, all-seeing father of gods and men: Zeus was the chief deity of the ancient Greek pantheon. His places of worship ranged from the household to Olympia, the greatest of all sanctuaries. His significance is reflected in the individual chapters dedicated to him in books on Greek religion and myth but this is the first attempt to capture him in the round, in a single volume, for many years.

In a study that is at once masterly and comprehensive, Ken Dowden presents a study of this fascinating god for the new millennium. Myth, cult and art are examined, as are philosophy, drama, theology, European painting and much more. Zeus is not just seen as a god of Greece itself, but also as a god of the developing Mediterranean world and of the Romans, when he became their 'Jupiter'. The importance of Zeus in the medieval period and modern times is discussed in a revealing section on reception.

The book contains many and varied illustrations, charts and maps and provides a thorough and accessible, as well as scholarly, introduction to the chief god in the Greek pantheon.

Ken Dowden is Professor of Classics, and Director of the Institute of Archaeology and Antiquity, at the University of Birmingham.

ZEUS

Ken Dowden

Routledge
Taylor & Francis Group

LONDON AND NEW YORK

First published 2006
by Routledge
2 Park Square, Milton Park, Abingdon, Oxon OX14 4RN

Simultaneously published in the USA and Canada
by Routledge
270 Madison Ave, New York, NY 10016

Routledge is an imprint of the Taylor & Francis Group

© 2006 Ken Dowden

Designed and typeset in Utopia by
Keystroke, Jacaranda Lodge, Wolverhampton
Printed and bound in Great Britain by
TJ International Ltd, Padstow, Cornwall

British Library Cataloguing in Publication Data
A catalogue record for this book is available from the British Library

Library of Congress Cataloging in Publication Data
Dowden, Ken, 1950–
    Zeus / Ken Dowden.— 1st ed.
        p. cm.
    Includes bibliographical references and index.
    ISBN 0–415–30502–0 (hardback : alk. paper) — ISBN 0–415–30503–9
    (pbk. : alk. paper)
    1. Zeus (Greek deity) I. Title.
    BL820.J8D68 2005
    292.2'113—dc22   2005009985

ISBN10: 0–415–30502–0 (hbk)
ISBN10: 0–415–30503–9 (pbk)
ISBN13: 978–0–415–30502–0 (hbk)
ISBN13: 978–0–415–30503–7 (pbk)

CONTENTS

CONTENTS vii

SERIES FOREWORD

For a person who is about to embark on any serious discourse or task, it is proper to begin first with the gods.

(Demosthenes, *Letters* 1.1)

WHY GODS AND HEROES?

The gods and heroes of classical antiquity are part of our culture. Many function as sources of creative inspiration for poets, novelists, artists, composers, filmmakers and designers. Greek tragedy's enduring appeal has ensured an ongoing familiarity with its protagonists' experiences and sufferings, while the choice of Minerva as the logo of one of the newest British universities, the University of Lincoln, demonstrates the ancient gods' continued emblematic potential. Even the world of management has used them as representatives of different styles: Zeus and the 'club' culture for example, and Apollo and the 'role' culture: see C. Handy, *The Gods of Management: who they are, how they work and why they fail* (London, 1978).

This series is concerned with how and why these figures continue to fascinate and intrigue. But it has another aim too, namely to explore their strangeness. The familiarity of the gods and heroes risks obscuring a vital difference between modern meanings and ancient functions and purpose. With certain exceptions, people today do not worship them, yet to the Greeks and Romans they were real beings in a system comprising literally hundreds of divine powers. These range from the major gods, each of whom was worshipped in many guises via their epithets or 'surnames', to the heroes – deceased individuals associated with local communities – to other figures such as daimons and nymphs. The landscape was dotted with sanctuaries, while natural features such as mountains, trees and rivers were thought to be inhabited by religious beings. Studying ancient paganism involves finding strategies to comprehend a world where everything was, in the often quoted words of Thales, 'full of gods'.

In order to get to grips with this world, it is necessary to set aside our preconceptions of the divine, shaped as they are in large part by Christianised notions of a transcendent, omnipotent God who is morally good. The Greeks and Romans worshipped numerous beings, both male and female, who looked, behaved and suffered like humans, but who, as immortals, were not bound by the human condition. Far from being omnipotent, each had limited powers: even the sovereign, Zeus/Jupiter, shared control of the universe with his brothers Poseidon/Neptune (the sea) and Hades/Pluto (the under-world). Lacking a creed or anything like an organised church, ancient paganism was open to continual reinterpretation, with the result that we should not expect to find figures with a uniform essence. It is common to begin accounts of the pantheon with a list of the major gods and their function(s) (Hephaistos/Vulcan: craft; Aphrodite/Venus: love; and Artemis/Diana: the hunt and so on), but few are this straightforward. Aphrodite, for example, is much more than the goddess of love, vital though that function is. Her epithets include *Hetaira* ('courtesan') and *Porne* ('prostitute'), but also attest roles as varied as patron of the citizen body (*Pandemos*: 'of all the people') and protectress of seafaring (*Euploia, Pontia, Limenia*).

Recognising this diversity, the series consists not of biographies of each god or hero (though such have been attempted in the past), but of investigations into their multifaceted aspects within the complex world of ancient paganism. Its approach has been shaped partly in response to two distinctive patterns in previous research. Until the middle of the twentieth century, scholarship largely took the form of studies of individual gods and heroes. Many works presented a detailed appraisal of such issues as each figure's origins, myth and cult; these include L.R. Farnell's examination of major deities in his *Cults of the Greek States* (5 vols, Oxford, 1896–1909) and A.B. Cook's huge three-volume *Zeus* (Cambridge, 1914–40). Others applied theoretical developments to the study of gods and heroes, notably (and in the closest existing works to a uniform series) K. Kerényi in his investigations of gods as Jungian archetypes, including *Prometheus: archetypal image of human existence* (English trans. London 1963) and *Dionysos: archetypal image of the indestructable life* (English trans. London 1976).

In contrast, under the influence of French structuralism, the later part of the century saw a deliberate shift away from research into particular gods and heroes towards an investigation of the system of which they were part. Fuelled by a conviction that the study of isolated gods could not do justice to the dynamics of ancient religion, the pantheon came to be represented as a logical and coherent network in which the various powers were systematically opposed to one another. In a classic study by J.-P. Vernant, for example, the Greek concept of space was shown to be consecrated through the opposition between Hestia (goddess of the hearth – fixed space) and Hermes (messenger and traveller god – moveable space: Vernant, *Myth and Thought Among the Greeks*, London, 1983, 127–75). The gods as individual entities were far from neglected however, as may be exemplified by the works by Vernant, and his colleague M. Detienne, on particular deities including Artemis, Dionysos and Apollo: see, most recently, Detienne's *Apollon, le couteau en main: une approche expérimentale du polythéisme grec* (Paris, 1998).

In a sense, this series is seeking a middle ground. While approaching its subjects as unique (if diverse) individuals, it pays attention to their significance as powers within the collectivity of religious beings. *Gods and Heroes of the Ancient World* sheds new light on many of the most important religious beings of classical antiquity; it also provides a route into understanding Greek and Roman polytheism in the twenty-first century.

The series is intended to interest the general reader as well as being geared to the needs of students in a wide range of fields from Greek and Roman religion and mythology, classical literature and anthropology, to Renaissance literature and cultural studies. Each book presents an authoritative, accessible and refreshing account of its subject via three main sections. The introduction brings out what it is about the god or hero that merits particular attention. This is followed by a central section which introduces key themes and ideas, including (to varying degrees) origins, myth, cult and representations in literature and art. Recognising that the heritage of myth is a crucial factor in its continued appeal, the reception of each figure since antiquity forms the subject of the third part of the book. The volumes include illustrations of each god/hero and where appropriate time charts, family trees and maps. An annotated bibliography synthesises past research and indicates useful follow-up reading.

For convenience, the masculine terms 'gods' and 'heroes' have been selected for the series title, although (and with an apology for the male-dominated language), the choice partly reflects ancient usage in that the Greek *theos* ('god') is used of goddesses too. For convenience and consistency, Greek spellings are used for ancient names, except for famous Latinised exceptions, and BC/AD has been selected rather than BCE/CE.

I am indebted to Catherine Bousfield, the editorial assistant until 2004, who (literally) dreamt up the series and whose thoroughness and motivation brought it close to its launch. The hard work and efficiency of her successor, Matthew Gibbons, has overseen its progress to publication, and the classics editor of Routledge, Richard Stoneman, has provided support and expertise throughout. The anonymous readers for each proposal gave frank and helpful advice, while the authors' commitment to advancing scholarship while producing accessible accounts of their designated subjects has made it a pleasure to work with them.

Susan Deacy, Roehampton University, June 2005

LIST OF MAPS

LIST OF ILLUSTRATIONS
AND CREDITS

PREFACE

What could be easier to write, for someone who has spent his working life in Greek religion and mythology, than a short book on Zeus aimed at a broad but discriminating readership? The answer is 'almost anything'. There is no knowledge of Zeus without confronting the detail of myth and literature, and getting a real sense of the place of the art or without taking seriously what it was to worship, revere and respect this greatest of Greek gods. There are no halfway houses – Intermediate Zeus is impossible.

There has been a lot to tell and I apologise in advance if some of it is tough going. We are after all sweeping through a history from the Indo-European peoples whom we can dimly sense worshipping their god *Dyēus pətēr* in the fourth millennium BC to the cute names that software engineers adopt in order to market abstrusely powerful computing 'solutions' as our third millennium AD begins. In between, among the Greeks the worship of Zeus was universal, but locally modulated and infinitely rich: it matters what they did in Boeotia at the Great Daidala every fifty-ninth year or at the feast of grim Zeus Laphystios. It matters too how Zeus spread to nations newly arrived in the world of accredited Greek culture, or Romans who wanted to think about the real Jupiter, or Syrians worshipping Baal. So a sense of geography and chronology, indeed of the unfurling map of history, is unavoidable.

In writing on myth once, I commented how there is no right order in which to present such material. At best one achieves a rhetorical success. This book has been specially difficult and I have written it at least three times in different orders. I will be happy if readers feel that the book conveys a sense of the onward march of history whilst grouping themes as though it were giving a synchronic account, an overview, of how Zeus fitted together, aspect by aspect, at a given time.

Writing this sort of book requires a wide expertise, wider than any of us has. I am aware of many of my weaknesses and wish I could have given more attention particularly to iconography and to archaeology. But with the best will in the world I would not surrender a single page of this book to make room. I believe in the authentic voice of people of long ago, whether in Greek and Roman times or in medieval times (and I believe in letting them speak for themselves). It is a miracle that we have their literature after so long and can come so close to recreating their worlds and concerns. Some of this material becomes highbrow; but much too is what today we would call folk culture. It is a whole world, down to the very swear words they used.

All nations deserve respect. But the ancient Greeks have to be rescued from many evils – for instance the dying breed who would idealise all Greeks, or the trivialisers who treat them as people of fantasy, fit for computer games, role play and mindless notching up of the mythology. The Greeks were a people, like any other people today, and the peculiar tensions of their societies catalysed cultural phenomena to which we owe much in the European, and human, tradition. Their religion, however, thanks to our Christian history, has been treated as an interesting collection of customs with no inner content. I do not personally subscribe to the inner content of any religion. But if a religion thinks it reaches out for something other, something categorically different and beyond human understanding – and that is what religions on their own account do – then the religion of Zeus strove harder than most. The Greeks were not going through humanist motions, but were committed to their gods and their supreme god. Let this book be a bloodless offering to him!

This is also an offering to those who have been so kind to me in putting this book together. Illustrations have been a particular nightmare and key interventions, often beyond the call of duty, by European friends of culture in Bologna, St Petersburg, Rome, Berlin, Heidelberg, Paris and Glasgow have meant a lot to me. I am also grateful to anonymous readers (particularly at the design stage) and to Susan Deacy and Catherine Bousfield for their patience and constructive criticisms, to Geraldine Martin for her unflappability in resolving issues raised at the production stage, to my son James Dowden for heroic and speedy work on the indexes, and to Ken and Diana Wardle for corrections, practical help and sufficient wine.

The University of Birmingham
Christmas Eve 2004

CHRONOLOGICAL TABLE

This table is designed to help you follow this sequence of events and periods. Please be aware that I have had to make some arbitrary decisions about when periods begin and end, and about when events, particularly earlier ones, took place. Any uncertain date for an event is in italics.

Period	Year	Event
Before the Greeks 3500–2100 BC	*3500*	Final break-up of Indo-European language and society
Bronze Age (*Minoan* in Crete, *Mycenaean* in Greece) 2100–1200 BC	*1200*	Zeus at Knossos and Pylos
Dark Age 1200–776 BC	*800/700*	End of kingship in most of Greece
Archaic Age 776–480 BC	776	(allegedly) the first Olympic Games
	700	Hesiod, *Theogony* and *Works and Days*
	700/650	Homer, *Iliad* and *Odyssey*
	630	Mimnermos' poetry
	600	Alcaeus' poetry
	546–510	Tyranny at Athens (Peisistratids)
Classical Age 480–323 BC	480/479	Greeks defeat Xerxes (King of Persia)
	484–456	plays of Aeschylus

Period	Year	Event
	441–406	plays of Euripides
	435	Pheidias' statue of Zeus enthroned
	429–347	Plato
	384–322	Aristotle
	339–314	Xenokrates head of the Academy
Hellenistic Age (Greece) 323–31 BC	323	death of Alexander the Great
	335–263	Zeno (founder of Stoicism)
Republic (Rome) 509–31 BC	300	Euhemeros
	280–250	poetry of Aratus
	331–232	Cleanthes (Stoic)
	204–169	poetry and plays of Ennius
	47 BC	Varro's *Human and Divine Antiquities*
Empire, whilst pagan 31 BC–AD 312	29–19 BC	Vergil's *Aeneid*
	by AD 8	Ovid's *Metamorphoses*
	60s	Cornutus' *Compendium of Greek Mythology*
	117–138	Hadrian emperor
	150	Pausanias' *Guide to Greece*
	190–230	writings of Tertullian
Empire, whilst Christian; Late Antiquity 312–567	312–337	Constantine emperor
	391/2	Theodosius bans pagan cult
	393	last Olympic Games
	426	Augustine's *City of God*
	420–450	writings of Macrobius and of Martianus Capella
	470	Fulgentius', *Mythologiae*
	475	Pheidias' Zeus destroyed in fire at Constantinople
Middle Ages 567–1453	600–636	Isidore Bishop of Seville
	1200	Carmina Burana
	1321	Dante's *Divine Comedy*
	1360	Boccaccio's *Genealogies of the Pagan Gods*
	1380	Chaucer's *House of Fame*

Period	Year	Event
Renaissance 1453–1600	1470s	printed editions of Ovid's *Metamorphoses*
	1499?–1546	Giulio Romano, painter
	1545	Titian's *Danae* (Naples)
	1550	Fontainebleau mythological scenes (the court of Henri II of France is the New Olympus)
Modern 1600–2005	1744	Handel's *Semele*
	1876	Wagner's *Ring of the Nibelungs* first performed complete

Map I The regions of mainland Greece

WHY ZEUS?

INTRODUCING ZEUS

Zeus, king of the Greek gods, master of lightning, smiter of those who offend him, god of the sky who rules on Mt Olympus. Zeus the superlative: *kydistos, megistos, hypatos* – most glorious, most great, most supreme. Father of men and of gods, he sees all, he plans all. We cannot and may not understand his mind, but *nothing comes to fulfilment without Zeus*, as the Elders in Aeschylus' tragedy, *Agamemnon* (1487), intone.

Dare we think that Zeus still exists? Polytheists, people who believe in many gods, should have no problem thinking of him as an additional god or simply the Greek name for a key god of their own. For monotheists, why should he not be a way of talking about, a way of approaching, the one God? He is after all that single planning force that gives sense to Greek polytheism.

Yet to us Zeus is mere fiction: colourful, lustful, mighty and irresponsible. We know him from modern paintings, books of ancient art, sometimes the real thing in museums and from a mythology of his adulteries. How could the Greeks have worshipped such an empty god? Zeus rained, their crops grew. Zeus thundered, he was angry. A battle was lost, they had not sacrificed enough. A battle was won, they dedicated a trophy to Zeus Tropaios. Was that all?

From beginning to end Zeus has been unseen, operating the causal system of the universe in mysterious ways, and underlying every event. From the beginnings of Western literature in the works of Homer, he is a strange and remote force focused on our world and causing it to be as it is. The universe displays the justice of Zeus. And it is tough justice. Neither Homer nor the tragedians nor the philosophers thought they had his measure. Even a philosopher, Cleanthes the Stoic, might compose a hymn to him as he struggled to grasp something of Zeus's place in, or rather slightly outside, our world – in the ether somehow. The mythology was only a way of talking about Zeus, a *façon de parler*. No one believed that the gods actually had a palace at the top of a mountain in Thessaly. Mythology was always a parable, a transposition of the mysterious into another language. If the Greeks often treated their myth with a sense of fun that might shock generations brought up on scripture and holy books, that was at least partly because they did not take it quite so literally or naively. Ancient Greeks were no less sophisticated than ourselves.

THE EVIDENCE FOR ZEUS

We know about Zeus from myth, from cult and from art. The three fuse together to form the Zeus that Greeks constructed in their imaginations and revered. *Myth* wraps religious sites in an ambience of gods and heroes, and presents the origins in the past of current religious life. It is told from childhood onwards, forms the subject of performances – whether epic, drama or hymns danced out – and is at the core of ancient education and life. *Cult* is the unceasing recognition of the supremacy of the gods and our dependence on them: it embraces the home, the city and its countryside, and defines what it is to be Greek. Time itself is created by the rhythm of the festivals during the year, the spans of years between, for instance, Olympic festivals, and the ceremonies that highlight life stages, from birth to death. *Art* gives visible shape and its own sense to the ideas we have of the gods and to their mythology; it does much more than decorate temples and shrines: it is a vehicle for religious ideas to penetrate the whole world.

The mythology

Zeus is born, usually in Crete. He escapes being swallowed by his father Kronos when his mother Rhea puts a stone in his place. Meanwhile his baby cries are hidden by the noisy dancing of young warriors, the Kouretes (Curetes). He is looked after, alternatively, by Amaltheia the goat (or nymph) or the Kouretes. Kronos is bound and confined. An attempted counter-revolution by the Titans (who comprise Kronos and his generation) is defeated. This is the *Titanomachy*. The Titans are imprisoned in Tartarus. There are some more battles to make Zeus's authority absolute: sometimes a *Gigantomachy* (fight with the Gigantes, the Giants), and sometimes a battle with the deadly monster and enemy Typhon. He comes close to defeat in this battle.

His rule is now complete. When Prometheus steals fire from the immortals, Zeus has him chained to the Caucasus mountains and his liver is savaged by an eagle until Herakles (Hercules) shoots it – a sample of the order of Zeus.

He is married to Hera and it is cult more than myth that tells of his 'sacred marriage' with her (p. 31). But most of his children, of which there are many, are begotten in relationships with other women, who form a mighty list (p. 39) and constitute the larger part of his mythology. Semele foolishly prays for him to appear in his true form, which turns out to be the lightning bolt. Unlike other gods he has no human shape in which to appear and therefore, usefully for stories, can only appear in disguise, or transformed. So, to Alkmene, mother of Herakles, he appears as her husband Amphitryon; to Danae, mother of Perseus, as a shower of golden rain; to Leda, mother of Helen and the Dioskouroi, as a swan; to Europa as a bull. He also sends his eagle for Ganymede, a Trojan prince of exceptional beauty, so that he may be his cup-bearer in heaven.

He also dies, according to the Cretans. But that is an outrageous story that gave the Cretans the reputation for being liars (p. 35).

These are the stories. In the first part, 'key themes', we will see what some of them have meant, or seemed to have meant, to the Greeks. The myths are always for thinking with, and, as the Greek world expands, become a defining part of the prestigious Greek – and later Roman – culture which would eventually be adopted by new

Figure 1 The sanctuary of Zeus at Olympia, as imagined in a nineteenth-century engraving.

civilisations. This mythological portrait also becomes an ideological reference point: Zeus helps us think about kings and their roles, about emperors, about life and the rules of the universe that govern it. In the European tradition too, the subject of the second part, 'Zeus afterwards', the myths have their meaning: the world of myth does not divide into authentic ancient times on the one hand and later European manipulation on the other.

The cult

Zeus is the most widespread Greek god, and Greeks worshipped him in many different ways. At one extreme the head of household is praying in his courtyard, hands uplifted to heaven as the altar blazes with a few sticks. At the other extreme it is the time of the Olympic Festival, held every four years, at Olympia in the Peloponnese, and half the Greek world, and more besides, seems to be there. Something between the Vatican City in the jubilee year and huge Hindu festivals like the Kumbh Mela, you would have seen a sizeable apparatus of priests, officials, hostels, treasuries, sporting events, statues of victors and, in the middle, the great temples of Zeus and of Hera. On a more humble scale, a procession winds up a mountain, perhaps in Arcadia, Crete or Macedonia, to offer traditional gifts, to pray for rain or simply to recognise his supreme power. And now, in the little village of Erchia in the territory of Athens, it is the 4th of Thargelion, time for the people to go up their local hill, the *pagos*, and offer Zeus a sheep.

Regardless of whether Zeus is your city's patron god, he is continually worshipped at every level and your dependence on him is constantly acknowledged by the humility of ritual and the slaughter of animals.

The image

It was the job of sculpture and painting to capture the god and his meaning and to provide a visible focus for thinking about the god and adoring him. The first task was to provide a cult image, a statue which in past times was often wooden and rather notional ('crude' according to evolutionary prejudice). These often remained the most powerful in religious terms. Later, it was the custom to make statues out of stone or bronze and these became more lifelike in the sense that they looked more exactly like people; they were 'anthropomorphic'. Pheidias' great statue of Zeus at Olympia was 'chryselephantine' – *gold and ivory* were applied around a central wooden core to create the pale skin and contrasts such as hair and rich clothing. These then served as a focus for worship and contemplation. But temples also came to be decorated with scenes from the mythology and you might find the god on metopes that filled the gaps between the stone representations of the ends of roof joists, on the body of the temple behind the colonnade and, of course, on the pediment. You might also find free-standing statues of Zeus at any religious site.

Greek painting is largely lost to us, and it is impossible to know whether there were striking images of Zeus on the interiors of temples or public buildings. His stories certainly appear on pottery, which derived much of its inspiration from painting. At mealtimes and at drinking parties, and in all domestic and ceremonial contexts, vase-painting would have provided another way, beyond the epic and tragic texts that Greeks met in education and in performance, for images of Zeus and his mythology to be constantly at hand.

The omnipresence of Zeus – portrayed, talked about, thought about, worshipped – cannot be exaggerated. And the physical representation, as is typical of Christian and Hindu art and life, forms a necessary anchor. It is deeply revealing that in the Middle Ages, when Zeus was no longer seen in art, the book of Albricus had to be written to describe the appearance of the ancient gods (p. 124).

EXPLAINING ZEUS

In our modern world it is hard to grasp Zeus. And we should not underestimate the influence that writers since the nineteenth century have had on our ideas, for better and for worse. If we set down some of these ideas now, we may be able to stand back from them when we need to and recognise disembodied echoes of these views in modern writing about the god.

Playing with words: the name 'Zeus'

Can his name give us any information? 'Zeus' is an unusual case because it is actually relatively clear where it comes from, unlike the names of the other Greek gods. In 1786 it was discovered that Greek was part of a family of related languages. Our word 'three' looks like the Greek *treis* or the Sanskrit *trayaḥ* or the Latin *tres* because it *is* the same word. Likewise, the 'Tue' in Tuesday is the same as *Zeus* or *Dyāuḥ* or *Ju*-piter (Greeks called on 'Zeus father', *Zeu pater*, as well): Tuesday for us is Zeus's day. These words can be traced back to common linguistic ancestors, the 'Proto-Indo-Europeans', who perhaps lived north of the Black Sea, around 3500 BC. Their **Dyēus* belonged to a group of words that led to:

- *dies*, the Latin word for 'day' (the English word is actually unrelated);

- the Greek adjective *endios*, referring to a peak time of day usually envisaged as midday;
- the Greek adjective *eudios*, referring to good weather as opposed to storm;
- many Sanskrit words built on the root *div-* referring to heaven, shining and day.

This is fascinating: we have in some way recovered an ancestral god of the Indo-European peoples, a named god in what was presumably a polytheistic system and the senior ('father') god at that. All Greeks have this god because he was there at the beginning before there were any separate Greeks. His role appears to be based in nature, expressing the brightness of the sky – and the disruptions of that sky by rain, storm and lightning – an elemental feature in human experience. Even if Zeus does not *mean* 'sky', he is so entwined with it that Greeks can say that 'Zeus rains' (p. 54) and attribute atmospheric phenomena to him.[1]

But we should control our enthusiasm: however scientific and pragmatic this link may seem, its significance is in fact quite limited. *Dyēus* does not tell us about the Zeus that ancient Greeks worshipped, happily ignorant of Indo-European etymology. For that we need facts about the Greeks, their systems and structures of thought. Classical Greek religion is the product of two millennia of change since Indo-European times. Wherever *Dyēus-* or Zeus-worshippers migrated, they found new Zeuses around them and, as they also identified this or that god as 'Zeus', so the identity of Zeus changed and had to form part of a new system. The cultures that preceded the Greeks in Greece contributed to every aspect of the lives of the new, merged, population. It is for this reason that so many of the gods of Greece cannot be etymologically linked with Indo-European, and it may also help explain why there were so many female gods dominating Greek cities. When we come to look at Zeus's cults we will find them very varied: we can thank poets and thinkers for swinging the pendulum back and seeking to restore unity to a god named Zeus.

Despite the efforts of poets, however, the variety is still visible. So, Zeus in Crete absorbed the cult of a divine child, guarded in mythology by the young warrior Kouretes. This god was one who could die. At

Dodona (Epirus) his wife is Dione rather than the usual Hera. His children should be the 'youths of Zeus', the Dioskouroi (p. 44) Castor and Pollux, but his parenthood is not at the forefront of their mythology. He may indeed have been 'father of gods and men' in Indo-European times – this description is found at least in both Greek and Sanskrit. But the development of an organised family of gods, preferably 12, for him to preside over looks more like the mythologies of the Near-Eastern cultures with which the Greeks came into contact and from which they got this idea. Indeed, but for the additional employment provided for him by this Near-Eastern model he might have found it harder to survive; the Sanskrit Dyāuḥ and the proto-German *Tiwaz have almost faded away: we can say something about Woden whose name survives in the word 'Wednesday', but what can we say of the god of Tuesday? Zeus has derived more vigour from the young, violent and successful storm god found in various Near-Eastern cultures.

Nature and evolution

All personal gods come from nature gods

Welcker, *Griechische Götterlehre* i.324 (1857)

[The Greek people] very soon progressed to secure personification and complete anthropomorphism of the gods

Preller, *Griechische Mythologie* i.2 (1854)

Indo-European etymology was an early nineteenth-century enthusiasm. So were Nature and Evolution. Nature, which had bubbled to the surface in Romantic poetry in the first half of the nineteenth century, seemed important to scholars too: many of the forms of experience characteristic of earlier civilisations had resulted, they thought, from the religious way in which man stood in awe of nature. Evolution is something we most readily associate with the theories of Darwin and the emergence of *Homo sapiens*, but it went far beyond these. Language, as we have seen, had been found to have evolved till we had the privileged languages of Western Europe. Indeed, not just man but his whole civilisation evolved. Stages in this evolution could be seen in its relics in modern times – in the 'primitives' and 'savages' that Empire existed to colonise, who, frozen in time, contrasted starkly with the life of the mind practised by the scholars of the great European universities.

Ideas such as these were in the air as A.B. Cook wrote what is still the single most monumental book on Zeus, in three heavy, diffuse volumes. He wrote the preface to the first volume on 22 July 1914, around three weeks after the assassination of the Archduke Ferdinand and within days of the outbreak of the First World War. So it was that Cook originally looked for 'The European Sky God' (Cook 1914: i.xii) until he was advised by Farnell in Oxford that 'the unity of an ancient god consisted less in his nature than in his name' (ibid.: i.xii), thus privileging study of the history of words. This did not, however, stop Cook from tracing 'the evolution of Zeus from Sky to Sky-God' and seeking 'to determine the relations in which he stood to the solar, lunar, and stellar cults of the Mediterranean basin' (ibid.: i.xiii).

So, Cook's Zeus, as a person, an anthropomorphic god, was the product of a three-stage evolution 'in which the feelings, the will, and the intellect played successively the principal part' (ibid.: i.13f.):

1. *feelings*: 'the awe felt by early man as he regarded the live azure [Cook means the sky] above him';
2. *expression of will* 'when the community was parched with drought and the magician by his own passionate self-projection made the rushing rain-storm to satisfy the thirst of man and beast';
3. *the work of intellect*, 'expressing heaven in terms of earth', and leading to 'the clear-cut form and fashion of the weather-ruling king'.

This vision of man's progress is presented as a modification of the formula which Frazer had recently used in the second edition of his colossal *Golden Bough* in struggling to give belated sense to the mountains of evidence he had collected, tracing an evolution in man's dependence from magic to religion to science. Rather contrary to Frazer's ideas was the sense which prevailed in a religious country such as England then was that Christianity was itself the destined outcome of the evolution of the religious mentality. This appears very frequently, usually in suppressed form, in classical scholarship and it can be seen at work in Cook's belief that this evolution of Zeus led to 'nothing less than the rise of faith in a personal God, the Ruler and Father of all' (1914: i.9). Faith and personal gods had nothing to do with Greek religion, but a lot to do with Christianity.

Gathering the facts – the empirical approach

Cook had probably not understood Farnell's advice very well. Farnell, back in 1896, had published the first volume of *The Cults of the Greek States*, including chapters on Zeus. His approach was generally much more factual and much less speculative than Cook's – which is one reason why, over a century later, these volumes are still useful. 'The main scope', he wrote, 'of the present work is not the question of origin, but a survey of the most important texts and monuments that express the actual religious conceptions of the various Greek communities at different historical epochs' (1896: i.1). He collected data more than he theorised, though the categories into which the data falls do give something away. He explicitly rejected the theoretical basis on which other scholars were working, namely 'the view that the myths are allegorical accounts of physical phenomena, and the mythic figures are the personification of the elements and the powers of nature' (ibid.: i.3), because, 'as applied to the origins of Greek religion and the explanation of its development, the theory has produced only inconsequence and confusion'.

Even Farnell, however, was not immune to the evolutionary environment of those times: 'we can distinguish the more primitive from the more advanced stages of the cult, if we accept the most probable hypothesis that the physical aspect of the god is the earlier, and that the savage character which is preserved in cults and myths is prior to the more moral and spiritual' (ibid.: i.36).

Viewed from a different perspective, Farnell can be seen as part of a long-drawn movement away from myth towards ritual and cult practice. This reflects the characteristic evidence of scholars: we move from a world where the prime material was creative literature

– prose or poetry, read by people who were sensitive to it – away to a different world where the prime material was found by archaeologists, ethnologists and those who, in effect, quarried in literature. This tendency is already apparent in the privileging of folk practices in Mannhardt's *Wald- und Feldkulte* ('Rituals of Wood and Field', 1st edn 1875/7).[2] Similarly Frazer, in his *Golden Bough* (1st edn 1890), is initially heavily dependant on Mannhardt but progressively he embroiders his work with the spurious evolutionary patterning which we have seen above. But it reached definitive expression in the replacement of the standard volumes on Greek religion in the German *Handbuch der Altertumswissenschaft* ('Handbook of Antiquity'), which Otto Gruppe had written under the title *Griechische Mythologie und Religionsgeschichte* ('History of Greek Religion and Mythology', 1906), by Martin Nilsson's more conservative and empirical *Geschichte der griechischen Religion* ('History of Greek Religion', 1st edn, i. 1941, ii. 1950). Cult and the facts about cult were now what mattered above all. Mythology was a distraction which could not be scientifically related to the real facts of cult.

Specialism and the art of interpretation

As the mountain of data grows, it becomes harder and harder to get a clear idea of Zeus, particularly if one must now abandon Victorian ideas like nature and evolution as a means of patterning the information. Already when reading Cook, reviewers thought it was hard to see the forest for the trees, though Cook was quite insistent on Zeus the Sky God leading men's thought on the upward path of religious evolution.

One antidote to the data mountain is to write studies that look at some particular aspect of Zeus. To mention a few examples: in 1931, a pupil of Nilsson's, H. Sjövall, wrote a book, *Zeus im altgriechischen Hauskult*, on Zeus in household cult; in 1981, H. Verbruggen did a study of Zeus in Crete, *Le Zeus crétois*; and in 1990 K.W. Arafat looked at Zeus on Athenian red-figure vases.[3] But we learn more about the god and the Greek thought-world from the splendidly trenchant and faithfully grim volume of Hugh Lloyd-Jones on *The Justice of Zeus* (1971).

At another extreme, critical and scientific standards in the humanities have led to the creation of huge databanks. The encyclopedia to end all encyclopedias is the revision of A. Pauly's *Realencyclopaedie der Altertumswissenschaft* (in a mere six volumes by 1866), begun in 1894 by G. Wissowa and completed in 1980 (in 85 volumes). One part of Schwabl's splendid entry on Zeus appeared in 1972, listing every epithet and appellation, and the other in 1978, presenting a huge survey of the evidence in literature and art. In a comparable encyclopedic vein are the articles in the *Lexicon Iconographicum Mythologiae Classicae* on Zeus (in vol. 8, 1997) that collect and classify every single instance of Zeus's representation in Greek, Etruscan, Roman and more marginal art. This work has been fundamental in helping us to find our way around heroes and gods in ancient art, and, like Farnell, it will be lastingly useful because it gives us the facts as straight as it can.

It is much rarer to try to grasp the essence of the god that underlies these manifestations. Something like this was attempted by C. Kerényi in his *Zeus and Hera: archetypal image of father, husband and wife* (1976 – the German original dates from 1972). Kerényi, who at times worked closely with C.J. Jung, looked for the psychological wellsprings of Zeus and Hera and the way in which the archetypes deep within human nature condition the creation of myth and indeed all our ideas. It would have been an impressive approach if it had worked.

A different story begins with W.F. Otto, who wrote enthused books crystallising the distinctive nature of various Greek gods, giving the impression he even believed in them. Though he seemed idiosyncratic in the 1930s, his work has been a lasting inspiration for those who want to look beneath the surface and understand the credibility, and raw power, of Greek gods. Through his occasional scattered comments on Zeus in *The Homeric Gods: the spiritual significance of Greek religion* (1929, English translation 1954) we gain an inkling of Zeus's transcendent, all-encompassing, indescribable power. This points the way towards two final scholars.

J.-P. Vernant has not written a book on Zeus, but he has helped us to understand the god and the system of Greek religion. He has sought to detect the underlying patterns of thought that gain expression in mythology and religion, such as that of Zeus. Characteristically he has taken a particular interest in the thoughtful mythmaking of Hesiod (around 700 BC). Here we find ourselves looking at the special intelligence of Zeus, his *metis*, at his consequent relationship to Athene, the goddess of wisdom who springs from his head, and at Prometheus who challenges his world order by empowering man through the gift of fire. Vernant has also emphasised how gods such as Zeus offer ways of categorising and dividing up the world. If he is closely associated with the sky, its lightness and its darkness, then that is because it is a vehicle by which his special overwhelming power becomes apparent to us. What matters is not that he is a sky god but that he is a particular type of power (Vernant 1982: 95).

Books on Greek religion usually include a (not always insightful) chapter on Zeus. But one work has proved definitive in modern times and speaks for a generation: Walter Burkert's *Greek Religion: archaic and classical* (1985, first published in German in 1977). Sheer power and supremacy – a vision so close to Otto's and Vernant's – drive Burkert's Zeus forward through every manifestation: 'all sovereignty among men proceeds from Zeus . . . Zeus stands above all faction . . . Zeus is therefore uniquely qualified to be the god of all Greeks . . . Zeus was the only god who could become an all-embracing god of the universe . . . (and for the philosophers) Zeus is the world as a whole' (Burkert 1985: 130 f.).

Unity in diversity. This is what we must now wrestle with as in a new millennium we try once more to form a portrait of the whole god and see how he has remained a force to bargain with even in modern times. He has many, widely differing manifestations. But he is not a miscellany. There is one Zeus.

OVERVIEW: FIRST IMPRESSIONS OF ZEUS

As we begin, we are faced with the following questions:

- Can we learn the nature of Zeus from the origins of his name? If not, is he only a miscellaneous product of historical accident?
- Did religious perceptions evolve from primitive awe at nature to envisaging 'the clear-cut form and fashion of the weather-ruling

king'? But if they did not, how can he embrace both a personal and an impersonal world?

- Did Zeus evolve from a god in physical shape to something higher, and did Greeks advance from primitive cults and myths to 'the more moral and spiritual'? But can a 'higher' god not be envisaged in a physical shape?
- Should we set aside all this myth and nature material and look instead at his worship in all its diversity, for instance collecting and sorting his cult names? But what conclusions will we reach and how can the mythology be irrelevant to Greek religion?
- Have we now passed the point where we can, or would wish to, reach a deeper understanding of Zeus? Or can we still grasp him through the psychology underlying how he is depicted, or through some intuitive grasp of his transcendent power?

A final word on some of these competing ideas. First, cult. If you want to say that any one aspect of Zeus is more important than the others, maybe you should indeed choose the cult. The cult is what Greeks did, both privately and publicly. It is how they performed Zeus and how they dramatised their relationship to this awesome power. Without the cult, they would have a Zeus no different from ours. But at the same time, the cult is part of a larger text: it speaks a ritual language and draws together occasions and needs, but there are other languages. One is the language of myth and of poetry. Another is the language of sculpture and painting that surrounded Greeks in their day-to-day lives. Yet another is the language of philosophy, which wrestled with the language of myth and poetry and finally reached an understanding through allegory, because they needed to make sense of the traditional myths and of the poets whom they rightly valued. Alongside this is the lost language of ordinary people, who will have picked up elements of these other languages, absorbed the art and watched the ritual and often performed it. As we can see from fragments of their language, they will have talked piously of the 'rain of Zeus' and would vigorously have cursed by him. All these ideas and performances swirled round the Greeks as they worshipped Zeus, and gave a depth of meaning to their activity.

Second, the division of Zeus. A key to understanding Zeus is that he is at once a weather god, that is a god who looks after a particular function in nature, and the ultimate god, who is cause of everything. This is entirely intelligible and widely paralleled, because the sky from which weather comes is, quite simply, above us and everywhere. There is no need to trace an evolution from a weather god to a supreme god – all that does is to work out the logical connections between the two (which we do below in 'Zeus from Weather to Fate'), or worse to separate out the constituent elements of his supremacy. The images of the thunderbolt and sceptre do all the work that is necessary to hold these two aspects together.

Third, Zeus is also *part of a system*[4] at any one time: he relates to all other ideas and pictures that people have about their lives and to all the other gods. It is from the totality of gods, not just from one of them, that we develop a science or theology of the universe. Zeus, however, underpins that system and in a sense is the only god that is totally indispensable. His character is therefore special: he is remote, invisible and inscrutable. Greek pagans were religious too.

KEY THEMES

I

ENVISAGING ZEUS

You recognise gods by their attributes. In the case of Zeus this means above all the thunderbolt that he wields, causing the flash of lightning, the sound of thunder and the impact as it strikes. Lightning can be recognised in art by its double lotus shape (see figs 5, 6, 8). This is based originally on Near-Eastern art, which had depicted a fork of lightning – sometimes doubled. But it was imported into Greece as part of a repertoire of ornamental motifs and in the process was beautifully transmuted into a double lotus flower. Zeus is already holding the thunderbolt in Homer's *Iliad*:

> Then it was that the father of men and gods
> was seated upon the peaks of Ida with its springs
> having come down from the sky; and he was holding the
>   lightning in his hands.

Iliad 11.182–4

Sitting down is not a matter of convenience but one of status: it is majestic to sit, and both gods and kings sit on a *thronos*, a chair indicating their status. Around 650 BC Homer conjured up a vivid picture of Zeus enthroned with thunderbolt and thus foreshadowed the development of Western art. He captured the spirit of Zeus in a way that set an agenda for sculptors, who by the nature of their art must wrestle with freeze-frame moments. This was the Zeus that dominated the centre of the east pediment of the Parthenon.

Another distinctive thing about Homer's Zeus is that he is *aigiochos*, which later Greeks thought meant 'he who holds the *aigis*', where the *aigis* (*aegis*) is a shield made with goatskin. It is not exactly clear why he should have this attribute in particular – and indeed the word should strictly mean 'riding a goat'![1] Nevertheless, this goatskin shield is good for raising storms (some writers even use *aigis* to mean storms):

> Then Kronos' son took the *aigis* with its tassels,
> sparkling, and covered Ida over with clouds
> and, flashing lightning, he thundered mightily and shook it,
> and gave victory to the Trojans and routed the Achaeans.

Homer, *Iliad* 17.593–6

There seems to be a sort of shake of the tambourine to this *aigis*, and certainly the *aigis* Athene is carrying at *Iliad* 2.448 has a hundred solid gold tassels. When Zeus is associated with animal skins, it is usually sheep- or ramskin: the *Dios kodion*, 'Zeus's fleece', was an important part of the apparatus for purification, for instance in initiation into the Eleusinian Mysteries.[2] The Golden Fleece too belonged to a ram sacrificed to Zeus and is connected with the cult of Zeus Laphystios at Halos (Thessaly). And at the time of the rising of the Dog Star, Thessalian noblemen and their sons used to go dressed in fresh ramskins to the peak of Mt Pelion – to the cave of Cheiron the Centaur and the shrine of Zeus Akraios. Perhaps in other cults, in days gone by, goats had been his cult animals. And maybe waving goatskins, not so different from clouds in appearance, had some place in the rain magic of days gone by.

In art, the earliest surviving Zeus of which we can be certain is a decorative figure on a pithos lid (LIMC 12) of around 700 BC, recognised as Zeus because of a bird in the left hand and a thunderbolt in the right. Although this is, in effect, from the time of Homer, this was perhaps not yet the standard depiction. At what became a key site, Olympia, the earlier statuettes manufactured for dedication to Zeus seem to depict a warrior god rather than the lightning god.[3] This is what we might expect of a society in the unstable times of the eighth and seventh centuries BC, just like the corresponding god, *Tiwaz, became a warrior god in unsettled Germanic cultures.

The standard Zeus results from a particular reading of the warrior god: he is increasingly seen as a wielder of lightning thanks to the

Figure 2 Zeus Keraunios. 11-cm bronze statuette of c. 480 BC, reproduced at approximately life size (National Archaeological Museum, Athens).

international (or at least inter-state) influence of epic poets with their theogonies, titanomachies and heroic poems like the *Iliad* – tales of gods being born, older gods being subdued and mortals dying. Beginning around 600 BC and going well into the fifth century, we repeatedly see the *Zeus Keraunios*, 'Zeus of the thunderbolt', especially in those 10–20-cm statuettes left by the devout at Olympia as testimony to their beliefs: here (fig. 2) Zeus strides, his right hand ready to hurl the thunderbolt (a mortal would be holding a spear), whilst his eagle perches on his left hand, an icon of supremacy in the skies. This is Zeus captured in action.

If not in action, Zeus may sit majestically on a *thronos*. *Zeus enthroned* is already in Homer and was soon established as an artistic type, though we must wait for the sixth century BC for undeniable depictions of this motif, when he can be seen on three clearly related black-figure cups from Laconia (fig. 3) where, dressed in a highly patterned robe, and wearing long hair and beard, his eagle swoops in to meet him.

Figure 3 Zeus enthroned. Laconian cup from Italy, c. 560 BC (Louvre).

We learn for instance from Pausanias that the oldest bronze statue was from the early sixth-century BC; it depicted Zeus Hypatos ('Highest') at Sparta and was made of hammered bronze plates fitted together with nails (Pausanias 3.17.6, 8.14.7; LIMC 55). What survives is obviously the tip of an iceberg. The great statues, particularly the imposing ones of Zeus enthroned, are all lost, though occasionally we pick up echoes and impressions of them on coins or through Roman reproductions.

Figure 4 Zeus enthroned. Drawings reconstructing Pheidias' statue of Zeus at Olympia: with the Nike (left) life-size (drawing of F. Adler), and (right) three times life-size (drawing of W. Schiering).

The masterpiece was Pheidias' colossal statue for the temple at Olympia (fig. 4; LIMC 89). He even included a depiction of his boy-friend, Pantarkes, and wrote 'Pantarkes is beautiful' on a finger of the statue, so it is said.[4] This gives us the rough date of the statue because we know that Pantarkes won the boys' wrestling in 436 BC. The statue comes vividly to life in Pausanias's description:

> The god is sitting on a throne made of gold and ivory. A garland lies on his head, in the form of olive shoots. In his right hand he carries (a statuette of) Victory, itself too of gold and ivory, with a ribbon and a garland on the head. In the left hand of the god there is a sceptre, richly decorated with every sort of metal; and the bird sitting on the sceptre is the eagle. The god's sandals too are of gold and the robe likewise. On the robe there are embroidered animal figures and flowers, lilies. The throne is decorated with gods and precious stones, and also with ebony and ivory. And there are depictions of animals painted on it and figures worked in it. There are four Victories in the form of dancers at each foot of the throne, and two further at the base of each foot . . .

Pausanias, Tour of Greece 5.11.1f.

With this sensational sculpture the Homeric image reaches classical fulfilment and according to the story, which I believe, Pheidias actually took Homer's poetry as his model (Dio Chrysostom 12.25). Now the lightning bolt is replaced in the Zeus-enthroned genre by the goddess Nike (Victory), whose proportions, unfortunately, we do not know. This is a modernising change, resting on a more anthropomorphic rendering of Zeus's supremacy. The goddess Nike is somehow more sophisticated than a thunderbolt and more suited to this static pose.

Thunderbolt, eagle, sceptre and now Nike – these are the attributes of Zeus by the fourth century BC. Sometimes too he holds a shallow libation-dish (*phiale*) reflecting the worship that he himself received in domestic cult. He is now more normally 'statuesque' in modern terms, and less a thunderbolt-hurler except on some coins. He has almost become more serious, in the wake of Pheidias' classical and human conception and the philosophers' demands.

Against this background, the Zeuses of the late fourth-century BC sculptor Lysippos sought atmosphere through archaism. The colossal bronze Zeus in the agora (central marketplace) at Tarentum (LIMC 224),[5] an unprecedented 40 cubits high (around 17 m), deliberately echoed those nude, striding, thunderbolt-hurling archaic statues, but presented more decorum with its *himation* (cloak) and an eagle on a column to provide both literal and metaphorical stability (LIMC 8.1, p. 344). The statues he made for the *agorai* (shopping centres) at Argos and Sikyon, however, seem from imitations on coins to have been good old-fashioned heroic nudes and the one for Megara even depicted thunderbolt-hurling.

OVERVIEW

This then is Zeus when he is depicted on his own and when he is the exclusive focus of contemplation. The image projects his power: standing to wield the thunderbolt, or seated in majesty, this is the most powerful of all the gods. In an anthropomorphic religion he had been clearly envisaged as far back as Homer. This stabilises in the art, with its insistence on regular attributes – the lightning, the eagle. But since the statue of Pheidias gave new life to Homer's portrait, his iconography has changed for ever. Every later portrayal has Pheidias' Zeus in mind.

2

ZEUS'S RELATIONSHIPS WITH GODS AND MORTALS

ZEUS IN THE BRONZE AGE

Zeus is a special god. He may in fact be the only god to have survived from Indo-European times, when there must have been a polytheistic range of gods, a pantheon, just as there was in the Greece we know. In the 3,000 or so years in between, they had been modernised, replaced, updated. It is in the millennium before classical Greece, in the Late Bronze Age ('Mycenaean' Greece), that Zeus first comes into sight.

Amongst the earliest evidence is a tablet found at the Mycenaean palace at Pylos written in the 'Linear B' script perhaps around 1200 BC.[6] It seems to say something like this:

> <something about> the Diwion [Zeus-shrine] and bring gifts and lead the porena
> to Zeus 1 gold vessel, 1 man; to Hera 1 gold vessel, 1 woman; to Drimios [we don't
> know who he is] Son of Zeus 1 gold vessel, 1 <man?>

The *porena* must be gifts that walk – that's why they are *led*, not *brought*. They look like the man and woman – are they even human sacrifices?[7] The Diwion of Pylos (assuming it is the same one in each case) is a familiar part of this world, featuring on two other tablets, where Zeus receives gifts of around a litre of olive oil and possibly some clothing (Hiller 1978: 1004). We have no idea whether this is a palace shrine, some open-air place or something more ambitious (though that would be very unusual as far as we can tell from the archaeology).

There appears to be some sort of priest or attendant too at Pylos – the *Diwieus*. Already Hera appears in close association with Zeus, though there is also a goddess Diwia, who appears to have a priestess, the *Diwieia*.

Meanwhile at Knossos, a tablet (Knossos Fp1) tells us about an offering of oil to Zeus Diktaios ('of Mt Dikte'). His name must have been applied to a being already worshipped in a pre-existing shrine on Mt Dikte with the result that another variation entered the system of Greek religion. The sending of offerings 'to (Mt) Dikte' conjures up long processions of Greek-speaking peoples in the later second millennium BC. Grain and oil appear to be the usual gifts for Zeus, whether Diktaian or not. A month, *Diwios*, is named after him, which survives in the month *Dios* of later Macedonia, Aetolia and Thessaly; and this must mean that his festival, evidently the *Diwia*, took place at that time of the year.

So already we have many elements that will be familiar later: the god Zeus; an epithet associating him with a place, a mountain; a month, and therefore probably a festival; a precinct or special place, the Diwion; a priest; probably a consort (whether Hera or Diwia) and apparently a son, implying a mythology of a divine family. The son of Zeus has echoes in mainstream Greek tradition. The name of the god 'Dionysos' looks as though it must, one way or another, once have meant 'son of Zeus'.[8] And the 'Dios-kouroi' (Dioscuri) are certainly 'Zeus's sons': their place in an Indo-European god-system as twin horsemen is assured by their parallel in Sanskrit literature, the twin Aśvins – who are amongst the offspring of the primal god of begetting, *Prajāpati* (this is in the ancient epic, the *Mahābhārata* 1.30–2).[9]

FATHER, BROTHER, HUSBAND

The function that has above all preserved Zeus since Indo-European times is that of *father*, the function which is enshrined particularly in the 'vocative case', the form of the word used when addressing the god, as one must:

Zeu pater [Zeus father] . . .

Iliad 1.503 etc. – nine times in Homer's two epics

O father of ours, Kronides [son of Kronos], highest of rulers . . .

Athene speaking, *Iliad* 8.31

Zeus father, ruling from [Mt] Ida, most glorious, most great . . .

Iliad 3.276

Zeus father who is lord over men and immortals . . .

Odyssey 20.112.

These examples are from the epic but they run through Greek literature and life – as when we find written on a vase at the end of the 6th century BC, 'O Zeus father, may I become rich.'[10] This form of address also appears in Latin: when he does something or you address him he is *Iuppiter* (Jupiter, 'Jove-father'); but when he plays a less significant role in the sentence, he is merely *Iovem* (Jove). Jupiter rules over gods and men; we worship Jove.

If he is 'father', that is not just a pleasing aspect of family life and it does not make him into some creator god on the Judaeo-Christian model – that came later. He is father because he has unquestioned authority over the family of gods, and over a sort of extended household made up of both gods and men (Lloyd-Jones 1971: 33). It is in a way proof of this that he is in fact, as we will see below, father of some gods and father of some men, notably those at the beginnings of nations. But of course he is the brother, surprisingly the youngest, of Poseidon, Hades, Demeter and of his wife Hera.

If he is a head of household, that means he has a wife as well as children. At Dodona his wife must have been Dione, a name containing the root of his own name (*Di-*), a sort of 'Zeus-ona' and rather reminiscent of the Roman *Diana*. But, maybe because of the fusion of the religion and culture of the Zeus-worshippers as they arrived in Greece with those of the peoples who already lived there, the usual wife is Hera. One may wonder why he marries his sister. Brother–sister marriages happened amongst the pharaohs of Egypt. Did Late Bronze Age Greek royalty behave like this too? Or is the myth itself borrowed from somewhere like Egypt? Perhaps it is just that a marriage so early in the genealogy of the gods tends to be incestuous, and Kerényi (1976: 112) is right: 'the theme serves to play a cosmogonic part as the procreative union of a "first couple"'.

The idea of a primal marriage is more than myth – it has an important role in cult. In Nauplion there was a spring, Kanathos:

Here the people of Argos say that Hera, when she is washed yearly, becomes a virgin. This is from the Rite which they conduct for Hera and is one of the secrets.

Pausanias 2.38.2f.

Thus the magic of cult brings us back to the starting point for a theogony, or for a marriage, and the marriage of Zeus and Hera is a way of restarting the clock. It is what we refer to as a *hieros gamos*, a 'sacred marriage' which can be ritually enacted.

There were many locations in Greece where this marriage of Zeus and Hera was supposed to have taken place.[11] A striking instance, where we know something of the festival surrounding it is in Boeotia. Here Plataea celebrated the Daidala in every sixth year and Boeotia as a whole celebrated the Great Daidala in every fifty-ninth year. Festivals which occur at such lengthy intervals, in both Greek and other Indo-European cultures, take on the character of festivals of renewal, where society makes a new start and in extreme cases the world may seem to begin again. In the case of the Daidala this sexual act and marriage takes place on Mt Kithairon, next to Plataea, on the border with Attica, and that is how Hera comes to be called Hera Gamelia ('of the rites of marriage') and Hera Teleia. The adjective *teleios* refers to the completion of the transition from betrothal to marriage and the completion of adulthood through marriage.[12] At the Daidala, however, Hera's favours have to be won. According to the 'aetiological' (explanatory) myth, Hera had fallen out with Zeus, and Zeus did not know what to do. A local hero now advised him: either Kithairon, who is the person that exists in myth to have Mt Kithairon named after him, the 'eponym' of Mt Kithairon, or Alalkomeneus, the eponym of Alalkomenai, further away in Boeotia, a wily first man. Following this advice, he dresses up a wooden statue, calls it Daidale (*daidala*, Pausanias says, is what they used to call *xoana* – wooden statues – in ancient times), and lets it be known that he is going to marry this Daidale. Hera then arrives in rage and jealousy, but discovers the truth, thinks it a great joke, is reconciled with Zeus and herself goes through the marriage with him.[13] So there is a festival with a procession leading a wooden statue of Hera from the town of Plataea up Mt Kithairon, where the *hieros gamos* is to take place. And it is to achieve this that Zeus's marriage to Hera must constantly be undone – in order to be renewed.

Pausanias's Daidale story looks as though it owes a lot to Homer's picture of Zeus's stormy relationship with Hera. But it may be the other way round. Homer's picture is an odd one until we realise that it is this need in cult to prepare for a new marriage that drives the portrayal of the marriage as practically broken down. Homer preserves the cult dynamics quite faithfully: rage and jealousy in *Iliad* 1, wiped out for the time being by the *hieros gamos* on Mt Ida in Book 14. But the trickery in this case is of course Hera's, not Zeus's.

Real marriages in Athens often happened in the month of Gamelion (around February), the month of the Wedding Festival, the Gamelia. This involved prayers and offerings to Zeus Teleios and Hera Teleia whose *hieros gamos* was celebrated in the Theogamia on the 27th of the month and served to model and complete the marriage now to be enacted on earth.[14] A scatter of evidence suggests, as Kerényi observes, that mortal participants somehow sanctified their own marriages in this process and made them special, as sacred as that of the gods.

ZEUS BORN AND DYING

The birth of Zeus is not a moment of key significance as it is, say, for Jesus Christ. He is primarily there to rule and to order the world, not to have an exemplary biography. If we have stories of his birth that is because there has been a merger between the god Zeus and a divine child god, offspring of a 'Great Mother', who was there long before Zeus. However, the importance attributed to the divine child by local cults, and the pivotal role of the mountain in both cults, must have been such as to compel them to fasten their myth to Zeus.

So it is that Zeus is born in Arcadia to Rhea: in a rather tortured myth, she is at a cave at the peak of Mt Thaumasion ('wonderful') as she is *about* to give birth and at Mt Lykaion where she *does* give birth.[15]

That neatly mops up two cult sites with evidently inconsistent claims. But of course both are wrong, because the successful cult place in this competition was in Crete and he can then be proudly proclaimed Zeus *Kretagenes* ('Crete-born'). Thus in Hesiod she gets sent to Lyktos (Lyttos) in Crete with its cave, almost certainly the one above Psychro, where Zeus of Dikte may have been worshipped in early times. But this site died out around 500 BC and the most influential association was with Mt Dikte itself, not the modern Mt Dikte placed by modern mythmakers near the cave at Psychro, but the real one known to ancient geographers in the far east of the island in the territory of Praisos – which also included the shrine of Zeus Diktaios at the site known today as Palaikastro. Dikte sounds like *tiktei* ('gives birth to') and the myth tells that in a cave on Mt Dikte the infant Zeus's cries were drowned out by the noisy weapon-clanging dance of the Kouretes,[16] evidently reflecting in myth a ritual dance of warrior youth whose initiation practices were typically associated with caves. Thus a number of cult ingredients – song, dance, youths, mother goddess come together and come into focus as a colourful myth almost para-doxically recounting the infancy of the father of gods and men, the king of the immortals. The only problem is that the caves in the east of the island do not seem to have been cult places – that element has come from Mt Ida in the centre of the island, or indeed from Psychro.[17]

As stories from different sites amalgamate, a rich and inconsistent mythology is formed. Zeus was perhaps suckled by a goat, who acquired the name of 'Amaltheia', and Zenobius in the second century

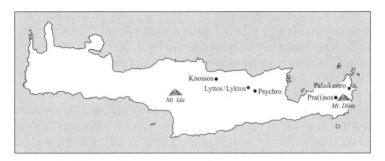

Map 2   Crete: Zeus's myth and cult

AD said Zeus set her amongst the constellations. At Praisos they believed it was a sow that protected Zeus by grunting a lot and indeed they sacrificed to it. Another story tells of bees in a cave that no one may enter; once a year a brilliant light shines out from the cave as the 'blood of Zeus' from his birth boils over; here live 'holy bees, nurses of Zeus' on whose honey Zeus fed. The Holy Bees might just be a title of priestesses of some sort in a cult where Zeus is born anew every year. But the liveliest surviving evidence is an actual cult hymn found in the temple of Zeus Diktaios at Palaikastro. Colourfully christened the *Hymn of the Kouretes* by modern authors, it is in fact an energetic hymn summoning Zeus to give fertility and prosperity to the land and people. Its theology is quite quirky:

> Yo!
> Greatest Youth [*Kouros*], I say hail!,
> Son of Kronos, all-powerful joy,
> Come!
> Leading the *daimones* ['spirits', mini-gods]
> To Dikte annually make your way and
> rejoice in the song
> that we weave with the lyre
> and mix with flutes
> and standing we sing around your
> well-bounded altar
> Yo! [etc.]
>
> *Hymn of the Kouretes* 1–12

One may guess that this hymn to the 'Greatest Youth', with his troupe of demons, was in fact still performed in the third century AD, the date of this inscription, by youths in the territory of Praisos as an event in local folk culture.[18]

There was a parallel cult at the Cretan Mt Ida, a wooded mountain – which is what (*w*)*ida* means. It is confused with Dikte by Alexandrian authors who had never been there.[19] Apollonius of Rhodes talks of a '*Diktaios* grotto' (1.509, 1130) and an '*Idaios* cave' (3.134) as though they were the same thing, namely a 'Cretan cave' (2.1233). So mythology struggled and it was left to Diodorus (5.70) or his sources to tidy this up: Zeus was *born* in the cave at Dikte *but brought up* in the cave on Ida (Nilsson 1967: i.320 n.3). Certainly the latter had an increasing influence and in Lyttos too Zeus could be referred to as *Widatas* ('of Ida').

Greek paganism was fairly open and tolerant. It had trouble, however, with the concept of gods dying, as gods are by definition immortal. This only happens in marginal and strange cases. Adonis, if a god, dies. In a story of Plutarch's (*Decline of Oracles* 419b–d), travellers in Egypt were told 'great Pan is dead'. Ares and Aphrodite are wounded by Diomedes in *Iliad* 5 in a supreme act of exaggeration by Homer, telling too how once Ares had nearly died (5.388). But it was another thing to have a tomb of Zeus, whose location, like the birthplace, varies between Dikte and Ida. That just shows Cretans were liars (Callimachus, *Hymn* 1.8). But it also shows very clearly how local cults introduce variant and inconsistent elements into the portrait of a Greek god; indeed the portrait of a Greek god is formed in the first place by the accretion over centuries of different characteristics and stories. If the god is born every year he will need to die too.

TITANOMACHY, TYPHON, GIGANTOMACHY

Zeus's control of the order of the universe is underlined by stories which involve establishing that order or defeating onslaughts on it. This sort of story is found first in our surviving literature, in Hesiod, who may be described as an 'orientalising' author, refreshing Greek mythology with quite a lot of Near-Eastern material – and this seems to be where these stories originated.

In the beginning were Heaven and Earth (Ouranos and Gaia). They beget the one-eyed Cyclopes and a series of persons known collectively as the Titans, including Kronos. Kronos castrates Ouranos and a new régime is born. Kronos then eats his children until a stone is substituted for Zeus (the stone was still on display at Delphi in the second century AD). Zeus recovered his brothers and sisters whom Kronos had swallowed and in a great battle – the Titanomachy – defeats the old régime. His crucial weapon in this battle, the thunderbolt, is made by the Cyclopes, which gives him the firepower for victory and an emblem of that victory. This is described in Hesiod (*Theogony* 617–731) and had been described in the *Titanomachy* of Eumelos of Corinth, a lost poem of around 700 BC.

The battle with the Titans, as described by Hesiod, is passingly mighty: Zeus throws around plenty of lightning and thunder, the earth sizzles and the rivers and sea boil (*Theogony* 693–6). All that really matters is that the battle occurs and has an outcome, not the quality of the fighting and the plot over a rather standard ten years. The key part is played by his allies the Hundred-Handers (*Hekatoncheires*), Kottos, Briareos and Gyges. In Eumelos, it would seem, the sea monster Aegaeon-Briareos 'blazed fire from fifty upper bodies and clattered so many shields *against* the thunderbolts of Jove'.[20] This version is closer to the pattern of Near-Eastern myths like the myth from Ugarit (on the coast of what later became Syria), cited by West, in which Baal fights the seven-headed dragon Yammu (the sea).[21]

In any case, in the end most of the Titans are sent to Tartarus, apart from Hyperion the Sun, and others – mainly Titanesses including Leto, Themis and Mnemosyne. This must be the myth from which Homer gets Zeus's repeated threat to send other gods to Tartarus (Gantz 1993: 45). It is a supremely powerful and assertive thing to send someone to Tartarus and in time[22] there develops a word for it, *tartaroö*, or, more thoroughly, *katatartaroö* – '(utterly) to tartarise'.

Zeus's special enemy is Typh(a)on (Hesiod, *Theogony* 306), or Typhoeus (820–80 – the joints in Hesiod's text show rather badly). This monster shows up after the Titanomachy, embodying disorder and unintelligibility in his physique: 100 heads, which quite apart from other disagreeable aspects (snakiness), pour out a confusion of voices, between god-talk and bellowing bull (Hesiod, 831f.). Zeus needs all his strength to defeat him and finally to smite him down in some scorched place called Aidna. It was not long before this had transmuted to Mt Etna in Sicily, where the flames of Typhon appear awesomely through the volcano. The tale too was repatriated to the east in the Hellenistic Age, with its larger horizons. Now Typhon, who already in Pindar and Ps.-Aeschylus' *Prometheus Bound* had come from Cilicia, moved a little further to become the dragon of the holy mountain, once Mt Hazzi of the Hittites, by then Mt Kasios in Syria (which rose above where Ugarit had been). In this version Zeus had his sinews stolen by Typhon and, helpless, was finally rescued only by the intervention of Hermes and Goat-Pan (Aigipan), or in Nonnos' epic *Dionysiaka* (fifth century AD), Kadmos, founder of Thebes.

The Archaic Age, when this sort of poetry first flourished, was also the age of the hoplite – the heavily armed soldier who fought in formation with his fellows. As these men fought and died, sometimes the straps of their shields were decorated with metal bands of almost cartoon-strip scenes such as a hoplite might associate with. Found at Olympia where they were dedicated 2,500 years ago, several depict Zeus's battle with Typhon, the cosmic parallel for the hoplite's work (see fig. 5).

Figure 5 Zeus strikes Typhon, panels from shield-strap covers, sixth century BC (LIMC Typhon 17–18).

Titanomachies captured the imagination of Archaic Greece in poetry, but it was to *Gigantomachies* that sculpture tended to turn, battles against *Gigantes* (see fig. 6).

Gigantes are a race of beings, apparently men, not necessarily what we understand as 'giants', at least at first (rather like the mysterious *Nephilim* of *Genesis* 6.4, themselves translated as 'Gigantes' in the Greek Septuagint). No one really tells their story outright, though Herakles' role in it was known to the author of Ps-Hesiod *Catalogue of Women* (*fr.* 43a.65, sixth century BC). It is left for later authors[23] to piece together a story that the gods met the Gigantes in battle at Phlegra, a place in Thrace, out in the northern barbarous regions beyond Greece, off the map. To defeat them, the gods needed the assistance of two demigods, Herakles and Dionysos – playing the role of the helpers in the Typhon myth.

Figure 6 Zeus in battle against the Gigantes, calyx crater c. 450BC (Antikenmuseum, Basel).

You often see the Gigantomachy in the sculptural decoration of Archaic temples: the statement of the authority of the gods, made by the temple itself, is reinforced by the myth told upon it. It was everywhere in the sixth and fifth centuries BC (all dates approximate): the temple of Artemis at Corfu (early sixth century BC), the Treasury of the Siphnians at Delphi (525 BC), the west front of the 'Alcmeonid' temple of Apollo at Delphi (500 BC), an anonymous treasury at Delphi (early fifth century BC), the Treasury of the Megarians at Olympia (510 BC), the east pediment of the Archaic temple of Athene on the Acropolis at Athens (520 BC), probably other sites at Athens in the late sixth, metopes from various temples at Selinous in Sicily (first half of the fifth century BC), the Olympieion at Agrigento in the second quarter of the fifth, a frieze at Sounion on the temple of Poseidon (450 BC), of course the wonderful metopes of the Parthenon, and finally the metopes of the Heraion at Argos (410 BC). Or not quite finally, because the frieze of the great altar of Zeus at Pergamon in the early second century BC, superbly recalling canonical Archaic and classical sculpture, displayed a Gigantomachy on a grand baroque scale.

These, then, are stories that serve to lead up to the reign of Zeus and to praise him for his power. They establish the awesome and indisputable character that requires us to recognise him as the most important of the gods. This is a special mythic language, borrowed from the Near East, where people were comfortable with concepts of powerful and awesome kingship. In this sublimated form, however, the Greeks found Hesiodic orientalism to their taste and it matched their expectations of superbeings. Gods, and to an extent heroes, could exhibit extremes that humans in a civilised Greek world might shun. That was because they were greater and it went to constitute their greatness. Violent and unassailable power underpinned a higher order, the justice of Zeus.

THE SEXUAL ACTIVITY OF ZEUS

He was so addicted to sex that he lusted after all women and fulfilled his lust on all women.

Clement of Alexandria, *Exhortation to the Greeks* 2 (27 P.)

What is this Olympian palace to me? I will go to earth
and leave behind my father's *aither* and living
in our own Thrace I shall not see my mother grieving
in anguish, nor Zeus the marriage-spoiler!

Ares speaks in Nonnos, *Dionysiaka* 8.61–4

Zeus the adulterer

Zeus spends a lot of mythic time in adultery. You can think of this as a projection of male fantasies of what it would be like not to be constrained by society or morality. But there are other reasons that will become apparent when we sort these myths into categories. In so doing, I am aware that each myth has its interest and that we will have to skim very fast over them. We also need to bear in mind that Greeks told their myths in whatever way seemed useful for the purpose in hand. There was no Greek bible of myth, and details and precise names do on occasion vary. Zeus may not be the only, or even the usual, father of the offspring I attribute to him below – it is simply that someone in antiquity said he was and they had a reason.

Generally when a god has sex, the reader should bear in mind the words Homer makes Poseidon speak to Tyro after the event:

> Rejoice, woman, in (this) love; as the year comes round
> you will bear splendid children, since not in vain are the beds
> of the immortals . . .
>
> *Odyssey* 11.248–50[24]

In most myths the point of intercourse with a god is the offspring that results. (In the case of Tyro it is Neleus, the ancestral king of Pylos, whose particular cult of Poseidon is memorably described at the beginning of *Odyssey* 3.) Conversely, if someone wishes proudly to claim that some hero or tribe is descended from Zeus, another adultery will usually be added to his list. This is how family trees ('genealogies') work. It is nevertheless remarkable how few children Zeus has by Hera and how insignificant they are. Perhaps rape and seduction account better for the distribution of offspring across Greece. If this is so, we reach the important conclusion that Zeus the rapist and adulterer is actually a product of the needs of what one might term 'international' poetry as it came together in the allegedly 'Dark Age' (say, 1200–776 BC). This was in fact a formative age, which had to combine different local traditions for the growing and dynamically self-aware market all over the Greek world. As worlds grow, they struggle to accommodate the new and to recover their unity through various cultural expressions, including religion and mythology. In the Dark Age Zeus's adultery reflects the changes of gear as the traditions of one Greek society combine with those of another. In the Hellenistic and Roman Ages the scope of the Greek world would suddenly expand again and Zeus would have to become Baal and Jupiter (pp. 107–9).

The lack of legitimate offspring casts particular light on the *hieros gamos* ('sacred marriage') of Zeus and Hera. Evidently it is the act of marriage that is foregrounded, not the procreation of children. Greek mythology as it is known to us did not generally set up a Divine Triad or Holy Family, though there were parts of the Greek world where *Zeus,*

Hera and Dionysos were worshipped together, for instance on Lesbos. This of course reflects the structure we saw in the Late Bronze Age with Drimios son of Zeus (p. 28ff). The Romans, under Etruscan influence, picked up this sort of patterning too and set up a great temple to *Jupiter, Juno and Minerva* (Zeus, Hera and Athene), the so-called Capitoline Triad, on the Capitoline Hill in Rome, dedicated in '509 BC'. And it would rise again in Greece when a new version of Egyptian religion was invented in the third century BC for the Mediterranean market, focusing on *Isis, Osiris and Horos/Harpokrates* (mother, father and son). Christianity too would eventually pay attention to this model.

Zeus begetter of gods

In the case of gods we need to know the parents of each in order to place them, to understand them, almost to register them. If it matters to us who our families are, it matters much more to a traditional society. 'Theogony' is the account of the 'births of gods', as in the *Theogony* of Hesiod (around 700 BC). It is therefore a particular form of genealogy. To generate gods, you need a really important god as a father, and preferably divine mothers if a satisfactorily qualified god is to be the result; just as a citizen father and a citizen mother are required to make a citizen Athenian child.

Zeus begets Apollo and Artemis, Aphrodite, Ares, Athene, Dionysos, Hermes. In fact he begets all the Olympian gods[25] that are not his brothers and sisters – they are the children of Kronos (Hestia, Demeter, Hera, Hades, Poseidon). Genealogy makes the Olympian gods into a tightly knit system, a close group, a team: they are depicted as a specially close family. These gods as a matter of historical fact all had their separate origins, mostly lost to us, but visible in their differing traditional mothers. Zeus's official mythological wife, Hera, is usually the mother only of Ares in this group – and otherwise only of the minor goddesses Hebe ('youth/peak of condition' – she becomes Herakles' wife on Olympus) and Eileithyia (an ancient birth goddess). Dione, Zeus's consort from Dodona, is used as the mother of Aphrodite. Sometimes too she is the mother of Dionysos, though usually it is a mythological mortal, Semele. A mysterious Maia, a daughter of Atlas, is Hermes' mother, and Leto is the mother of Apollo and Artemis. The story of Athene, from Hesiod onwards, is that Zeus produced her on his own, out of his own head, because he had swallowed *Metis*, ('Intelligence', a personification more than a goddess).[26] This gives rise to some fine depictions on vases showing Hephaistos splitting his head open with an axe.

The *Theogony* of Hesiod is an unusually original and inventive poem, both in its original parts and in the parts that someone added as the poem circulated (line numbers over 900). Hephaistos may seem to be a son of Zeus and Hera in Homer's *Iliad*, but late in the *Theogony* (927) he is begotten by Hera without male assistance, presumably to account for his lameness. Aphrodite is Zeus's daughter in the *Iliad* (5.370 and 428), but Hesiod wants her born from the froth of Ouranos' genitals as they floated, severed, on the sea (*aphros* = 'froth', *Theogony* 191) and that is the version we all remember, with thanks to Botticelli.[27] Hesiod's Horai too are remodelled. In Athenian cult the Horai (Seasons) were Thallo and Karpo ('Vigorous-growth' and 'Fruitful'), but in *Theogony* 901–3, they press home a less seasonal message: these children of Zeus and *Themis* ('that which is religiously lawful') are Eunomia, Dike and Eirene – 'Law-and-order', 'Justice' and 'Peace' (West 1966: 406f.). This shows the danger of taking a text, particularly an influential one, as simply relaying 'Greek mythology' to us or just reading flat statements out of a handbook of mythology. Each text has its own agenda. It says something too that the Moirai (Fates) are the children of Zeus and Themis at *Theogony* 904: at 217, by the real Hesiod, they had been gloomy children of Night, like the baneful Keres ('Dooms'). Other Hesiodic abstract children of Zeus include the Charites ('Graces') and the Muses, daughters of Memory (*Mnemosyne*).

This approach leads to mystic writers, 'Orphics', who in the sixth and fifth centuries BC made Ananke (Necessity) the mother of Adrasteia (Inescapability), Rhea the mother of awesome Persephone, Queen of the Underworld, and Persephone herself mother of the dying god Dionysos Zagreus. The exotic mythologising of the Orphics formed a counterweight to the development of what we call philosophy, which rested on extending mythmaking to generate the same impressive weight of worldview. It will not surprise us that Zeus coupled with Rhea in snake-form.

In the mainstream not Rhea but Demeter bears Persephone to Zeus and she also bears Nemesis. Persephone is married to her uncle, Hades, a familiar pattern of marriage for instance in classical Athens.[28] Nemesis seems like an abstraction ('righteous anger', cf. below), but she also had long-standing cult as a real divinity at Rhamnous in Attica. It is right therefore for her to have an important mother.

Zeus also begets gloomier figures. Amazingly, he is the father of Tantalos and Tityos, two of the sinners who were powerful enough to offend the gods and be punished in Hades forever. He is also father to Hekate, a rather shadowy goddess who does not belong to the canonical set of 12 Olympians and is often just treated as a form of Artemis. However, she had a real enough cult in the right places for the famous proto-historian Hecataeus of Miletus to be named after her and for Hesiod to be interested in her. This outsider, some-times identified with Artemis, appropriately becomes the goddess of crossroads (a place of danger), the dead as they haunt this world, and witches. Lesser gods too may, to our surprise, have mattered enough to be born of Zeus: the rustic Pan or Goat-Pan (Aigipan), and the Dactyls ('Finger' gods) of Mt Ida in Crete or Phrygia, dwarfs numbering five or ten like fingers, who invented iron-working.

The Dioskouroi are, as we have seen, 'sons of Zeus'. He begets them by Leda and they have particular cult in Sparta, where to say *tō siō*, 'the (pair of) gods', is to name them. They are embedded in the pre-Dorian mythology as sons of the Spartan ruler Tyndareus. Here, however, Zeus, disguised as a swan, has sex with a married woman, Leda, and we can see that her marriage is not incidental but itself has a purpose. Mortal marriage is no obstacle to divine parentage, something which must take its origin ultimately from the pretensions of real royal genealogies – just as the Egyptian tradition led to the story that Zeus Ammon was the real father of Alexander the Great, rather than merely his father Philip. Boeotia too had its own version of the Dioskouroi, the twins Amphion and Zethus. It is therefore no coincidence that Zeus is their father too. It must also be said that once gods become plural they do tend to get confused with other plural sets. The Dioskouroi are found in cult as the 'Lords (*Anaktes* or *Anakes*) Dioskouroi', or just as

'Lords', and become interlaced with the Kabeiroi (or their alias, *The Great Gods*), the Kouretes (who danced in armour round the baby Zeus), and the Korybantes (also begotten by Zeus). Dioskouroi, Kouretes, Korybantes – all *youth* (*kouros/koros*) gods, projections of youths as a class in society, trainee warriors. This is worth thinking about when looking at Zeus and the phatries at Athens (p. 66).

Their sister Helen has a special position in Greek myth: 'though a huge number of demigods was begotten by Zeus', she is the only mortal *daughter* of Zeus (Isocrates, *Helen* 16). Her sister Clytaemestra was after all merely the daughter of the mortal Tyndareus, but Helen is the daughter of Zeus himself.[29] Helen is believed by some originally to have been a goddess, perhaps a tree goddess, Helen Dendritis ('of the tree') in Sparta. But if we turn aside from cult, she seems to have a long history: her functional counterpart in Sanskrit and other mythologies is a daughter of the Sun, existing to be captured and then to be recovered by her brothers, the twin youth gods.

Birth from Zeus is doubly important for inscribing foreign gods, such as Britomartis (an Artemis on Crete) or Velchanos (an old Cretan god sometimes alternatively made into Zeus Velchanos), into Greek mythology and culture. They gain a sort of cultural citizenship through genealogical adoption. Another son is Belus, obviously Baal, the 'Lord' god of the Phoenicians and Syrians. He becomes a son of Libya, presumably because of Carthage, a Phoenician colony. And if Zeus begets a Herakles by Asteria, he is really incorporating the birth of the Phoenician Herakles, Melqart, by the Phoenician goddess Astarte.

Zeus begetter of mortals

Turning now to mortals, many of Zeus's children exist for 'aetiological' reasons, to *explain the origins* of geography and nations. This usually works by creating eponyms, persons that exist in order that people and places may be *named after* them. These names may be obscure to us, but they mattered crucially for those who lived in these landscapes. I hope you will find map 1 on p. xxvi useful.

In northern Greece, his offspring included Thebe and Lokros, accounting for Thebes (Boeotia), and the Locrians (Locris). Thessaly was possibly the most important centre for Zeus-worship (that is why Olympus is on its borders) and specially exploited ancestry from Zeus: delightfully, his son Meliteus ('Honeyman'), was fed on honey by the bees, before founding Melite (Phthiotis). The Haemones (Pelasgiotis), the Magnesians and the Myrmidons (the tribe of the *Iliad*'s Patroclus) traced their ancestry back to sons of Zeus – Haemon, Magnes and Myrmidon. Their neighbours the Macedonians did the same with Macedon. In the northwest, his oracular site at Dodona (Epirus) goes back to his son Dodonaios, and the tribe that gave the Romans and us the name 'Greeks' goes back to his son Graikos. Down in *central Greece* we find a Megaros (who alone survives the Flood, in order to found Megara), and in the *Peloponnese* the ancestors of major tribes – Achaeus (Achaeans), Lakon (Laconians) and Arkas (Arcadians), and some cities and hamlets – Lakedaimon (Sparta, Laconia), Argos and a minor Olenos. The same language is used in Greek-settled Sicily to create Akragas (Agrigento) and to interpret the Palisci, who are Zeus's children by (Mt) Etna. Wherever Greeks went they used this language, accounting for Cretans, Thracians, Bithynians, Carians, Lydians and Dardanians – a tribe in the Balkans identified by epic tradition with the Trojans. But when we are talking about this sub-variety of Trojans, their leader is Aeneas, the son not of Zeus but of a mighty goddess of Asia Minor, brought into the Greek fold by being named as Aphrodite.

Even where the hero is not an eponym, he may nevertheless be a founding father or one who is a key figure in the mythic and cultural history of a place or region. Then too Zeus may be his father. So we can see from the *Iliad* that Sarpedon, the leader of the Lycians, matters dearly to Zeus. And Perseus too, son of Danae, may once have been a key figure in the mythology of Mycenae.

The colour of myth: golden rain and other stories

However, myths have a life of their own and in some cases the genealogical purposes cease to predominate and may even recede altogether. This is what leads to vibrant myths, important for literature, art and music from classical times to the present day, as we shall also see in the second part of this book.

Zeus gave up his affair with the sea nymph Thetis because the son was destined to be more powerful than the father. Thus Thetis married Peleus, and Achilles, the greatest of the Homeric heroes, was born. What is left behind is the soft spot that Zeus has for this daughter of Nereus, colouring her appeal in *Iliad* 1. In the fifth century BC that literary interest takes off, in Pindar and Aeschylus. In art Thetis offers less interesting opportunities, however, than the theme of his abduction of Europa from Sidon (Phoenicia). There, Zeus is transformed into a bull riding the waves with Europa on his back. This is a favourite scene from as early as 560 BC (LIMC Europe 22) up to the wall-paintings of Pompeii. It must have figured, too, in early poems such as the *Europeia* of Eumelos. This is a momentous myth because Europa's brother Kadmos must search for her and in the process transform his nationality from Phoenician to Greek (Euripides, *fr.* 819 Kannicht²) – in order to found Thebes. This myth therefore negotiates the boundaries between Europe (to which she gives her name) and Asia, between Greek identity and the identity of the Phoenicians, to whose mercantile supremacy the Greeks succeeded, travelling the seas for trade and discovery.

Io was a virgin priestess of Hera at her shrine near Argos until Zeus loved her. Then, whether through the wrath of the goddess or thanks to a failed attempt at concealment by Zeus, she is turned into a cow. Like many of Zeus's romantic themes this has no place in monumental or dedicatory sculptures; rather it takes off in fifth-century red-figure vases, just as tragedy is beginning and fuelling the already buoyant market for myth on pots. Zeus enthroned reaches out to poor Io, transformed into a cow, in a *kalpis* of around 470 (LIMC Io 11). On a *pelike* of around 440 it looks as though Zeus has met Io (horns and cow-ears mark her out) at a party (LIMC Io 62)! Around 330 BC there was a painting by Nicias – lost, like all the famous Greek paintings – where the effects of Zeus's actions were depicted but not Zeus himself. Nicias' painting then led to the frescoes of her at Pompeii, which we do have. A parallel case is Kallisto ('Prettiest'), a nymph in the company of Artemis until Zeus makes love to her. Unable to hide her pregnancy from the wrathful goddess, she is turned into a bear, shot and transformed into the Great Bear constellation in the sky – though not without somehow first giving birth to Arcas, the first Arcadian. Zeus is rare too in depictions of Kallisto, though there is a late third-century AD silver ladle that depicts him seducing Kallisto whilst disguised as Artemis (LIMC Kallisto 4).

Figure 7 Danae receives the golden rain, red-figure krater c. 490/80 BC (Hermitage, St Petersburg).

Akrisios had an oracle that his daughter Danae's son (Perseus) would kill him, another of these myths that portray anxieties about roles within the family. In this fantasy, Akrisios locks Danae in a bronze tower, but there is no escaping Zeus, who descends in the form of fertilising golden rain. Danae does appear in art after 500 BC, with the beautiful hair that attracted Zeus, sometimes neatly tied up in a *kekryphalos* (net headdress), and her robe outstretched to welcome the golden rain.[30] Some fourth-century BC funerary *lekythoi* (oil-jugs) even suggest she symbolises the contact that the dead make with the divine at death. But it is the fantasy of the *golden rain* that continually attracts artists, from Roman wall-paintings and mosaics through to modern European painting.

These are well-loved stories, full of colour and action. Many of them are told with lightness of touch and superb wit by Ovid in the *Metamorphoses* (complete by AD 8), a repertoire of myth from the creation to the present day told in 15 books in a relentless sweep with huge energy and in beautiful Latin. In Book 1 we meet Io, Book 2 Callisto and Europa, Book 3 Semele and Danae. Or we can enjoy Jupiter's (Zeus's) tours of inspection when he visits the world in disguise in the Lycaon story (Book 1) and the story of Philemon and Baucis (Book 8) and restores justice: Lycaon serves him child casserole and is punished by transformation into a wolf; Baucis and Philemon offer simple hospitality and earn the gift of dying at the very same moment as each other.

Underneath the colourful stories, there are some more serious messages. Zeus patrolling the world is an implementation of his function as controller of the world order and distributor of a sort of justice, of which we will see more below. The transformations and disguises doubtless each have their own origins, but they have in common that Zeus is an unseen force of incalculable power. Only Semele seeks to see that power as it really is and her mortal frame cannot withstand the thunderbolt that *is* Zeus. We for our part need to be careful to recognise when that power is at work, in whatever form.

In several cases we see myth homing in on a moment fraught with danger for the virgin. She meets Zeus, the embodiment of the dangerous and powerful male, perhaps the husband depicted as alien and illegitimate. Her beauty exposes her to him and the result is suffering and transformation. The stories focus on these vivid expressions of the end of maidenhood. We do not find stories of incorporation back into the community as a mother with all the authority of womanhood and as part of a female citizen order which meets to celebrate great rituals such as the Thesmophoria. Anxiety makes memorable myth.

Zeus's most famous, and last (Diodoros 4.14.4), son was Herakles. In his case Zeus literally replaces the mortal father and visits Alkmene, disguised as her husband Amphitryon whilst he is away at war. Comic potential was found in this myth, even as early as Aristophanes' *Birds* in which the birds threaten to cut off the gods' airspace so that, when they have erections, they will be unable to visit the likes of Alkmene, Alope or Semele (554–9; Alope was a conquest of Poseidon, the other two of Zeus). But we know the story best from the excellent Roman comedy of Plautus, the *Amphitruo*, based on a lost Greek play, deriving ultimately from the so-called 'Middle Comedy' (fourth century BC) when mythological burlesque took off. A farcical rendition of this theme is depicted on a south Italian vase of the late fourth century BC (LIMC Alkmene 2) showing Zeus and Hermes padded up grotesquely as 'gibbering' characters (*phlyakes*), carrying a ladder to climb up to Alkmene in the window! A different part of Alkmene's story must, very unusually, be reconstructed from other depictions on south Italian vases (LIMC 3–7). It seems that they are reproducing some tragedy, quite probably Euripides' *Alkmene*. Now Amphitryon is angry at the unfaithfulness of Alkmene, she flees to an altar, he builds a pyre around it and in the nick of time Zeus causes clouds to quench the fire. It looks as though a rule is upheld: tragic Zeus does not appear on stage; but a comic Zeus can.

Leaving this excitement behind, Herakles represents in myth an extreme of aspiration and Freudian denial of the father. He is a hero, not really the son of his mortal father. He seeks through his prodigious labours to transcend the human condition represented by that father altogether. Successfully, because he is the only hero to be stripped of his mortality – in agonising flames of a funeral pyre on the peak of Mt Oeta. This hero becomes a god like his real father, Zeus.

Zeus and Ganymede

'Loving boys is something enjoyable since once Ganymede too was loved by the Son of Kronos, king of the immortals.'

Theognis 1345f.

No story of Zeus's seductions would be complete without Ganymede, the son of the Trojan king Tros (or alternatively Laomedon) and the most beautiful boy on earth.[31] Zeus abducts him and compensates his father with a gift of splendid immortal horses. The role of Ganymede is then to be the server of wine for Zeus. This story in fact reflects ancient initiation customs known from an instance in Crete.[32] There a person of high status ritually abducts the prime boy of the adolescent age group (the *kleinos*, 'famous') and gives expensive presents. Among the required presents given to the boy is a drinking-cup. It is hard to catch the tone of this ritual: the boy is actually undergoing a sort of apprenticeship rather like our picture of a squire to a knight. Cup-bearing looks like part of the picture. So does sex. The Cretan *kleinos* had to say whether the sex had been acceptable (as opposed to violent) and inscriptions found on Thera certifying such acts seem to belong in the same ritual context.

These customs are only known in any detail from one account of 'a unique custom' in Crete. So, the ritual basis for the myth had more or less died out. But the myth, as myths do, had taken on a life of its own and provided a model in heaven for a form of homosexual relationship with an adolescent. This sort of relationship was in itself acceptable within certain parameters in classical Athens: here, the associated gift-giving was also ritualised, and the Athenian politician Alcibiades in his youth was not so unlike the Cretan *kleinos*. Thus what the myth says about Zeus is not meant to be something disgraceful and perverted – though it certainly becomes so for readers not sharing that culture, like the Christian Clement of Alexandria writing around AD 200:

Your gods didn't even keep off boys! – one of them [Herakles] loving Hylas . . . another loving Ganymede. Let your women fall down before these gods! Let them pray that their husbands should be like this, so well-behaved that they may become like the gods by doing what they do! Let your boys get used to worshipping them so that when they become men they may have the gods by them as a clear example of perversion.

Clement of Alexandria, *Exhortation to the Greeks* 2 (28 P.)

In art, however, this myth of abduction becomes a celebration of beauty admired even by the gods. At first, around 560, Ganymede is simply a member of the Olympian court (LIMC Ganymedes 57). Then on Athenian fifth-century vases (fig. 8) he becomes a standard Athenian boyfriend, courted and half-reluctant. Some time in the

Figure 8 Zeus woos Ganymede, red-figure cup by the Penthesilea Painter, c. 460/50 BC (Museo Archeologico Nazionale, Ferrara). Lightning bolt and sceptre tumble as Zeus adopts fifth century Athenian ways; the boy holds a cockerel, the usual present from a lover.

fourth century Zeus's eagle appears as the vehicle of abduction (Gantz 1993: 560). We first hear of it in a statue of Leochares and it may well be that it was from art, with its sense of the attributes of Zeus, that this particular motif originated rather than from poetry. One doubt remains, however, as Gantz observes: if you see the eagle abducting Ganymede, is it Zeus's bird or is it Zeus himself in the form of an eagle? By Roman times Ganymede wears a Phrygian cap to mark him as an easterner, like Attis or Mithras, and is often accompanied by the eagle rather than riding on it (see fig. 9). In a religious context, the myth of abduction can model the successful escape of the soul to the divine at death and it is for this reason that it appears on the stucco ceiling of the great underground basilica at the Porta Maggiore in Rome, which has been thought to be a Pythagorean place of worship. It is also why

Figure 9 Ganymede and the eagle, Roman sarcophagus, second century AD (LIMC Ganymede 109). Ganymede with Phrygian cap and the eagle that grants immortality to the sleeping dead – part of the décor of death.

it is appropriate for funerary monuments, in particular sarcophagi such as the one depicted here in fig. 9.

OVERVIEW

The mythology of Zeus, from all over the Greek world, is one dominated by his sexual adventures. We have seen how these can be understood in different ways. On one level, the mythology reflects some of the psychology of Greek males in their male-dominated societies. On another level, they display his enormous and irresistible power to command the service of beauty wherever it is found. But most important, they cause him to be the foundation of the society of gods and the society of men, because when you for instance trace a Greek people back to its origin, the answer is so often Zeus. He has been Zeus father since Indo-European times.

The god that is worshipped with such magnificence is the same god that is found, often in disguise, in acts which no society would sanction. This tension, which has arisen from the mythological need to explain the foundations of our societies, can be played in many ways: as something mysterious and unfair about the rule of the gods, as for instance in tragedy, or as something jarringly comic, bringing the gods literally down to earth. Of this Ovid is the master in his *Metamorphoses* and this is the tradition which we will see energise Western European art.

The way he was depicted in art became defined in the Archaic Age. This was a time of frequent wars and battles and one very open to the establishment of a régime through military action. This was the time when titanomachies and gigantomachies caught the imagination, and sculpture advertised to the age of the hoplite the ways in which Zeus's reign had been secured.

So the diverse mythology of Zeus has its origins in his authority and in social organisations. But once established, the better-known myths have a colour of their own and present a wonderful range of opportunities to the creative artist.

3

ZEUS FROM WEATHER TO FATE

WEATHER, LIGHTNING

It is easy when thinking about loftier roles of Zeus to forget a central role in cult: in both literature and life he is the sky and weather god. The sky especially is his realm. According to Poseidon in *Iliad* 15. 187–93, a lottery shared out the universe between three sons of Kronos: Poseidon got the sea, Hades the 'misty darkness' where he rules over the dead, and Zeus 'the broad sky in the ether and clouds' (192) – leaving the earth and Olympus as common ground.

Zeus can be held to be responsible in an astonishingly direct way for weather phenomena. Somehow Macrobius (*Saturnalia* 1.15.14, *c.* AD 440) had come across the titbit of information that Cretans called day 'Zeus'. That was rather odd, but it was commonplace to view Zeus as raining:

> Zeus rains and from heaven there is a great
> storm and the streams are stiff with water.
>
> Alcaeus, *fr.* 338.1–2 Lobel-Page

Zeus does not send rain, he actually rains.[33] So, in Aristophanes' comedy, *Clouds*, the simpleton Strepsiades is confronted by a wonderfully overdrawn sophistic Socrates and cannot understand how Socrates can claim that Zeus does not exist:

> Soc.: What Zeus? Don't talk nonsense at me. There is no Zeus.

STREPS.: What do you mean? *Who rains then?* That's what you can tell me for starters.

Aristophanes, *Clouds* 367f.

It is also traditional that he 'lightens', i.e. himself does lightning as we see in Homer:

As when the husband of Hera with her lovely hair *lightens*
making a large and awesome rainstorm or hail
or blizzard when snow sprinkles the ploughland . . .

Homer, *Iliad* 10.5–7

The rainstorm and snowstorm are particular to him: they are Zeus's rainstorm (*Iliad* 5.91) or Zeus's snow flurries (19.357). And the clouds are Zeus's and the rays of sunlight are Zeus's.[34] I think we should hear in this the expression of piety in a traditional society, a sort of religious humility faced with the weather. More generally, Homer's Zeus brings clouds together (he is *nephelegereta* – 'cloud gatherer') and specialises in black clouds (he is *kelainephes* – 'black-clouded'). Together with lightning we now have the ingredients for all sorts of storms, particularly those that spring up out of a clear sky or cluster around a mountain as rainclouds do, demonstrating beyond doubt that there is a great god at work:[35]

As when from the high peak of a great mountain
lightning-gatherer Zeus stirs a dense cloud
and all the peaks and jutting crags shine out
and the glens, and the awesome *aither* is torn apart from heaven down . . .

Iliad 16.297–300

The poet is a little overexcited here – it is clouds that are gathered, not lightning, and I'm not too sure about how you rend the ether in quite this way – but the effect is wonderful and we sense the majestic power of Zeus. These ways of attributing weather to Zeus are not just poetic, but also part of ordinary speech, even if sometimes a more cautious 'the god' is substituted for Zeus in these expressions, a vaguer method of speaking that survived even the conversion to Christianity. An inscription describes rainwater as 'water from Zeus'. What was odd was to go a step further, as some Orphics did, and say a shower was the *tears of Zeus*.[36]

In Homer no fewer than 26 epithets link Zeus with thunder and lightning. Most often he is *erigdoupos*, a resounding word meaning something like 'very thundering' (*Iliad* seven times, *Odyssey* three), and *terpikeraunos*, 'rejoicing in lightning' (*Iliad* eight times, *Odyssey* seven). *Terpikeraunos* may even contain within it a long-lost Indo-European word for a god of lightning and of the oak tree that lightning so easily explodes, known for instance to Lithuanians as Perkunas. There is no such thing as a thunderbolt, because lightning is not an object that is thrown, and we cannot literally be thunderstruck or struck by lightning, as if by an object. But for the Greeks thunderbolts were real and Zeus had his manufactured by the Cyclopes on their anvils under Mt Etna in Sicily:

> Trusting in these [thunder and lightning bolts] he is lord over mortals and immortals.
>
> Hesiod, *Theogony* 506, cf. 854

This is the missile Zeus uses to sink Odysseus' ship (*Odyssey* 12.416), and, as we have seen, it is his hallmark. So, from praying for rain we reach a mythology of him fighting giants in cosmic battles for control of the universe.

The electricity of the sky is awesome and invites cult. Places where lightning struck were very special and practically showed the god descending. In Arcadia we find fifth-century BC inscriptions dedicating a spot to Zeus *Keraunos*, 'Zeus lightning' or Zeus *Storpaos*, 'Zeus of lightning' (*IG* V 2.288, 64). Elsewhere you might find Zeus *Astrapaios*, or *Keraunios* ('of lightning', both), or *Keraunobolos* ('lightning thrower'), or *Kataibates*, 'descending', or, at Gytheion (Laconia) *Kappotas*, 'falling'. At Gytheion a stone was on display in the second century AD, which in our modern mythology we call a meteor.

Though his storms are conspicuous, we should not overlook his serenity. He lives in the *aither* (Latin *aether* or *ether*), the brilliant upper atmosphere, fiery and shining, up above the clouds (see below). Repeatedly, he is *aitheri naion*, 'dwelling in the ether'.[37] And if he is responsible for downpours, he is also responsible for the droughts that occur for lack of them – 'of rains and of droughts Zeus is the steward' (Isocrates, *Busiris* 13).

THE MOUNTAIN

Nearest to the sky, rising mightily from the horizontal earth are mountains. And a Greek of the late second century AD might believe (rather like the Victorians)[38] that

> the first men dedicated mountain peaks to Zeus as his statues, Olympus and Ida and any other mountain that is close to the sky.
>
> Maximus of Tyre, *Oration* 8.1

There are many Mt Olympuses in the Greek world, including Asia Minor (modern Turkey), whether because Olympus was just a pre-Greek word for 'mountain' or because, as I think, migrating Greeks considered it important to have an Olympus where they lived (this is far from the only Thessalian place name to pop up elsewhere). The most important Mt Olympus, and an impressive one whose highest peak reaches 2918 m, is situated on the borders of Thessaly and Macedonia as you enter the main part of Greece.

The idea developed that there were two levels of air: the lower air (*aer*) and the upper fiery air (*aither*, as we have just seen). It seemed to Cook that a mountain such as Olympus, visibly rising above the

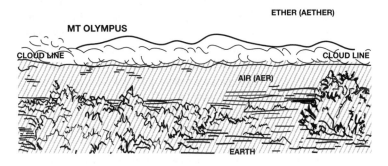

Figure 10 Ether, Air and Olympus (after Cook 1914: i.100f. and pl. ix).

rainclouds, must have been seen as reaching the very ether where the gods lived. It is a tempting thought. Certainly, ancient writers commented on how the ashes from sacrifice at extreme height on the peak of Mt Olympus were undisturbed by rain or wind, and letters which it was the custom to write in the ashes remained till the next occasion.[39] They surely had in mind the magical lines of Homer:

> . . . Olympus, where they say the secure seat of the gods for ever
> abides; it is neither shaken by wind nor ever soaked
> by rain nor does snow come there, but it is utterly clear weather,[40]
> cloudless, and a bright radiance is cast over it
> and on it the blessed gods rejoice for all time.
>
> Homer, *Odyssey* 6.42–7

Scholars used to be inclined to locate the cult of Zeus on the mountain on the northernmost peak. In more modern times there has been a simple stone shrine there of his replacement (see p.119), St Elias, to which processions wended their way. But in fact the substantial remains of cult – ashes (could the excavators still make out the letters?), inscriptions to 'Zeus Olympios', pots, pedestals, fourth-century BC coins – were found in 1961 further south on the peak of St Antonios (2817 m) during the building of an observatory.[41] In any event, we should not be looking for anything too grand, because much of the cult activity took place at the city named after Zeus, Dion (the later form of the Mycenaean *Diwion*), which stood at the foot of the mountain on the northern side. Dion, the major Macedonian festival centre, has been being excavated for some years but it was only in 2003 that Professor Pantermalis and his team discovered the sanctuary of Zeus itself. Astonishingly, the cult statue, of Zeus Hypsistos ('Highest'), was still in place (fig. 11).[42] Its head may be missing but it is recognisably of the Pheidian type, as you can see by comparing it with figs 4 and 12. That left arm is reaching for its sceptre!

'Olympus' is central to the identity of Zeus, and this may well derive ultimately from the strong commitment to worship of Zeus in Thessaly and Macedonia. This may explain the naming of other mountains in the Greek world as Olympus too, as well as underlie the description of the gods as 'Olympian' (or 'having Olympian homes') in Homer and

Figure 11 Artist's impression of the Zeus enthroned from Dion.

the poets and the frequent worship of Zeus Olympios elsewhere, for instance at Olympia.

Mountains were the focus of Zeus cult elsewhere too. This explains for instance a Zeus Aenesios of Mt Ainos on Kephallenia, the Zeuses who we see dominating mountains at the heart of states (pp.68–71), and a number of Zeuses, particularly in Boeotia, who are called *Keraios, Karaios, Karios*. This has led to an ancient Greek mythology of Karians (a nation of Asia Minor) living in Boeotia, but the explanation looks simpler – this is a god of the *kara* ('head'), i.e. the mountain peak, who in other states might be called *akraios*. Athens had a particular love of mountain sanctuaries, as Pausanias notes (1.32.2), though offerings are fewer and farther between after 300 BC: On Mt Hymettos there was a Zeus Hymettios, on Mt Parnes a Zeus in bronze, on the 'not very big mountain' Anchesimos there was a Zeus too. Elsewhere there were altars of Zeus Ombrios, 'of rain showers', and Zeus Semaleos, 'who gives signs' – evidently weather signs, perhaps cloud formations or, more immediately, lightning and thunder (Parker 1996: 30–32).

These shrines are not centres of habitation and we must therefore envisage processions of people and sacrificial animals to them. So in the case of Mt Olympus, it may well be that the procession would start at Dion. In another case, on Cos, there is an association of those who make a monthly, voluntary journey together to Zeus Hyetios ('of rain').[43] One might also envisage special journeys in time of need, as happened at Mt Lykaion (Arcadia):

If a drought lasts for a long time and by now their seed in the grounds and their trees are drying up, in such circumstances the priest of Zeus Lykaios prays at the water [of Hagno, a spring on the mountain] and makes all the sacrifices that custom requires; he then lowers an oak branch to the surface – not deep into the spring – and as the water is stirred water vapour rises from it, like mist, and after a short while the vapour becomes cloud and draws other clouds to it until it makes rain fall on the land of the Arcadians.

Pausanias 8.38.4

At the top of the mountain there would have been an altar and ashes from previous sacrifices, maybe a statue or two and perhaps offerings of coins and other objects. At Megara the rock was carved to provide a giant throne from which the god might be envisaged as viewing the human world below; this throne gave rise to the story of Xerxes watching the battle of Salamis from a mountain top between Megarid and Attica, but it faces the wrong way for that (Cook 1914: i.145). Occasionally, and strikingly, a temple might grace the mountain top if for instance its centrality eventually justified the expenditure of funds – much as the Parthenon of Athene caught the eye on the Athenian acropolis (156 m). A temple of Zeus Polieus was built by the brutal tyrant Phalaris on the loftier acropolis of Akragas (Agrigento in Sicily; 350 m), and another of Zeus Larisaios on the Larisa (the acropolis,

289 m) was built at Argos. Above Glisas in Boeotia, on Mt Hypatos ('Highest', 730 m) rose the temple of Zeus Hypatos (Pausanias 9.19.3). And on Rhodes there was a temple of Zeus Atabyrios on Mt Atabyrion (1215 m – there was another temple of Zeus on the Rhodian acropolis or, rather, plateau). These are not the only examples but they are probably the major ones.

CONTROL OF TIME AND EVENTS

Zeus controls the weather on a given day. Particular changes in the weather, especially lightning, may have significance and be called a 'sign from Zeus', *diosemia* – as we see when 'thrice from the Ida mountains Zeus thundered, giving a sign to the Trojans' (*Iliad* 8.170f.). But he also steers the sequence of days and what happens to anyone on any particular day. So Hesiod in his *Works and Days* talks of Zeus completing the 60 days after the winter solstice (565), and Eumaeus the (obviously pious) swineherd can speak of 'all the days and nights that are from Zeus' (*Odyssey* 14.93). And the days of the months have a particular significance in the final section of Hesiod's *Works and Days* (765–828) – we must take note of 'the days from Zeus' (765).

Times of year we tell by our astronomical clock, watching the constellations which Zeus himself has fixed in heaven as signs to us. This is what Aratus tells us in his *Phaenomena*, a work of the third century BC consciously building on the work of Hesiod 400 years earlier. The Greek word for a sign is *sema* and revealingly it also becomes the word for a constellation.

This leads us to a form of expression in the epic which takes 'day' into the realm of fate. Homer speaks of such things as the 'due day (for death), evil day, pitiless day, day of slavery, day of freedom, day of return' (Schwabl 1978: 1022). It is Zeus who manages these key days, which determine our own thoughts and behaviour if we are to believe the disguised Odysseus:[44]

> The thinking of men on earth is such
> as the day that the father of men and gods brings on.

> Homer, *Odyssey* 18.136f.

There are indeed moments when we wish to attribute our thoughts to others. Clearest in this regard is the apology of Agamemnon to Achilles in the *Iliad*:[45]

'. . . I am not responsible,
but Zeus and Moira [the destiny he allots] and the Erinys [vengeful demon] that
   walks in the mist,
who at the assembly implanted wild *ate* [destructiveness] in my mind
on the day on which I myself took his prize [Briseis] from Achilles.'

Homer, *Iliad* 19.86–9

It is his own fault that he is describing, and he knows it. But it is how the world is, it is Zeus.

~ If Zeus sends signs by weather and by the stars, and if he manages the whole course of human life, then it makes sense that he should sometimes communicate with men in various indirect ways to express his will. Messages come from him, borne by Hermes in the *Odyssey* and Iris in the *Iliad*. Iris is the rainbow, a beautiful icon of the gods' communication with man. Zeus sends dreams too, such as the one that misleads Agamemnon in *Iliad* 2. 'Let us send', says Achilles (*Iliad* 1.62f.), 'for a diviner or a priest, or a dream-interpreter – for dreams too are from Zeus.'

When we think of oracles we think of Apollo and Delphi. But Zeus too had oracles, at Dodona and Olympia. We first hear of Dodona from Achilles as he prays to a very distinctive Zeus:

Zeus lord, Dodonaian, Pelasgian, dwelling afar,
ruling over wintry Dodona; and around you the Selloi
dwell, the interpreters, unwashed their feet, their bed on the ground!

Iliad 16.233–5

This is the principal oracle of Zeus in classical times. The Selloi are an archaic priesthood, bound by ancestral tabus. Their unmediated contact with the ground has a number of parallels including those with the equally antique and tabu-ridden priest of Jupiter in Rome, the Flamen Dialis. The site itself goes back a long way: remnants have been found of Late Mycenaean pottery and of wooden huts.[46] Here, thanks to the rustling of Zeus's sacred Oak and the work of the Doves, presumably priestesses, the will of Zeus and his wife Dione may be ascertained by states or by those who wondered whether to keep sheep, emigrate or find a stolen piece of cloth. At least they might find out which god or hero it is best to pray to.

Oracles, however, are an unusual tool in Zeus's otherwise indirect and distant management of the universe. The oracle at Olympia was dead by the time of Pausanias (c. AD 150) and only appears once or twice in the historical record, though these mentions are interesting. We hear of its being manoeuvred outrageously by King Agesilaos of Sparta in 388 BC (Xenophon, *Hellenica* 4.7). Agesilaos asked it to allow him to refuse a sacred truce offered by the Argives, and, having succeeded, went to Delphi and asked Apollo if he agreed with his father (Zeus). Apollo had to say yes – this was after all the god who had cried:

Give me my lyre and my curving bow!
And I shall deliver to men the unfailing will of Zeus!

'Homer', *Hymn to Apollo* 131f.

A second item of interest is found in Plutarch's *Life of Agis* (§11, c. AD 100). Every nine years the Spartan ephors would watch the skies for a shooting star and, if they saw one, suspend the kings until an oracle from Delphi or Olympia allowed them to resume. This echoes the way in which every nine years Minos had to converse with Zeus (see Chapter 4). Kingship is something that runs out and needs to be restored from its source, Zeus.

With his control of day-by-day events, Zeus is naturally the god of decisive moments. Victory (*Nike*) and the supreme means of achieving it, the thunderbolt, are embedded in his iconography (see Chapter 1). This applies both to war and to sport, the means of training warriors. At Olympia they even sang in honour of the thunderbolt:[47]

Following previous beginnings,
now too we shall sing loudly the so-named joy of proud victory,
the thunderbolt,
the fire-thrown weapon
of thunder-raising Zeus,

the blazing bolt that fits
every success.

Pindar, Olympian Ode 10.78–83

Greeks were sensitive to the point at which the fortune of battle shifted or *turned*. The word for this was *trope* (usually translated 'rout') and the god who determined the point at which the battle turned was of course Zeus *Tropaios*. To celebrate this, a dedication was made, usually at the very spot, called a *tropaion*, which leads to our word 'trophy'. *Tropaion* is however an adjective and applies to the *bretas*, the crude wooden statue that trophies in effect were. In their simpler form they were made from an oak tree roughly lopped of its branches, with the captured weapons displayed on it, just as ancient Germanic tribes displayed sacrificed prisoners on trees. These distinctive monuments were set up primarily to Zeus Tropaios, though of course dedications could be made to any god. Once set up it was tabu to move them. They evidently constituted a fully dedicated religious place.[48]

OVERVIEW

In this chapter we have seen the links between the sky god and the god who controls life and the universe. The control of weather and its unexpected changes, particularly the mighty exhibitions of thunder and lightning and blackening of the skies, joins seamlessly with the control of time, day by day, and the unexpected changes this brings to our lives. Yet behind all is the unrivalled power of the god whose realm is the fiery ether into which only the tallest mountains reach. Zeus receives honour high up mountains, and processions of needy mortals will on occasion make their way there to do him reverence. But he is always in the background determining the due time for everything and in so doing deciding the outcome of battles as of everything else.

ZEUS AND THE ORDER OF SOCIETY

ATHENS

Athens, the city for which we have the best evidence, did not exploit Zeus as much as many other states, but even here we can see ways in which Zeus subtly orders society.

Heading out of Athens, across the River Kephisos, is an altar of Zeus *Meilichios*, 'the gentle', a worrying word in Greek religion, because what is at issue is purification and release from *miasma*, religious pollution. This altar is where the great hero of Athens, its king Theseus, was once cleansed of his killings (Pausanias 1.37.4) and it was the site of the Diasia, the major Zeus festival in Athens. The story goes (Thucydides 1.126) that Cylon had attempted a coup d'état around 632 BC and had been advised by the Delphic oracle, in one of those legendary ambiguous responses, that he should carry out his plans during the major festival of Zeus. It is remarkable that Cylon in this legend thinks not of his home Athens but of the Olympic Games, which is why his coup fails. The less obvious answer, closer to home, was that the *Diasia*, held on the 23rd of Anthesterion, in late March, was the major *Athenian* festival of Zeus. In this festival all the Athenian districts ('demes') united in worship. Most people made the so-called 'local offerings', namely baked animal shapes, but those that could afford them sacrificed real pigs, though they did not feast on the meat because in this case the whole animal was to be burnt; it was a 'holocaust' in the Greek technical sense, as was appropriate to gods of the underworld.

The festival was described in antiquity as 'performed with a certain loathsomeness' and accompanied by grim expressions. This was the public side. Domestically, it was a day of family meals, hospitality and of giving children presents. Thus it was like holding Good Friday and Easter on the same day, and indeed it was much the same time of year. So Zeus Meilichios, god of the grim forces from which one seeks purification, was also a god of joy and warmth, whose worship intertwines, as one can see from the remains of cult, with that of Zeus Philios ('of friendship')[49] and Zeus Soter ('who saves'). His depiction is often as a snake, a creature of the earth – which contains the dead and propagates the new. The sense of the ending of a year seems to belong with this festival – February in Rome was a month of purifications so that their new year might begin with the spring month of March. The Diasia has something of this feel, and the local communities, meeting outside the city, on its margins, may have returned to their city and their demes invigorated.

Some have thought that the Meilichios functions are so separate from others that they originally belonged to a separate god (cf. Nilsson 1967: i.412, 414). But Zeus is the overseer of the whole world order and is the special protector of its compartments and structures, like the demes in this case. Killing disrupts the structure and so he is the god from whom purification may appropriately be sought. This is the same Zeus who protects suppliants (Zeus Hikesios), who will uphold the relationships of friendship (Zeus Philios) and guest-friendship (Zeus Xenios).

Zeus may also oversee the entrance of boys into the male community as they cross from childhood and the community's structure is changed. A phratry is the 'brotherhood' of adult men into which new entrants are incorporated and is the only context in which Greek uses the Indo-European word for 'brother', also ours. In Athens we know that Zeus Phratrios and Athene Phratria were worshipped and there were some precincts, maybe including a state super-precinct, and that phratries proudly worshipped varying gods, such as Zeus Xenios, Apollo Patroos ('ancestral'), Apollo Hebdomeios ('of the number seven'). Quite how this all adds up, we do not know, but it may well be that all phratries were engaged in the worship of both the normal gods and their own special gods. What we hear is that Zeus

Phratrios played a central part in the enrolment process: to oppose the enrolment you might 'take the sacrificial victim away from the altar'; to carry it through on the other hand you had to 'take a voting pebble from the altar of Zeus Phratrios while the victims were burning'.[50] Clearly the electricity that powers changes in status and the alteration of the adult male community must flow uninterrupted from Zeus Phratrios.

ZEUS CENTRAL

Please consult map 1.

Among other Greek peoples Zeus was the central god. He had a special role when particular sets of cities and tribes united to express their common identity.

Every four years the people of the areas of Elis and Pisa, as well as Triphylia, a people supposedly sacred to Zeus, assembled at midsummer at the time of a full moon for a festival notable for its games. The festival took place at a cult site which goes back to Mycenaean times and was known as the *Olympia*, the festival of Zeus Olympios. The Olympic Games were so powerful a gathering of the athletic young, all competing to display their prowess, that the festival exceeded the boundaries of the state and the whole of Greece was invited. This is why we describe this festival as *panhellenic* ('all-Greek'). What started as a local festival of shared identity came to be a place where the whole of Greece could express its common ideals, something of which has been carried over into the modern Olympic Games.

The primary force behind this festival was centripetal and multi-tribal from the beginning. Comparable in intention was the annual meeting of the 12 divisions of the Achaeans to deal with matters of common interest, who met near Aigion at a grove of Zeus called *Amarion* (probably 'Meeting-place') where Zeus Amarios presided over the assembly-cum-festival.[51] This is a familiar structure among the Indo-European peoples: in the case of Germanic tribes, the unificatory meeting of sub-tribes is called the 'Thing'. There is also a tendency to divisions into 12 (Dowden 2000: 278, 282–4). Even the Etruscans met in this way. To modern political eyes, this is the annual meeting of a 'league' or 'federation', but this may be more of a recreation of the tribe from its first origins, from the womb, and a recreation of its identity, something which required a powerful sacrifice – there are persistent reports of human sacrifice at such Germanic and Slavonic meetings.

Greek mythology associates human sacrifice with some Zeus sites, though it looks as if it was not actually practised in historical times. When the Messenians finally escaped Spartan subjection in 369 BC, Ithome became the citadel of the town Messene, and Zeus Ithomatas was adopted as their principal god. In the nature of national identities, this is likely to have been hallowed by tradition. But Zeus of Ithome is also the god to whom a Christian writer (Clement, *Protrepticus* 3) alleges that 'King Aristomenes the Messenian' sacrificed the King of the Spartans, Theopompos, and 300 of their warriors, apparently way back in the eighth century BC. If there is anything in this story, it might refer not simply to an atrocity, or war crime in our terms, but also to an early custom, paralleled in Germanic culture, of sacrificing enemy troops. This would then point us to another Zeus cult in which human sacrifice had its part in asserting the identity of a super-tribe. This key cult was proud of its fine bronze statue from early in the fifth century BC, the work of Hageladas of Argos. This statue was an emblem on its later coinage, which gives some idea of its centrality to Messenian identity.

The most celebrated site where human sacrifice is supposed to have occurred is in southern Arcadia on Mt Lykaion, which 'other Arcadians call Olympus or the Sacred Mountain' (Pausanias 8.38.2). Here they made their way up between two massive pillars surmounted by gilded eagles, the particular companion of Zeus Lykaios as we see on coins, past the sanctuary that no man might enter on pain of stoning, up to the altar, an artificial mound 30 m in diameter and 1.5 m high on the very summit of the mountain. Here, with the whole Peloponnese spread out before them, they would sacrifice to Zeus Lykaios 'in secret; and it was not a pleasant idea for me to ask any more questions about the sacrifice. Let it be as it is and as it was from the beginning' (Pausanias 8.38.7). In Ovid (*Metamorphoses* 1) we find the story that the king Lycaon had slain a prisoner and served him to Zeus and was punished by being transformed into a wolf. But there is also a story

(Plato, *Republic* 565d) that if a person tasted human flesh mixed with meat at the shrine of Zeus Lykaios, he would be turned into a wolf. The story is developed in Pausanias (8.2.6):

> Indeed they say that since Lykaon someone regularly turns from man into wolf at the sacrifice of Zeus Lykaios, but he does not become a wolf for life. While he is a wolf, provided he abstains from human meat, in the tenth year thereafter, they say, he again becomes a man instead of a wolf. But if he tastes it he always remains a beast.

The third-century BC writer Apollas knew of a person who had done just this, something to which Pliny the Elder (8.82) reacts with exasperation:

> It is amazing just how far Greek gullibility can go – there is no lie so outrageous that it lacks someone to testify to it. So, Apollas, who wrote the *Victors at Olympia*, tells how Demaenetus the Parrhasian was at the sacrifice that the Arcadians were still then doing for Zeus Lykaios with human victims. He tasted the entrails of the sacrificed boy and turned into a wolf. The same was in the tenth year restored and trained as an athlete for the boxing and left Olympia a victor.

However, archaeologists have found no human bones and, for all the claims and insinuations, no one witnessed either a metamorphosis or a human sacrifice. Here at what was once the great centralising festival of the local Arcadians, a boy was ritually made into a wolf – just as in myth at Argos, Io became a cow, and in ritual young girls at Brauron in Attica became 'bears'. This is a special type of priesthood held by a young person making the transition from childhood to adulthood. It is not so far from the world of Zeus Phratrios, guarding the boundaries of the adult community.

Mt Lykaion is not particularly near a town, except Megalopolis (15 km away), which was founded in 368/7 to unite the Parrhasian Arcadians in their 40 hamlets into a force that could resist the Spartans from whom they had just been freed. This cult of Zeus Lykaios had previously been their vehicle of identity and unity and now it increasingly found a purpose as a focus for all Arcadians, proud to be Arcadians rather than just the inhabitants of this or that town.

Appropriately, Zeus was guarantor of both these Arcadians and the Messenians of Mt Ithome against the Spartans. It becomes clear, however, that these are genuine choices when we see that Megalopolis and its effective territory of Parrhasia were Zeus-worshippers, but Mantinea, further away in Arcadia, maintained a deliberately distinct identity through its devotion instead to Poseidon. A branch of the Mt Lykaion cult was also set up in the city of Megalopolis, a pattern we shall see repeated below (Koroneia). We must envisage these communities as uniting in their worship of Zeus at the festival of the Lykaia – perhaps around April – and its games, which followed the normal pattern of men's events and boys' events by the time we learn about them and had their own hippodrome. Werewolf stories are only a quaint echo of what this cult meant to its participants.[52]

A similar situation arises with the cult of Zeus *Laphystios*, Zeus the 'Devourer'. On his altar, on Mt Laphystion, 20 stades from Koroneia (Boeotia), Athamas was going to sacrifice Phrixos and Helle before the ram with the golden fleece rescued them. And legend associates the lands of Orchomenos, Koroneia and Haliartos with each other and with this mountain, evidently a major focus for their identity – and that of the 'Pan-Boeotians' – as expressed through cult. Schachter (1994: iii.105) refers to the Zeus of Koroneia as the 'pan-Boeotian ethnic god' and thinks that he appears on several Boeotian coins. The cult of Zeus Laphystios, and the story of the intended sacrifice of Phrixos, is also found at Halos in Thessaly, looking over the Pagasaean Gulf towards Mt Pelion. Given the southwards migration of the Boeotians, the cult probably originates there in their original homeland and is part of a pattern of bringing old names to new places. The same profile emerges in both locations of the pairing of town and mountain: at Koroneia and Mt Laphystion; at Halos and Mt Pelion, where there was a cult of Zeus Akraios ('of the peak') – another title borne by Zeus Laphystios at Koroneia. The shrine of Zeus Akraios on Mt Pelion doubled as the shrine (cave) of Cheiron the Centaur and, as we have seen, the sons of Thessalian nobles went there annually dressed in ramskins,[53] distant cousins of Athenians worshipping Zeus Phratrios.

In later editions of his *Golden Bough*, Sir James Frazer used the tale of Athamas' attempted sacrifice of Phrixos as yet another piece of

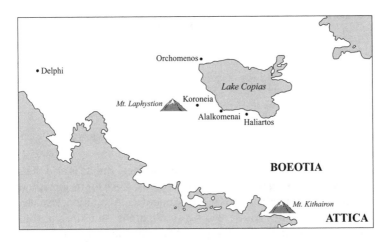

Map 3 Cities of Boeotia

evidence for his view that once there had been a widespread custom of creating priest-kings for a period until finally they were sacrificed.[54] We may not believe Frazer any more, but the human sacrifices which seem merely symbolic in Greek myth and cult – on some of our views play-acting the end of youth so that adulthood may begin – look more likely to have once actually happened when we look beyond the Greeks to other nations. Zeus Devourer may indeed once have been a sinister god.

More marginal were the Nemean Games, every two years in honour of Zeus *Nemeios* – marginal because Nemea was not much of a place: it belonged to Cleonae, on the other side of the Pierced (*Tretos*) Pass through the mountains from Argos. Here too, under the authority of Zeus, a panhellenic festival developed from what may have been the towns around a mountain coming together for worship and sport: a little to the north, there is Mt Apesas where Zeus Apesantios was first worshipped by Perseus, the founder-hero of Mycenae (Pausanias 2.15.3), itself on the Argive side of the Pierced Pass. Thus the Nemean Games may originally not have been so different from the other festivals we have looked at in this section, and once again we see a panhellenic festival emerging from the sense of shared culture between local populations.

KINGS AND THE JUSTICE OF ZEUS

Zeus lord . . .

Iliad 3.351 – three times in Homer

Lord of lords, most blest
of the blest and most accomplishing [*teleiotaton*]
of ends [*telos*], happy Zeus . . .

Aeschylus, *Suppliant Women* 524–6

Zeus, as we saw earlier, is father of gods and men. But he is also their lord (*anax*) and king (*basileus*). We celebrate Greece for its invention of democracy, but other forms of government were common. Usually, in fact, Greek states were ruled by an oligarchy. But kingship did not have to wait for the Kings of Macedon and the successors of Alexander the Great. They are everywhere in Homer – from a lord, i.e. great king, Agamemnon, to the kings, for example minor kings, eg Diomedes. And Homeric kings rest on the reality of kings in Greek society – both in the Late Bronze Age in the palaces of Mycenaean Greece and Minoan Crete, and in the Dark Age and the beginnings of Archaic Greece.

Homer would agree with Hesiod that 'kings are from Zeus' just as bards are from the Muses and Apollo (*Theogony* 94–6). That is why kings or princes such as Patroclus, Ajax, Agamemnon, Menelaus and, most frequently, Odysseus are described by Homer as *Zeus-born* (*diogenes*). Herakles on the other hand is described as 'Zeus-born' because he is. In the case of kings, you can if you wish explain this by the supposition that the king's line goes back to Zeus, but that only re-expresses what the epithet amounts to: kings rule with an authority that comes from Zeus. And as his managers, they are also subject to surprise audits, as we will see below. A king is also *diotrephes* – nourished by Zeus, reared and made into who he is by Zeus.[55] These are quite emphatic epithets and we must not think they just mean vaguely 'divinely favoured' – the word for 'god' in Greek is *theos* and the Greeks do not have any of the Latin *di* or *deus*-shaped words that I think we sometimes subconsciously and wrongly hear in these Greek epithets. *Dio-* means Zeus.

If authority derives from Zeus, it must also, on occasion, be renewed from Zeus. Nine years seems to be the cycle. According to Odysseus (*Odyssey* 19.178f.) Minos used to be or become king every nine years, 'he who communed with great Zeus'. According to a dialogue attributed to Plato (*Minos* 319e) he had to give an account of his rule to Zeus every nine years and learn more. This seems to fit with a pattern of renewal of the whole of society which had once been practised by the Indo-European cultures (Dowden 2000: 286 and ch. 14 *passim*; Schwabl 1978: 1394). Divine renewal, and Zeus as its source, is one aspect that has had a long shelf life. It reappears in the case of the Spartan kings, as we have seen.

Before the development of states in the contemporary sense, there was no codification of law; law was therefore owned by individual leaders. So it is that in Homer and Hesiod kings hear law cases and issue judgments (*themistes, dikai*). It is then a matter of concern whether those judgments are 'straight' or 'crooked'. As Zeus is a projection in heaven of kings on earth, it follows that he is responsible for the declaring of justice and its implementation, so long as we bear in mind that this is not Christian or philosopher's justice, but rough and ready managerial justice.[56]

In the *Odyssey* we learn that gods unspecified walk the earth in the shape of strangers to check up on men's respect for law (17.485–7). In Hesiod (*Works and Days* 248–55) it is eerier: three myriad immortals (i.e. 30,000 of them, but he wasn't counting), cloaked in mist, police mortal men; but these mortal men are kings, because the three myriad immortals, Zeus's 'guards', are checking up on their standards of justice. This story of a divine inspection of mortals has parallels in Near-Eastern cultures: the Persian god Mithra supervised contracts, and the Hebrew God with two companions visited righteous Abraham and Sarah and, next stop, the unjust towns of Sodom and Gomorrah (*Genesis* 18–19, 21).[57] These similarities are not coincidental: they form part of a pattern of cultural borrowing from the East. But here and now in Greek culture this has become Zeus's role, and this is what matters, to manage justice by mysterious intervention and inspection. It is not just battles but the whole dispensation of human life that is controlled by Zeus.

Modern writers have tried to claim that the *Odyssey* has a different view from the *Iliad* and that Hesiod is different again. Increasingly, however, we can see that it is the particular character of each work rather than changing Greek conceptions that are at issue. The story of a man's return against all the odds generally puts different demands on its gods than a tragedy set on the battleplains of Troy (Lloyd-Jones 1971: 30–32). And Hesiod's *Works and Days* weighs in with moral severity to create its distinctive atmosphere. This is shown for instance by a passage in which Homer's *Iliad* can turn to Hesiodic concepts of justice and an Odyssean sense of respect for the gods:

> . . . as when the black earth is all weighed down in by pelting rain
> on an autumn day, when water is poured out torrentially
> by Zeus, when he is annoyed and enraged at men
> who use violence in the agora to deliver crooked judgments
> and drive out *dike*, without any respect for the gods.

Iliad 16.383–8

Here Homer enjoys adding a dash of Hesiodic colour to his epic, neatly quarantined in the alternative register of the simile.[58]

The ground is already laid for Zeus as manager of mortal lives in the remarkable scene at the beginning of the *Odyssey* where Zeus speaks (1.29–38):

> He had been thinking in his spirit about doughty Aegisthus
> whom Agamemnon's son far-famed Orestes had killed.
> That is what was in his mind when he uttered words among the immortals:
> 'Oh dear, how mortals blame the gods!
> They say that misfortune comes from us, when they themselves
> By their own recklessness suffer grief beyond measure [*moros*]
> Take how Aegisthus recently beyond measure married
> Agamemnon's wooed wife and killed him on his return
> Knowing full well it meant sheer destruction – because we had already told him
> Sending Hermes . . .

There is an order in things and a due 'measure' or 'proportion' (*moros*), which is monitored by Zeus and about which he worries. This is not fate, though: the word usually translated as fate, *moira*, is a related word denoting that proportion, or the divine power that dispenses it, the 'Fates' in a soft sense. Zeus, according to this view, does not blast Aegisthus with a thunderbolt – he simply warns because he knows the order of things, that Aegisthus will have it coming to him.

This is the scene on which, 600 or so years later, Ovid builds the opening action of the *Metamorphoses* (1.163ff.). His gods stride along the Milky Way into a 'Palatine in the sky' to hear Jupiter, the Roman Zeus. Jupiter reports with outrage how Lycaon, King of Arcadia, has wickedly tried first to kill him, then to feed him human meat. Ovid's poetic décor is elaborate: Lycaon's house is brought down by 'avenging flame' (1.230), namely the thunderbolt; Lycaon changes into a baying wolf; and the earth is destroyed in the great flood, the cataclysm. But it remains a case of the gods patrolling the earth in disguise, a motif which also appears, in more of an Abraham-and-Sarah mode, in the story of Philemon and Baucis (8.617ff.). Ovid did not invent these stories and it appears that the tale of Zeus's entertainment by Lycaon goes all the way back to a pseudo-Hesiodic text, though one that no longer survives (Hesiod, *fr.* 163 Merkelbach-West; see West 1997: 123). That means it was probably circulating as one of the works badged 'Hesiod' by the mid sixth century BC.

Hesiod preaches the tough justice of Zeus. Pandora opens the box of evils, showing mortal weakness and the particular weakness, in a man's mythology, of woman. This is, however, simultaneously the order that Zeus has laid down and Hesiod concludes that 'there is no way to escape the mind of Zeus' (*Works and Days* 105), just as he comments later (483f.):

> The mind of Zeus, holder of the *aigis*, varies from time to time
> and it is painful for mortal men to understand.

Hesiod's Zeus does more than just set up the world. He monitors the ways of men and replaces each age of men with the next (*Works and Days*, e.g. 140, 144, 158). When the day comes he will destroy our age as well (180), though in his wisdom he is not quite at the point of doing that, we hope (273). The behaviour of kings and their administration of justice is a special concern of Hesiod's in *Works and Days*. This is what 'wide-seeing' Zeus (*euryopa*, 229, 239), or the 'all-seeing eye of Zeus' (267), is monitoring through a variety of agents, whether Justice (*Dike*, a maiden who is born of Zeus, 256), Oath (*Horkos*) or the 30,000 spirits. Whole cities perish around unjust rulers (240).

We should not think that Greeks were particularly literal-minded about their mythology. Zeus hurls no thunderbolts in Homer (except at Odysseus' ship, a relatively realistic setting) and he influences the human world in an altogether more subtle way, depicted by the poet as the operation of a family of gods. Homer always tones down the mythic register. Everyone presumably knew from the lost epic *Thebaids* that Kapaneus had exhibited contempt for the gods when he was one of the Seven Against Thebes and that he was in consequence personally smitten by Zeus's bolt. He is mentioned a number of times in the *Iliad* and Homer positions a son of his, whom he calls Sthenelos ('Strongman'), next to Diomedes in the *Iliad*, to tempt his audience to recall the reckless bravado of Kapaneus and to allow Diomedes in contrast to state the new morality that had led to the success of his new generation – the *Epigonoi* or 'Successors' – in their quest to capture Thebes:

> We actually captured the seat of seven-gated Thebes,
> the two of us leading a smaller host against better walls,
> putting our trust in the portents of the gods and the aid of Zeus
> – where *they* perished from their own recklessness.

Iliad 4.406–9

The audience knows the unmentioned thunderbolt story but maybe Homer doesn't take it too literally. What matters is that leaders understand the justice of Zeus. That is why Diomedes is called Diomedes, 'Counsel of Zeus'.

HISTORICAL KINGS

Kings largely disappeared from the Greek scene during the Dark Age. The most notable exceptions were in Macedonia and at Sparta. In Sparta they retained a pair of kings, something which seems to be reflected in the twin Dioskouroi whose home was Sparta. Elsewhere, power was levelled out and passed to aristocratic oligarchies with occasional interruptions in the Archaic Age (776–480 BC) by 'tyrants', a sort of dictator. Such tyrants were of necessity alert to their public image, and keen for instance on building programmes. It is no co-incidence that Cylon's abortive attempt to seize power in Athens (above p. 65) was associated in legend with a festival of *Zeus*.

Indeed, the role of Zeus at Athens might have been different if the sixth-century BC tyranny of Peisistratos and his sons had survived longer. Apparently on the foundations of a substantial earlier temple they had begun a temple of Zeus Olympios. The original temple had been built, it was said (Pausanias 1.18.7f.), by Deucalion, the Greek Noah, and the fissure was still shown where the flood waters dis-appeared and a new world had been created – a world which, as the neighbouring temple of Kronos and Rhea serves to remind us, was under the new régime of Zeus. But the half-finished new temple became for later generations 'a symbol of arrogant Pisistratid display' (Parker 1996: 68). Assertion of monarchic authority through the image of Zeus became problematic in the formative years following the fall of the tyranny (510) and the testing times of the war against the Persian Great Kings Darius (490) and Xerxes (481–79): in Greek, the 'king' usually referred to the King of Persia – it was a word in exile, because Greeks had law and freedom, not kingship and slavery (Herodotus 7.101–4). This attitude privileged instead the divinity of the Acropolis, Athene, for whom the democracy constructed her Parthenon and its environment – though not without acknowledging the background presence of Zeus Hypatos ('most high') with an altar next to the Erechtheion that received only cakes (Pausanias 1.26.4). It would not be until the king of Syria Antiochus Epiphanes (148–138 BC) that there was further work on the temple of Olympian Zeus, or until the Emperor Hadrian that an Athens now long comfortable with monarchy gratefully saw it completed and furnished with a colossal ivory and gold statue (Pausanias 1.18.6).

In Macedonia, Zeus was held to be the father of Macedon himself, just as Woden was the ancestor of the Anglo-Saxon kings, and there was perhaps more prominent cult of Zeus in Macedonia than else-where.[59] With Alexander the Great's conquests (334–323 BC), royalty returned to huge areas of the Greek world and the Egyptian and Near-Eastern monarchic worlds now became part of the enlarged Greek world. Just as Peisistratos had sought to express his sovereignty through a new temple of Zeus Olympios at Athens, now the kings who succeeded Alexander – Ptolemies in Egypt, Seleucids in Syria and, rather later, the Attalids in Pergamon found uses for Zeus in their projection of their power. So for instance when ruler cult was created among the Greek kings of Syria and Babylon, Zeus was called into service. This started with Antiochus I's deification of his father Seleucus in 280: an inscription from the reign of Seleucus IV (187–175) reveals there was a priest of Seleucus Zeus *Nikator*, 'Victor', together with Antiochus Apollo *Soter*, 'Saviour' (Nilsson 1974: ii.167). Zeus and his son Apollo modelled the world of earthly sovereigns.

The huge altar of Zeus at Pergamon (now in Berlin), one of the glories of Hellenistic sculpture and certainly the largest surviving work, was erected by the Greek king Attalos I. The cult of this city intertwined the worship of Zeus with reverence for the kings in many ritual ways. The message of the altar is that Attalos, through his defeat of the Gauls in 226 BC and creation of this powerful new state based on Pergamon, had repeated the battles of Zeus which established the current order. In the sculpture, fine 'dying Gauls' echo Giants defeated by Zeus and Athene. In this way Attalos also attached Pergamon to the cultural heritage of Athens, where he made dedications of sculpture on similar themes.

Kingship, then, continued to be supported by Zeus, just as emperors and kings in late antiquity and in Europe would be specially protected by the Christian God.

THE NEEDS OF OUTSIDERS: STRANGER, SUPPLIANT, OATH

We turn now from order within societies to international conventions. Homer's *Odyssey* proclaims the need to respect not only the bonds that are internal to society, but also those that protect outsiders and ensure that different states and their inhabitants have the means to coexist with each other. Zeus guarantees all bonds of friendship as Zeus Philios and, above all, these inter-state bonds, as a sort of religious Red Cross. Nausicaa knows that 'All *xenoi* and beggars are from Zeus' (*Odyssey* 6.207f.), a line which Odysseus himself picks up at 14.251 and which, a millennium later, was a favourite line of the pagan emperor Julian when he hammered home the point that pagans should not leave Christians a monopoly on charity.[60] *Xenia* is the relationship of reciprocal hospitality between persons of different states, and both parties are known as a *xenos*, regardless of who is the host and who the guest on any particular occasion. To ask which is the guest is like asking which of two friends is the recipient of a good turn. Zeus Xenios, then, enforces respect for these relationships. This is why Nausicaa's statement is tinged with the worry that the *xenos* may be a god in disguise, inspecting the earth, precisely as we see at *Odyssey* 17.485-7 when there is talk of 'gods in the form of foreign *xenoi*'. This is also why Odysseus, even though he knows in his heart that Polyphemos is a savage, still appeals to him:

> . . . but we, reaching your knees,
> have arrived as suppliants, in the hope you might provide us with a *xenion* or in some other way
> give us a gift, which is the *themis* [religious right] of *xenoi*.
> Be respectful, my good man, of the gods: we are your suppliants [*hiketai*].
> And Zeus is avenger of suppliants and *xenoi*,
> Zeus Xenios, who stands beside respectful *xenoi*.
>
> *Odyssey* 9.266-71

A whole culture underlies this passage: the 'arriver' (*hiketes*) is the Greek for a suppliant and he performs the ritual of supplication by getting down and grasping the knees of the person supplicated; the *xenion* is a present whose giving solemnly creates the bond of guest-friendship and the obligation, when possible, to reciprocate; and *themis* is the uninfringeable divine law or order, quite different from the *dike*, the order or justice that a good ruler or a good society maintains. Zeus can be Zeus Hikesios, Zeus Xenios; he has children by *Themis*. It is a terrible sin, requiring expiation, when a person kills a *xenos*. So for instance Herakles killed his *xenos* Iphitos:

> It is said that Zeus, appalled at the *xenos*-killing, instructed Hermes to take Herakles and sell him as *dike* [in effect, 'penalty'] for the murder. He took him to

Lydia and sold him to the queen of the place, Omphale, at a price of three talents. The story is in Pherekydes.

Pherekydes of Athens, FGrH 3F82

Thus there are conventions and there are sanctions which can only be exercised by god. Nowhere is this truer than in the case of oaths. The mightiest, and most persuasive, oath is naturally by the mightiest god and Zeus Horkios (of oaths, *horkoi*) is its guarantor:

The statue of Zeus in the Council-Chamber [at Olympia] is the most terrifying of all the statues of Zeus to unjust men. He is called Horkios and has a thunderbolt in either hand.

Pausanias 5.24.9

Double thunderbolts strike fear into the oath-taker who perjures himself next to the statue as he swears over slices of boar's flesh, just as in the great oath of Agamemnon at *Iliad* 19.258: 'Let Zeus know first, of gods the highest and best'. Oaths were not always by Zeus and he was in any case often combined with forces of earth and sea (e.g. Ge and Poseidon), but if an oath was worth swearing it was often worth swearing by him. Thus the thunderbolt stood for the deadly recoil of ultimate power taken in vain by those who did not understand the world's order.

ZEUS IN THE HOME: PRAYING, DRINKING AND SWEARING

The bard Phemius is anxious to avoid Odysseus killing him. One option he considers in order to achieve this objective is to claim asylum:

to go out of the *megaron* and sit at the altar of great Zeus
Herkeios, a properly made altar where many
were the thighs of oxen that Laertes and Odysseus had burnt.

Odyssey 22.334–6

So the geography is clear: this Greek palace, like any Greek house, has its living room (*megaron*) and outside, a fenced area (*herkos* is a boundary fence, or the area so enclosed) with an altar of Zeus of the Fenced-off Area (*Herkeios*). This is where the family would do its sacrifices and is the outward-facing religious point in the house, to which in this case a suppliant flees. Zeus is the ultimate father of the family and head of household, reflecting the key person in the home, the *oikos*, in Greece. Like an Agamemnon or an Odysseus, the head of household would sacrifice at his altar of paternal Zeus Herkeios, though it may be doubted whether epic oxen thighs would be much in evidence, rather than sheep or pig. In the simpler rustic surroundings of Eumaios's hut, however, there is no altar and the pig is sacrificed indoors at a blazing hearth (*eschara, Odyssey* 14.420). But you can talk about an *eschara* too when you focus on the part of the altar that burns, something which is to the forefront of your mental image, as it is for Pausanias when he describes the slaughter of Priam by Neoptolemos at the *eschara* of Zeus Herkeios.[61] This was a particularly vile and irreligious act.

This is also a defining cult for citizenship. When the suitability of a candidate for *archon* (magistrate at Athens) was scrutinised, Aristotle tells us (*Constitution of the Athenians* 55) that they were asked not only about their fathers' and mothers' families but also about the location of their cult of paternal Apollo or Zeus Herkeios.

Zeus in the house is also frequently known as Zeus *Ktesios* ('of the possessions/stores'), which seems to relate above all to the larder, where a lexicographer says an image of him had to be set up. This then replicates the pattern of household cult known from Roman religion, in which there is a division between the gods of the area of land (*Lar* or plural *Lares*) and the gods of the store cupboard (*Penates*). Close to the latter is the god of the hearth, *Hestia* in Greek (*Vesta* in Latin), though the personal focus is often on Zeus *Ephestios* ('at the hearth'). The Romans also had public Penates as though the state itself were only a large household. This may be the sort of thinking that underlies an altar of Zeus Ktesios in a temple at a large village in Attica or his worship at the Piraeus (the port of Athens), and similar considerations may apply to public worship of Zeus Herkeios, worshipped on the Athenian acropolis itself.[62] Zeus *Ktesios* can be depicted with, or as, a snake, which matches well with the folk views of harmless snakes: they were manifestations of the beneficent spirit of a given place and should be fed. But you could also make statuettes of Zeus Ktesios at home like this:

> Put a lid on a new two-eared [i.e. handled] *kadiskos* [type of jar], drape its ears with white wool, and from the right shoulder and from the brow dress it with a saffron [mini-robe?], and pour in 'ambrosia'. Ambrosia is pure water, olive-oil, mixed grain – that's what you put in.

Autokleides, Exegeticon (fourth/third century BC)
FGrH 353F1, emended

Libations were important in the home too. Hector must first pour a libation to Zeus and the other immortals before he can drink himself (*Iliad* 6.259f.).[63] At parties and social gatherings three bowls of wine would be mixed, none to be touched before a libation. The first libation was, we are told, to Zeus Olympios and the Olympian gods, the second to the heroes (who protect their local people from their graves) and the third, the 'complete' (*teleios*) would be to Zeus Soter – yes, the Zeus responsible for *saving* the state in war as the priesthoods and inscriptions of so many states testify, but also simply 'Zeus saviour third, who guards the home of pious men'.[64] This libation is the exquisite backdrop to the awful words of Clytaemestra as she tells how she killed Agamemnon:

> I strike him twice, and in two wailings
> his limbs give way, and, fallen,
> I put in a third – in votive gratitude to
> the Zeus beneath the earth, *soter*, of the dead.

Aeschylus, Agamemnon 1384–7

If we had a microphone to catch ancient Greek and Roman speech, we might be struck by the amount of mild swearing that went on. We have already seen how characters in the *Birds* of Aristophanes are always swearing *ne ton Dia* ('By Zeus!'), as they do in all his plays, and occasionally with a bit more emphasis, I think, *ma ton Dia!* Thus their conversational practice reflected practice in major oaths. Socrates was a bit perverse in swearing 'By the Dog' instead, which is a humorous oath by the dog-headed god of Egypt, Anubis. Equally, if you were appealing to someone, then it was most effective to plead *pros Dios* ('In the name of/for the sake of Zeus'). Romans in this respect were not much different – certainly an expostulatory *pro Iuppiter!* ('oh/wow Jupiter!') is commonplace. Latin *per Iovem* ('In the name of Jupiter!') is not infrequent, though Romans did like to heap up the things in whose name one appealed: 'I beg of you, In the name of gods and men – and my foolishness, and your knees . . .' (Plautus, *Miles Gloriosus* 541).

This sort of expression contributes in its subliminal way to a background noise of piety. It would be interesting to know whether changes in that piety could be measured by changes in the swearing volume. If you set Greek texts of the classical period alongside Greek texts of the imperial period it does look as though something has changed. In Aristophanes, Demosthenes and Plato (fifth-fourth century BC) there is quite a lot of by-Zeusing. In Dio Chrysostom, Plutarch and Lucian (first–second century) there is a good deal less. In Plotinus and Himerius (third–fourth AD) there is none, and in Libanius (fourth AD) it is restricted to the artificial and archaic environment of the declamations. There are really only two possibilities: either literary Greek prose had become divorced from common speech and sentiment; or the by-Zeusing piety had passed away.

The gods infiltrated ordinary life in other ways too, as can be seen from the problems with which the Christian Tertullian wrestles:

> The Law prohibits the naming of pagan gods, but that does not mean to say that we can't pronounce their names when conversation forces us to. You often have to say things like 'you'll find him in the temple of Asclepius', or 'I live in the Isis quarter', or 'he has been appointed priest of Jupiter'. I'm not worshipping Saturn if I call someone by this name, any more than I'm worshipping Marcus if I call someone Marcus.

> from Tertullian, *On Idolatry* §20

This may seem obvious enough, but any expert on brainwashing will immediately recognise the insidious effects of this naming culture. The pagan world was all around you: you lived near the temple of Zeus and your Greek friends were very often named after him. They might be 'gift of Zeus', *Diodotos, Diodoros, Zenodotos, Zenodoros, Diozotos*;

or 'born of Zeus', *Diogenes, Diognetos*; or 'glory of Zeus', *Diokles*; or 'son of glory of Zeus', *Diokleides*; or 'beloved of Zeus', *Diiphilos, Diphilos, Zenophilos*; or 'wisdom of Zeus', *Diomedes*; or 'honour/ worship of Zeus', *Diotimos, Zenotimos* – or *Dieitrephes, Diogeiton, Diophanes, Diophantos, Zenobios, Diomedon, Diopeithes* – or just plain 'Zeus-o', *Dion* or *Zenon* like the philosopher Zeno.[65]

And the plant world too bore his name. A carnation is *diosanthos* 'Zeus's flower' (hence the Latin botanical name *dianthus*), and a sweet chestnut is 'the acorn of Zeus', *diosbalanos*. A herb, field basil, is *dioselakate*, 'Zeus's spindle', and what better name for a wild flower than *diospogon* 'Zeus's beard'?

Other complaints of Tertullian are that contracts required oaths by gods if they were to be enforced, and that foolish well-wishers might *bless* the unfortunate Christian in the name of their gods. Gibbon thought this might refer to a 'Jupiter bless you' on sneezing.[66] This could well be right; a poem in the *Greek Anthology* tells us about a certain Proclus:

> . . . nor does he say *Zeu, soson!* ['Zeus save us!'] if he sneezes: he can't hear his nose: it's too far from his ears.
>
> Anonymous, *Greek Anthology* 11.268.3f.

All this, together with continuing reference to 'Zeus's rain' or the habit in late antiquity, maybe modelled on the Christian Lord's Day, of not working on Thursdays (the day of Jove, *Jovis dies, jeudi*) meant that it was no simple matter to eradicate Zeus or Jove from the life and culture of the pagan world (Dowden 2000: 158, 164).

OVERVIEW

There has been a kaleidoscope of practices in this chapter. We started at Athens, where we saw the social cohesion and organisation brought about by Zeus: among his various functions the strangely grim Zeus Meilichios stood out, whom all the demes joyfully assembled to worship as spring began. In other places, at Olympia, or just outside Achaean Aigion, or on Mt Lykaion, Ithome or Laphystion, we saw whole peoples meeting in all their tribes and subdivisions to assemble their identity; we also saw a grimmer side, with perpetual hints that once there had been human sacrifice. From there we turned to another aspect of the social order, another guarantee for society, namely the special relationship of kings with Zeus, himself the ultimate projection of kingship in heaven. This is a relationship that he specially monitors (just as he monitors the ways of men at large) in order to maintain the 'straightness' of justice and in order to maintain a world that observes due proportion. Real kings become rare in Greece after the Dark Age, but tyrants and Macedonian kings and the Hellenistic monarchs tend to have a special connection with Zeus, which they promote. Finally we turned to the supra-state relationships of reciprocal hospitality and supplication that Zeus oversees and to the oaths that he enforces; and we saw how he even governs the rhythm of familiar and domestic life, from the altar of Zeus Herkeios in the courtyard to swearing and the naming of weeds. Truly Zeus pervades every aspect of human society.

THINKING ABOUT ZEUS

THE VISION OF HOMER, AND THE ARCHAIC POETS

If religion is often a serious thing in our modern cultures, it is not surprising if we find it hard to understand the more playful parts of Homer's writing about Zeus. Thetis appeals to Zeus to help her son Achilles; Zeus promises but is worried that this will annoy Hera, who already gives him a hard time for helping the Trojans; indeed Thetis had better go before Hera notices – but he is too late, she already has (*Iliad* 1.517–61). Meanwhile, we think of the story that Zeus only gave up Thetis because her son would be more powerful than his father (p. 46). Now Zeus threatens violence, as though it were a case of wife-beating in heaven, and Hera's son Hephaistos the bronze-smith says gods should not fight over men; he tells how he was flung from heaven by Zeus on an earlier occasion and landed in Lemnos where the 'Sintian men' looked after him. Now, she smiles and the gods roar with 'unquenchable laughter' as they watch lame Hephaistos bustling around serving wine. These are not the stories we tell of gods in modern credal religions ('faiths'). Perhaps the Greeks took their religion less seriously?

But it is not like this. That gods should not fight over men is a cliché, uttered more imposingly by Apollo to Poseidon (*Iliad* 21.463–6). This must be a common epic situation: gods are always actually fighting over men and why they do it is a problem, to Homer and his audiences as well as to us. This is the strange thing about gods, which only Epicurus rejected: despite their lofty status and powers they are still strangely interested in us. Gods are known to support cities, because otherwise there would be no point in cities paying special reverence to particular gods. Hera accuses Zeus of helping the Trojans, because she supports key Greek states ('Argos, Sparta, and Mycenae with its broad streets', *Iliad* 4.52) and Apollo misleads Achilles in *Iliad* 21 because he supports Troy. If gods support cities and if cities come into conflict, then gods must necessarily fight each other, because if they did not, to whom else would we appeal? No one can doubt that they fight, even if Homer built this up into a grand battle that was too much for Plato and like-minded philosophers to stomach (*Iliad* 20 and 21).

On Lemnos there was a special cult of Hephaistos, who manufactured fire on the peak of Mt Mosychlos (in reality his priests may have used bronze mirrors), and that is why there is a myth of the special obligation Hephaistos owes to the Sinties and of the fall of the fire god to earth. This is not a random invention by Homer but a foundation for, or a reflection of, real cult which he has worked brilliantly into his rhapsodic account of daily quarrels among the gods.

So this scene speaks and it tells us about Zeus. He is the key to how events turn out: if you, Thetis, want a shift in the direction of battle, or if you, Hera, think that the battle is going in the direction of the Trojans, you look to Zeus. His influence is depicted here as based on exceptional brute power of the leading male in the household. But it is not simply that he is a hyperman amongst supermen: he is *different*. We can see this when we look at how precisely he controls the outcome of the battle.

Gods are less visible than we assume: men cannot readily identify them, because they operate in disguise or unseen. And Zeus is different again: not once in the poem does he walk the human earth. He never travels anywhere, except to Mt Ida in *Iliad* 14. His major interventions are to weigh a person's doom in the scales – this is *psychostasia*, 'soul-weighing'. By some unexplained process this is simultaneously the will of Zeus, and failure at the scales precipitates the doom of the unfortunate Sarpedon or Hector. I do not believe that this is something separate, determined by an impersonal force which constrains Zeus, 'fate' – Greeks had no such concept in those days.[67] Rather, his judgment, however human and reluctant in its presentation, is always a matter of weighing and of determining the right time.

Achilles is in no doubt that mortals should look to Zeus for the source of their fortunes and happiness. There are two *pithoi* (massive storage jars) on Zeus's threshold which colourfully embody the world of possible evils and possible successes. He draws from these jars and gives man one of two things – a mixture, or all bad. Such, says Achilles, is human life, that we suffer on the earth and that they up there live without care. This is a window on the harshness of life as it appears to us at blacker times and in blacker moods, and there is a strong feeling of revelation in these lines as the *Iliad* takes stock of itself and raises the question of closure. Like many portraits of how the gods work and what they do, this is not part of a systematic theology – we are offered a piece in a possible jigsaw, a snapshot from the world as it seems at some moments. We do not conclude from such passages that 'the Greeks believed' that your destiny was assigned to you at birth by Zeus, king of the gods. It is simply one way of viewing it.

Poets, particularly in the Archaic period, are fond of gloomy presentations of the gulf between man and gods, something which has led some scholars to talk of an 'archaic world view'.[68] Homer would in fact have been entirely comfortable with these postures. Achilles' pots are the basis of Mimnermos' comments (*c.* 630 BC):

> . . . there is no
> man to whom Zeus does not give many ills.

Mimnermos, fr. 2.15f. West

This clear sense that Zeus's influence over events is pervasive and thoroughgoing is underlined a generation later by Alcaeus in a papyrus scrap (*fr.* 39 Lobel-Page), where he appears to be saying that it is not possible for mortal men to escape what is determined and that it was a wise man who said that 'contrary to the fate laid down by Zeus [the *moira* of Zeus] not even a hair' could be moved. A special word for Zeus is *telos* – end, target, completion, fulfilment. This is already embedded in Homer, *Iliad* 1.5, where Zeus's plan was *accomplished* (*eteleieto*). Solon (*c.* 600 BC) complains that men do not think long enough about acts of violence 'but Zeus oversees the *telos* of everything' (*fr.* 13.17 West). And Semonides of Amorgos (*c.* 650 BC), rarely a cheerful writer, hammers home the message:

Boy, it is Zeus the deep-thundering who holds the *telos*
of all things that exist and disposes them as he will.
Men do not have mind, but day by day
they live the lives cattle do, knowing nothing
of how the god will bring each thing to fulfilment [*ekteleutesei*].

Semonides of Amorgos, fr. 1.1–5 West

Zeus of line 1 has become a rather vaguer 'the god' in line 5. It is worth remembering when you read Greek literature that Zeus is not always named: he is 'the god' par excellence.

Gods are acutely aware of the gulf between us and them, and, looking upon mortals, feel 'disdain mingled with slight pity' (Lloyd-Jones 1971: 3). This reaches classic expression in the astounding climax of the fight over Patroclus' body, when Homer puts centre stage the pair of horses which Achilles inherited from his father Peleus and lent to the now dead Patroclus. They are immortal and, standing bereft on the battlefield, serve to expose the gulf that separates us:

As the pair of them lamented, the son of Kronos [Zeus] saw them and took pity
and, moving his head, spoke to his heart:
'Poor creatures! Why did we give you two to lord Peleus,
a mortal, when you are unaging and immortal?
Was it that you might, amidst men in their wretchedness, suffer grief?
There is nothing anywhere more lamentable than man
of all the things that breathe and crawl upon the earth . . .'

Homer, Iliad 17.441–7

But the gods, and above all Zeus, are far from the concerns of men, however serious those concerns seem to us. While Achilles and Agamemnon fall out with disastrous consequences, Zeus and Hera's argument, which is meant to be read in the light of that of Achilles and Agamemnon, evaporates into rollicking, almost irresponsible, laughter. The laughter of the gods marks their *difference*. This is how Homer can present Zeus, with calculated paradox, as reacting to the battle between the gods themselves like this:

He laughed in his heart
from joy to see the gods coming together in strife.

Iliad 21.389f.

Such an apparently shocking comment points to a very different religious sense:

> We ourselves are accustomed to think of the divine being as preoccupied with man and his needs and are little concerned with his existence beyond humanity. But here the spiritual eye seeks a higher world which is no longer troubled for man's sake; and it stands enthralled before the vision of its perfection. Only in a remote reflection are we still able to grasp this vision, but even so it remains powerful. However zealously an Olympian may concern himself for men and their needs, the son of eternity always returns to the majesty of his heavenly splendor. There, in the ethereal heights, there is neither pain nor anxiety, neither age nor death. In the rapture of imperishable youth, beauty, and grandeur they stride through the spaces which shine for them eternally. There they encounter their peers, brothers and sisters, friends and loved ones, and one god takes joy in another, for the splendor of perfection rests upon each figure. To be sure, partisanship for men and peoples sometimes leads to a vigorous argument, but dissension never endures for long, and no day ends without bringing the gods together in festive pleasure for the common enjoyment of their divine existence.
>
> Otto 1954: 129

It was Otto's greatest merit to try to see into that alien idea of religion.

At the same time, we catch in Homer the beginning of a lightness of poetic touch in describing the gods in general and Zeus in particular. Zeus is seduced by Hera in Book 14 of the *Iliad*, overpowered by Sleep (*Hypnos*) and lust (Aphrodite). The whole scene is daring and dazzling, and became deeply offensive to serious-minded philosophers. As the flowers spring up beneath them on Mt Ida ('dewy lotus and saffron and hyacinth, dense and soft', 14.348f.), we students of classical antiquity can learnedly see that the scene has originated in a ritual *hierogamy*, as we saw above (p. 31). That explains where Homer got his tools from, but it does not explain away the rhapsodic licence with which he used them or the cultural collision course he had set up between the poets and the philosophers.

THE PRESOCRATIC THINKERS

. . . speaking in such a 'serious' way he diverts myths into what he says is mystic discourse about the gods.

Eusebius, *Praeparatio evangelica* 3.pref., talking about Plutarch
(*fr.* 157 Sandbach)

Before we turn to the stage, we look at how thinkers had addressed the question of Zeus before the dramatists wrote. The first philosophers, the so-called 'Presocratic' philosophers, in their attempts to think about the nature of the universe and the way it worked, advanced on mythology as we see it in Homer and, above all, Hesiod by constructing a more abstract world, which the gods of myth and cult found it harder to enter. Simultaneously, the quest for more 'scientific' explanation drove them towards fewer first principles, and in theology towards what looks to us like monotheism more than the polytheism of the cultures in which these thinkers lived. When their way of thinking has been digested, its effect is therefore to add weight to the tendency in Greek religion towards 'kathenotheism', thinking about one god as special on some occasions whilst not denying the existence of others. Time and again that special god is Zeus. Though he may lose ground as a mythological being, his special nature, transcending that of the other gods and planning the direction of everything, commends him. Even when he is not mentioned, you can sometimes feel him controlling the shape of philosophers' speculations on the ultimate divinity.

Towards the end of the sixth century BC, Theagenes of Rhegium introduced the philosophical way of saving unacceptable poetic mythology: the battle of the gods in Homer's *Iliad* (Book 20) was an *allegory* for the conflict between the elements that make up the universe. And if Heraclitus (*c.* 500 BC) proposed that the universe was fundamentally an immortal fire (*fr.* B30 *DK*), then it is hard not to think of the *aither*,[69] the special realm of Zeus. So, Heraclitus' statement that 'Thunderbolt steers everything' (*fr.* 64) must tell us about the force of the heavenly fire, effectively allegorising the mythology of Zeus. This sits neatly with the view that 'the One Wise, the only one, is both willing and unwilling to be spoken of by the name of Zeus' (*fr.* 32). Thus the oneness of Zeus, and his special role distinct from the other gods, enables thinkers from the Presocratics to the last Neoplatonists to associate him with their single, topmost, universe-ordering principle. In the fifth century BC, the Pythagorean Philolaos put this in a geometric way: Zeus was responsible for the angle of the dodecahedron that gave unity to this 12-sided figure, which must reflect the 12 Olympians (*fr.* A14 *DK*). Empedokles, also in the mid fifth century, associated Zeus and Hera with two of the four elements; perhaps Hera was earth rather than air, which became common later, but there is no doubt that Zeus was fire (*fr.* B6 *DK*).

Now that Zeus had been liberated from his human shape and had become the most vital element in the universe, it was possible for a new mystic language to appear. By 500 BC poets had begun composing texts under the name of the mythical Thracian bard 'Orpheus'. One of the early Orphic poems is a hymn to Zeus reflecting his new cosmic role:

> Zeus is first, Zeus of the flashing lightning is last,
> Zeus is the head, Zeus the middle, by Zeus are all things accomplished.
> Zeus is male, Zeus is an immortal nymph,
> Zeus is the foundation of earth and starry heaven . . .
>
> *Orphica fr.* 21a Kern[70]

The first two lines were known to Plato and are discussed in a papyrus from Derveni in Greece dated to the late fourth century BC. This is bold writing, and the strange third line must refer to the power of Zeus to create – therefore he is both male and female. In a way he had demonstrated this through giving birth on his own to Athene. This sort of poetry now tries to break free of the limited traditional mythology. It also begins a stylistic manner, the repetitive appeal to the power of Zeus's name, the ultimate encapsulated in a monosyllable.

THE TRAGIC STAGE

Tragedians can think in any way they choose about Zeus and in any way that suits the character they have mouth the words. But one fact is immediately striking: *Zeus never appears on the tragic stage*, just as in Homer he never appears on earth. Thus any talk of Zeus in anthropomorphic terms is in fact in some way metaphorical. And extremes can be reached:

> Zeus is the aither, Zeus the land, Zeus the heaven,
> Zeus is everything and whatever is higher than this.
>
> Aeschylus, *Heliads fr.* 70 Radt

We cannot know how these lines came to be spoken. The *Heliads*, 'Daughters of the Sun', was presumably about the grief of these sisters of Phaethon at his death following his doomed attempt to drive the Sun's chariot. But they look like a statement of pantheism (that god is everything and everything is god), something which has become possible after the Presocratic philosophers.

We know more about the characters in Aeschylus' *Agamemnon* who talk about Zeus. The Chorus of old men, in their entrance piece (*parodos*), know that the power of Menelaus and Agamemnon comes from Zeus (43) and that Zeus sent them to punish Paris. But the execution of this justice will, they recognise, be grim for Greeks as well as Trojans (60–67), as is typical of the justice of Zeus. Later, as the Chorus sings of how Agamemnon had to sacrifice his own daughter so that the fleet might sail against Troy, they reach the limits of their understanding of Zeus in lines that rather defy translation:

> Zeus whoever he is, if he likes to be called this,
> this is what I address him as.
> I cannot get close to it, though I measure out everything,
> except [by calling him] Zeus, it the frustrating burden of thought
> is truly to be cast aside.
>
> *Agamemnon* 160–66

The old men think of how the myth tells that Zeus came to power through a violent succession and reach a thought that, whilst not the message of the play, is the sort of jangly semi-proverbial expression that old men might think profound:

> (Zeus) who guided mortals to think sense,
> who made *pathei mathos* a rule.
>
> *Agamemnon* 176–8

Mathos is 'learning'; *pathos* is 'experience/suffering'. *Pathei mathos* is 'learning by what happens to you'. What the old men are really wrestling with is the difficulty of understanding the mind of Zeus, i.e. of seeing the justice in what he accomplishes. But they know there is a justice to look for.

It is Zeus Xenios (of guest-friendship) that actually drives the Greeks against the Trojans in *Agamemnon* (362), and the Trojans as a result have the 'blow of Zeus' to tell of (367). Plainly they have been smitten, not by picturesque thunderbolt but by human agency operating to uphold principles, if cruelly. In this case it is the principle of guest-friendship that bonds different human societies together and is not lightly to be sundered. In the same way, the ghost of king Darius realises, in Aeschylus' *Persians*, that in their attack on Greece through their unrestrained violence [*hybris*] they created a 'crop of destruction [*ate*] from which to reap a lamentable harvest' and Zeus comes in as 'the punisher of excessively boastful conceptions' (*Persians* 821f., 827f.).

The view of Zeus in *Prometheus Bound* (whether the play is by Aeschylus or by another hand) adopts a different, Hesiodic, tone. In this wonderfully excessive play, opening in the 'uninhabited desolation' of Scythia, three gods march onto the stage – Hephaistos, Might and Violence. The latter two are the agents of the, as always, unseen Zeus, embodying aspects of the power of Zeus already in Hesiod (*Theogony* 385–8):

> also she brought forth Kratos [Might] and Bia [Violence],
> wonderful children. These have no house apart from Zeus, nor any
> dwelling nor path except that wherein God leads them, but they
> dwell always with Zeus the loud-thunderer.

Zeus's problematic justice is on display in *Prometheus Bound* but he must also have been behind the freeing of Prometheus in the lost *Prometheus Unbound*, perhaps along the lines long ago sketched by

Hesiod (*Theogony* 529–31) where Herakles shoots the bird that gnaws Prometheus' liver[71]

> not without the will of Olympian Zeus who reigns on high, that
> the glory of Herakles the Theban-born might be yet greater than
> it was previously over the plenteous earth

What predominates in the account of Zeus given by characters under the microscope of tragedy is a sense of his distance and the difficulty of understanding his world order:

> Zeus really ought, if he is (actually) in heaven,
> not make the same person (constantly) unfortunate.
>
> Euripides, *fr.* 900 Kannicht[2]

> You see him who high up here the boundless *aither*
> and the earth embraces in his moist arms
> – consider this Zeus, deem this god.
>
> Euripides, *fr.* 941 Kannicht[2]

ZEUS IN PLATO AND ARISTOTLE

Plato is indeed deeply concerned with the soul and with a world beyond this physical world of appearance and futile pleasures. His vision, however, drawing on the work done by the Presocratic philosophers, does not take named gods particularly seriously, except in order to correct the improper ideas of the poets about the behaviour of the divine. He does sometimes suggest that the gods need to be understood as ways of talking about things which are much deeper. One particularly striking instance, which has a Christian afterlife we will see in the next section, is the discussion of the meaning of the names Zeus and Kronos in his *Cratylus*. Here playful, or experimental, etymologies are used to suggest philosophic views of the divine nature:

> Some people call him *Zena*, others *Dia* [these are 'accusative' forms of the word *Zeus*] and if we put them together we reveal the nature of the god . . . for there is

> no-one who is more responsible for us and everyone else *living* [*zen*] than the
> leader and king of the entirety. So it turns out that this god is correctly named,
> *through* [*dia*] whom it is possible for all creatures to *live* [*zen*].
>
> Plato, *Cratylus* 396a–b

Plato, in his unhappiness with mythology in the *Republic*, takes particular exception to myths of Zeus, evidently because this is the nearest one can come in the traditional mythology to the sort of fundamental divine force to which Plato is actually committed. Because 'the god' is good (379b), Zeus cannot, as Achilles thought, dole out evil from the pots in heaven (379d; *Iliad* 24.527). Nor does 'the god' change his appearance, and as a result the gods do *not* travel in disguise about the world (381d; *Odyssey* 17.485). As for the notorious Ouranos, Kronos and Zeus mythology, Plato thinks it is untellable even if it does have some ulterior significance (377e–378a), and the same goes for the tales of gods fighting each other and the tale of Zeus throwing Hephaistos out of heaven (378b–e; *Iliad* 20, 1.590–94). Among myths criticised elsewhere, it is interesting that in the late and rather conventional treatise, the *Laws* (636c–d), the myth of Zeus and Ganymede is said to be made up by the Cretans to justify their perversions. This both anticipates later criticism of the myth, especially by Christians, and picks up the sort of ritual we found in Crete (p. 50).

In the *Timaeus*, where Plato talks about the construction of the Universe, he assigns the traditional gods a very small place in it. The 'Demiurge' (manufacturer god) has done his work and then Plato proceeds to the other gods. The sole mention of Zeus is: 'From Kronos and Rhea proceeded Zeus and Hera and all the ones we know are said to be their siblings, and others who are their offspring in turn' (41a). However, the language Plato uses of the Demiurge is the language that later in the Platonic tradition is applied to Zeus (Schwabl 1978: 1338). We may add that this is not surprising, given that Plato is really trying to reconceive what a Zeus should be. If Zeus was 'father of men and gods', the Demiurge is 'maker and father of this entirety' (28c), but in accordance with the doctrine of the *Republic* he is responsible only for good (30a), and therefore the question for Plato has clearly been whether the term 'Zeus' remains valuable or is simply too inaccurate. He seems to have judged the latter on this occasion.

It is consistent with this view that Plato's Zeus is generally in the mythic or conventional register. The conventionally pious man, Euthyphro, believes Zeus is 'the best and most just' and then proceeds to say how Kronos deserved to be bound and Ouranos deserved castration (*Euthyphro* 5e–6a)! The legislation that Plato envisages in the *Laws* will have its Zeus *Horios* to protect boundary stones, its Zeus Homophylos (of 'tribe-together') to protect social cohesion, its Zeus Xenios to protect strangers (all 843a). It will also have a temple of Zeus and Hera where penal taxation on those indulging in excessive dowries can be dedicated (774d). Plato could be as revolutionary as he liked in his thought, but in reality there was no real world conceivable without the apparatus of gods in general and Zeus in particular. And Aristotle is of much the same view when he opines that the whole anthropomorphic apparatus of gods is for popular consumption, for the maintenance of law and for the general good (*Metaphysics* 1074b1), or that kingship is projected onto them from present and historical experience of kingship among men and 'if men make gods resemble them in appearance, they do the same with their lifestyles' (*Politics* 1252b23–7).

SOME HELLENISTIC POETS

Zeus remained a living force in Greek literature long after the Classical Age of the fifth and fourth centuries BC. As Alexander the Great's conquests changed the world, and his successor as king in Egypt, Ptolemy I Soter, set up a great library in Alexandria – the New York of the ancient world – to collect the books that constituted Greek culture, poets who sought to define and continue that culture found their own place for Zeus. That is what I will look at briefly in this section.

We know the story of the Argonauts from Apollonius of Rhodes. His *Argonautica* is surer than Homer that Zeus plans – indeed the hero Jason is surer that Zeus intervenes in detail to ensure justice (2.1179f.), and the narrator himself supposes that Zeus takes measures following the criminal murder of her brother Apsyrtus by Medea (4.557f.). Indeed Apollonius seems to have invented (Gantz 1993: i.351) a particular reason for the torment of the prophet Phineus:

> . . . but he did not pay any attention even to Zeus himself
> revealing with precision the holy mind to men.
>
> Apollonius of Rhodes, *Argonautica* 2.180f.

The mind of Zeus is not just too difficult for mortals to understand – it is also secret (as Phineus himself now realises, 2.311–6). The knowledge of god has become a dangerous thing, as it was in the mystery religions that were now expanding and were founded on the secrecy observed by their initiates, and as it would be in Gnostic religions in the first centuries AD, where man's Fall resulted from the fatal attempt to know God prematurely.

The poet Aratus opens his poem on the constellations, the *Phaenomena*, with a mighty hymn to Zeus (1–5), playing the pantheistic themes we saw developing earlier:

> From Zeus let us begin! Him we men never leave
> unsaid. Full of Zeus are all the streets,
> all the marketplaces of men, full the sea
> and harbours. In every way we are all dependent on Zeus.
> For we are of his race too . . .

But Aratus's task is to show how the stars can guide human activity *to the extent that it is 'themis'* (religiously permissible, 18). The mind of Zeus is a great Mystery, not lightly to be revealed.

Callimachus' collection of poetic *Hymns* too opens with a hymn to Zeus. Here we have a work which characteristically of its age and environment collects local traditions particularly on the birth of Zeus: he was born in the Parrhasia region of Arcadia, he decides, not in Crete.[72] Callimachus enshrines the established culture and toys with it. But the climax comes when we turn to Zeus's relationship to royalty:

> From Zeus come kings, since there is nothing more divine than
> the lords of Zeus; so you [Zeus] selected them as your speciality.
> You gave them cities to protect while you yourself sat
> on acropolises, watching over those who govern
> the people with crooked judgments and those who do the opposite.
> [. . .]
> . . . and it is fitting to judge

by our ruler, for he has gone far above (others):

in the evening he fulfils that which he planned in the morning . . .

Callimachus, Hymn to Zeus 78–82, 84–6

'Our ruler' is Ptolemy II (285–247 BC) and this is the new world of monarchs and Zeus (p. 78).

STOICS AND OTHERS: ALLEGORY AND EUHEMERISM

If Plato and Aristotle had swung away from traditional religion, it was the job of later philosophers to find a way of accommodating this central feature of Greek cultural life. Plato's successor Xenokrates (head of the Academy from 339 to 314 BC) did just this. For him (*fr.* 15 Heinze) the first principle in the universe was the monad, that single ultimate source of things; it could be viewed as male, as odd (as opposed to even), as divine; and it could be called Zeus (in the *Zena* form). This then combined with the dyad, the principle of plurality, which might be viewed as feminine, as mother of the gods and as the world soul.

It is a short step from this, then, to the Stoics. The founder of Stoicism was Zeno of Kition, whose own name is derived from Zeus. The ultimate principle for him was the fiery breath that animates everything, ourselves included, something to which one need build no temples for it is within us (*fr.* 146).[73] This fiery air was the aether and that was what Zeus really was. It was also the *logos*, the 'reason' or 'word' (as in St John's Gospel), that pervades the universe, the soul, nature, fate, god, the mind of Zeus, the necessity of the universe – interchangeably (*frs* 158, 160). This is the Nature according to which we must live. Other gods amount to other elements: Hera the air, Poseidon the sea, Hephaistos fire, and other gods to other aspects of the physical universe (*fr.* 169); Aphrodite is the binding force of parts to each other and the Dioskouroi 'correct reason and worthy dispositions' (*frs* 168, 170).

Cleanthes, his successor, carries this to an extreme, with his remarkable *Hymn to Zeus*, some of which I present below:

Most glorious of the immortals, of many names, all-powerful forever,

Zeus, originator of Nature, governing everything with law,

Hail!: it is right [*themis*] for all mortals to address you,

for from you have they gained an imitation of an echo,

they alone of all mortal things that live and crawl upon the earth.

Therefore shall I hymn you and forever sing your power.

You all this world, swirling around the earth,

obeys, wherever you lead it and willingly is ruled over by you.

Such an assistant do you have in your invincible hands,

the forked, fiery, ever-living lightning-bolt.

Through its stroke all deeds of Nature are done

and with it you steer the common reason which circulates

through all things, mingling with great and minor lights,

and with it you have become so much the highest king throughout.

Nor does any deed happen on earth without you, spirit [*daimon*],

neither across the divine vault of the ether nor on the ocean,

except all the things that bad people do through their foolishness.

Cleanthes, *Hymn to Zeus* 1–13 (*SVF* i.537, *HP* 54I)

As with Homer's Zeus, there is a categorical distinction between him and the other gods. The rest are all destructible and in the last resort only aspects of Zeus himself,[74] as are we, because we are 'of his race', as both Cleanthes and Aratus remind us. Did Aratus borrow from the Stoic, or Cleanthes from the poet? Whatever it is, there is a sense of a new enthusiasm for Zeus fuelled by a far-reaching philosophy of the universe.

Finally, the Stoic L. Annaeus Cornutus, a contemporary of Nero's, shows us how Plato's *Cratylus* had been incorporated into this way of thinking:

Just as you are governed by your soul, so the universe has a soul which holds it together and it is called 'Zeus'. It is alive, with primacy and for ever, and is responsible for the life [*zen*] of things which live. For this reason Zeus is said to be king over the universe, just as the soul in us and our nature might be said to be king over us. We call it Zeus [*Dia*] because *through* [*dia*] it everything comes into existence and is preserved.

Cornutus, *Compendium of Greek Theology* 2

With this depth of allegory, the story of the stone that Kronos was given instead of Zeus assumes new significance: it was the earth itself formed as the foundation of an infant universe (*ibid.* 6). However, Cornutus finds it necessary to account for a great deal of the known cult of Zeus, which is still very much alive. We are told why he is called 'father of gods and men', 'cloud gatherer', 'deeply thundering', why he holds the aegis (because of the rushing storms):

> and they call him *soter* [saviour] and *herkeios* and 'of the city' and 'paternal' and 'of common kin' and *xenios* and *ktesios* and 'of counsel' and 'trophy-holder' and 'of freedom' – he has infinitely many names of this type because he extends to every capability and condition and is the cause of, and overseer of, everything. This is why he is also called father of Justice [*Dike*] . . . and of the Graces . . . and of the Seasons [*Horai*].
>
> Cornutus, *Compendium of Greek Theology* 9

The sceptre in his hand is not just a symbol of royal power but also of stability and support; the thunderbolt in his right hand needs no explanation; 'often he is depicted holding a Nike' because he cannot be defeated. The eagle is his bird because it is the fastest bird. And so it goes on, overwhelming in its devotion despite the intellectual detachment of the philosophy.

A generation later, around AD 101, the great orator Dio Chrysostom, only a year or two after returning from exile to his home city of Prusa in northeast Turkey, delivered his *Borysthenitic Oration* and, reaching the climax, told (36.39–61) of the creation of the universe itself in a myth he imaginatively claimed had been created by the Magi of Persia, though it looks rather Platonic and Stoic to anyone else's eyes. The universe is a chariot powered by four horses, of which the highest and outermost is sacred to Zeus himself. Sun, moon and stars are a mere part of its fiery brilliance. It is of course the ether. Next come the horses of Hera (air), Poseidon (water) and Hestia (an unusual choice for earth). But the horse is only an image for the soul of the charioteer 'or rather the thinking and ruling part' of that soul. This *nous*, the most intellectual and divine part of the soul, had at the beginning of time in a lightning flash been the demiurge (creator) of the universe that now exists. A fiery air resulted and in union with Hera, in this most complete sexual act, he released the entire seed of the universe. 'This is the blessed marriage of Hera and Zeus that the children of the wise sing in secret rites.' And when the demiurge looked at his act of creation he did not simply rejoice, no,

> seated on Olympus, his dear heart laughed
> from joy to see the gods

'all of them now born and present'. Thus Dio deflects that much criticised passage of Homer (p. 89 above) into a mystic, philosopher's reading of the beginnings of the universe. And though he expresses it with his own flair, this is not really original, but something that any educated person of AD 101 would recognise and applaud. Only children or the uneducated would by now take Zeus literally.

Other awkward moments in Homer led to no less inspired solutions. One was where Zeus had challenged the other gods (*Iliad* 8.18–22):

> Come, try, you gods and all you goddesses:
> hang a golden chain from heaven
> and hold on to it, you gods and all you goddesses
> – you won't drag down from heaven to the ground
> Zeus highest counsellor, not even if you labour very hard . . .

Aristotle took this unseemly tug of war and used it as an image for the nature of motion (*On the movement of animals* 699b37). Motion is relative to something fixed and unmoving and this applies to the Universe, which moves under the influence of the unmoved mover – a single, focal god, by implication Zeus in an Aristotelian Homer. What Aristotle was using as a casual illustration was used more determinedly in later mystic tradition, and by the time of the last Neoplatonists, such as Proclus,[75] there is a doctrine that the ultimate divine force driving the universe, the One, is tied or connected to all the forms of being beneath it through a *seira* ('chain', the word Homer uses), or rather a series of chains. Though lower forms of being may display a baffling multiplicity, what makes them intelligible and valuable is their link to the divine. This idea has a continuing popularity today as the 'Golden

Chain', or the 'Great Chain of Being'. Just remember: Zeus is at the other end!

Rationalisation is a different approach, designed to reduce myth to straightforward actual events, and one to which Greek culture was indeed susceptible. We ourselves know that myth is one thing and history quite another. But for Greeks, who had no history before the fifth century BC except by word of mouth, myth occupied the space that older history does for us. Thus the division between history and myth was not real versus mythical, but reliable modern versus more fanciful old. They had no trouble for instance in thinking of Herakles as a real person of long ago. How far could this go? It is one thing, as Hecataeus did in his *Genealogiai* (1F27), to say that Herakles did not bring Eurystheus a dog from Hades (Cerberus) but a snake from Taenarum that was so poisonous it was called 'the dog of Hades'. But would anyone claim that Zeus actually once walked the earth? This was the problem in classical times, that rationalisation would deal with things that were unrealistic in myths of heroes, but gods were gods and therefore what was unacceptable in their behaviour could only be dealt with by allegory. Nevertheless, this final frontier was crossed by Euhemeros of Messene.

Euhemeros lived in the wake of the conquests of Alexander and was a friend of Cassander, King of Macedonia (317–298 BC). The conquests of Alexander closed the gap between men and gods and sometimes led to gods being assimilated to him. Dionysos was often supposed to have conquered the world and reached India as Alexander had, but Euhemeros took a new and trenchant line in his *Sacred Record* (*Hiera Anagraphe*). In this work he told of his travel to a mythic land, Panchaia, one of a group of islands many days' sail across the Ocean south of Arabia:

> Here he saw the inhabitants, the Panchaioi, who were of exceptional piety and worshipped the gods with utterly magnificent sacrifices and remarkable gold and silver offerings. The island was sacred to the gods . . . and there was in it on a high hill, at its peak, a temple of Zeus Triphylios, founded by Zeus himself at the time when he was king of the whole world, when he was still amongst men. In this shrine there was a gold pillar on which, in Panchaian letters, there was written down a summary of the achievements of Ouranos and Kronos and Zeus . . . before

> Zeus, succeeding Kronos as king, married Hera and Demeter and Themis. From them he had the following children: the Kouretes from the first, Persephone from the second, and Athene from the third.
>
> Euhemeros *FGrH* 63F2 (as reported by Diodoros)

Characteristically of an age in which royalty and ruler cult was taking off, Euhemeros was asking what difference there was between a king and a god if both were distinguished for their acts as Benefactor (Euergetes) and Saviour (Soter) of mankind because of their Kind disposition (Eumenes). As rulers became remote, gods came closer.

This fantasy is evidence for a weakening commitment to the gods and their worship. Euhemeros himself was later reviled as an *atheos*, a 'godless' person, not quite an atheist in our sense. For all we know he could have believed in a more abstract divinity as much as Plato or Epicurus. He did, however, by taking this final step, make 'universal history' (a total history, from the beginning) more possible than it had been. Thus the first major universal history had been that of Ephoros in the 340s/330s BC. He had begun with 'the return of the Herakleidai', after the Trojan War, on the grounds that verifiable history started there. What might seem to us like good method is of course really a gap waiting to be plugged. Euhemeros had provided the toolset and Dionysios Skytobrachion (probably second century BC) deployed it vigorously to deal with the *Campaigns of Dionysos and Athene*, the Amazons, the Argonauts and the Trojan War. Now Diodoros of Sicily could take a quantum leap forward and deal with the gods themselves in his universal history, the *Historical Library*. For the following information on Zeus, we are indebted to the inhabitants of Atlantis (a source of Skytobrachion's that doesn't command confidence):

> The son of Kronos, Zeus, followed the opposite style of life to his father and showed himself reasonable and kindly [*philanthropos*] to everyone to the extent that the masses called him 'father' [*Zeus father, then*]. Accounts of how he took over the kingdom vary – either on the willing abdication of his father or because the masses chose him out of hatred for his father. Kronos launched a campaign against him with the help of the Titans but Zeus won in the battle and, on becoming Lord of all lands, he visited the whole world, doing good to (*euergetein*) the race of men . . .
>
> Diodoros, 3.61.4

And they call him *Zen* (a variant form of 'Zeus') because he caused men to *live* (*zen*) well.

Along with this rationalisation goes a process of dividing gods and heroes up into several with the same name. This is designed to eliminate inconsistencies of parentage or of chronology in universal history. There are, it turns out, three Zeuses:

> Those who are called 'theologians' count three Zeuses. Zeus 1 and 2 were born in Arcadia. The father of Zeus 1 was Aether and they say Persephone and Dionysus are his children. The father of Zeus 2 is Ouranos (Heaven), who is said to have given birth to Athene, whom they say was the leader in, and inventor of, war. Zeus 3 was a Cretan, the son of Kronos, and his tomb is on display on that island.
>
> Cicero, *On the Nature of the Gods* 3.53 (but with Greek god names)

The tomb of Zeus on Crete ceases to be a curiosity, and becomes the proof of Euhemerism.

It can be seen that Euhemeros had a lasting impact. This included an impact on an emerging nation, the Romans. Arguably their most important early writer, certainly the most versatile, was Ennius (239–169 BC). In his lost Latin piece, the *Euhemeros*, he 'translated and followed' the *Sacred Record* and brought this work thereby to the attention of Romans, such as Cicero (*Nature of the Gods*, 1.119) and Pliny the Elder who tells us that the Babylonian god Zeus Belos was the founder of astrology (*Natural History* 6.121). But it is perhaps more important in the long run that Christian authors writing in Latin took up this approach with enthusiasm.

Lactantius (*c.* AD 240–*c.* 320) apparently succeeded in finding a text of Ennius's *Euhemerus* and quotes the following from it:

> When Jupiter had travelled round the earth five times and had distributed empires to his friends and relations, and made laws for men and done a lot of other good things, having now acquired undying fame such that he would be remembered for ever, he passed from life in Crete and departed to the gods. His tomb is in Crete, in the town of Gnossus, and on it is written in Greek letters ZAN KPONOY, i.e. in Latin 'Jupiter son of Saturn'.
>
> Ennius, *Euhemerus* (Euhemeros *FGrH* 63F24)

These Euhemerist views were part of the Christian toolset, particularly in north Africa, practised by authors such as Tertullian, Minucius Felix, and Lactantius' teacher Arnobius. Augustine would use it in his *City of God* (7.18 and 7.27) and from these authors it passed into the medieval tradition (see 'Zeus afterwards' below).

SYNCRETISM

Greeks had always had to deal with the question of who the gods of foreigners ('barbarians') actually were. So, Herodotus in describing the gods of the Scythians says without thinking it at all problematic that 'Zeus in Scythian is quite rightly in my opinion called Papaios' (4.59). It is a natural assumption that as all Greeks worshipped Zeus, then all foreigners did as well: Homer's readers doubtless shuddered when Polyphemos tells Odysseus, 'We Cyclopes aren't bothered about Zeus the aegis-bearer' (*Odyssey* 9.275). No nation is really this barbaric. So it is that as the world with which Greeks are acquainted grows larger and as Greek culture spreads ever wider, we discover quite a number of Zeuses who express local divinities in the common (Greek) language. Identification of gods with each other is known as *syncretism*. This became crucial as the Greek world was extended under Alexander the Great. A need had in effect arisen for a common religious currency which could ease the free trade of religious ideas.

This trend is boosted by the activities of Alexander himself. The scene is the oracular shrine at the oasis of Siwah northwest of Egypt. This belonged to Ammon, long brought into the Greek system as Zeus Ammon. Here Alexander is pronounced in Egyptian fashion to be the son of the god, and inheritor, therefore, of the position of the pharaohs. Ammon is, however, an alien Zeus, at whom Lucian pokes fun in the second century AD (*Council of the gods* 10), and which Lucan comments on in the first century:

Jupiter, so they say, but not brandishing thunderbolts
and not similar to ours, but with twisted horns, Hammon.

Lucan, *Civil War* 9.513f.

Principal gods, whatever their attributes, have a tendency to become the local Zeus. In what is now northwest Turkey, then Phrygia and the surrounding lands, a local god of importance, Sabazios, is usually made a Zeus (rather than a Dionysos). His cult embraced snake-handling, gained some favour under Attalos III of Pergamon (in 135/4) and later became a focus for associations of individuals. These were called Sabaziasts and enjoyed the riddling depictions of toads, turtles, lizards and frogs crawling over sculpted hands.

Down in Syria a range of divinities popped in and out of identification with Zeus. Each one is a 'lord' (*baal*). So the lord of what in Greek is Mt Kasios, but Saphon in Syrian, is Zeus Kasios or Baal Saphon. This is the mountain where Zeus had his battle with Typhon. Here, in the Hellenistic world the traditions which had first given rise to the Zeus-Typhon myth were rediscovered and what might have seemed like an identification of convenience between one god of the weather and another on a Syrian mountain genuinely reflected a real constituent of Zeus's identity. Another, a major storm and rain god, Adad in Babylon and Assyria, but Hadad in Syria and Phoenicia, was presented in Greek as Zeus Adados.[76] Another version of this god was the sun god at Heliopolis (Baalbek in the Lebanon) and visitors today may still marvel at the remains of the huge and glorious temple to Jupiter of Heliopolis, or Adad, built by emperors from Antoninus Pius (AD 138–61) to Caracalla (AD 211–17) and destroyed by Theodosius in 379. Its striking cult statue, wearing a robe strangely decorated front and back with busts (for instance of Sun and Moon), however, escaped destruction and could still be seen in the 560s. Inscriptions to Jupiter Heliopolitanus are found as far afield as Hadrian's Wall. This was a great oracular shrine consulted even by Trajan. Thus we see a movement in theology towards a great syncretistic god, embracing Zeus, local gods and the Sun, both in the Zeus of Heliopolis and in Zeus Sarapis. The Syrian Zeus-Adad, of which another instance is to be found at Hierapolis (Bambyce) and whose cult is described by Lucian in his *On the Syrian Goddess*, was sometimes worshipped as a bull, like the Canaanite god of *Exodus* 32 worshipped as a golden *bull-calf*. This also takes us back to the formative stages of Greek myth, if we think of the story of Zeus who in bull form snatched Europa from Tyre.

In the same part of the world, Jews were usually bitterly opposed to syncretism, as we can see from Elijah's supposition that 'Baal' is a different god, that of the Canaanites, who must be shown up as powerless to deliver fire or rain (*1 Kings* 18). It was therefore a deliberate provocation by the Seleucid king Antiochus IV Epiphanes, in the course of a bloody repression, to dedicate the Temple on the Mount at Jerusalem to Zeus Olympios and another on Mt Gerizim to Zeus Xenios (*2 Maccabees* 6.2). This was in the context of the revolt of the Maccabees in 168/7 BC against modernising, or rather hellenising, forces. It is possible that Antiochus actually had a policy to draw up a consistent pattern of worship of Zeus in his kingdom, tied to the cult of the ruler (Préaux 1978: ii.577). But Jerusalem was clearly a step too far.

A different merger took place in Egypt, embracing the strong native religious tradition. Independently of Greek culture, the sacred bull Apis appears to have been identified with the god of the dead and in particular of the dead pharaoh, Osiris, resulting in the powerful god Sarapis (or in Latin, Serapis). But under Ptolemy I, Greek religious experts identified him in turn with the Greek god of the dead Pluto, whose iconography was adopted. This powerful god, based in the Memphis Serapeum with its monk-like *katochoi*, was identified with various Greek gods but above all, because of his authority and his association with rulers (the Ptolemies in this case), with Zeus. Once again a single god becomes a special focus for veneration and for understanding the world order, and inscriptions of the Roman Empire, particularly from the second century on (Vidman 1969: 343), will honour 'Zeus Sun Great Serapis' or proclaim that there is *One* Zeus Serapis.

GREEK THOUGHT ABOUT ROMAN JUPITER

Jupiter is a special case of syncretism: he is, and becomes, the Roman equivalent of Zeus. As we have seen (p. 9) the words Zeus *pater* ('father') and Jupiter are in origin the same words as each other, deriving from the common Indo-European culture of their linguistic ancestors. Much will obviously have changed in the 3,000 years since

us. The universe is not random, there is something wis‹
ns, and it determines fate. In the poetic discourse these ar‹
ds of Jupiter, but really this is the divine mind that infuses th‹
vorld and universe in which we live. It is within this traditior
can understand the oracle from the shrine of Zeus Ammon
byan desert, as imagined by Lucan (AD 39–65) and admired by
Epistle 10 §22)

e is no seat of (the) god but earth and ocean and air
heaven and virtue. Why should we seek further for the gods above?
ter is whatever you see and whatever you are moved by.

Lucan, Pharsalia 9.578–80

d be wrong, however, before closing, to overlook the rela-
between Jupiter and the emperor. There is a strong sense
in the Aeneid that Jupiter reflects the beneficent control of the
world by Augustus. Indeed the whole of the Roman emperor
rted from the declaration that on his death Julius Caesar had
a god, Jupiter Julius, whose Flamen Dialis – as the time-
d priest of Jupiter was called – would be Mark Antony. Jupiter
e the chosen image of the emperor Septimius Severus too (AD
), whilst others preferred to be Mars or Hercules.

OVERVIEW

e beginning, then, the superficialities of epic poetry cloak a
depth of reflection on the nature of the divine, and the
es of that understanding are progressively teased out by later
s. He is the controller of an often grim world order. Presocratic
s then liberated Zeus from his mythic dress and saw in him the
nciple of the universe, perhaps even fire. The impious battle of
s in Homer had only been an allegory for these scientific or
phic truths. It is against these backgrounds that tragedy is
, where characters struggle to find meaning in acute crises and
r the mystery of Zeus. Plato and Aristotle have no time for the
Zeus, but are deeply influenced by the evolving philosophic

then. However, as Romans and Italians came into contact with Greeks settled all around Italy (for instance at Naples, *Neapolis*, 'New City') and as they entered the stage as a world power, Roman enthusiasm for Greek literature and culture at all levels of society drew the Roman Jupiter back towards Zeus, just as in Greece the poets once had to some extent reunited the different Zeuses of different Greeks.

It is beyond my scope to start anew at this point on Jupiter and Roman culture. But I do want to show how thought about Jupiter continues in the West the story of Zeus.

Ennius, effectively the father of Latin literature, had a character in his tragedy, *Thyestes*, speak up in grandiose philosophic mode:

> aspice hoc sublime candens, quem invocant omnes Iovem
> Just look at this shining on high, whom all invoke as Jove.

Ennius, *fr.* 153 Jocelyn, in Cicero, *Nature of the Gods* 2.4

This is Zeus the awesome ether, faithfully transposed from Euripides (p. 95 above).

More striking still are the lines of Valerius of Sora (tribune in 82 BC), where thought going back to the earliest Orphic poetry finds new, and startling, expression in the hands of this 'most literary of all those who wear the toga' (Cicero, *de oratore* 3.43):

> Iuppiter omnipotens regum rerumque deumque
> progenitor genetrixque deum deus unus et omnes!
> Jupiter all-powerful over kings and the world and the gods,
> begetter and mother of gods, one god and all gods!

Valerius Soranus, in Augustine, *City of God* 7.10

These splendid lines were quoted by the polymath Varro (116–27 BC) in a dialogue *On the Cult of the Gods*. Varro himself was a key figure in the development of views about the gods at Rome with his ency-clopedic masterpiece, the *Human and Divine Antiquities* in 41 books, dedicated to Julius Caesar (the chief priest) in 47 BC. Resting on Greek views and terminology, he divided discourse about the gods ('theologia') into three types:

1. *mythicon*, concerning myth, which is the discourse of poets;
2. *physicon*, concerning nature and science, which is the discourse of philosophers;
3. *civile* (i.e. *politicon*), pertaining to the state, which is the language of nations and their political leaders.

This presents a number of problems for the religious person: even Varro admitted that in myth (1) 'there are many things made up contrary to the dignity and nature of the immortals'. As for civic religion (3), statues cannot possibly correspond to the reality of the divine nature and neither can gods that have resulted from assigning divine status to great men of the past, as Euhemeros alleged for gods of cult (see below). Thus the only reality for educated men such as Cicero and Varro is (2), the philosophical.[77]

What, then, for Varro is the real nature of Jupiter? So far as we can tell, he took on board the views of Greek thinkers like the Stoic philosopher Poseidonios. Jupiter is 'the mind of this world who fills that whole mass which is constructed from the four elements and moves it' or perhaps he is the aether/heaven that embraces the air/earth (Juno) that lies below. His thought is reflected in Augustine's dismissive comments:

> Let Jupiter at once be all the gods and goddesses, or, as some wish, let them all be parts of him, or, as it appears to those who have decided he is the mind of the world – a view shared by many great teachers, let them be his virtues.
>
> Augustine, *City of God* 4.11

Augustine mentions a line of Vergil's in this context:

> . . . for god pervades everything
> – lands, stretches of sea, and the deep heaven.
>
> Vergil, *Georgics* 4.221f.

This is an important point, because it makes clear that Vergil – the same man who talked about souls being purged till they consisted only of 'aetherial perception and the fire of unadulterated air' (*Aeneid* 6.746f.) – was engaged knowingly in an exercise in mythical theology

in his *Aeneid* in the 20s BC. His Jupiter is n
more than Homer's had been), but belong
how it works and what man's place is in
quest for the virtuous life.

At the same time, the story is built on
Trojan War and its aftermath. It draws
particular Homer, whose *Iliad* and *Odysse*
scenes and even phrases in the book, ar
of anthropomorphic gods interacting witl
Jupiter commands the gods, determines t
appealed to by other gods, but, true to Zet
directly. He speaks, *fatur*, and his word is
fatum, the Latin for 'fate'. The distance fro
him properly, is less than one might im
Aeneid 1:

> Smiling at her [Venus] the begetter of men anc
> with the expression with which he makes calm
> kissed the lips of his daughter and then spoke
> 'Do not fear, Cytherean [Venus], they stand uns
> fates: you will see the city and the promised wa
> of Lavinium, and you will carry high [*sublimem*]
> great-hearted Aeneas; nor has my decision cha

In the poetic mythology, a god smilingly k
and gives her reassurance. But this is a civi
sky and the storm, to whom nations may p
as in Valerius of Sora, he is the begetter of a
of the first century BC, take the view that H
in his formula *father of gods and men*. C
mode, we know that Jupiter is responsible f
fiery element of the universe, most purel
which the poet here calls *caelum* ('sky'). It
stars, high up, the *sublime candens* of En
Aeneas will fly after death. He will be tak
and perhaps in the Stoic sense he will join tl

and Ze
that pla
the wor
whole v
that we
in the L
Dante (

The
and
Jup

It woul
tionshi
already
Roman
cult sta
becom
hallowe
would l
193–21

From t
hidden
myster
thinker
thinker
first pr
the go
philoso
writter
grope f
mythic

Figure 12 The emperor Augustus depicted as the Zeus of Pheidias. 1.85 m tall. Early first century AD.

Zeus. Hellenistic poets we look at continue the sense of Zeus in epic or drama, but also worry about the limits on our knowledge and the dangers of exceeding them. Like any other writers they are part of their age and the hymn that opens Aratus's *Phaenomena* is very like the great hymn of Cleanthes the Stoic. Stoics were more comfortable with accommodating Zeus into their theology and deployed allegory freely. But a new solution emerged with Euhemeros: the mythological gods were in origin great men, like the great Hellenistic kings. This was later a godsend for the Christians, who could now, with the authority of Greek thinkers, undermine the basis of Greek worship. Finally, we looked at the thought underlying the encounter of Zeus with non-Greek cultures. Typically the gods might be identified or merged – this was syncretism. But in the Roman case we can see how an understanding of the less mythic and more philosophic approach to Zeus, as canonised in Varro's tripartite theology, helps us with Roman views of Jupiter. It was the Roman Jupiter, after all, that would pass on the tradition of Zeus into the culture of Europe, as we shall next see.

ZEUS AFTERWARDS

6

PHASES OF HISTORY

When dealing with a long stretch of time such as the millennium and a half since the end of the classical world, it is convenient to divide that time into different periods. However, periods do not begin and end cleanly and such breaks obscure continuities. The Roman Empire came to an end. But when? Conventionally, the sack of Rome by Alaric and the Visigoths in 410 marks the spot. But pagan writing about the universe and rather metaphorical gods continued unabated through-out fifth-century north Africa, and the apparatus of the western Roman state continued in one way or another, however limited, till the Lombards invaded Italy in 567.

If the 'Dark Ages' followed the end of the Roman Empire, that is to emphasise rather emotively the end of a particular urban economy and a particular European union. Yet exaggeration is all too easy in what in fact are the Early Middle Ages. The Christian Church becomes the bearer of culture and cities do not cease to exist or people to think about the world around them. Even if Christianity prescribed a good deal of the thought-world, this can be viewed as a shift in language: it was usually possible to take a view of the pagan gods other than instant dismissal. Indeed, as pagan gods had ceased to be serious competition, writers might, if they chose, bring them within their philosophy or astrology.

'Renaissance', too, is a dangerous term. It denotes 'rebirth', of something which has been dead or dormant, namely in this case 'civilisation', which had perished with the Roman Empire; the fall of Constantinople to the Turks in 1453 could, on this view, trigger an outflow of intellectuals who came bearing classical civilisation to a West grateful to receive it. This is not wholly without truth and it is certainly the case that in art it became possible to depict pagan gods where Virgin, Child and Saints had predominated for many years and to reintroduce a more natural and realistic art on the basis of rediscovered ancient works. But it does misrepresent the vibrancy of ideas in the written culture of the Middle Ages, however much ideas tended to be couched within a traditional framework of education and of Christianity. And it seriously misrepresents the exciting climate of ideas in the 1200s and 1300s, vital centuries without which there would have been no 'Renaissance', no matter how many Constantinoples fell.

I will be concerned with these periods and some of their legacy in the modern world in this section. But as I cannot tell every story, I have chosen to focus on the culture of Western Europe (the context in which this book itself has arisen). I can only mention in passing that there is another story to be told about the Greek east and about Arabic receptions and developments of Greek philosophy.

CHRISTIANITY TERMINATES ZEUS?

Early Christians had spared no pains to overturn devotion to Zeus, the chief pagan god. With the adoption by Constantine of Christianity in 312, the road now lay open for the end of paganism. But it was not a simple matter, as repeated decrees show. One from Constantine II and Constans in 346 instructed that temples everywhere should be closed and sacrifices stopped (*Codex Theodosianus* 16.10.4.). In 353 night sacrifices are banned again after being allowed by Magnentius (16.10.5). In 356 sacrifice and idolatry are banned (16.10.6). A further seven decrees of Theodosius in 391/2 repeat the banning of every form of pagan worship in every possible place – temple, shrine, in the home and on the land.

However, what really told against paganism in this climate was not worthy decrees of pious emperors, but money. Zosimus (*New History* 4.59) reports a discussion Theodosius is said to have had with the Senators at Rome around 393, in which he turns from exhortation to hard economic fact: it cost too much to keep up the pagan sacrifices (*so they were being kept up*) and the money was needed for the defence budget. Paganism had always been expensive and the number of ruined temples attested to that. So it was for Zeus: the last Olympic Games, which needed ample funding, were held in 393. The temple burnt down in 426 and there would be no money for repair. Instead, a rudimentary Christian church was built where Pheidias' workshop had been. Earthquakes, particularly in 522 and 551, finished it off.

The statues have their own story as they continued to be revered in a sort of museum culture; the temples tended to be protected too. But they were no longer sacrosanct. Constantine, constructing the effectively new city of Constantinople, needed to import culture and tradition; so for instance he sacrilegiously took the Zeus from Dodona and the Athene from Lindos and put them in the new Senate House. Rather later, Pheidias' legendary statue of Zeus from Olympia became the star piece in the major collection of Lausus, who was the Grand Chamberlain of Theodosius II (402–50). This collection, which also included for instance the Aphrodite of Knidos, was entirely destroyed in a fire of 475.[1]

This was, however, not quite the end. If Zeus was not worshipped under his own name, then people did not cease to need the services he had provided for millennia. On the mountain tops, where once Zeus had been worshipped, such as Mt Olympus and Mt Lykaion, a particular saint often received worship instead. This is the prophet Elias, sometimes St Elias, known in English as Elijah, who in a grand confrontation with the prophets of Baal called forth from the very summit of Mt Carmel a mighty rainstorm to flood the drought-ridden land, who smote the men of Ahab with lightning from a hill top, and who, when he died, rose to heaven in a 'fiery chariot'.[2] These are the qualities our Zeus replacement needs and they led to strange new mythologies in popular Greek culture: thunder is the prophet Elias driving across the sky, perhaps in pursuit of a dragon. Oddly, Mt Carmel itself, which is 'between Judaea and Syria', was the location of an oracle which was consulted by Vespasian in AD 69 as a step towards becoming emperor (Tacitus, *Histories* 2.78). This shows how underlying religious phenomena are not so much displaced as contested for by different religions: the religion of the Canaanites is really being mapped onto the monotheism of the Jews through the figure of Elijah; the mountain top weather god Zeus of the ancient Greeks is then translated into a Christian scriptural language as the prophet Elijah.

JUPITER IN WESTERN EUROPE 500–1200

At the summit of the citadel there was a temple of Jupiter and (Juno) Moneta.

Wonders of the City of Rome, §24 (*c*. AD 1150,

describing the Capitol Hill)

Classical texts in Latin continued to be read in the West after the end of the Roman world. As literacy became possible only in monastic and church contexts, the acceptability of classical literature to Christians was a key question. Undoubtedly the derivation of medieval education from pagan classical systems helped preserve a respect for the texts. The pagan texts also benefited from the support of leading church-men and from the practice of copying manuscripts in monasteries, without which little would have survived, given that most of our manu-scripts date from the ninth century or later. In addition, the view that Charlemagne and his advisors took of the culture a new Roman emperor should promote led to what is now called 'the Carolingian Renaissance' and the promotion of literary activity beyond that required by the Church. Thus the ancient gods retained a presence and were from time to time discussed.

At the same time there was sufficient interest in classical mythology for books in which it played a large part to survive and be read. Central to this tradition were three learned works of the fifth century AD – the *Commentarii* ('Notebooks') on Cicero's *Dream of Scipio* by Macrobius (prefect of Italy in 430), Martianus Capella's *Wedding of Philology and Mercury* (perhaps around 450) and Fulgentius' *Mythologiae* (perhaps in the generation following Martianus). It would be beyond the scope of this book to go into detail, but suffice it to say that these works kept the pagan gods alive in a literary way and suggested they had a greater significance than as objects of idolatry and sacrifice. Jupiter represented maybe fire, maybe life, maybe the soul of the world.[3] This Neoplatonism, the last and most otherworldly stage in the development of Plato's philosophy in the ancient world, is in effect the opposite of Euhemerism and, reaching for ultimate truths about man and the divine, does not obviously contradict Christianity in the way that pagan cult practices did.

Jupiter for Macrobius is the sky (i.e. ether) and his sister-wife Juno, the air: 'sister because air is born of the same seed as the sky, wife because air is subject to the sky' (*Dream of Scipio* 1.17.15). Martianus raises the stakes. Personified Arithmetic speaks to us in Book 7 of the eternity of the monad, that unitary number without which other, plural things cannot come into existence and which subsists even when they are gone:

> This father of all things is rightly called Jove, because it bears witness to the causative power of that prototypical and intelligible form. And after its example we speak of one god, one world, one sun, a single moon, and also the four single elements that exist . . . Some have called this Harmony, some Piety or Friendship, because it is so bound together that it cannot be cut up into parts; however it is more correctly called Jupiter, because the same is the source and the father of the gods.
>
> Martianus Capella, *Wedding of Philology and Mercury* 7.731

It is revealing that the material of which this is part is repeated in Isidore of Seville's *Book of Numbers* 'except for material relating to the pagan gods'.[4] This highlights the pagan tensions inherent in the scientific and educational material which the Middle Ages inherited and valued. On the other hand the sense of an individual god to be worshipped among others is very weak in these last pagan texts, and in Martianus they are harmless allegories – these authors have fulfilled the tendency already present in Plato to view the objects of the mind as the true target of religion, rather than sacrifice to gods in temples, now in any case closed. Neither Macrobius in his *Dream of Scipio* nor Martianus, however, speaks a word about the Christian God, Christ or Moses. Religion has become sublimated for the intellectual classes of late antique Roman Africa.

Fulgentius' driving concern, particularly in the *Mythologiae*, is to find the philosophic sense in a large range of myths of gods and heroes. This is his Jove and Juno as two of the four elements:

- first, Jove as fire: this is why he is called Zeus in Greek – Zeus in Greek can mean either life [*zen*] or heat [*zein* – to seethe, boil], either because they mean that all animate things have vital fire, as Heraclitus holds, or because this element is hot;

- second, Juno as air, which is why she is called Era in Greek; and although they ought to have made air masculine, nevertheless she is the sister of Jove for this reason, that these two elements are very much associated with each other, so she is the wife of Jove too, because air, when it is wedded with fire, blazes.

Fulgentius, *Mythologiae* 1.3 (bullet points added for clarity)

This is a text of sustained popularity up to the Renaissance and it filled the gap of 'science' without alleging false gods, providing another instalment for the virtual encyclopedia that has dominated the imagination of so many teachers and writers over these centuries. The world could be known if there were enough comprehensive works and certainly Isidore's *Origines* (or *Etymologiae*) covered every imaginable aspect of culture and learning. Isidore (*c.* 570–636) was Bishop of Seville in a Visigothic renaissance in Spain and his *Origines* spread like wildfire across Europe. From our point of view he is interesting for maintaining and propagating the Euhemerist way of looking at ancient gods. This had once, as we have seen, been argued in order to decry the gods but later it seems to have given them a reason to survive in Christian culture (Seznec 1953: ch.1.). Isidore's account of the 'Gods of the Pagans' begins like this:

(1) Those whom pagans declare to be gods are revealed once to have been men, and, in line with each one's life and achievements, they began to be worshipped after their death amongst their own people – like Isis among the Egyptians, Jupiter amongst the Cretans . . . (9) amongst the Greeks Cecrops . . . was the first to call upon Jupiter, discover statues, set up altars, sacrifice victims, when that sort of thing was unheard of in Greece. . . . (34) Jove is named after *helping* [*juvando*] and Jupiter is the sort of *helping father* [*juvans pater*], i.e. there for everyone. They also gave him the personal title of Jove *Optimus* [*best*], despite the fact that he committed incest with his family and sexual outrages on others. (35) They sometimes depict him as a bull because of the abduction of Europa – he was in a ship whose sign was a bull; sometimes he is supposed to have sought congress

with Danae through golden rain – so you can understand that the virtue of a woman has been corrupted by gold; sometimes in the form of an eagle because he snatched a boy to abuse him.

Isidore, *Origines* 8.11

A final strand to consider here is that of astrology, which, even if it got short shrift from Isidore (3.27) as mere superstition, continued to fascinate in an age whose notion of science was very different from ours. It had in any case been integrated by the end of antiquity into the whole system of knowledge. Astronomy, from which it was barely distinguishable, was part of the advanced core curriculum, the *quadrivium*. Jupiter (Zeus) was more than a label for a planet, he *was* that planet, something which fits on the one hand with the non-Euhemerist strand of thinking, which itself tended to meditate on sun, stars and universe.[5] On the other it connects with the euergetist (benefactor/do-gooder) character of Euhemeros' Zeus: the planet Jupiter is predominantly beneficent and health-bringing.[6] This mythic-astrological lore was so well embedded that it was impossible to remove the pagan names from the planets and constellations and William of Conches, the tutor of Henry Plantagenet around 1122, even justified knowledge of pagan myth on this basis: if we did not know the story of Jupiter taking on bull form to abduct Europa, we would not know how to find Taurus in the skies (Seznec 1953: 51). Astrology became specially influential from the twelfth on to the fourteenth, through interaction with Byzantium and with the Arab world that had taken such an interest in Greek philosophy and science.

1200s, 1300s: RENAISSANCE BEFORE THE RENAISSANCE

Knowledge of the Classics was pretty commonplace among the literate and their audiences by the end of the Middle Ages. One of the most delightful pieces of evidence is the collection of songs in a manuscript of 1230 or earlier from Benediktbeuern in the foothills of the Alps, the so-called *Carmina Burana*. Celebrated in the remarkable rhythmic work of Carl Orff in 1938, these medieval poems have a place for Jupiter in their lightly worn classical mythology: laughing (*risu Jovis*, 'with the laughter of Jove'), sometimes ruling, once the planet. The Archpoet tells us that 'men may look at appearances, but the heart is open to Jove', which seems rather Christian (191, stanza 22): *homo videt faciem, sed cor patet Jovi.* He makes a good rhyme too, as when the singer indignantly denies he has been unfaithful:

Unde juro Musas novem,	So I swear by Muses nine,
quod et maius est, per Jovem,	and, more than that, by Jove,
qui pro Dane sumpsit auri,	who for Danae took the form of gold,
in Europa formam tauri.	and in the case of Europa the form of a bull.

Carmina Burana 117, stanza 4

A lot of the knowledge of mythology was coming from Ovid's *Metamorphoses*, which was by now interpreted in ingenious allegorical ways. A key work in this tradition was the *Book of Albricus the Philosopher on the Images of the Gods*, which some thought, probably rightly, was by Alexander Neckham (1157–1217). Also spelt Alexander *Nequam* (Latin for 'the Wicked'!), this was a philosopher and encyclopedist whose mother suckled Richard Lionheart and who was the first man in history to mention the glass mirror and the magnetic compass. Under the pen name Albricus, then, he told what gods looked like, important in an age when all the statues had gone, and he told what their stories meant.

This was in turn an important source for the truly massive rhyming poem, the *Ovide moralisé* of around 1300, which brought these materials to a wider market than even a Latin work could:[7]

Of Jupiter and his shape:

Jupiter, son of Saturn, to whom the sky and its rule was assigned by lot, should be painted seated in great majesty on a throne of ivory, holding in his right hand the royal sceptre and in his left the thunder. He casts down some giants that he has defeated and prostrated beneath his feet. Beside him stands an eagle, wings extended, who between his feet is seizing a young boy named Ganymedes.

Ovide moralisé: 'Texte du commentaire de Copenhague',
de Boer v.394, from 'Albricus'

At the heart of this project is the idea that if 'our blessed Saviour and Redeemer Jesus' used parables and comparisons, then it was legitimate so to use Ovid. It follows, however, that we are not extracting a single definitive meaning from Ovid but in a way using him as a text which can be turned to good effect in a sort of moral preaching and accordingly a variety of different interpretations is suggested for each myth, for instance that of Ganymede:

- Explanation 1: Jupiter was a king of Crete (10.3368) who defeated the Phrygians in battle and took Troy. Ganymede was very pretty and Jupiter took him away for his own pleasure *contre droit et contre nature* (3385).
- Explanation 2: *Jupiter est un element | sor touz est assis le plus hault* (3401–2): 'Jupiter is an element, above all he is seated the highest'. He is the hottest and driest and he is refreshed by the heavenly water-carrier Aquarius, figured in this myth as Ganymede.
- Explanation 3: Jupiter, now the creator god, for love of mankind – *pour amour d'umaine nature* (3411) – is prepared to descend from heaven and become that which he has never been, a man. Like an eagle he flies off to the skies, carrying the flesh that he has taken on. For Jupiter, it seems, is Christ.

In the Danae myth Jupiter is 'God our help, our father, our saviour, our king, our creator'. Danae is the virginity loved of God (4.5584), and the tower in which she is enclosed is the womb that God enters with golden rain, not violating the door, as he joins himself to our nature. The offspring is the *Aurigena* (born of gold, Ovid *Metamorphoses* 5.250), the valiant Perseus, and in fact *c'est Jhesu, vrai dieu et vrai home* ('It is Jesus, true god, true man,' 5610). It recalls the Annunciation (5611–3), that scene where the angel of God appears to Mary to announce that she will bear the Son of God. This is a favourite of European painting and the viewer of Danae amidst her golden rain should always bear in mind that what artists are painting is a secularised Annunciation; it is more than an opportunity to paint an impassioned nude.

Not everything runs so smooth in this inventive reading of classical myth. Io, long virtuous and loved by God, turns to carnal pleasure

– wine, food and sex (1.3956) and Argus is this world (3938). She is a pagan image of what Mary of Egypt meant to the Christian (4013).[8] Semele, by contrast, is a drunkard led astray by an even drunker old woman, Juno (3.872), unless she is the soul 'drunk and full of the divine love' (907), with a heavy stress on her motherhood of Bacchus.

To our taste this may be obsessed with Christian religion and overwhelms the carefree pagan sense of the text. But there is a pleasure of the crossword puzzle about working out these ingenious interpretations, a music in the jaunty rhymes and a fine demonstration of the never-ending power of classical mythology to make you think.

As might be expected, Italian authors were intensely familiar with secular Latin literature by 1300. Maundy Thursday 1300 is when the *Divine Comedy* of Dante is set (it was written 1306–21). This is a poem immersed in the Classics, famously citing with approval (*Inferno* 4.88–90) the work of Homer, Horace, Ovid and Lucan in that order – and Vergil is of course Dante's guide to the Underworld. Jove exists in the background, occasionally emerging thundering at the Giants he once defeated, or as the planet Jupiter, to which his name had been applied by misguided pagans. But even the *Ovide moralisé* doesn't quite prepare us for this theology:

o sommo Giove,	O supreme Jove,
Che fosti in terra per noi crocifisso.	who was crucified on earth for us.

Purgatorio 6.118f.

Nothing is without precedent: this equation of Zeus with Christ had also been made before by one John the Deacon, drawing the logical conclusions from Plato's *Cratylus* (see p. 95f):

And Zeus son of Kronos, father of gods and men, is to be understood as the only-begotten son of God: as he is responsible for life [*zoe*] he is called 'Zeus'. But as he is the son of God, he is called 'son of Kronos', because we should think of Kronos as that pure mind [*koros nous*][9] which we can neither see nor grasp, which had no origin . . . but Kronides, the son of this one, consubstantial and sharing his throne, and seated above those gods who are as a conceit called his sons, judging all humanity and for this reason called father of men and gods.

The poet and polymath Petrarch (1304–74) had the right books in his personal collection: the *Mythologiae* of Fulgentius and Alexander Neckham's *Albricus on the Images of the Gods*. Among much else he wrote in Latin hexameters an *Africa* on the second Punic War, so aware of the classical range of gods that we could be back in the world of Vergil:

> Jupiter in front of the others, proud on his august throne
> Holding sceptre and thunderbolt in his hands; and Jove's armour-bearer
>   [the eagle] in front
> In his claws raised the Idaean youth [Ganymede] above the stars.
>
> Petrarch, *Africa* 140–42 (in Seznec 1953: 173)

And his friend Boccaccio (1313–75) wrote the new Fulgentius, a *Genealogie deorum gentilium* ('Genealogies of the Pagan Gods', 1st edn 1360, later revised), which was vastly popular in the succeeding centuries. His account has its oddities, like the primal being 'Demogorgon', which he has got out of a suspiciously unknown author 'Theodontius' whom he cites everywhere.[10] But it settles down to the elegant enumeration of divine beings from the beginning and shows all the influences we have talked about. There are several Jupiters, as there have to be when you start from a Euhemerist basis. Jupiter 1 (*Geneal.* 2.2) is the son of Ether and Day, as Theodontius assures us. This Jupiter under the name of Lysanias introduced civilisation and pagan religion at Athens, according to the Greek Leontius (who?). And because he was an ingenious, sparky type of person they made out he was the element of fire and the son of the Ether. Boccaccio thinks he came to be called Jupiter because he was like the planet Jupiter, in its astrological character as described by Albumasar (ninth-century Arab astronomer), 'hot, humid, airy, temperate, modest and decent' and so on. Jupiter 2 is the son of Caelum ('Heaven', Ouranos) and Jupiter 3 a Cretan, the son of Saturn (Kronos). 'Some serious people think that he is called Jupiter because he is the *helping father* [see Isidore above, p. 122], but that only fits God himself.' In Greek he is pronounced *Zefs*, Boccaccio tells us, i.e. 'life' (*zen*, 'to live', see Fulgentius or Plato) but of course it is Christ who is the way, the truth and the life 'and that is how it really is'. Rationalisations and allegories appear from time to time. Jupiter is supposed to have snatched Europa in the form of a white bull, because that was the emblem painted on his ship (see Isidore above). If Jupiter kills Semele in the form of a thunderbolt, this means that 'fire i.e. Jupiter does not mix with air i.e. Juno except when as a thunderbolt it descends to the world below' (2.64).

Classical learning about Jupiter included England. To cite but one example, Chaucer, another reader of the *Ovide moralisé*, envisaged himself carried off by the eagle of Jupiter to the 'House of Fame' in the poem of that name (around 1380).[11] This motif of 'dreaming poet swept up by eagle of Jove' comes from Dante (*Purgatorio* 9.22–4) but the poem is in its own right an exhibition piece of classical learning, extending to the *Somnium Scipionis* and a summary of the *Aeneid*, including the scene from *Aeneid* 1 that we discussed earlier (p. 111):

> Ther saugh I Joves Venus kysse,
> And graunted of the tempest lysse [relief].

Chaucer, House of Fame 219f.

John Gower in his *Confessio Amantis* (*c.*1390) knew his Ovid too. For instance Jupiter at 5.6249 deflowers Callisto, and earlier Io:

> Ovide telleth in his sawes,
> How Jupiter be olde dawes
> Lay be a Mayde, which Yo
> Was cleped, wherof that Juno
> His wif was wroth, and the goddesse
> Of Yo torneth the liknesse
> Into a cow, to gon theroute
> The large fieldes al aboute.

John Gower, Confessio Amantis 4.3317–24

ZEUS AND THE RENAISSANCE

With the Renaissance, humanist thinkers were now consistently looking for philosophies and values beyond those the Church had supplied.[12] This was a time when the Neoplatonic philosophy which had dominated the end of pagan antiquity took on a new lease of life, though in such a way that it was not demonstrably, dangerously, inconsistent with Christian belief. However, this did not particularly benefit Jupiter, as Plato had always been more abstract in his treatment of divinity. Thus a neoplatonist like Marsilio Ficino (1433–99) or a humanist like Pico della Mirandola (1463–94) would talk more about mystic aspects of religion than about Jove, even if Marsilio (*Letter* 8) was comfortable with Jupiter as aether and Juno as air. At best this is a world of emblems, where Federigo da Montefeltro could commission a medal with the planetary sign of Jupiter governing the discordant signs of Mars and Venus, war and love, whilst his eagle carries their insignia – including, for Jupiter Tonans (thundering), a cannonball (Wind 1967: 95f., fig. 71)! With a similar if more literal mindset, Conrad Celtes, a German humanist, in a 1507 woodcut constructed a picture of Christian shape but pagan content (fig. 13; Wind 1967: 252f.): here Jupiter and Phoebus Apollo look like God the Father and God the Son, surrounded by Minerva and Mercury playing Mary and St John Baptist, and with the Dove (Holy Spirit) represented by Pegasus – both flew after all!

The now uninhibited return to the treasury of Greek and Roman civilisation above all gave new life to the mythology, which on the one hand was an engaging set of motifs, situations and passions, and on the other mysteriously suggested some deeper sense underlying these apparently trivial stories. It was exploited notably in art and music.

Classical mythological themes, like any others, had to be commissioned, and they do not start appearing till the 1400s. There is for instance in the antechapel of the Palazzo Publico at Siena a series of frescoes depicting classical gods (together with Roman republican heroes) painted by Taddeo di Bartolo around 1414, including a 'Jupiter with Lightning Bolts'. An anonymous 'Scenes from a Legend', attributed to the Master of the Griggs Crucifixion, depicts, among others, Callisto and must date to around 1430. Meanwhile, in the unlikely setting of the bronze doors of St Peter's, in the Vatican, Antonio Averlino (or 'Filarete') included in 1445 a depiction of the 'Rape of Ganymede', which clearly must have been allegorically meant, figuring as it did opposite the crucifixion of St Peter. He also did an Amalthea here, the goat that suckled Zeus.

Figure 13 Centre of a woodcut from a book on music of 1507
– a Christianised set of pagan gods.

Art existed in a sense ready-made in Ovid's *Metamorphoses* (p. 48), often described as the 'painter's bible'. It certainly underlay a great quantity of the depictions in art, particularly the *amours* of the gods and lent its wit to many of those representations. Already in the 1470s editions were being printed at Subiaco (near Rome), Venice, Milan and Leuven. But it is from 1500 that this market gets going. Guidoccio Cozzarelli took a break from mainly religious paintings to do a 'Callisto' presumably around 1500. The first Danae in her shower of gold seems to be that of Baldassare Peruzzi in a fresco of the Villa Farnese in Rome (1512), painted appropriately for the banker Chigi; there is also a Ganymede there. Giorgione (*c.* 1477–1510) did a Daphne, Europa and Ganymede. Correggio (*c.* 1490–1534) did Danae (unless it was Giorgione), Ganymede, Io and the infancy of Zeus. Titian (*c.* 1488–1576) did Antiope, Callisto, Daphne, Ganymede. Giulio Romano (1499?–1546) did practically every myth – including Europa, Ganymede and Semele. He depicted Jupiter's childhood, *amours* and offspring in a series of 12 paintings around 1533, of which six survive, four of them at Hampton Court Palace and one in the National Gallery (both

Figure 14 Giulio Romano, *The Infant Zeus Guarded by the Corybants on Crete*, mid 1530s.

London). And there is also an overwhelming *trompe l'oeil* 'Fall of the Giants' (1534) as they are cast from Olympus, or rather from a cupola, all over the Giants' Room of the Palazzo del Tè at Mantua. Here Sistine Chapel meets pagan myth. I reproduce, however, as figure 14, the joyful but glowering scene of the infancy of the thunder god himself from the National Gallery (London).

The visit of Jupiter and Mercury to Baucis and Philemon is a more sensitive and advanced subject, maybe. At any rate, apart from a painting (oddly) of Bramantino's *c*. 1500, it first emerges with Primaticcio's designs for Fontainebleau (see below) around 1550, and after that is welcome when it is attempted for the humble, often rather dark, but mysterious peasant environment in which the gods find themselves. There is a marvellous Rembrandt of *Philemon and Baucis visited by Mercury and Jupiter* (1658) in the National Gallery of Art, Washington, which you can find on the Web. I cannot on the other hand quite imagine what it would look like as a 'marionette opera', which is what Franz Joseph Haydn created, to the pleasure, apparently, of the empress Maria Theresa at Esterházy in 1773. But if a New England company could do *Tosca* that way,[13] then perhaps Baucis and Philemon would have worked fine.

The visit to Lycaon and his transformation into a wolf are surprisingly rare. There seems once to have been a painting of Raphael's. There is a Rubens oil-painting sketch (1636–8) for a fresco intended for a palace of Philip IV of Spain with a rather Christ-like Jupiter. After that there are some engravings, directly illustrating Ovid.[14] Perhaps kings and princes on the whole did not like tales of the punishment of kings.

The flavour of Jupiter's *amours* is summed up by Thomas Heywood's 1625 compilation of scenes from his plays as *The Escapes of Jupiter*. On the other hand Congreve's libretto of 1707, whose performance with music by John Eccles fell through, was taken up and modified by Handel for his own *Semele* (1744), a grandiose oratorio with flaming altars and dragons, but too sexy a plot for the tastes of his supporters. Coincidentally in Paris in 1709 another *Semele* was performed, by Marin Marais, the leading composer of the Versailles court. It probably represented a step up from the routinely diverting god-and-beloved stuff done by the court lutenist Louis de Mollier for performance by the comedians of the Marais in *Les amours de Jupiter et Sémélé* (1666) to a libretto of Claude Boyer. This was fashionable entertainment for the educated classes, complete with machines to wheel in scenery and fly in gods. Anyone who wants to catch the mood of Paris in those days, with premieres of Molière and Corneille, need only consult the lists of performances in those years that are now available on the Web.[15] Greco-Roman mythology was a sort of cultural uniform which made audiences comfortable about their elite status without unduly taxing them.

These myths were typically treated very lightly, setting an amusing counterpoint of triviality against the labour of having learnt Latin and read Ovid in education. There is a *Calisto*, for instance, of 1651 by Cavalli in which Jupiter, in his quest for Callisto, starts by regretting giving human beings free will. He then adopts a *falsetto* voice and dresses up as a goddess in order to convince Callisto he is Diana, which, incredibly, succeeds instantly. This is a superbly preposterous opera, whose one mystic moment is the transposition of Callisto into the stars as the Great Bear.

Of all the material we have discussed in the first part, it might seem that Pausanias's account of the *Daedala* at Plataia (p. 31f) was singularly unlikely to generate an opera. But it did produce a ballet *Platée ou Junon jalouse* ('Plataea, or Jealous Juno') by Jacques Autreau, which was made into a comic opera by Rameau in 1745 for the delectation of Louis XV and his son the future Louis XVI, complete with a tenor (m.) singing the part of Plataea (f.). This opera was revived by New York City Opera in 2000 and 'set in a seedy modern bar patronized by a colourful group of 20th century caricatures, including a black sailor, a masculine lesbian, a gaudy showgirl, a veiled baroness, and a bribe-taking cop'.[16] What settings of Pausanias does the twenty-first century hold in store for us?

There is, however, another dimension to this use of myths of Jupiter. Since the beginning Zeus had had a special connection with kings and repeatedly in more modern times we discover kings portrayed as Jupiter. Poets referred to Henri II of France (ruled 1547–59) and his court as *le nouvel Olympe* and this image was cultivated by the court itself acting out these roles. One has only to look at the frescoes in the palace at Fontainebleau to see this swirling world of gods, heroes and neoplatonic vision, for instance the 'Eagle abducting Ganymede' of 1551–6, designed by Primaticcio, who had worked under Giulio Romano, and executed by Niccolò dell' Abate. To take another example Rubens interlaced Henri IV and Marie de' Medici with Jupiter and Juno, even identifying them, in a cycle of 1622–5, which is mainly now in the Louvre. This usage both explains the popularity of Jupiter myths in court productions and makes some myths, like that of Semele, rather problematic. Was Handel in his *Semele* criticising the influence of Madame de Walmoden, the mistress of George II?

TWILIGHT OF THE GODS

In most histories of European civilisation, the French Revolution and the period of romanticism mark a turning point. From our point of view, however, they only prepare the ground for the modern period which has gradually turned its back on Renaissance values and asserted with new confidence a belief in progress, setting new value on the contemporary in comparison with the past.

In the nineteenth century, classical education continued to be central. The first Gilbert and Sullivan operetta was *Thespis*, in which Jupiter descends to earth to find out why the gods are no longer respected. But its first performance in 1871 was not exactly a success: it was booed not only by the audience but also by the orchestra! Despite 64 performances, it no longer survives. At the other end of a career, Richard Strauss's *The Love of Danae* of 1940 was his penultimate opera. Hofmannsthal's libretto brings together so much of the mythology of Zeus's *amours*. Danae, Semele, Leda, Europa, Alkmene – they are all there, in a work where Strauss is thought to have identified himself in a way with the god Jupiter, inconsistently raising his tone somewhere near to the Wotan of Wagner in his *Ring*.

Zeus-Jupiter is not mentioned in the *Ring of the Nibelungs* (first performed complete 1876). But he haunts it. Wagner's great cycle of operas is exceptional in posing large questions about the order of the world and putting in front of us the problems of being a flawed chief god, rather than just finding humour in a divine apparatus. The Wotan of Wagner implies the Zeus of Homer and the Jupiter of Vergil in the background, and the conflict with Giants recalls the establishment of Zeus's rule. But, truer maybe to Norse mythology's Ragnarök (which he understood as 'Twilight of the Gods'),[17] or to the final cataclysm of the Stoics in which the current universe will one day disappear, the portrait of Zeus is enhanced by a sense of the ending of the world and the ending of the rule of the gods. For the Greeks Zeus would rule forever. But modern times are less prone to images of stability.

Nowadays, as we browse the Web, the name 'Zeus' is often only a powerful monosyllable denoting total control, popular among those who give names to products. 'Zeus Technology is the world's expert on web server infrastructure.' 'Zeus Informatics was founded in 1998.' 'Zeus is a totally new concept in generating web traffic.' 'The Zeus for Windows programmers text editor has been specifically designed for software developers working in the Windows . . . environments. It offers a host of features that make the task of writing code easier and more productive.' And *Zeus Electronique Développement* deals with 'the study and manufacture of industrial electronic products.' More academically:

> We are a collaboration of about 450 physicists who are running a large particle detector at the electron-proton collider HERA at the DESY laboratory in Hamburg. The ZEUS detector is a sophisticated tool for studying the particle reactions provided by the high-energetic beams of the HERA accelerator.[18]

The Greco-Roman world has also become the stuff of fantasy, and every classicist first meets the classical world through the mythology. The film *Clash of the Titans* (1981), with its Norse Kraken-monster, clockwork owl, Ray Harryhausen's astounding special effects for 1981 and a hotchpotch of Perseus mythology, rolled in front of us a Zeus still controlling the world, whose human traits were not so very distant from the original Greek conceptions. It shows that we still respond, as the Greeks did, to a sense of irony and weakness in the running of the universe that is not really compatible with modern faiths. Zeus is an interesting casting problem too. Laurence Olivier was an epic choice for *Clash of the Titans*. This too is a world where Kevin Sorbo as Hercules (*Hercules: the Legendary Journeys*, television 1994–9) brings the lone gunslinger to the Greek world and occasionally communes with his irascible father, Zeus, played by another substantial figure, Anthony Quinn.

No fantasy is complete without a computer game. One such is *Zeus: Master of Olympus* in which you may compulsively 'build a city, challenge the gods, spawn a myth'.[19] I'm not sure, however, whether you will be able to put whatever you have gained from this book to much effect.

Finally, your direct line to Zeus. Who knows who was running the latter-day US oracle site *Ask Zeus!* or why? But its benefits were clear:

> Have a question? Don't trust earthly wisdom. Mortals make mistakes. Get your answers from the King of the Gods Himself. Omnipotence is cool![20]

Be warned, it suffered from the modern delusion that you should risk answers that aren't just yes/no and didn't recommend sacrifice to this or that god half often enough. On the other hand, authentically like Delphi, it backed the wrong side in politics. And it seems to have passed away, like the ancient god himself, as I add the last full stop.

NOTES

WHY ZEUS?

1 Rays of light (*Iliad* 13.837), fluttering snow (*Iliad* 19.357), see Schwabl 1978: 1014. Cretans even called day 'Zeus'.
2 As explained by Nilsson 1967: i.6.
3 I am also aware of J. Scheid and J. Svenbro, *The Craft of Zeus: myths of weaving and fabric* (Cambridge, MA 1996); the title is eye-catching but the book is not about Zeus.
4 'Any study which attempted to define the Greek gods independently from one another, as if they were separate and isolated figures, would be in danger of missing an essential point about them', Vernant 1982: 99.

KEY THEMES

1 As noted by West (1997: 115 and 1978: 366–8, 384), who thinks the *aigi-* in question may once have been a type of bird like the Himmelszeige ('heaven-goat') in rural German lore, a bird similar to the one Lithuanians believed accompanied the god of lightning, Perkunas. His Near-Eastern parallels, however, suggest that the word means 'riding the storms'.
2 Ramskin issues: Nilsson 1967: 110–13, 396 f.
3 E. Kunze, 'Zeusbilder in Olympia', *Antike und Abendland* 2 (1946) 91–113, section 2.
4 K. Brodersen, *Die sieben Weltwunder* (Munich, 1996) 63.
5 Strabo 6.3.1; Pliny, *Natural History* 34.40; Livy 27.16.8.
6 Tn 316, Hiller 1978: 1002; another tablet of this antiquity was found at Chania in Crete in the early 1990s (E. Voutiras in LIMC 8.1, p. 310) naming Zeus and Dionysos.

7 Possible according to Hiller 1978: 1002.

8 It is *Dios* 'of Zeus' plus a second element *nysos*, which is the problem. It would be easier if it belonged to a related language rather than Greek itself. P. Kretschmer proposed that it was Thracian (which rests on a misunderstanding of mythology), *Einleitung in die Geschichte der griechischen Sprache* (Göttingen, 1896) 241f. O. Szemerényi, *JHS* 94 (1974) 145 suggests transposition of the consonants in Indo-European **sunus* 'son'. This is questioned by West (1978: 373f.), who suggests he is a sort of male nymph.

9 Other parallels to the Dioskouroi, see P. Kretschmer, *Glotta* 14 (1925) 303 (Schwabl 1978: 1011).

10 Schwabl 1978: 1013, citing P.Mel. *fr.adesp.* 20f (938) P.

11 Schwabl 1978: 1233, on the basis of S. Eitrem s.v. 'Hera' in *RE* 8 (1913) 369–403, deduces a list such as Kithairon, Euboia, Attica, Argos, Hermione, Stymphalos, Kyme, Samos, Knossos. The Euboean instances are: (1) on Mt Ocha, rising high above Karystos at the south of the island; (2) on Elymion (Kerényi 1976: 140), an island of uncertain location (which is surprising given that it is supposed to have had a city on it) where there was a *nymphikon* (marriage grotto?).

12 Renewal: Dowden 1989: 201f.; 2000: 195f., 280–90. *Daidala*: Pausanias 9.2–3; Kerényi 1976 : 142; de Polignac 43. Mt Kithairon: Plutarch *fr.* 157 Sandbach ch.3. *Teleios*: cf. Pausanias 9.2.7, 8.22.2; marriage as a *telos*, fulfilment, Kerényi 1976: 104.

13 Plutarch *fr.* 153 Sandbach, Pausanias 9.3.

14 Deubner 1932: 117, 176–8; Kerényi 1976: 104–8; Schwabl 1978: 1074.

15 Pausanias 8.10.1, 8.36.2f.; Dowden 1992: 121f.

16 The evidence for this is admittedly very patchy in the archaic period (Gantz 1993: 42).

17 B. Rutkowski, *The Psychro Cave and other Sacred Grottoes in Crete* (Warsaw, 1996) 19. *Tikto*: Agathokles *FGrH* 472F1b (perhaps third century BC). Psychro and position of Dikte: West 1966 on line 477. Dikte in the east: Strabo 10.4.12. See also L.V. Watrous, *The Cave Sanctuary of Zeus at Psychro* (Liège, 1996) 18f.

18 Goat: myth later rationalised the goat into a nymph (Bremmer in *OCD*[3] s.v. Amaltheia), not vice versa, though perhaps the goat did not originally have a name (von Gärtner, in *KlP* s.v.). Praisos: Agathokles *FGrH* 472F1a; Schwabl 1978: 1208f. Blood and bees: Antoninus Liberalis 19; Schwabl 1978: 1209; Nilsson 1950: 542f. Annual rebirth: Nilsson 1967: i.321. Hymn: Nilsson 1950: 546f; Harrison 1912: ch.1, who should be read with some caution; Willetts 1962: ch.7.

19 West 1966 on line 477.

20 Vergil, *Aeneid* 10.567; M.L. West, *JHS* 122 (2002) 111.

21 On this type of myth, see also West 1997: 85–7, and J. Fontenrose, *Python: a study of Delphic myth and its origins* (Berkeley, 1959), and esp. 129f.

22 First, in Akousilaos *FGrH* 2F8 (early fifth century BC), unless these are the words of Philodemos (first century BC).

23 An ancient footnote ('scholion') on Pindar, and Apollodoros (1.6.1f.)

24 Similar lines in Hesiod, *Catalogue of Women fr.* 31 West-Merkelbach, the tradition from which Homer borrowed them.

25 The 12 Olympian gods are Zeus and Hera, Poseidon, Demeter, Athene, Apollo and Artemis, Aphrodite, Ares, Hermes, Hephaistos and Dionysos or Hestia.

26 Hesiod, *Theogony* 886–900, 924–6.

27 The reason is probably, as West says (1966: 212f.), that the worship of Aphrodite Ourania was used by someone to make her the daughter of Ouranos.

28 N.R.E. Fisher, *Social Values in Classical Athens* (London, 1976) 8, 10.

29 The possibly sixth century BC epic poem the *Cypria* (*fr.7*) makes her a child of Nemesis, on whose worship see above. Theseus is the Paris of the story that brings her to Rhamnous and the origins of all this variant mythology can be seen to be in cult.

30 There are depictions too of her being cast to sea in a chest with her infant son Perseus, but they do not involve Zeus.

31 Homer *Iliad* 5.266, 20.232; *Homeric Hymn to Aphrodite* 202.

32 Dowden 1992: 112–4, Strabo 10.4.21. A variant version of the myth in which Tantalos abducts Ganymede and takes him hunting (see Gantz 1993: 536) fits quite well with the Cretan ritual model.

33 Also at *Iliad* 12.26f.; *Odyssey* 14.457f. He 'rainstorms' at Hesiod, *Works and Days* 415, lightens at *Theogony* 690, and thunders at *Iliad* 8.133. See West 1978 on line 416 and Cook 1925: ii.1–4.

34 2.146, 13.837.

35 Other passages to look at: *Iliad* 2.412, 5.91, 11.493, 12.275 and 279–86, 15.192, 19.357–8; *Odyssey* 9.111, 11.405 (= 14.303).

36 Survivals: Schwabl 1978: 1017, citing B. Schmidt, *Das Volksleben der Neugriechen* (Leipzig, 1871) whose information on Zeus is, as Schwabl notes, largely taken over by the standard English-language book, J.C. Lawson, *Modern Greek Folklore and Ancient Greek Religion* (Cambridge, 1910); Cook 1925: ii.3. Rainwater: known from Athenian inscriptions such as *IG* I³ 84.34f. (418–417 BC); Orphics: Clement, *Stromata* 5.49.

37 *Iliad* 2.412, 4.166; *Odyssey* 15.523.

38 See pp. 11–13 above. This view is stated still more explicitly by Dio

Chrysostom: 'many barbarians, through poverty and lack of skill, call mountains and unworked trees and unshaped stones gods' (*Oration* 12.61 of c. AD 100).

39 Plutarch, *fr.* 191 Sandbach; Augustine *de Genesi ad litt. imperf.* 1.14 cited by Cook 1914: i.103n.2.

40 The word for 'clear weather' is *aithre* – but there were those who could not resist saying *aither* instead.

41 Cook 1914: i.103; E.Meyer in *KIP* s.v.Olympus (1).

42 I thank Dr Ken Wardle for this information.

43 *SIG³* 1107 of 200 BC, Nilsson 1906: 4; Nilsson 1967: i.394 n.2; Parker 1996: 32; Schwabl 1978: 1046, 1134.

44 These lines struck a chord. Archilochos paraphrases them at *fr.* 131 (with 132) West, as no less than six ancient authors noted; and they provided a model for Stoics discussing the influence of the divine surrounding atmosphere, the 'environment', on man – see R. Polito, in T. Wiedemann and K. Dowden, *Sleep* (Bari, 2003) 57f.

45 There is a whole discussion around this passage, see for example E.R. Dodds *The Greeks and the Irrational* (Berkeley, 1951) ch.1 and Lloyd-Jones 1971: 22–5. Solon *fr.* 13.75 West talks about Zeus sending *ate*, which results from excess wealth.

46 Selloi: Parke 1967: 21. Mycenaean huts: Schwabl 1978: 1114.

47 Schwabl 1978: 1020; there is, oddly, a good example at Aristophanes, *Birds* 1743–54.

48 *Bretas*: Euripides, *Heraclidae* 936f., *Phoenissae* 1250f., 1472f. Dedicated place: Vitruivus 2.8.15.

49 'Philios . . . because he brings all men together and wants them to be friends with each other', Dio Chrysostom 12.76; Jost 1985: 275.

50 Ps.-Demosthenes 43.14, 82; Parker 1996: 105f.

51 Strabo 8.7.4. From *hom-/ham-* 'together' and *ararisko* 'link up'. Later, this Zeus became *Homagyrios* ('of the Assembling together'), as the original sense of *Amarios* faded.

52 The Lykaia are briefly handled by Nilsson 1906: 8–10. The temple of Zeus Lykaios on Mt Lykaion received only a little worship by Strabo's time (8.8.2). For all other information in this paragraph see Jost 1985: 184, 267f., 295.

53 On these Boeotian cults see Schachter 1994: iii.105–8. Cult association: Pausanias 9.34.6, Strabo 9.2.29. Cult at Halos: Herodotus 7.197. Migration: Schachter's view that the title Laphystios travelled northwards is not in my opinion necessary. Naming: Strabo 9.2.29. Cheiron: see also Dowden 1989: 91.

54 In his abridged edition (London, 1922) ch.xxvi.

55 *Iliad* 2.196; Hesiod, *Theogony* 82.

56 This is based on the incisive account of Lloyd-Jones 1971: 6f. and *passim*.

57 West 1978 on lines 249ff., West 1997: 123ff.

58 This was a familiar type of thought in the Near East too: West 1997: 126f. Homer is sometimes viewed as borrowing from Hesiod, e.g. *Iliad* 18.39–48 borrowed from *Theogony* 240–62, according to M.L. West, 'The date of the *Iliad*', *MH* 52 (1995): 203–19 at 208.

59 See M. Oppermann in *OCD*³ s.v. Macedonia, cults.

60 Julian, letter to Arsakios archpriest of Galatia (22 Loeb, 84 Budé) 431a–b; fragmentary letter, possibly to Theodoros the archpriest, (vol. ii p.304 Loeb, no. 89a Budé) 291b–c.

61 Cf. Stengel 1920: 16. Pausanias 4.17.4, 10.27.2 (where *eschara* and *bomos* are used interchangeably).

62 Ktesios: Nilsson 1967: i.405. The village was Phlya or Myrrhinous, Pausanias 1.31.4; Piraeus: Farnell 1896: i.55. Zeus Herkeios also at Olympia and Argos, see Farnell 1896: i.54.

63 See also *Odyssey* 7.164 and 13.51.

64 Aeschylus, *Suppliant Women* 27f. See also Euripides, *Ion* 1032f.; Stengel 1920: 104; Farnell 1896: i.61 (and the evidence at 164–6). Third libation: Sophocles, *fr.* 425 Radt; Aeschylus, *fr.* 55 Radt; Hesychius, s.v. *tritos krater*; Athenaeus, *Deipnosophists* 692e–693c.

65 Information on Greek names is best taken from P.M. Fraser and E. Matthews (eds), *A Lexicon of Greek Personal Names*, vol. ii, M.J. Osborne and S.G. Byrne (eds), 'Attica' (Oxford, 1994).

66 Tertullian, *On Idolatry* §22f.; E. Gibbon, *The Decline and Fall of the Roman Empire* bk 1 ch.15 (London, 1910) 447 n.1.

67 Lloyd-Jones 1971: 5: '*Moira*, one's "portion", is in the last resort identical with the will of Zeus'.

68 This sort of thinking is characterised by Lloyd-Jones 1971: 36.

69 For the *aither*, see G.S. Kirk, J.E. Raven, M. Schofield, *The Presocratic Philosophers*, 2nd edn (Cambridge, 1983) 198: 'The pure cosmic fire was probably identified by Heraclitus with' *aither*. See also Lloyd-Jones 1971: 83.

70 See also West 1983: 89.

71 Lloyd-Jones (1971: 97–103) brilliantly speculates that the third play of the trilogy was the *Women of Etna* and that the outcome was Zeus sending Dike (Justice) amongst men. The problem, however, remains why Prometheus was released and it is difficult not to make the release the subject of the final play.

72 This was a deliberate and wicked choice, based on Arcadian traditions mentioned by Pausanias 8.8, 8.36: the Cretan version had captured the

market – one only has to look at Aratus, *Phaenomena* 31–5 (of course, 'if this is true', 30).

73 All references are to *SVF*, vol. i.

74 The view of Chrysippus and Cleanthes according to Plutarch, *de communibus notitiis* 1066a (*SVF* ii, Cleanthes *fr.* 536).

75 Cf. *Elements of Theology* 21; *Platonic Theology* 1.3;

76 Philo of Byblos, in his *Phoinikika*, drawing on genuine Near-Eastern material, also talks about Zeus Adados and about Astarte (Aphrodite), *FGrH* 790F2 10.31.

77 Varro's dialogue was one of the 76 books described as *Logistorici*, also called, after a leading character in it, the *Curio*. We learn about the *Antiquities* from Augustine's *City of God*, e.g. 6.5, 4.11. Statues and Euhemerism: Cicero, *de natura deorum* 2.62, 1.77ff.; Augustine, *City of God* 4.27.

ZEUS AFTERWARDS

1 The key piece on this collection is Cyril Mango, Michael Vickers, and E.D. Francis, 'The Palace of Lausus at Constantinople and Its Collection of Ancient Statues', *Journal of the History of Collections* 4.1 (1992) 89–98. On these statue movements, see also J. Elsner, *Imperial Rome and Christian Triumph* (Oxford, 1998) esp. 189–91.

2 *1 Kings* 18, *2 Kings* 1–2 and Mendelssohn's oratorio, *Elijah*.

3 This is already in Varro (Augustine, *City of God* 7.9).

4 Translated from J. Willis, *Martianus Capella* (Leipzig, 1983) 262.

5 As in Alexander Neckham (died 1217 – he is buried in Worcester Cathedral), *de rerum naturis* 1.7 ('on the seven gifts and the seven planets').

6 E.g., Ptolemy, *Tetrabiblos* 1.5; Macrobius, *Dream of Scipio* 1.19.19; Martianus 9.885, 'The planet Jupiter, health-giving for everything seeing that he is ruler of the (gods) above . . .'.

7 The five-volume edition, very short on prefatory material, by C. de Boer (Amsterdam 1915) argues to my mind quite implausibly (i.9–11) for a date in the 1320s. The 1290s seem just as viable. In Appendix II (v.387–429) he presents the 'Texte du commentaire de Copenhague', but it reads (v.389) extraordinarily like the author's preface. 'Alexander' is named with Fulgentius and Servius as a source (also v.389). This work was brought to the wider attention of scholars around 1340 through the *Ovidius moralizatus* of Peter Berchorius (Pierre Bersuire).

8 For Mary of Egypt see, e.g. http://www.ocf.org/OrthodoxPage/reading/ st.mary.html. She was a prostitute from the age of about 12 to 30.

9 By now, Plato's account of *koros* had been accepted and from Proclus on it was used as a technical word for 'pure', cf. Liddell-Scott-Jones, *Greek-English Lexicon* (Oxford, 1940), s.v. *Koros* (B) Adj.

10 On Theodontius, there is a piece by M. Pade, 'The Fragments of Theodontius in Boccaccio's *Genealogie Deorum Gentilium Libri*', in M. Pade, H. Ragn Jensen and L. Waage Petersen (eds), *Avignon & Naples: Italy in France – France in Italy in the Fourteenth Century* (Rome, 1997).

11 There are signs too that in this work, Chaucer was drawing on the *Ovide moralisé*: S. Delany, 'Chaucer's *House of Fame* and the *Ovide Moralisé*', *Comparative Literature* 20 (1968) 254–64.

12 In this section above all, I have gratefully made heavy use of Reid 1993.

13 http://www.marionettes.com/tosca.shtml.

14 One can find images of engravings by Agostino Musi (Agostino Veneziano) *c.* 1523, and by F. Foppens, 1677.

15 http://foires.net/cal/cal.shtml.

16 http://www.frenchculture.org/music/events/rameau-platee.html.

17 *Götterdämmerung*, but actually it means 'Destiny of the powers'.

18 Information from: http://www.zeus.com, http://www.zeusinformatics.gr/index_eng.html, http://www.cyber-robotics.com, http://www. zeusedit. com, http://www.zeus.fr, http://www-zeus.desy.de.

19 From Sierra Entertainment Inc., http://games.sierra.com/games/zeus.

20 http://www.zeusthunders.com; similar questions arise at http://askthe bigbrain.com/index-page2.html!

FURTHER READING

The only substantial book intended to give a complete account of Zeus is Cook 1914–1940. Cults of Zeus also occupy 144 pages of Farnell 1896. These are both period pieces in their way, but they do contain a huge amount of information that is not otherwise easily accessible. For those with German and access to good libraries, there are some copious resources, most notably the mountain of evidence collected by Schwabl and others for the huge German encyclopedia s.v. Zeus (Schwabl 1972, 1978). There is also a wide variety of information in Nilsson's (German) history of Greek religion (Nilsson 1967/74).

In English the definitive account of the figure of Zeus is that given by Walter Burkert in his history of Greek religion (1985), though its portrait can usefully be supplemented by the greyer tones of Lloyd-Jones 1971. Informative and well-defined briefer accounts have been done by Fritz Graf in *OCD*[3] 1636–8 and in K. van der Toorn, B. Becking and P.W. van der Horst, *Dictionary of Deities and Demons in the Bible*, 2nd edition (Leiden, 1999) 934–40. Detail about his cult must be gathered on rather a region by region basis, e.g. from Robert Parker, *Athenian Religion: a history* (Oxford, 1996) or Albert Schachter's volumes on Boiotia (Schachter 1994). For his oracle at Dodona, any general book on Greek oracles will give an account, but the standard account is Herbert Parke's, *The Oracles of Zeus: Dodona, Olympia, Ammon* (Oxford, 1967).

For inspiration, there is a lot to be said for sharing Walter Otto's visionary account of Greek religion (Otto 1954, regrettably there is no specific work on Zeus) and even for attempting to follow the more psychoanalytic-archetypal insights of Kerényi 1976. But more reliable, judicious and no less insightful is the work of Vernant, e.g. 1982: ch. 5 'The society of the Gods', which focuses on Zeus, or the analysis of Hesiod's Prometheus stories in ch. 8; or for a vigorous experimental telling of Zeus's rise to power, you may turn to J.-P. Vernant, *The Universe, the Gods and Men* (London, 2002), a cheap paperback either in English or in French (Paris, 1999).

For myth, it is best to begin with the first-century AD handbook: Apollodorus, *The Library of Greek Mythology*, translated R. Hard, Oxford, 1997. Ancient authors such as Homer and the tragedians are easy to find; for Hesiod, it is best to turn to: Hesiod, *Theogony, Works and Days*, translated M.L. West, Oxford, 1988. The best modern handbook, giving what myths exist and in what author or work of art you discover them, is: T. Gantz, *Early Greek Myth: a guide to literary and artistic sources*, Baltimore and London, 1993 (two volumes in paperback). The best introductions to the uses and study of myth are: K. Dowden, *Uses of Greek Mythology*, London, 1992 and F. Graf, *Greek Mythology: an introduction*, Eng. transl., Baltimore and London, 1993.

To get an idea of the part that Zeus and other divine figures play in art, T.H. Carpenter, *Art and Myth in Ancient Greece* (London, 1991) remains a straightforward introduction. The evidence is, however, piled up as exhaustively as possible in *LIMC* (university libraries only). If your interest is in Zeus on Athenian red-figure vases, then Arafat 1990 offers a detailed and methodical look at their iconography beside literary accounts of the myths involved. More generally, the use of myth in art is illuminated by Susan Woodford's excellent *Images of Myths in Classical Antiquity*, Cambridge, 2003.

Turning to European culture, Seznec 1953 is the authoritative text for pagan religion and the Renaissance and is full of fascinating detail; the more mystic side is dealt with by Wind 1967. To this we can now add L. Freedman's *The Revival of the Olympian Gods in Renaissance Art*, Cambridge, 2003. If you want to find European paintings, sculptures or even music on classical mythological themes, nothing is more useful than J.D. Reid (with C. Rohmann), *The Oxford Guide to Classical Mythology in the Arts, 1300–1990s*, 2 vols (Oxford, 1993), which lists alphabetically mythological figures (Zeus, Danae . . .) and gives a chronological catalogue of representations in the arts. More single-minded on music is D.M. Poduska, 'Classical Myth in Music: a selective list', *Classical World* 92.3 (1999) 195–276, which aims to amplify Reid and deal with works actually available on CD.

WORKS CITED

This bibliography is provided to help with references in the endnotes. E.g., 'Dowden 1992: 65f.' means my *Uses of Greek Mythology*, pages 65 and 66. For advice on further reading, please consult the 'Further Reading' section.

References to ancient authors. Ancient authors are referred to by 'books', 'chapters', 'sections', 'lines' – where a 'book' is about the size of one of our chapters and 'chapters' are correspondingly smaller. The authors themselves, except possibly Homer, divided their longer works into books. But it is scholars in recent centuries that have mapped out agreed chapters and other smaller divisions. So:

- Homer, *Iliad* 14.252 = Homer's epic the *Iliad*, book 14, line 252.
- Aeschylus, *Agamemnon* 1487 = Aeschylus's play the *Agamemnon*, line 1487.
- Strabo 3.6.5 = Strabo's *Geography* (it's the only work of his that survives, so there is no point in stating which work we are referring to), book 3, chapter 6, section 5.

The translations in this book are my own work. To explore ancient texts further there are several useful series of translations, notably *Oxford World's Classics* (Oxford University Press) and *Penguin Classics* (Penguin Books); but the most wide-reaching range of translations (with facing Greek/Latin text) is the *Loeb Classical Library* (Harvard University Press).

References of the form 'Alcaeus, fr. 338.1–2 Lobel-Page' refer to *fragments* of lost texts – on papyri or quoted by another author; here the standard edition is by Lobel, revised by Page. It is beyond the scope of this note to go into more detail.

K.W. Arafat, *Classical Zeus: a study in art and literature*, Oxford, 1990.

W. Burkert, *Greek Religion: archaic and classical*, Eng. trans., Oxford, 1985.

A.B. Cook, *Zeus: a study in ancient religion*, Cambridge, 3 vols. in 5 parts, 1914–40.

F. Cumont, *Recherches sur le symbolisme funéraire des romains*, Paris, 1942.

L. Deubner, *Attische Feste*, Berlin, 1932.

K. Dowden, *Death and the Maiden: girls' initiation rites in Greek mythology*, London, New York, 1989.

—— *The Uses of Greek Mythology*, London, 1992.

—— *European Paganism: the realities of cult from antiquity to the Middle Ages*, London, New York, 2000.

L.R. Farnell, *The Cults of the Greek States*, Oxford, vol. 1, 1896.

J.G. Frazer, *The Golden Bough: a study in comparative religion*, 2nd edn, revised, London, 1900.

T. Gantz, *Early Greek Myth: a guide to literary and artistic sources*, Baltimore and London, 1993 (2 vols in the paperback edition).

J.E. Harrison, *Themis: a study of the social origins of Greek religion*, Cambridge, 1912.

S. Hiller, 'Zeus in den mykenischen Texten', in Schwabl 1978: 1001–9.

M. Jost, *Sanctuaires et cultes d'Arcadie*, Paris, 1985.

C. Kerényi, *Zeus and Hera: archetypal image of father, husband and wife*, Princeton NJ and London, 1976 (marked 1975).

K. Latte, *Römische Religionsgeschichte*, Munich, 1960.

P.H.J. Lloyd-Jones, *The Justice of Zeus*, Berkeley CA, Los Angeles, London, 1971.

M.P. Nilsson, *Griechische Feste von religiöser Bedeutung mit Ausschluss der Attischen*, Leipzig, 1906.

—— *The Minoan-Mycenaean Religion and its Survival in Greek Religion*, 2nd edn, Lund, 1950.

—— *Geschichte der griechischen Religion*, 3rd edn, Munich, vol. 1, 1967; vol. 2, 1974.

W.F. Otto, *The Homeric Gods: the spiritual significance of Greek religion*, Eng. transl., New York, 1954, repr. London, 1955.

H.W. Parke, *Greek Oracles*, London, 1967.

—— *Festivals of the Athenians*, London, 1977.

R. Parker, *Athenian Religion: a history*, Oxford, 1996.

C. Préaux, *Le Monde hellénistique: La Grèce et l'Orient (323–146 av. J.-C.)*, 2 vols, Paris, 1978.

G. Radke, *Zur Entwicklung der Gottesvorstellung und der Gottesverehrung in Rom*, Darmstadt, 1987.

J.D. Reid (with C. Rohmann), *The Oxford Guide to Classical Mythology in the Arts, 1300–1990s*, 2 vols, Oxford, 1993.

A. Schachter, *Cults of Boiotia*, vol.3 [*BICS* Suppl. 38.3], London, 1994.

J. Schindler, 'Sprachgeschichte', in Schwabl 1978: 999–1001.

H. Schwabl s.v. 'Zeus I' in *RE* 10A (1972) 253–76, and s.v. 'Zeus II' in *RE* Suppl.15 (1978) 993–1411.

J. Seznec, *The Survival of the Pagan Gods: the mythological tradition and its place in Renaissance humanism and art*, Eng. transl., Princeton NJ, 1953.

P. Stengel, *Die griechische Kultusaltertümer*, Munich, 1920.

J.-P. Vernant, *Myth and Society in Ancient Greece*, Eng. trans., London, 1982.

L. Vidman, *Sylloge inscriptionum religionis Isiacae et Sarapiacae* [*Religionsgeschichtliche Versuche und Vorarbeiten*, xxviii], Berlin, 1969.

M.L. West, *Hesiod: Theogony: edited with prolegomena and commentary*, Oxford, 1966.

—— *Hesiod: Works and Days: edited with prolegomena and commentary*, Oxford, 1978.

—— *The Orphic Poems*, Oxford, 1983.

—— *The East Face of Helicon: West Asiatic elements in Greek poetry and myth*, Oxford, 1997.

R.F. Willetts, *Cretan Cults and Festivals*, London, 1962.

E. Wind, *Pagan Mysteries in the Renaissance*, revised ed., Harmondsworth, 1967.

ABBREVIATIONS

This provides the key to some shorthand references, particularly in the endnotes

fr.   'fragment', a snippet surviving from a lost work (e.g. because someone quotes it)

DK   H. Diels, revised W. Kranz, *Die Fragmente der Vorsokratiker*, 6. Auflage, Berlin, 1951.

FGrH   F. Jacoby (ed.), *Die Fragmenter der griechischen Historiker*, Berlin, 1926–30, Leiden 1954–8.

HP   A.A. Long and D.N. Sedley, *The Hellenistic Philosophers*, 2 vols, Cambridge, 1987.

IG   *Inscriptiones Graecae*, 14 vols (not all published), Berlin, 1873–1914.

IG I³   *Inscriptiones Graecae*, vol. I, 3rd edn, Berlin, 1981–98.

JHS   *Journal of Hellenic Studies*

KlP   K. Ziegler, W. Sontheimer, H. Gärtner (eds), *Der kleine Pauly: Lexicon der Antike*, Munich, 1975.

LIMC   H.C. Ackermann, J.-R. Gisler (eds), *Lexicon iconographicum mythologiae classicae*, Zurich, 1981–97.

MH   *Museum Helveticum*

OCD³   S. Hornblower and A. Spawforth (eds), *Oxford Classical Dictionary*, 3rd edition, Oxford, 1996.

RE   W. Kroll, K. Mittelhaus and K. Ziegler (eds), *Paulys Real-Encyclopädie der klassischen Altertumswissenschaft*, Munich, 1894–1980.

SIG[3] W. Dittenberger, *Sylloge inscriptionum graecarum*, 3rd edn, Leipzig, 1915–24.

SVF J. von Arnim, *Stoicorum veterum fragmenta*, 3 vols, Leipzig, 1905, 1903, 1903.

INDEX OF PERSONAL AND GEOGRAPHICAL NAMES

*On the whole I prefer to transcribe Greek names as they are written in Greek –
with, eg, –os at the end and* k*'s and* ai*'s rather than* c*'s and* ae*'s. But some words
are too naturalised in their Latin form. It is hard to be consistent.*

INDEX OF SUBJECTS

Related titles from Routledge

Medea

Emma Griffiths

Medea, the sorceress of Greek myth and Euripides' vengeful heroine, is famed for the murder of her children after she is banished from her own family and displaced by a new wife. Her reputation as a wronged 'everywoman' of Greek tragedy has helped engender her lasting appeal to the modern age. However, this firmly rooted status has also caused many of the intricacies of her timeless tale to be overlooked.

Emma Griffiths brings into focus previously unexplored themes of the Medea myth, along with providing an incisive introduction to the story and its history. Viewed within its context, the tale reveals fascinating insights into ancient Greece and its ideology, the importance of children, the role of women, and the position of the outsider and barbarian.

The critically sophisticated analysis, expressed in clear and accessible terms, proceeds to examine the persistence of the Medea myth through ancient Rome to the modern day. Placing the myth within a modern context and into analytical frameworks such as psychoanalysis, Griffiths highlights Medea's position in current classical study, as well as her lasting appeal. A vivid portrait of a woman empowered by her exclusion from society, alive with passion and the suffering of wounded love, this book is an indispensable guide to a fascinating mythical figure.

Hb: 0–415–30069–X
Pb: 0–415–30070–3

Available at all good bookshops
For ordering and further information please visit:
www.routledge.com